I, WITNESS

NORAH McCLINTOCK

MIKE DEAS

ORCA BOOK PUBLISHERS

Library and Archives Canada Cataloguing in Publication

McClintock, Norah
I, witness / Norah McClintock ; illustrated by Mike Deas.

Issued also in electronic formats.
ISBN 978-1-55469-789-2

1. Graphic novels. I. Deas, Mike, 1982- II. Title.
PN6733.M29I12 2012 j741.5'971 C2012-902258-6

First published in the United States, 2012
Library of Congress Control Number: 2012938210

Summary: When Boone witnesses a murder and several friends are killed, he must try and find the truth.

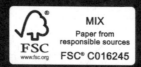

MIX
Paper from responsible sources
FSC® C016245

Orca Book Publishers is dedicated to preserving the environment and has printed this book on paper certified by the Forest Stewardship Council ®.

Orca Book Publishers gratefully acknowledges the support for its publishing programs provided by the following agencies: the Government of Canada through the Canada Book Fund and the Canada Council for the Arts, and the Province of British Columbia through the BC Arts Council and the Book Publishing Tax Credit.

Cover and interior artwork by Mike Deas
Cover design by Mike Deas and Teresa Bubela

ORCA BOOK PUBLISHERS
PO Box 5626, Stn. B
Victoria, BC Canada
V8R 6S4

ORCA BOOK PUBLISHERS
PO Box 468
Custer, WA USA
98240-0468

www.orcabook.com
Printed and bound in Canada.

15 14 13 12 • 4 3 2 1

To my friend Jason Taniguchi,
who introduced me to graphic novels.
—NM

To Nancy, with thanks.
—MD

gunfire

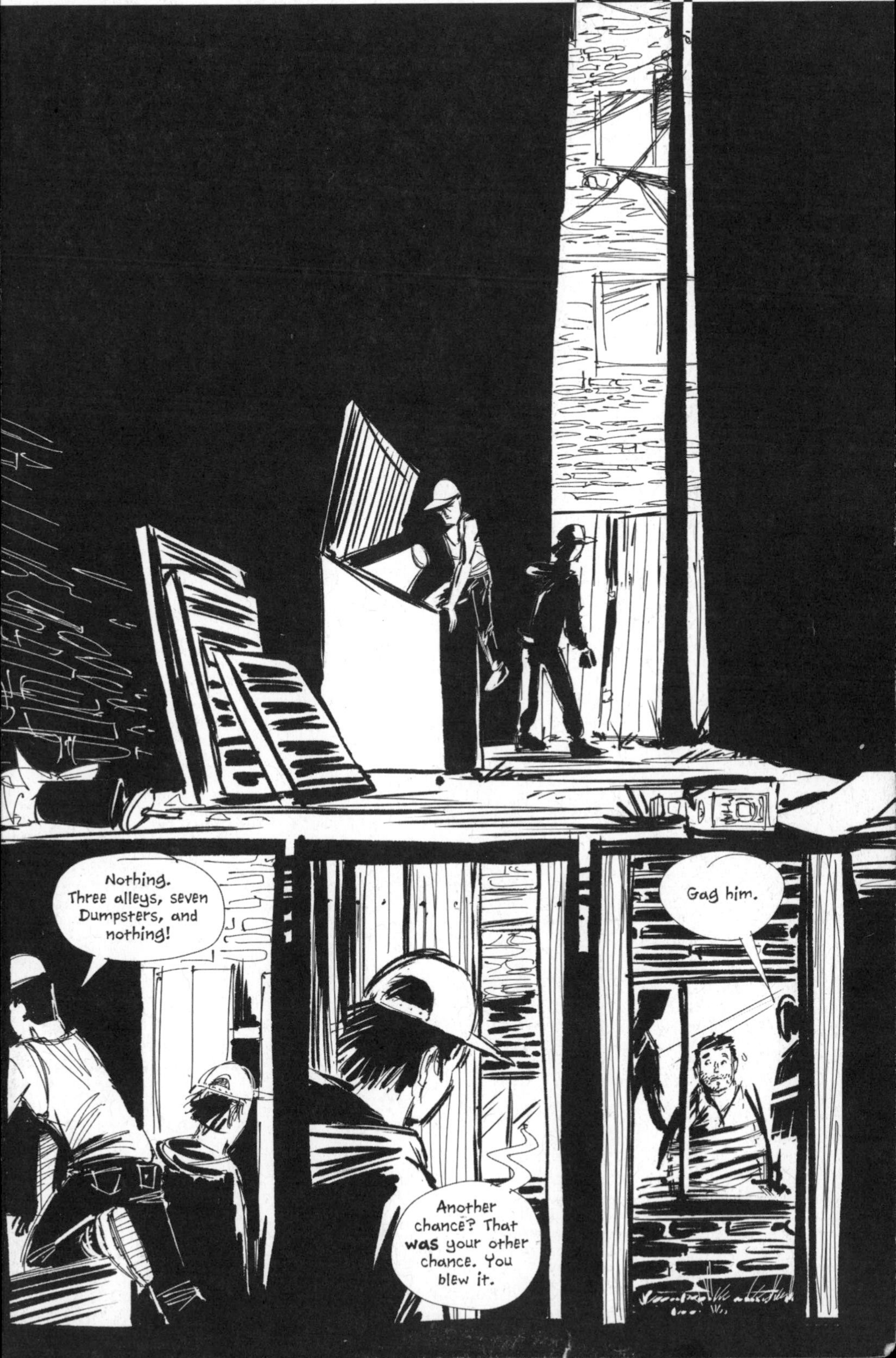
Nothing. Three alleys, seven Dumpsters, and nothing!
Another chance? That **was** your other chance. You blew it.
Gag him.

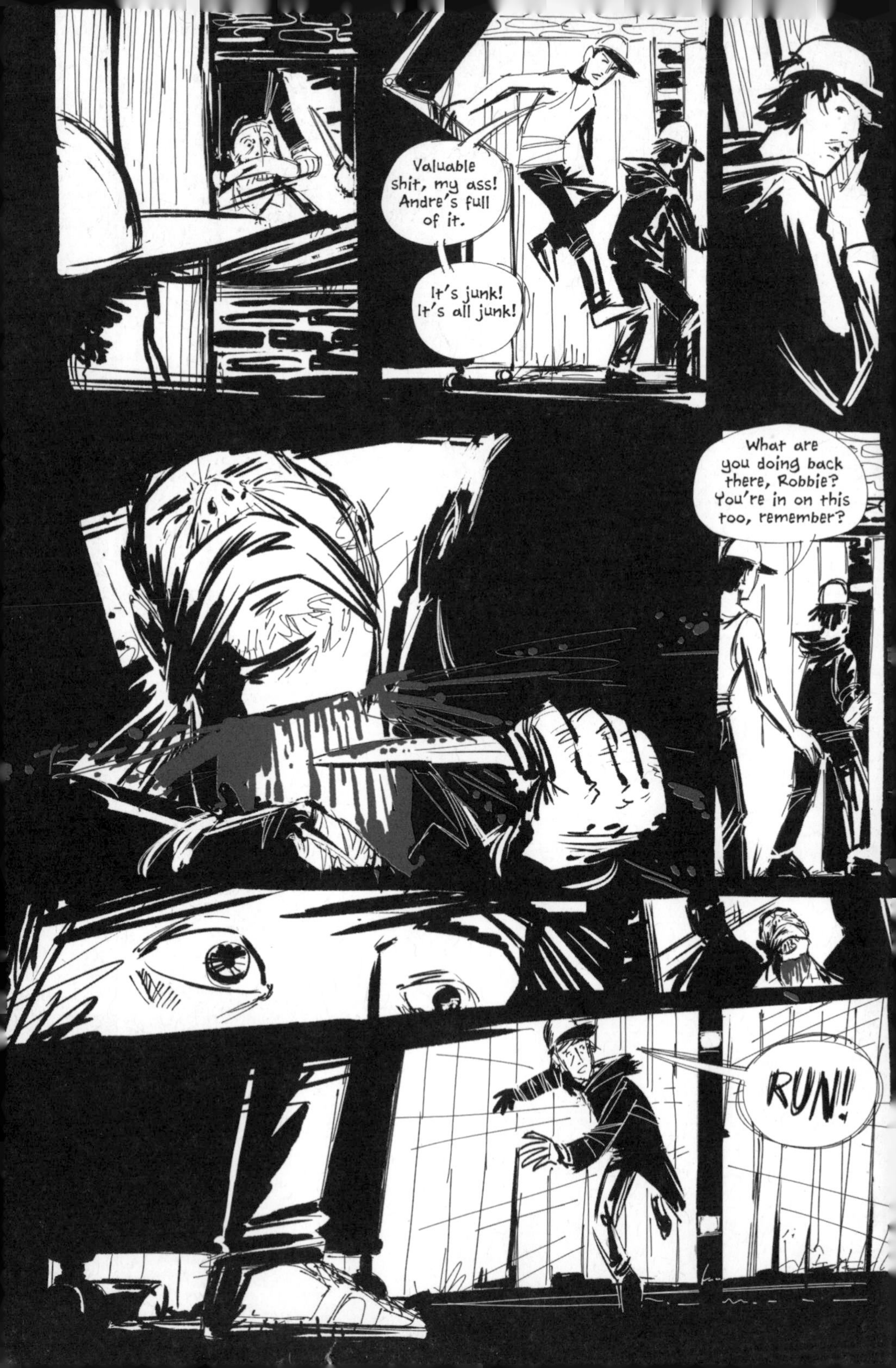
Valuable shit, my ass! Andre's full of it.
It's junk! It's all junk!
What are you doing back there, Robbie? You're in on this too, remember?
RUN!

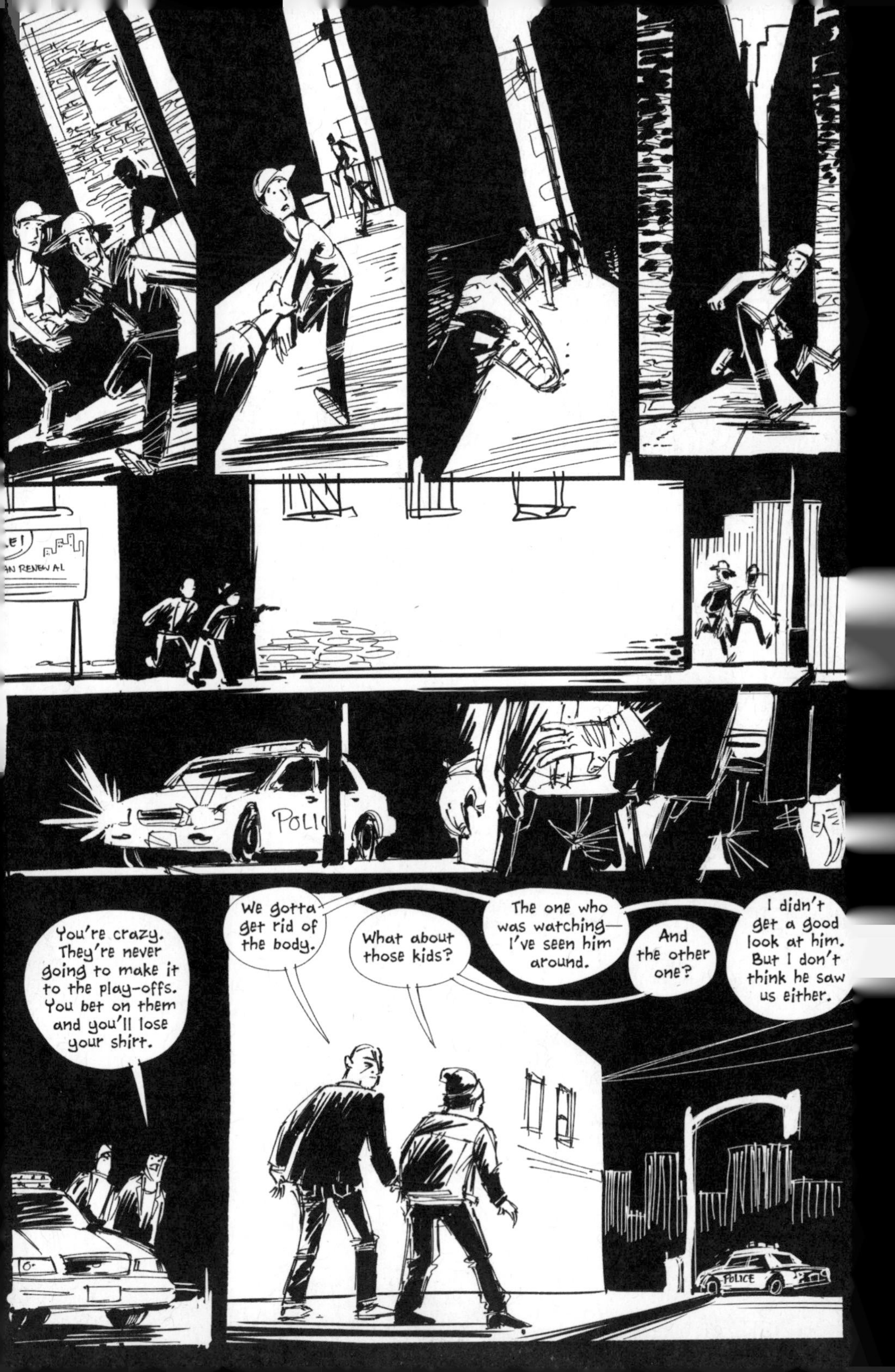

AN RENEWAL
POLIC
You're crazy. They're never going to make it to the play-offs. You bet on them and you'll lose your shirt.
We gotta get rid of the body.
What about those kids?
The one who was watching— I've seen him around.
And the other one?
I didn't get a good look at him. But I don't think he saw us either.
POLICE

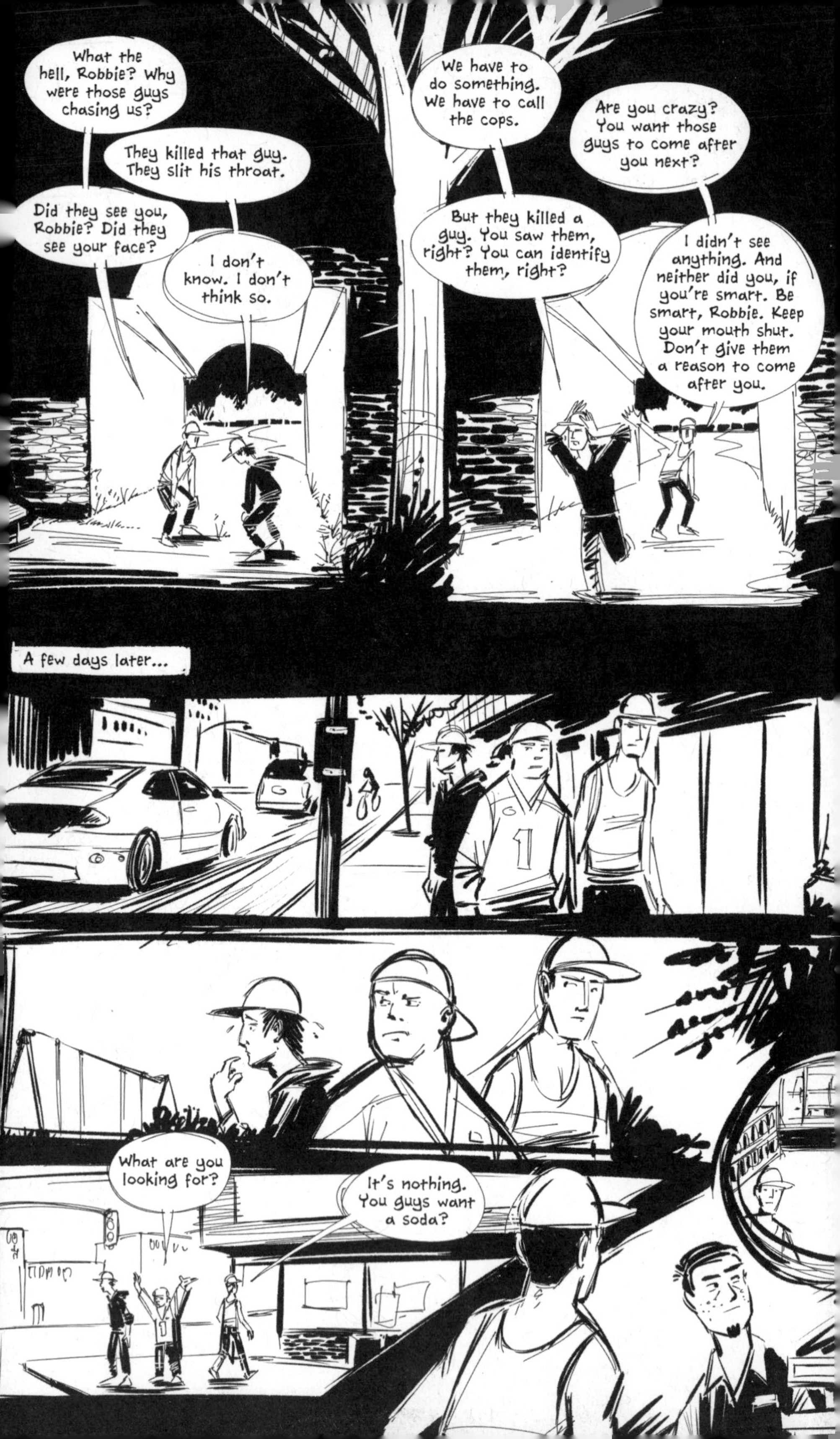
What the hell, Robbie? Why were those guys chasing us?
They killed that guy. They slit his throat.
Did they see you, Robbie? Did they see your face?
I don't know. I don't think so.
We have to do something. We have to call the cops.
Are you crazy? You want those guys to come after you next?
But they killed a guy. You saw them, right? You can identify them, right?
I didn't see anything. And neither did you, if you're smart. Be smart, Robbie. Keep your mouth shut. Don't give them a reason to come after you.
A few days later...
What are you looking for?
It's nothing. You guys want a soda?

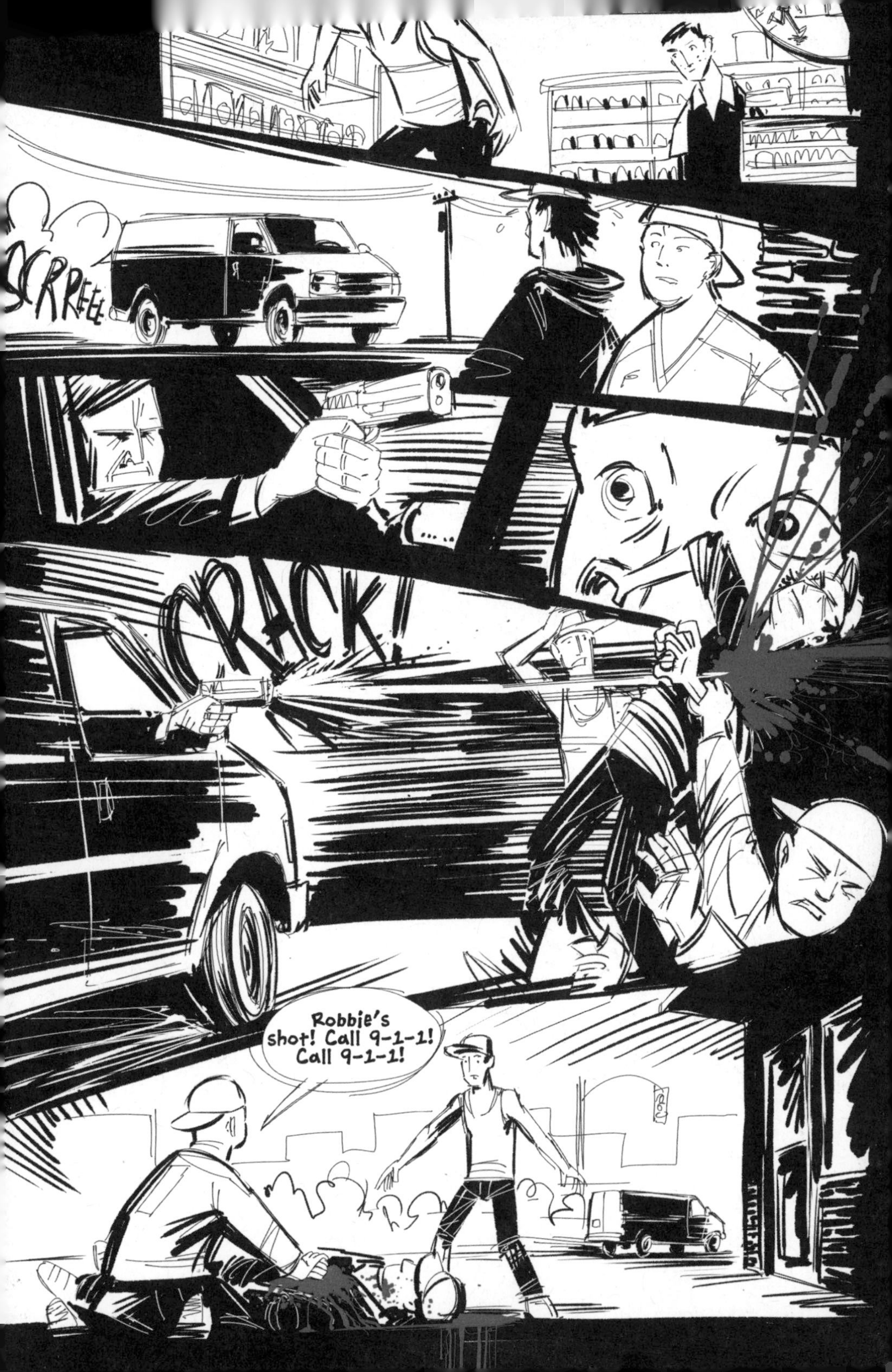
SCRREEEE
CRACK!
Robbie's shot! Call 9-1-1! Call 9-1-1!

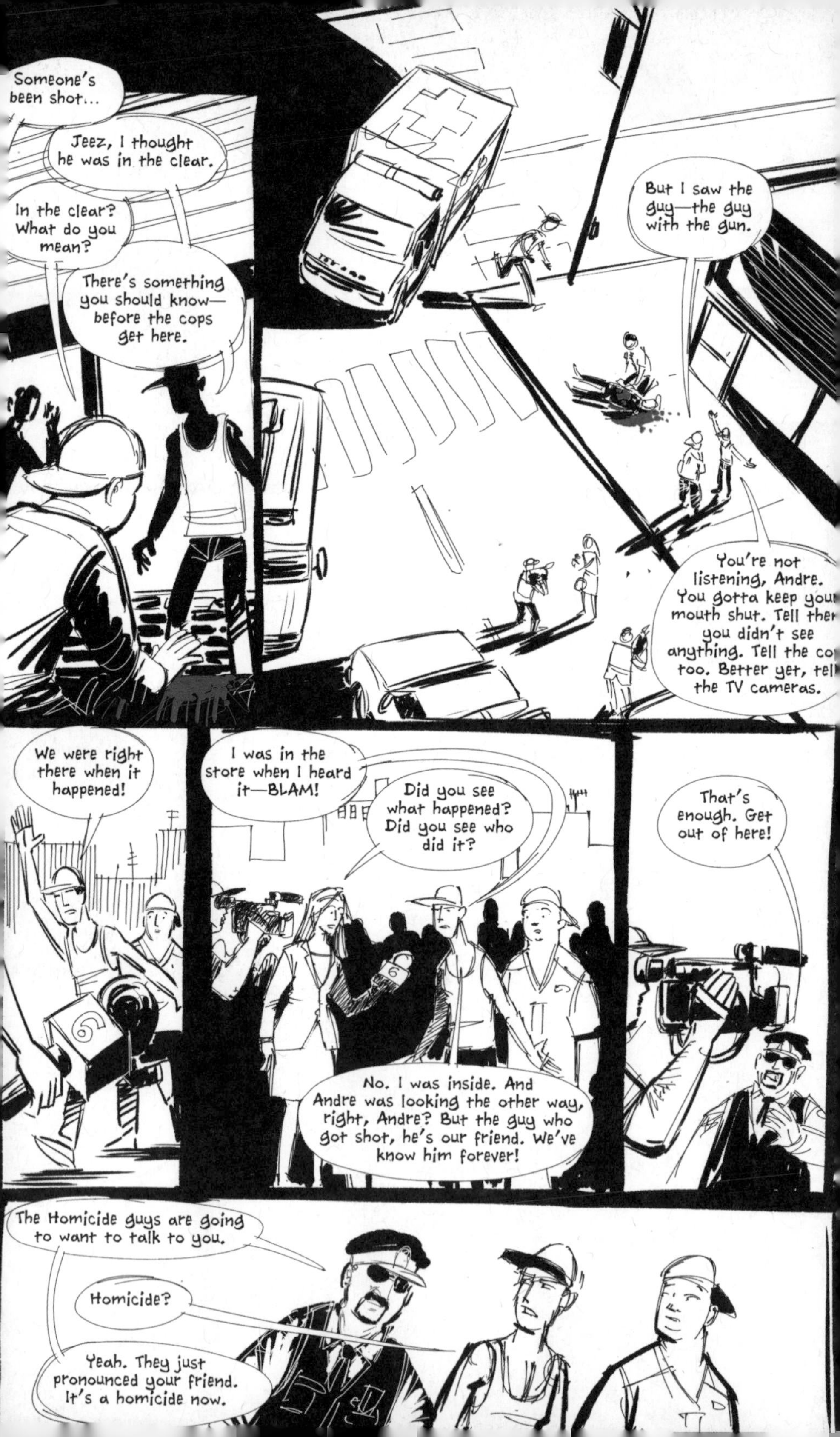
Someone's been shot...
Jeez, I thought he was in the clear.
In the clear? What do you mean?
There's something you should know— before the cops get here.
But I saw the guy—the guy with the gun.
You're not listening, Andre. You gotta keep your mouth shut. Tell ther you didn't see anything. Tell the co too. Better yet, tell the TV cameras.
We were right there when it happened!
I was in the store when I heard it—BLAM!
Did you see what happened? Did you see who did it?
No. I was inside. And Andre was looking the other way, right, Andre? But the guy who got shot, he's our friend. We've know him forever!
That's enough. Get out of here!
The Homicide guys are going to want to talk to you.
Homicide?
Yeah. They just pronounced your friend. It's a homicide now.

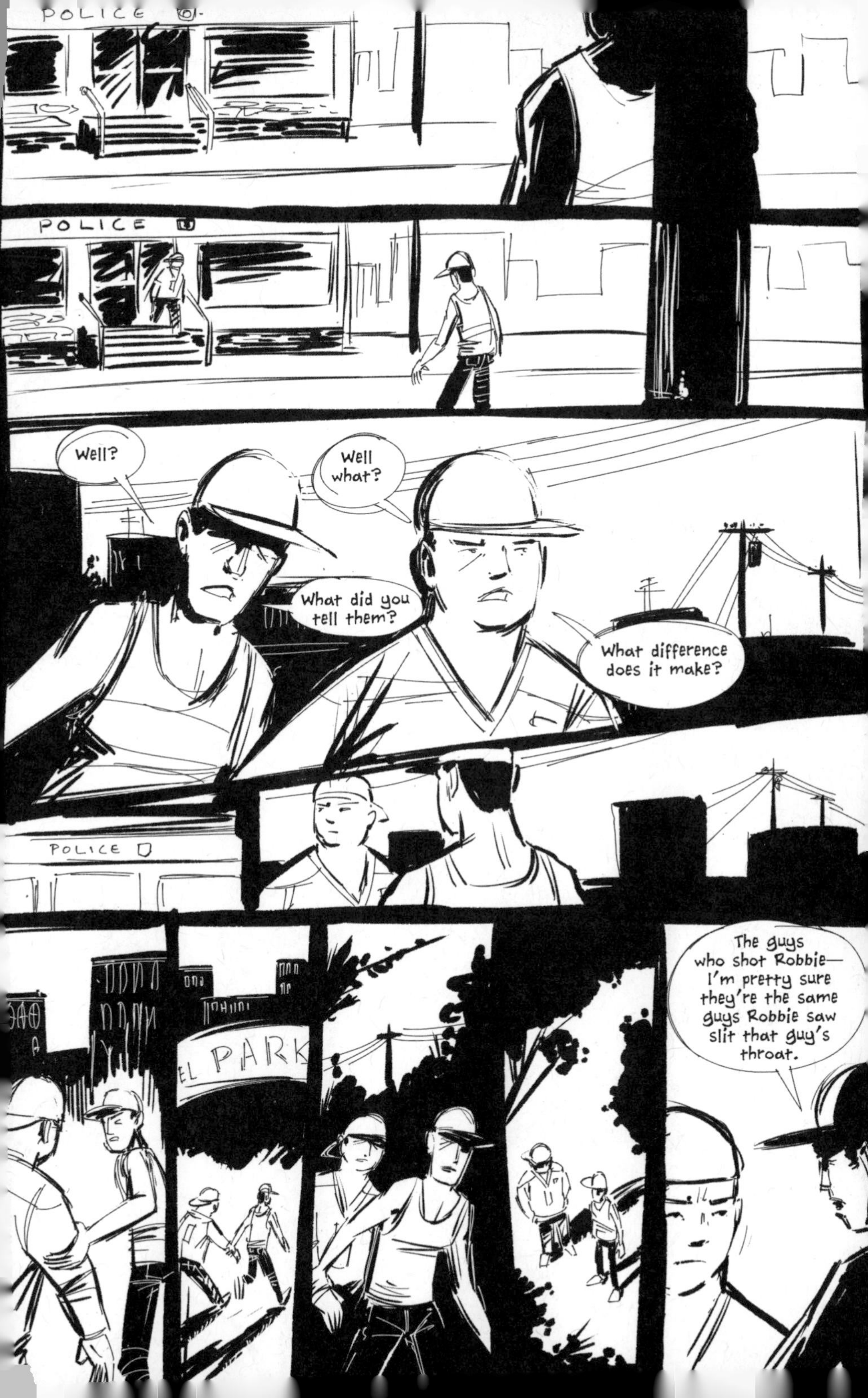
POLICE
POLICE
Well?
Well what?
What did you tell them?
What difference does it make?
POLICE
PARK
The guys who shot Robbie— I'm pretty sure they're the same guys Robbie saw slit that guy's throat.

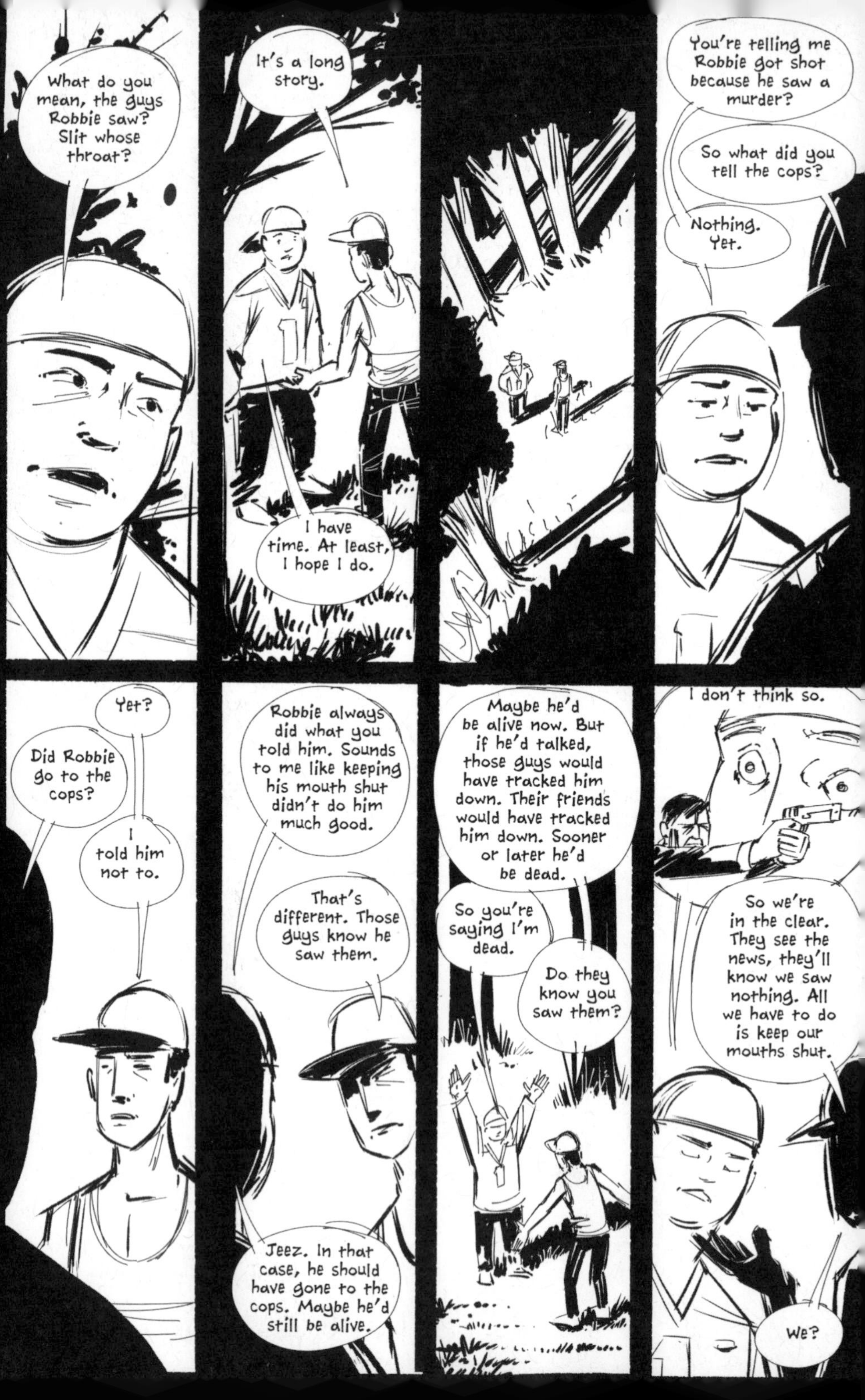
What do you mean, the guys Robbie saw? Slit whose throat?
It's a long story.
I have time. At least, I hope I do.
You're telling me Robbie got shot because he saw a murder?
So what did you tell the cops?
Nothing. Yet.
Yet?
Did Robbie go to the cops?
I told him not to.
Robbie always did what you told him. Sounds to me like keeping his mouth shut didn't do him much good.
That's different. Those guys know he saw them.
Jeez. In that case, he should have gone to the cops. Maybe he'd still be alive.
Maybe he'd be alive now. But if he'd talked, those guys would have tracked him down. Their friends would have tracked him down. Sooner or later he'd be dead.
So you're saying I'm dead.
Do they know you saw them?
I don't think so.
So we're in the clear. They see the news, they'll know we saw nothing. All we have to do is keep our mouths shut.
We?

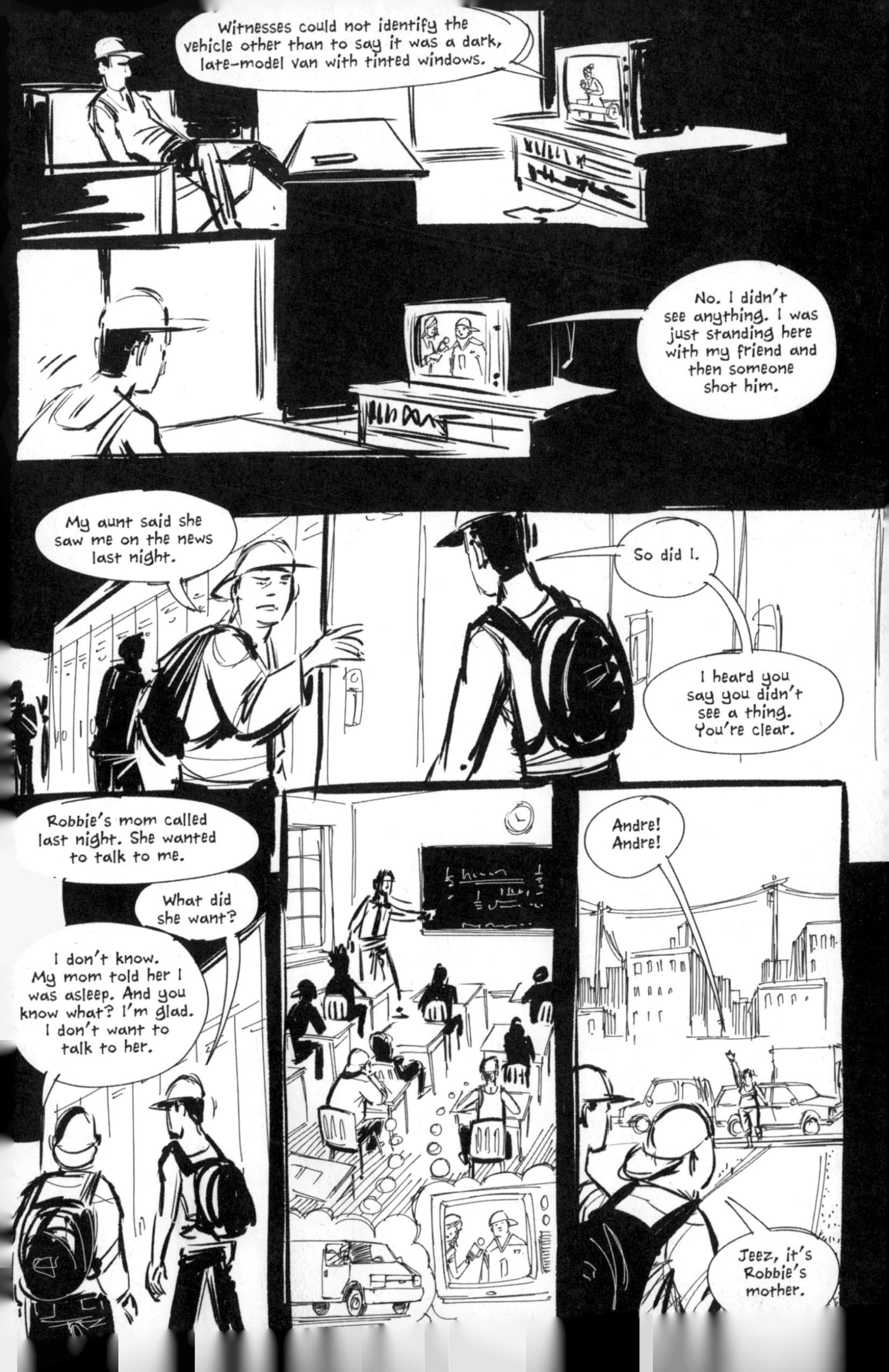
Witnesses could not identify the vehicle other than to say it was a dark, late-model van with tinted windows.
No. I didn't see anything. I was just standing here with my friend and then someone shot him.
My aunt said she saw me on the news last night.
So did I.
I heard you say you didn't see a thing. You're clear.
Robbie's mom called last night. She wanted to talk to me.
What did she want?
I don't know. My mom told her I was asleep. And you know what? I'm glad. I don't want to talk to her.
Andre! Andre!
Jeez, it's Robbie's mother.

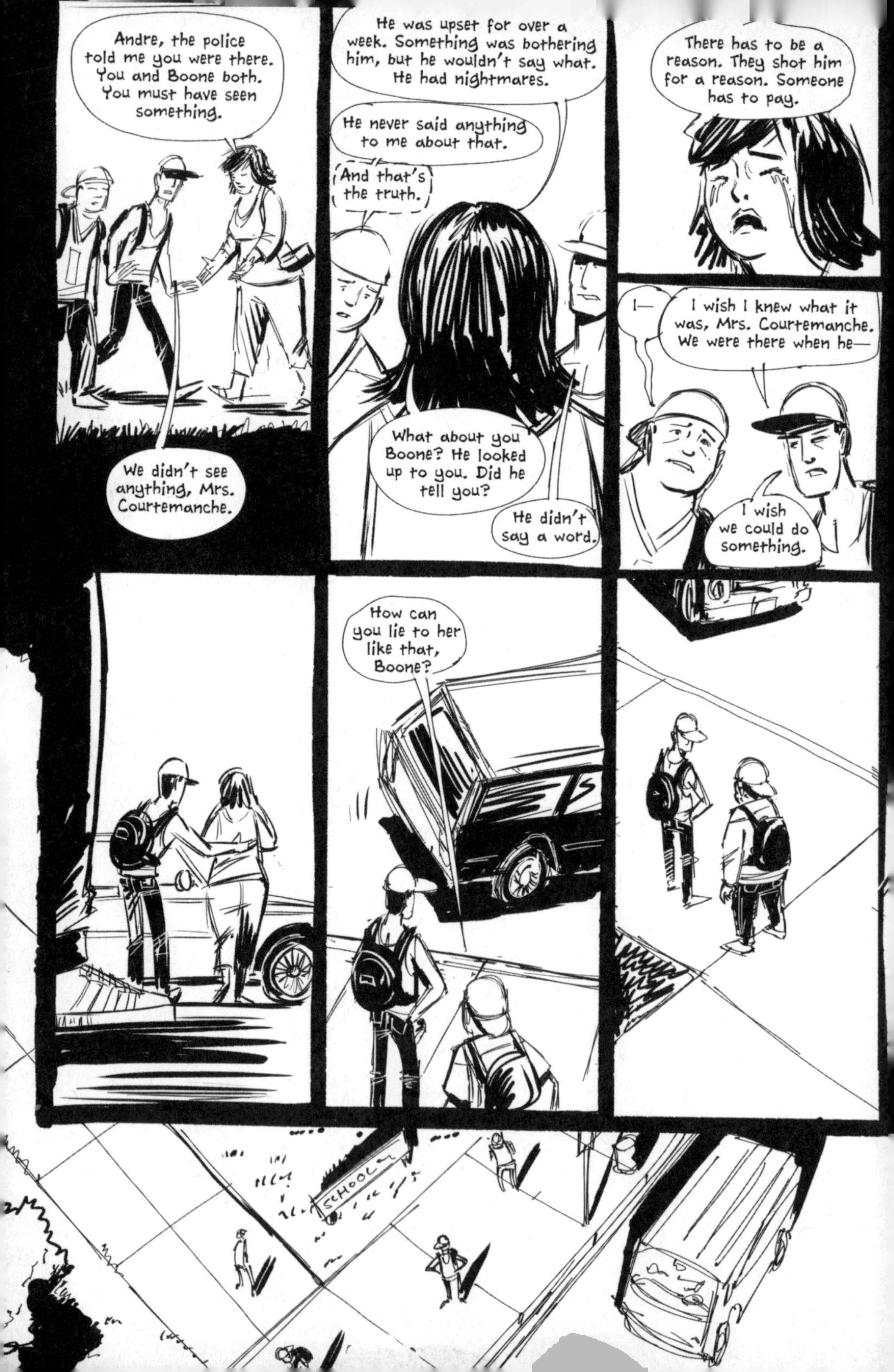
Andre, the police told me you were there. You and Boone both. You must have seen something.
We didn't see anything, Mrs. Courtemanche.
He was upset for over a week. Something was bothering him, but he wouldn't say what. He had nightmares.
He never said anything to me about that.
And that's the truth.
What about you Boone? He looked up to you. Did he tell you?
He didn't say a word.
There has to be a reason. They shot him for a reason. Someone has to pay.
I—
I wish I knew what it was, Mrs. Courtemanche. We were there when he—
I wish we could do something.
How can you lie to her like that, Boone?
SCHOOL

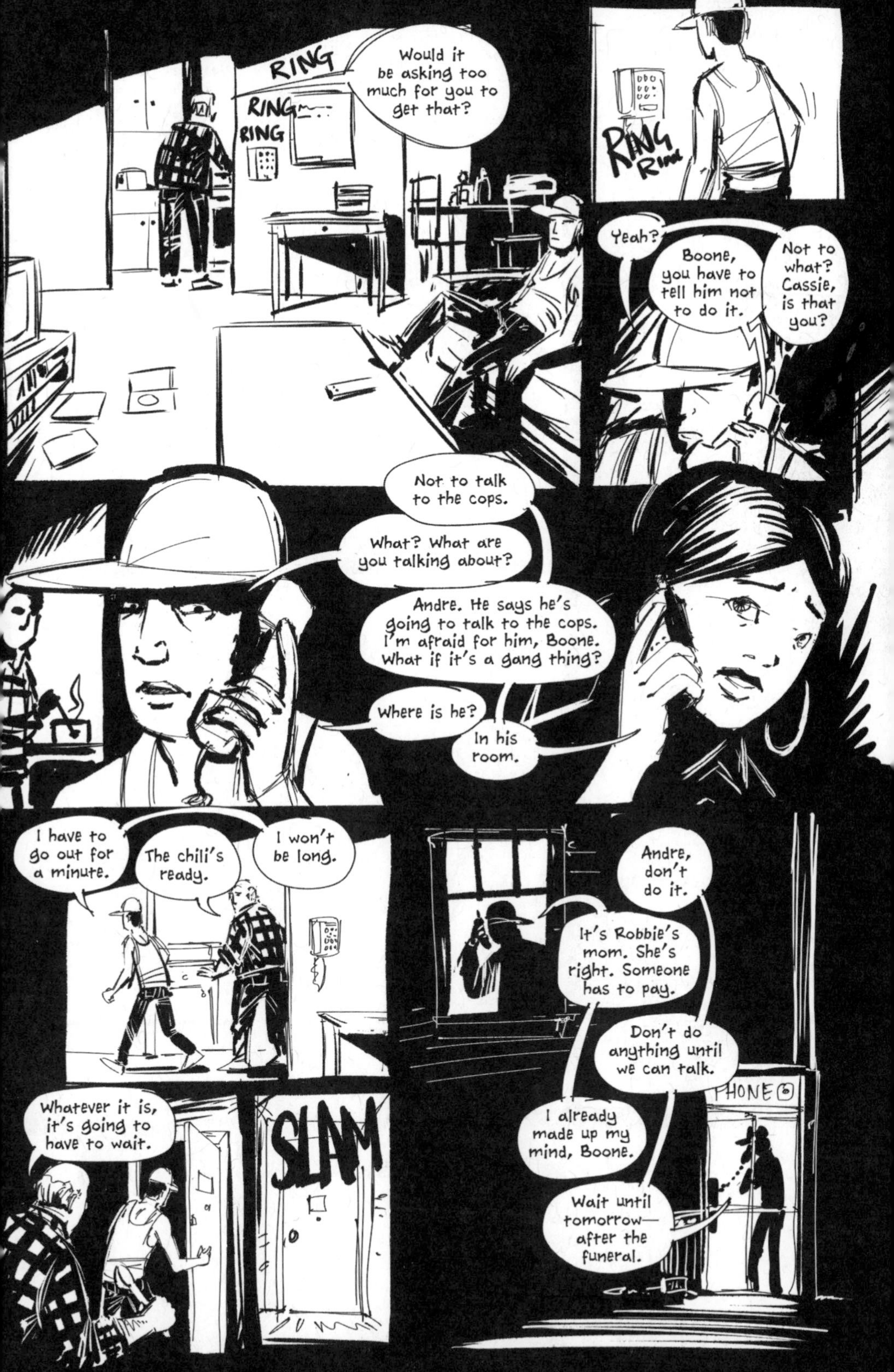
RING
RING
RING
Would it be asking too much for you to get that?
RING
Ring
Yeah?
Boone, you have to tell him not to do it.
Not to what? Cassie, is that you?
Not to talk to the cops.
What? What are you talking about?
Andre. He says he's going to talk to the cops. I'm afraid for him, Boone. What if it's a gang thing?
Where is he?
In his room.
I have to go out for a minute.
The chili's ready.
I won't be long.
Whatever it is, it's going to have to wait.
SLAM
Andre, don't do it.
It's Robbie's mom. She's right. Someone has to pay.
Don't do anything until we can talk.
I already made up my mind, Boone.
Wait until tomorrow— after the funeral.
PHONE

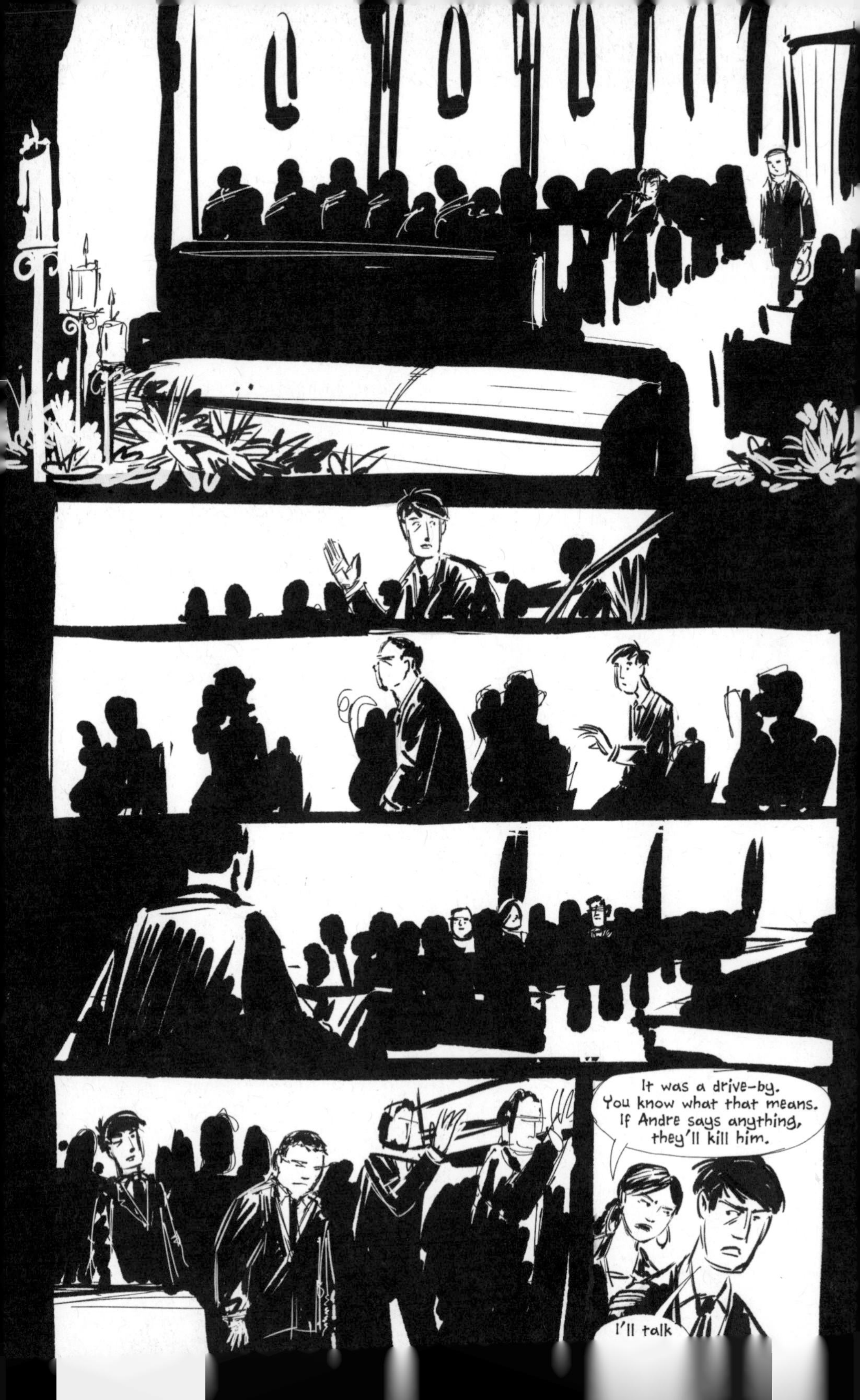
It was a drive-by. You know what that means. If Andre says anything, they'll kill him.
I'll talk

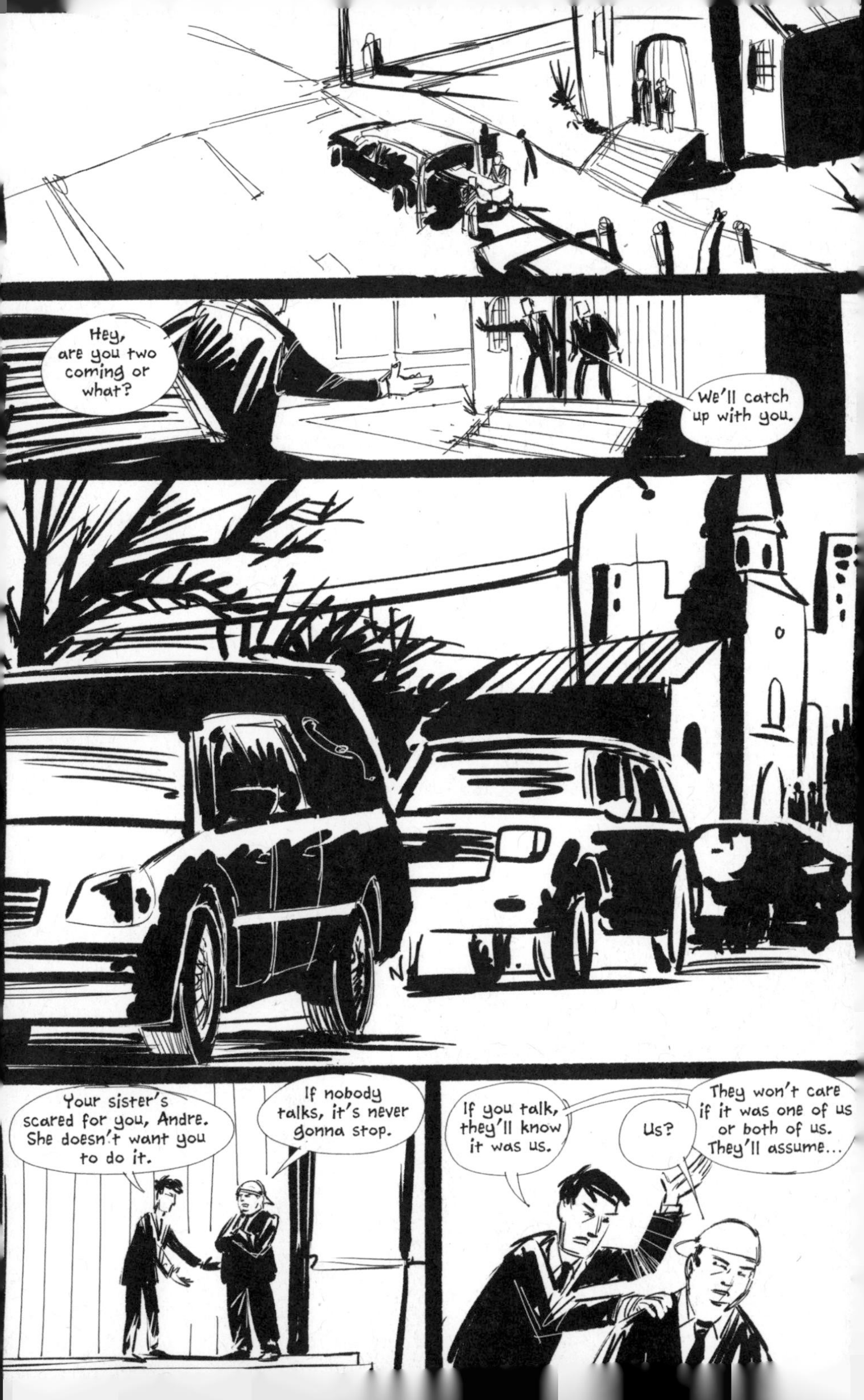
Hey, are you two coming or what?
We'll catch up with you.
Your sister's scared for you, Andre. She doesn't want you to do it.
If nobody talks, it's never gonna stop.
If you talk, they'll know it was us.
Us?
They won't care if it was one of us or both of us. They'll assume...

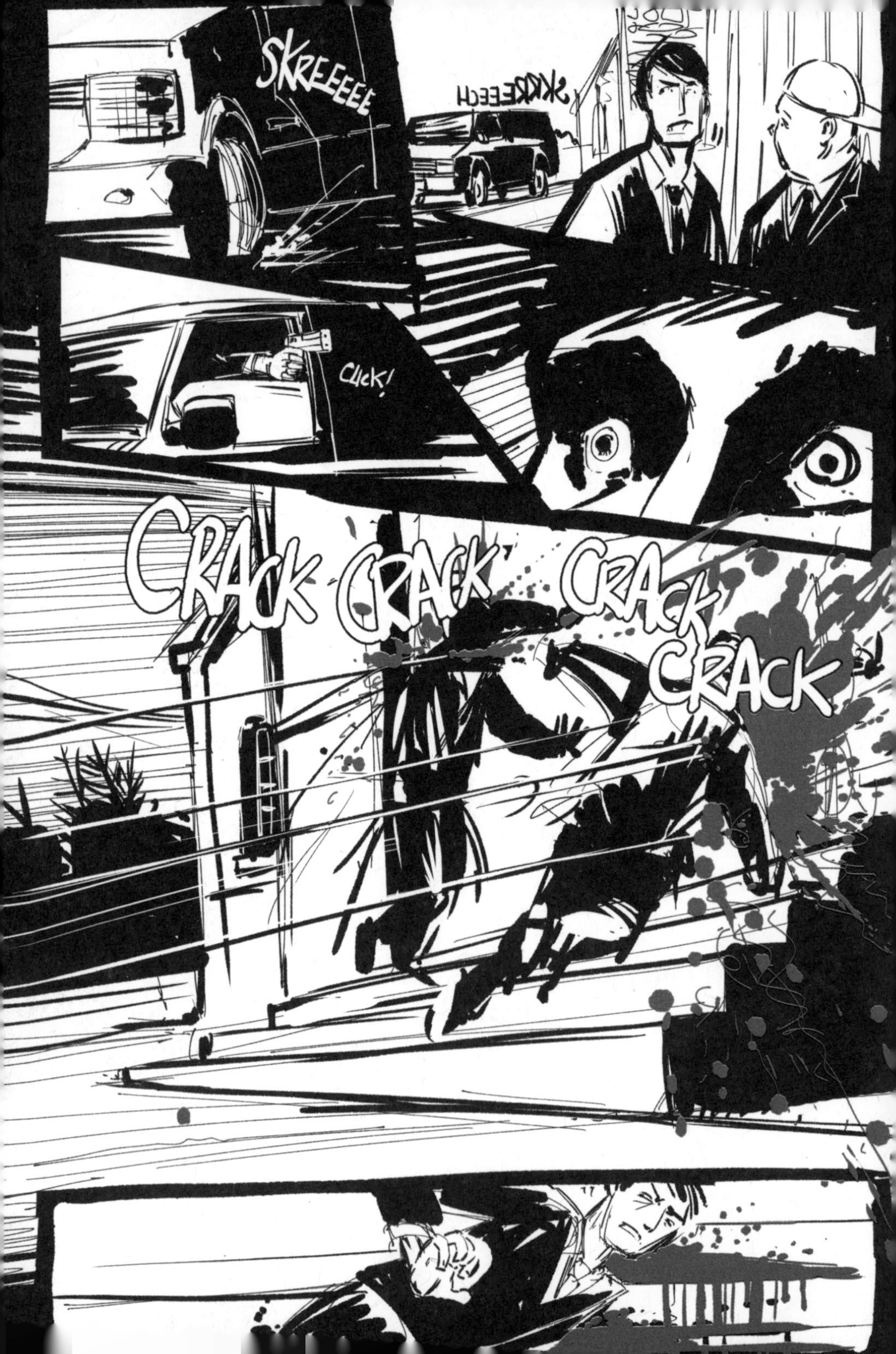
SKREEEEE
SKRREEECH
CLICK!
CRACK CRACK CRACK
CRACK

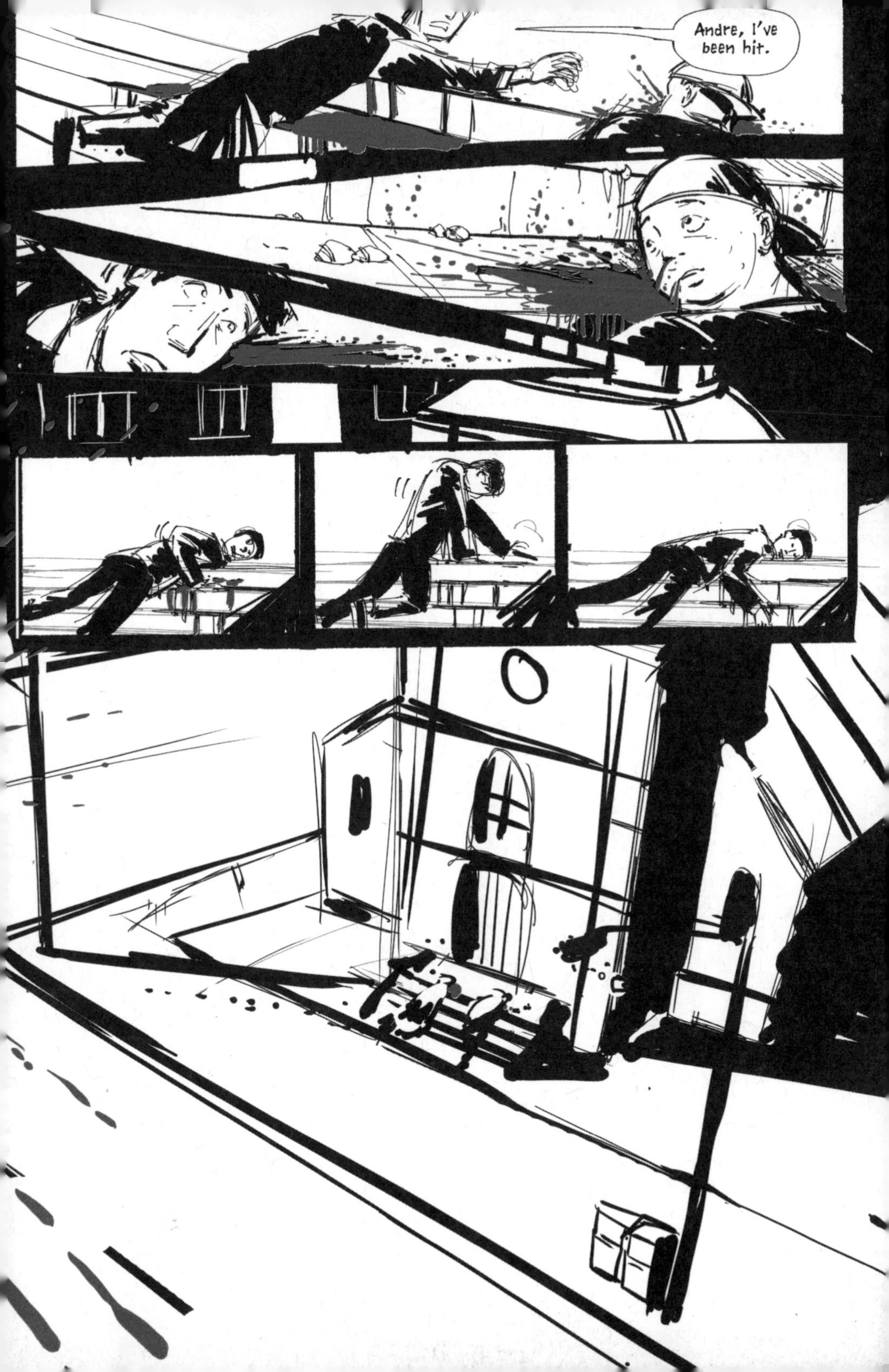
Andre, I've been hit.

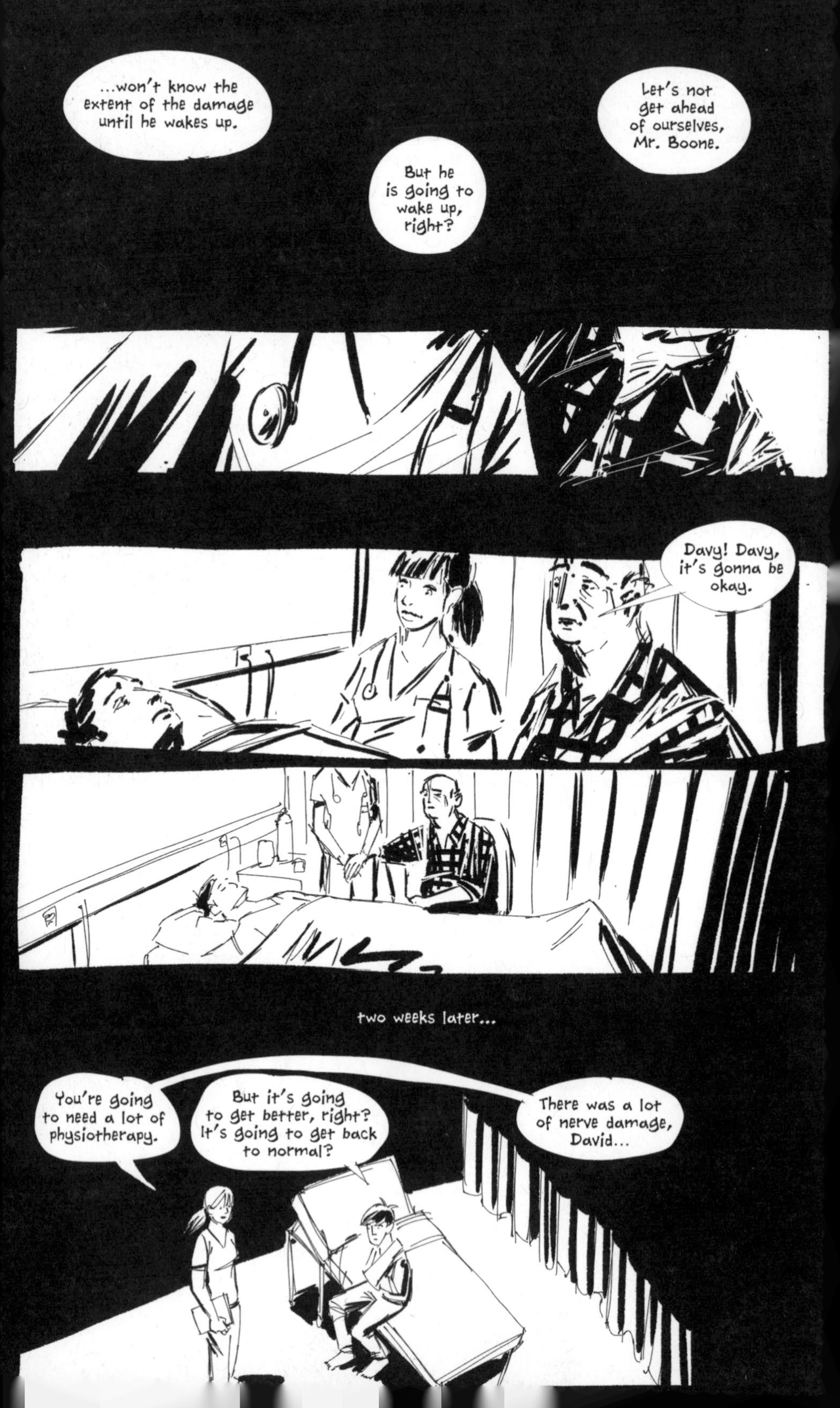
...won't know the extent of the damage until he wakes up.
But he is going to wake up, right?
Let's not get ahead of ourselves, Mr. Boone.
Davy! Davy, it's gonna be okay.
two weeks later...
You're going to need a lot of physiotherapy.
But it's going to get better, right? It's going to get back to normal?
There was a lot of nerve damage, David...

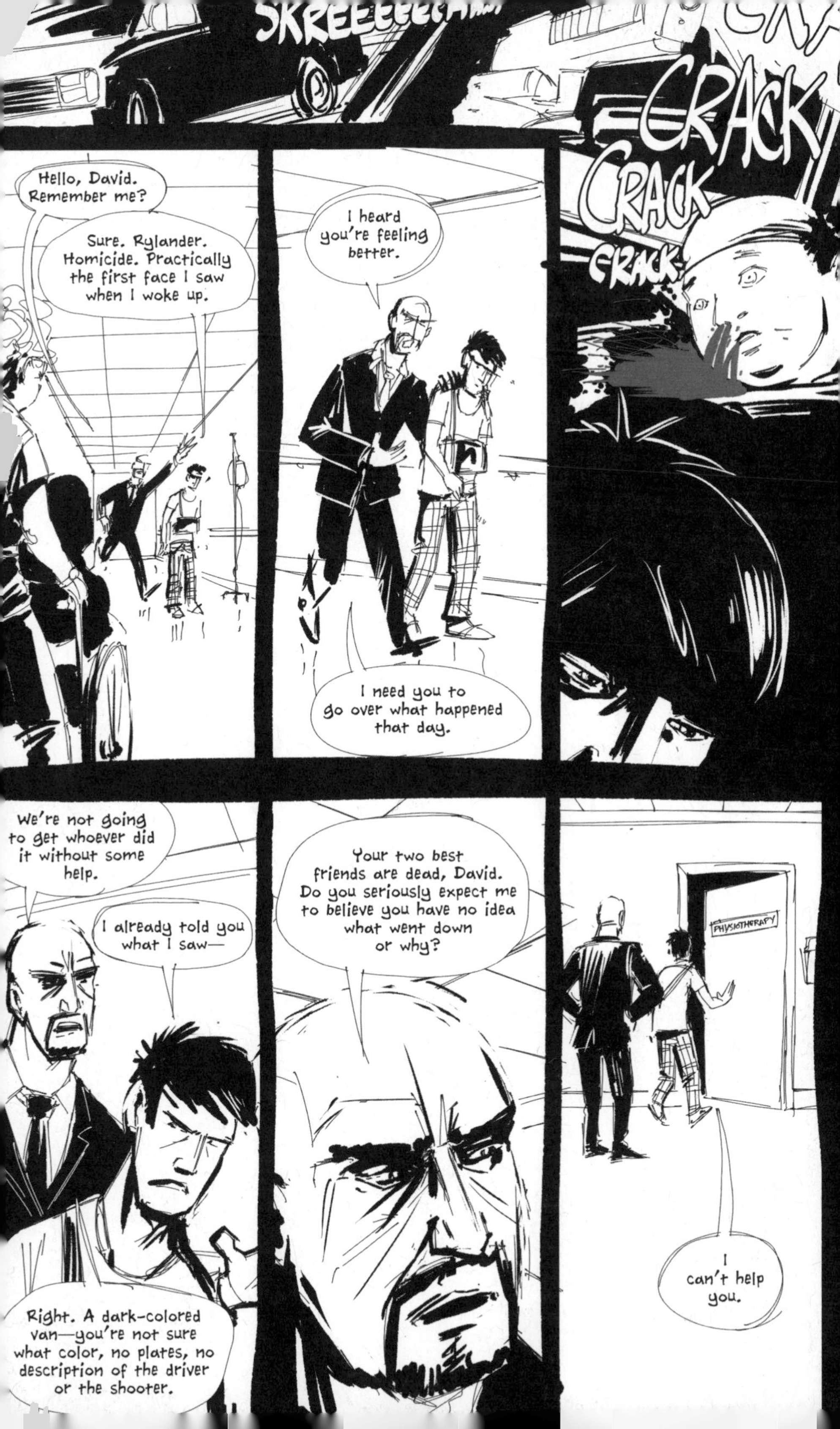
SKREEEEECH
CRACK
CRACK
CRACK
Hello, David. Remember me?
Sure. Rylander. Homicide. Practically the first face I saw when I woke up.
I heard you're feeling better.
I need you to go over what happened that day.
We're not going to get whoever did it without some help.
I already told you what I saw—
Right. A dark-colored van—you're not sure what color, no plates, no description of the driver or the shooter.
Your two best friends are dead, David. Do you seriously expect me to believe you have no idea what went down or why?
PHYSIOTHERAPY
I can't help you.

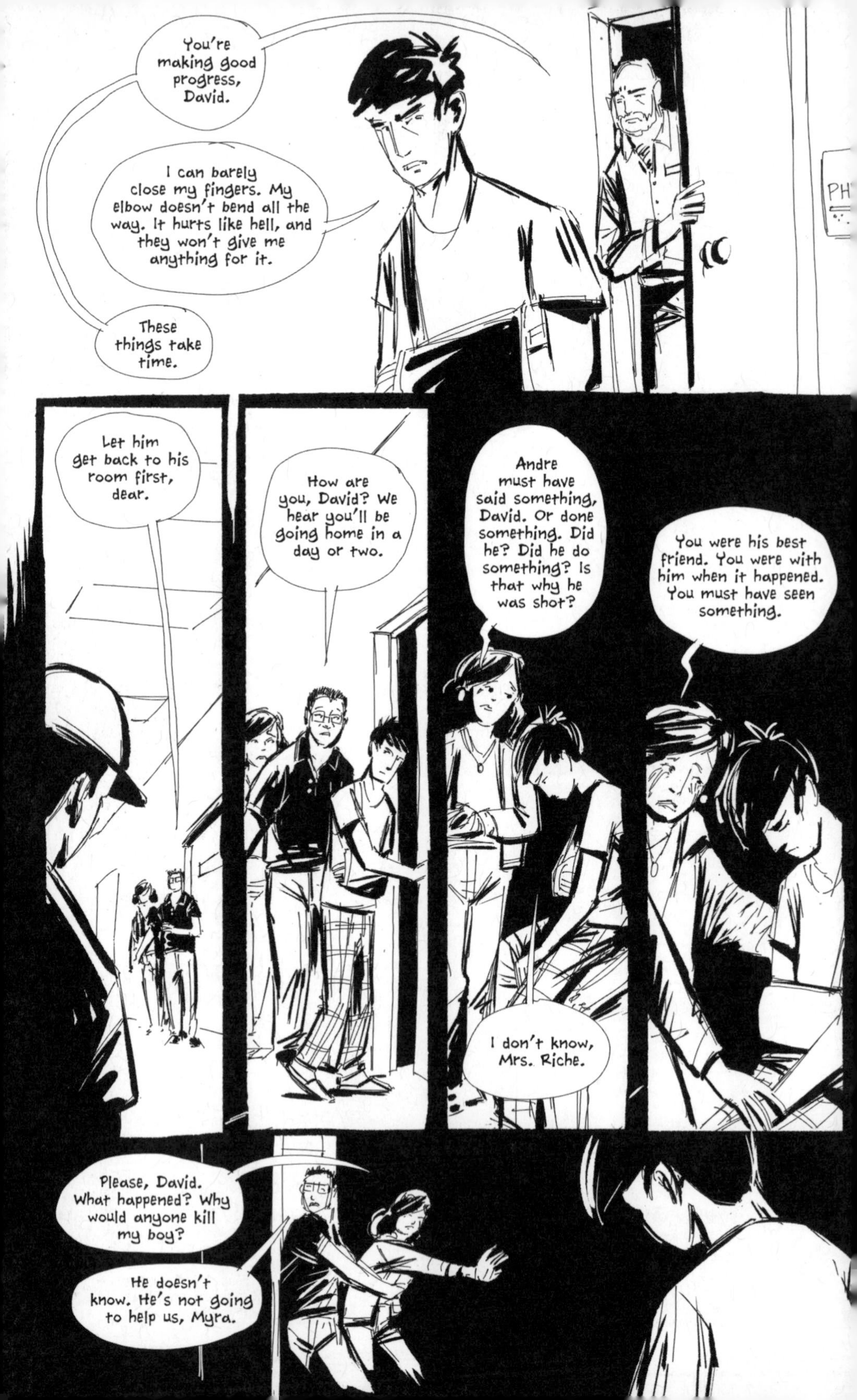

You're making good progress, David.
I can barely close my fingers. My elbow doesn't bend all the way. It hurts like hell, and they won't give me anything for it.
These things take time.
Let him get back to his room first, dear.
How are you, David? We hear you'll be going home in a day or two.
Andre must have said something, David. Or done something. Did he? Did he do something? Is that why he was shot?
I don't know, Mrs. Riche.
You were his best friend. You were with him when it happened. You must have seen something.
Please, David. What happened? Why would anyone kill my boy?
He doesn't know. He's not going to help us, Myra.

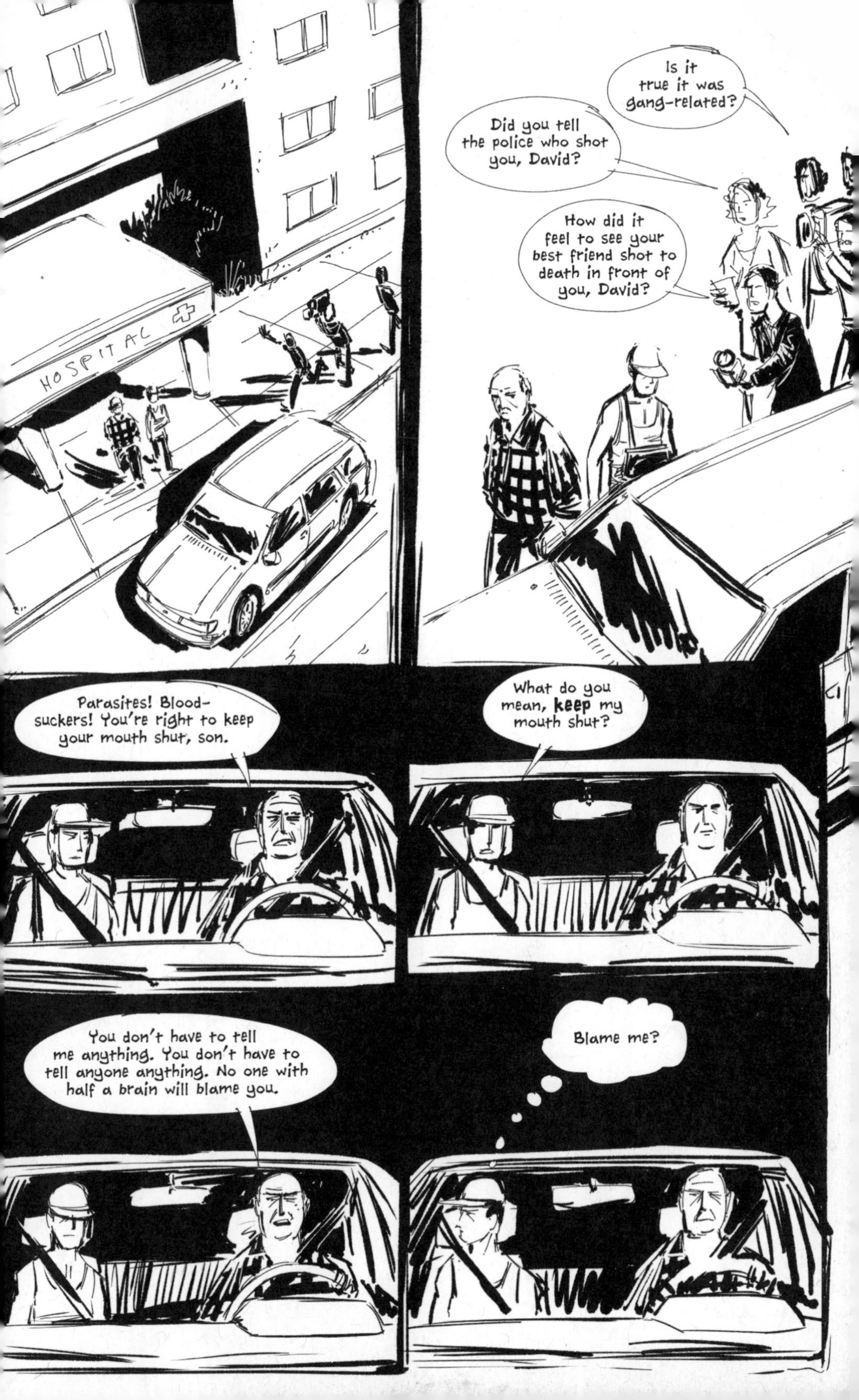
HOSPITAL
Is it true it was gang-related?
Did you tell the police who shot you, David?
How did it feel to see your best friend shot to death in front of you, David?
Parasites! Blood-suckers! You're right to keep your mouth shut, son.
What do you mean, **keep** my mouth shut?
You don't have to tell me anything. You don't have to tell anyone anything. No one with half a brain will blame you.
Blame me?

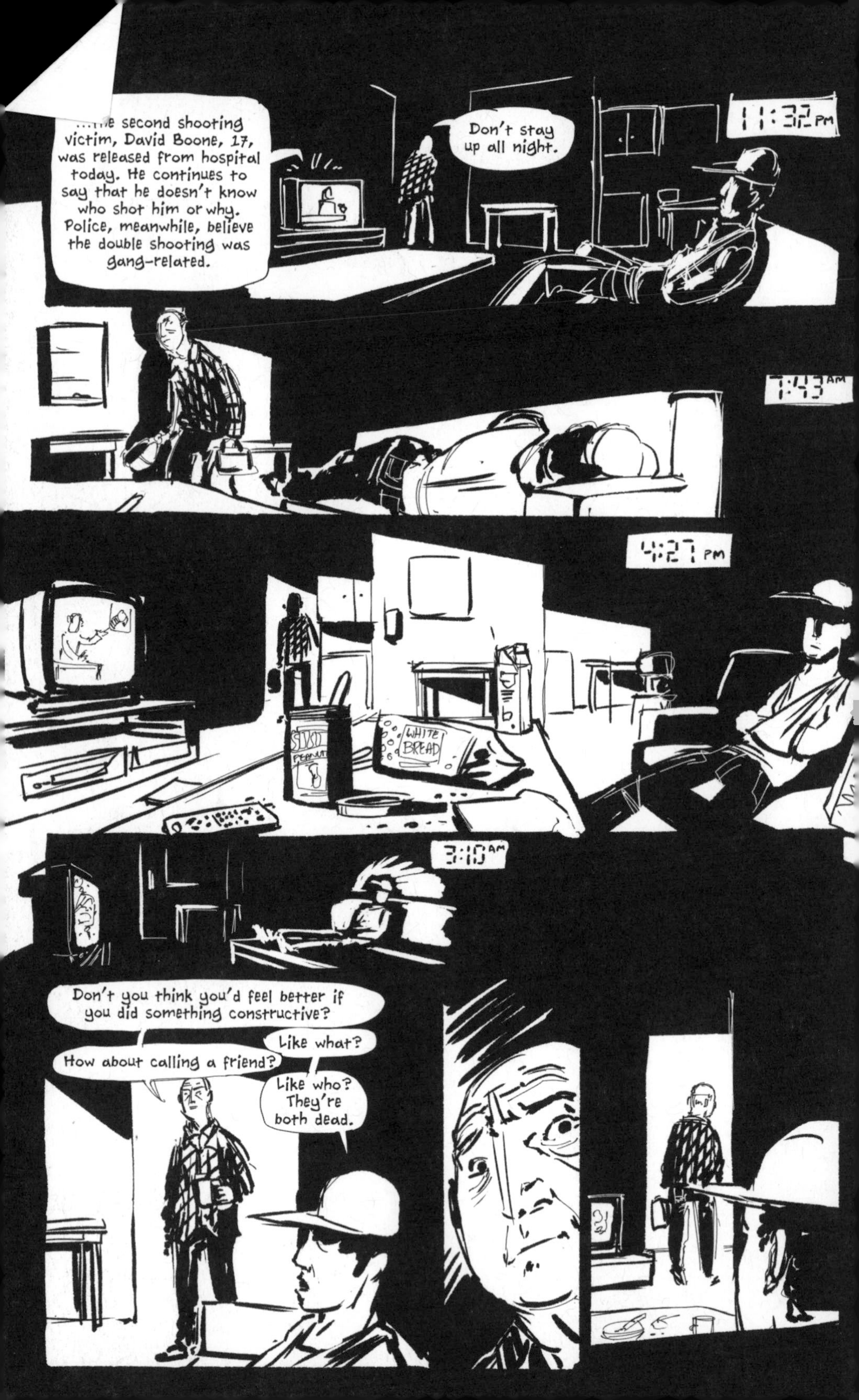
...the second shooting victim, David Boone, 17, was released from hospital today. He continues to say that he doesn't know who shot him or why. Police, meanwhile, believe the double shooting was gang-related.
Don't stay up all night.
11:32 PM
1:43 AM
4:27 PM
WHITE BREAD
PEANUT
3:10 AM
Don't you think you'd feel better if you did something constructive?
Like what?
How about calling a friend?
Like who? They're both dead.

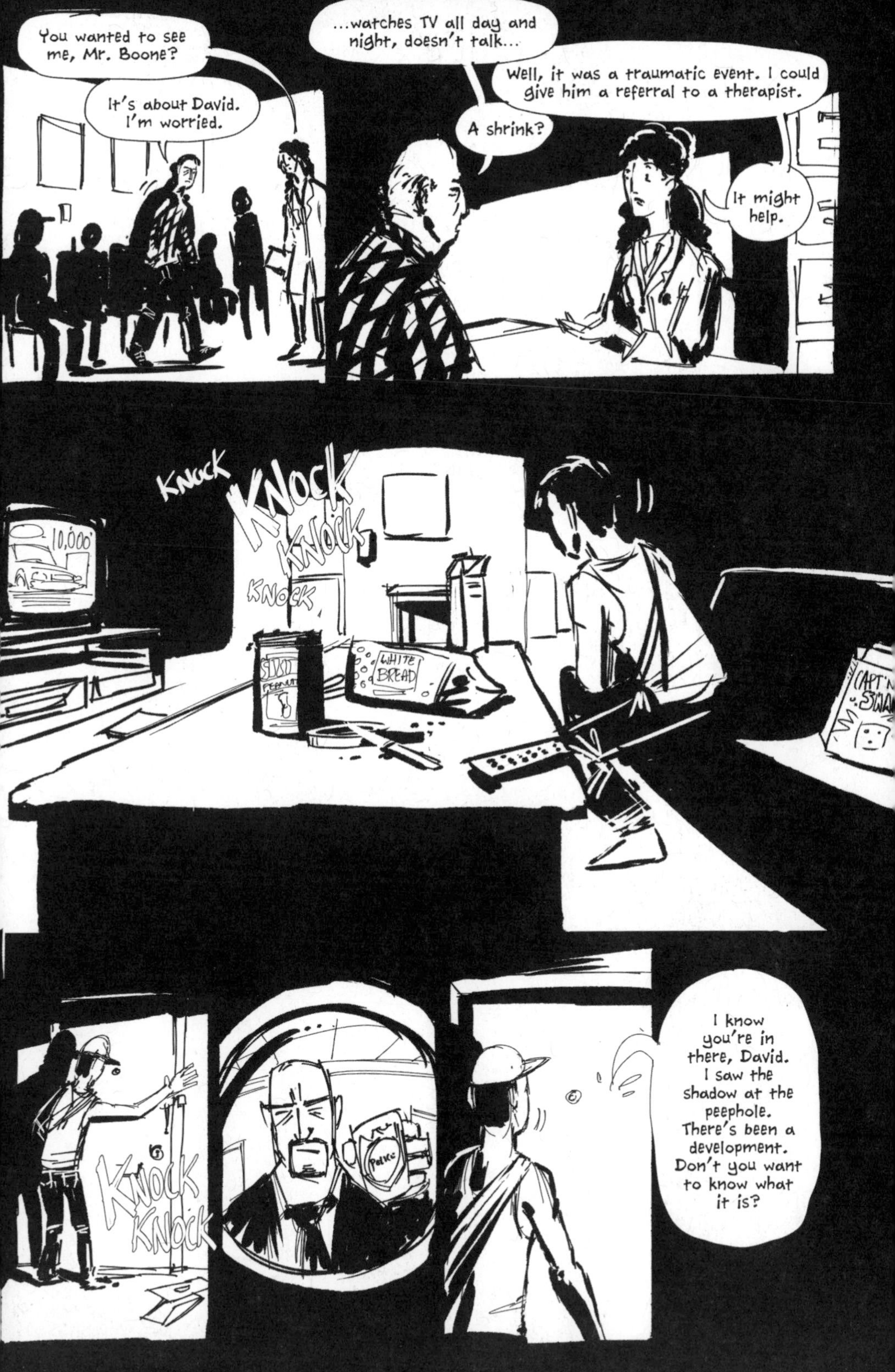
You wanted to see me, Mr. Boone?
It's about David. I'm worried.
...watches TV all day and night, doesn't talk...
Well, it was a traumatic event. I could give him a referral to a therapist.
A shrink?
It might help.
KNOCK
KNOCK
KNOCK
KNOCK
10,000
WHITE BREAD
KNOCK
KNOCK
I know you're in there, David. I saw the shadow at the peephole. There's been a development. Don't you want to know what it is?

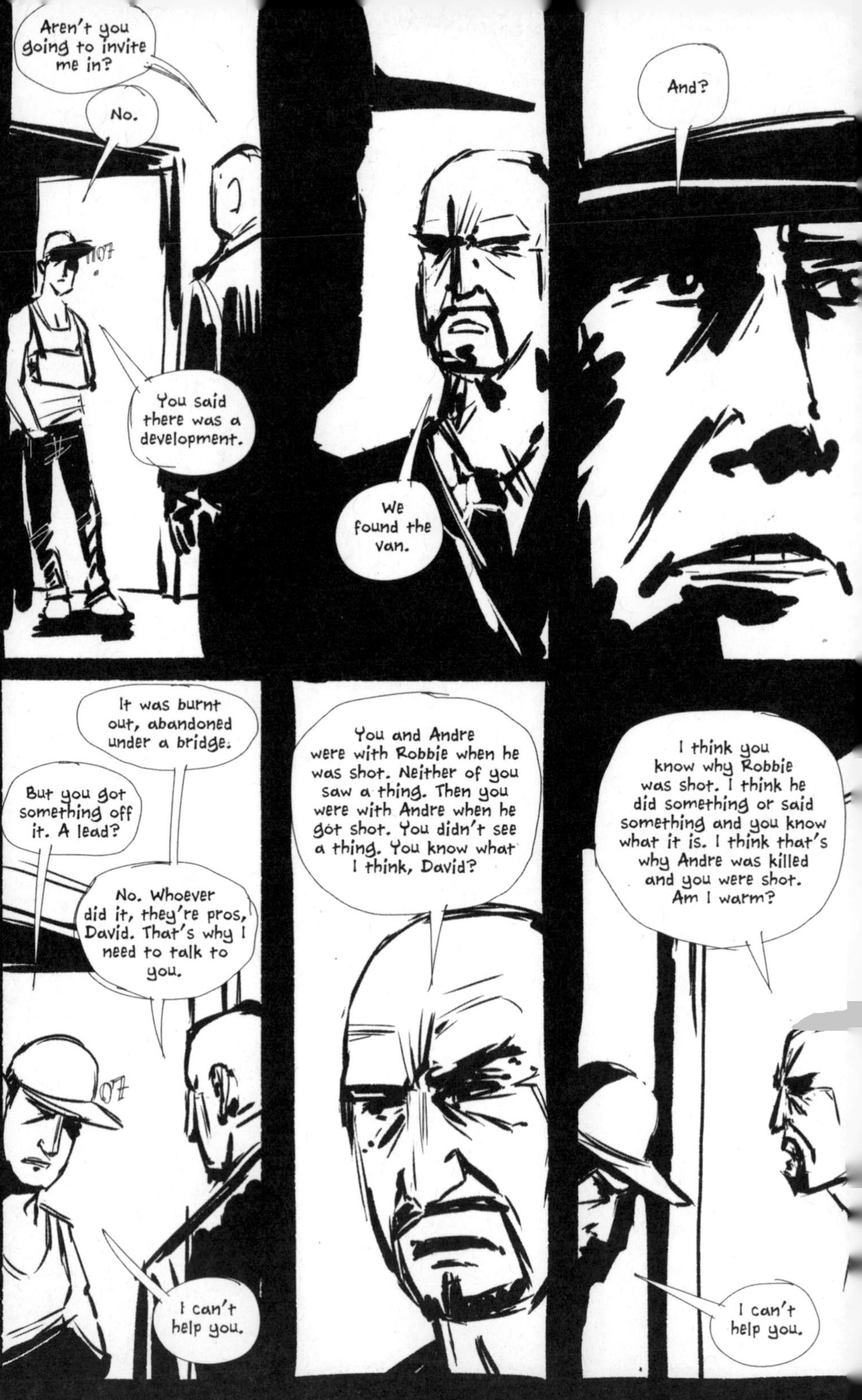
Aren't you going to invite me in?
No.
You said there was a development.
We found the van.
And?
It was burnt out, abandoned under a bridge.
But you got something off it. A lead?
No. Whoever did it, they're pros, David. That's why I need to talk to you.
I can't help you.
You and Andre were with Robbie when he was shot. Neither of you saw a thing. Then you were with Andre when he got shot. You didn't see a thing. You know what I think, David?
I think you know why Robbie was shot. I think he did something or said something and you know what it is. I think that's why Andre was killed and you were shot. Am I warm?
I can't help you.

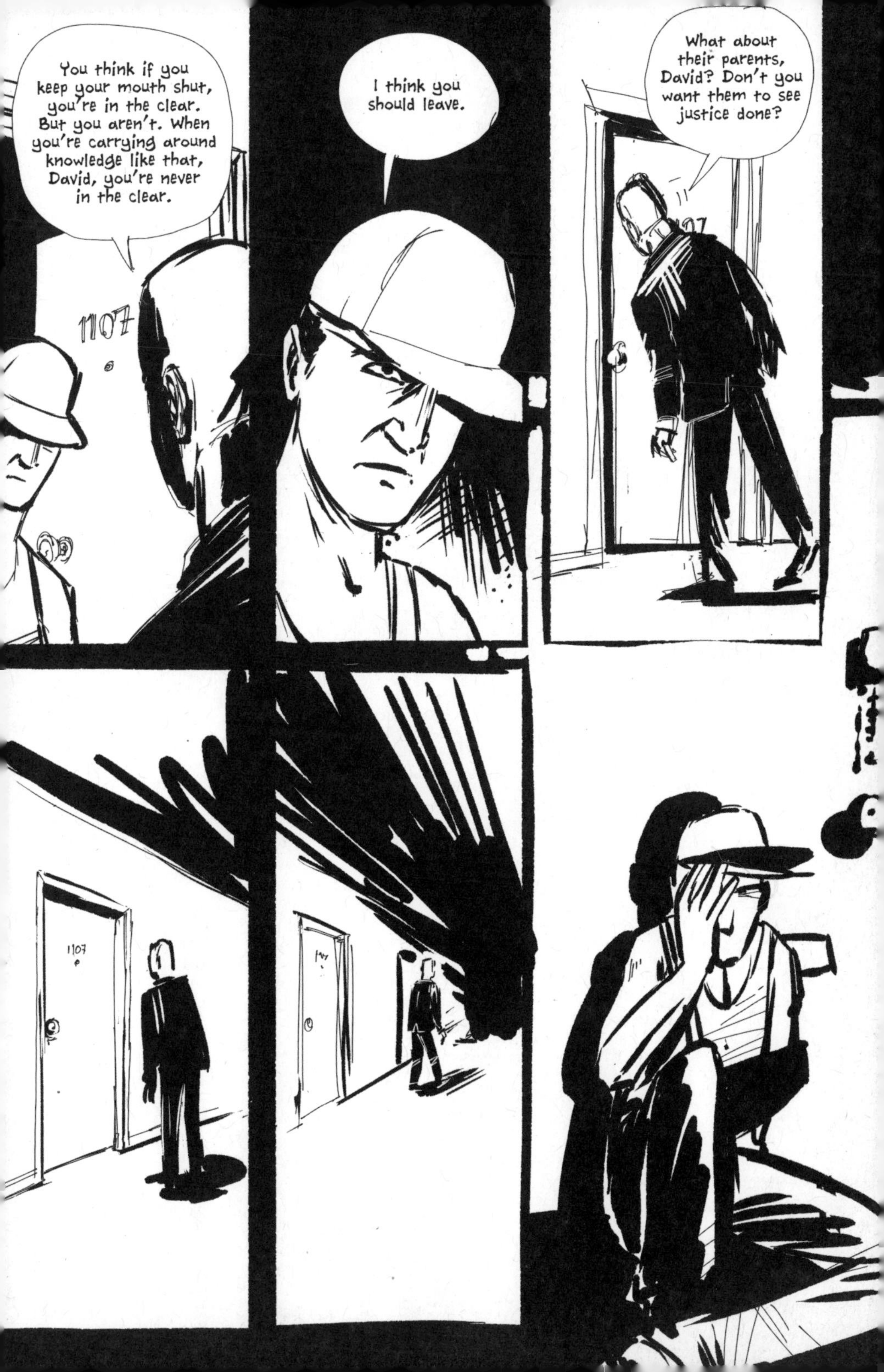
You think if you keep your mouth shut, you're in the clear. But you aren't. When you're carrying around knowledge like that, David, you're never in the clear.
I think you should leave.
What about their parents, David? Don't you want them to see justice done?
1107

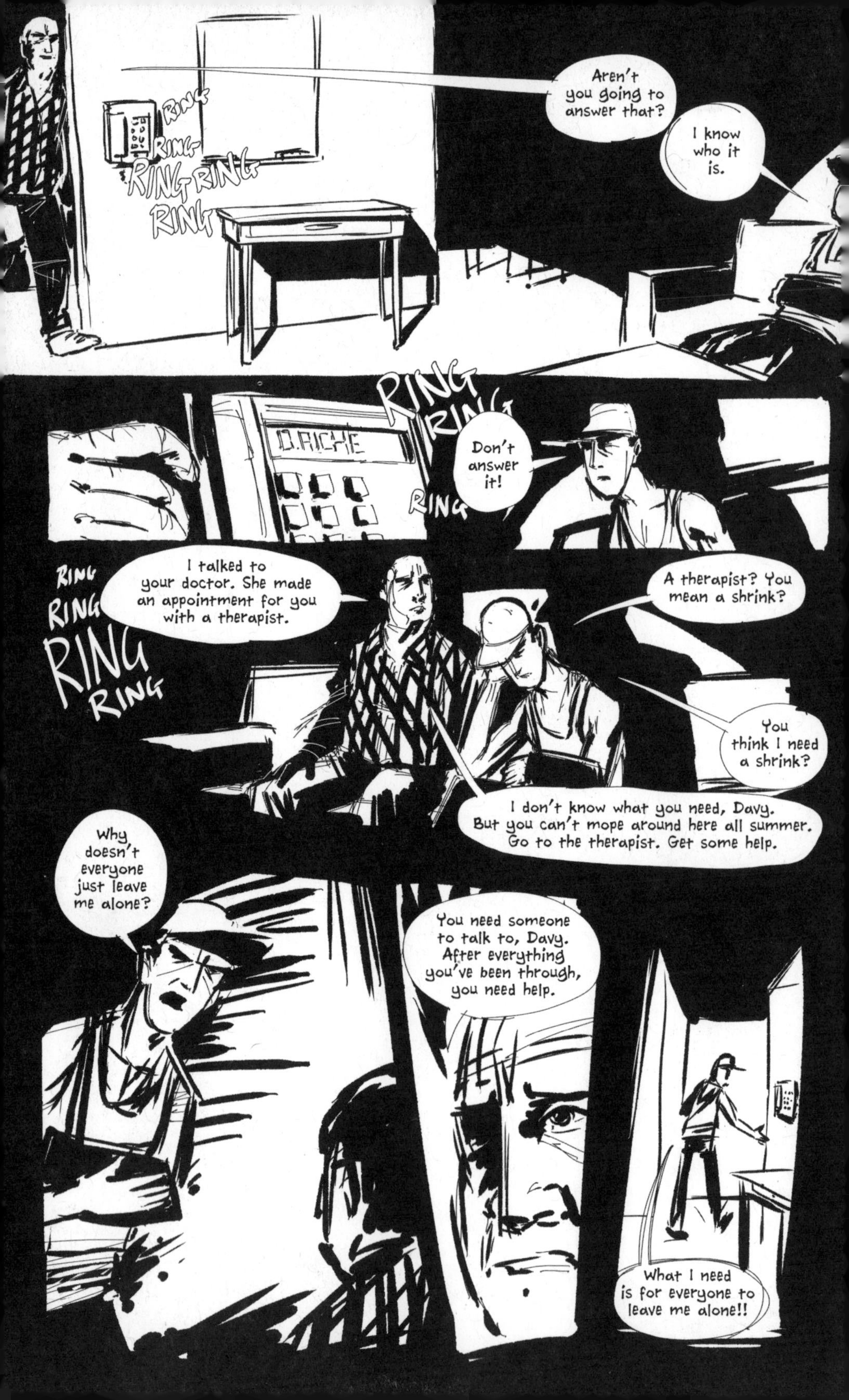
RING
RING
RING RING
RING
Aren't you going to answer that?
I know who it is.
D.RICHE
RING
RING
Don't answer it!
RING
RING
RING
RING
RING
I talked to your doctor. She made an appointment for you with a therapist.
A therapist? You mean a shrink?
You think I need a shrink?
I don't know what you need, Davy. But you can't mope around here all summer. Go to the therapist. Get some help.
Why doesn't everyone just leave me alone?
You need someone to talk to, Davy. After everything you've been through, you need help.
What I need is for everyone to leave me alone!!

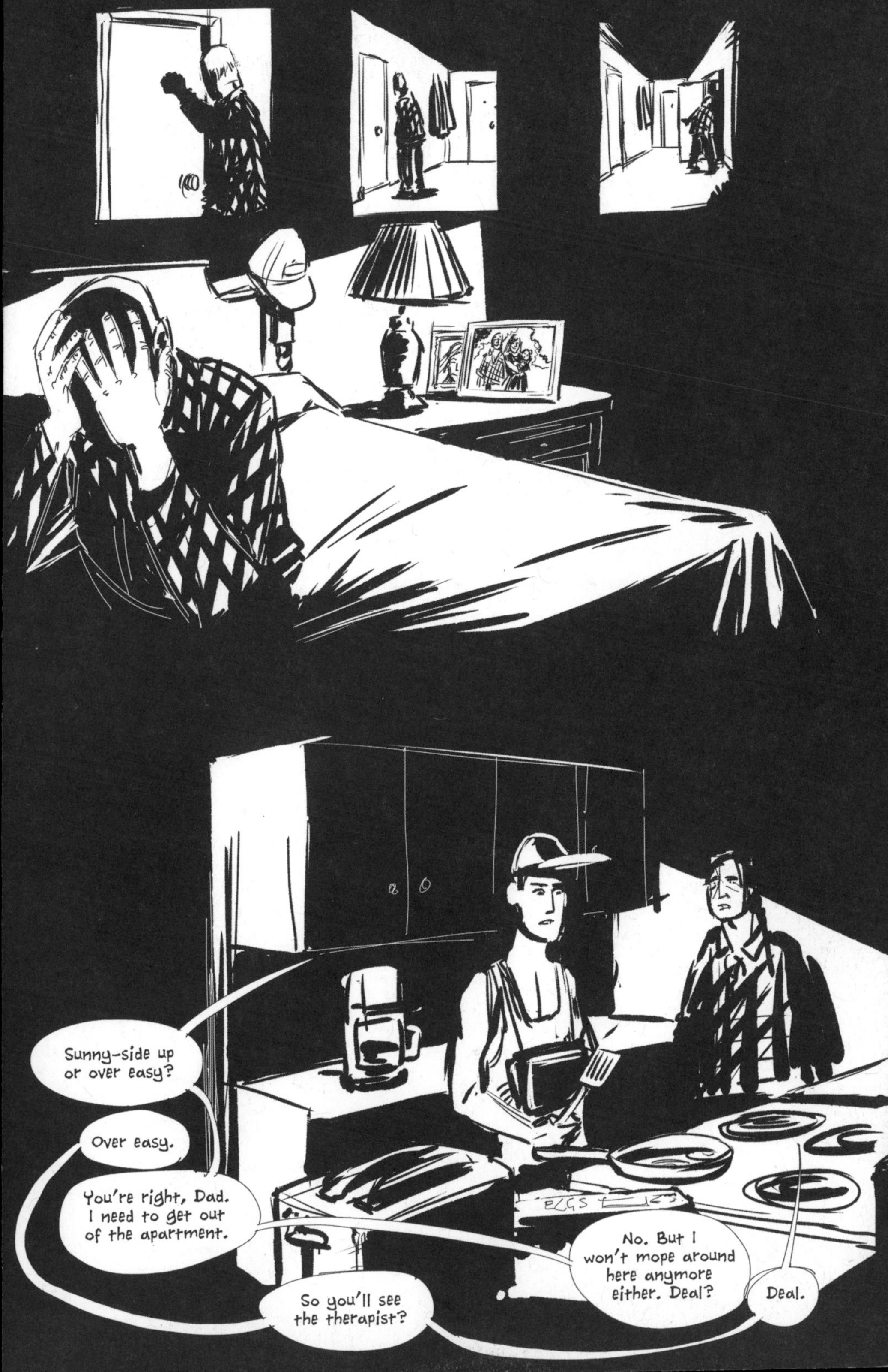
Sunny-side up or over easy?
Over easy.
You're right, Dad. I need to get out of the apartment.
So you'll see the therapist?
No. But I won't mope around here anymore either. Deal?
Deal.

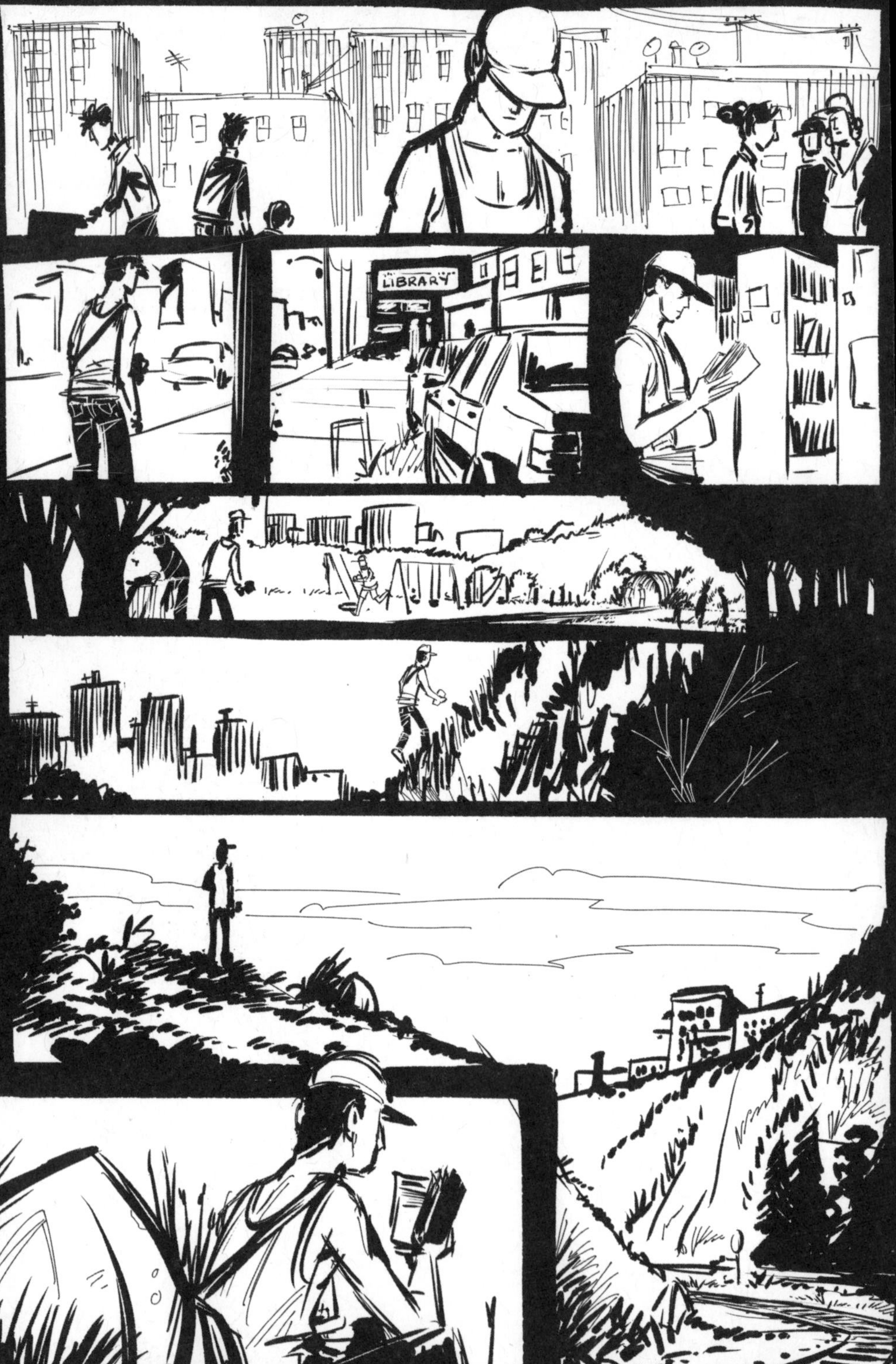
LIBRARY

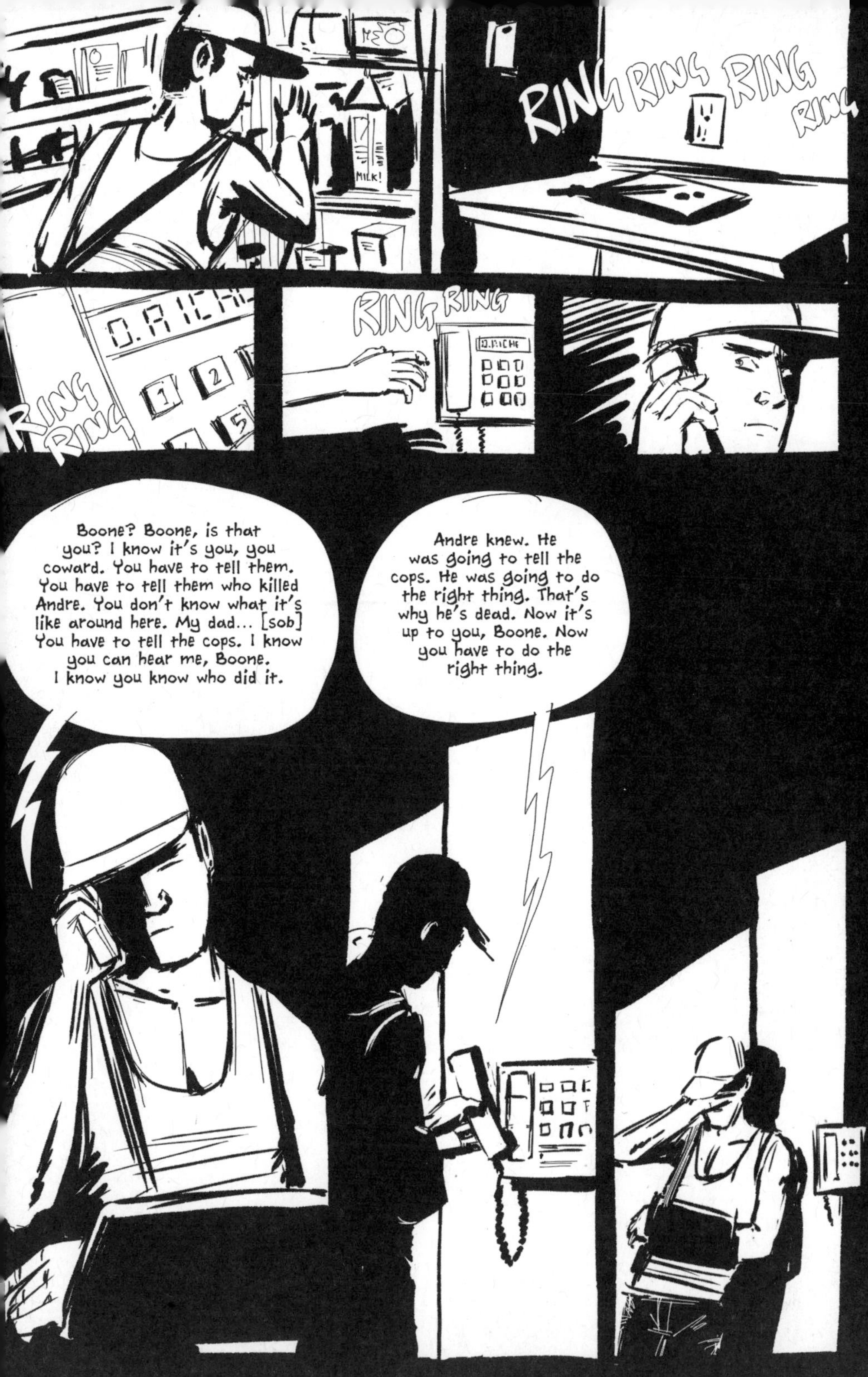
MILK!
RING RING RING RING
D.RICHE
RING RING
RING RING
Boone? Boone, is that you? I know it's you, you coward. You have to tell them. You have to tell them who killed Andre. You don't know what it's like around here. My dad... [sob] You have to tell the cops. I know you can hear me, Boone. I know you know who did it.
Andre knew. He was going to tell the cops. He was going to do the right thing. That's why he's dead. Now it's up to you, Boone. Now you have to do the right thing.

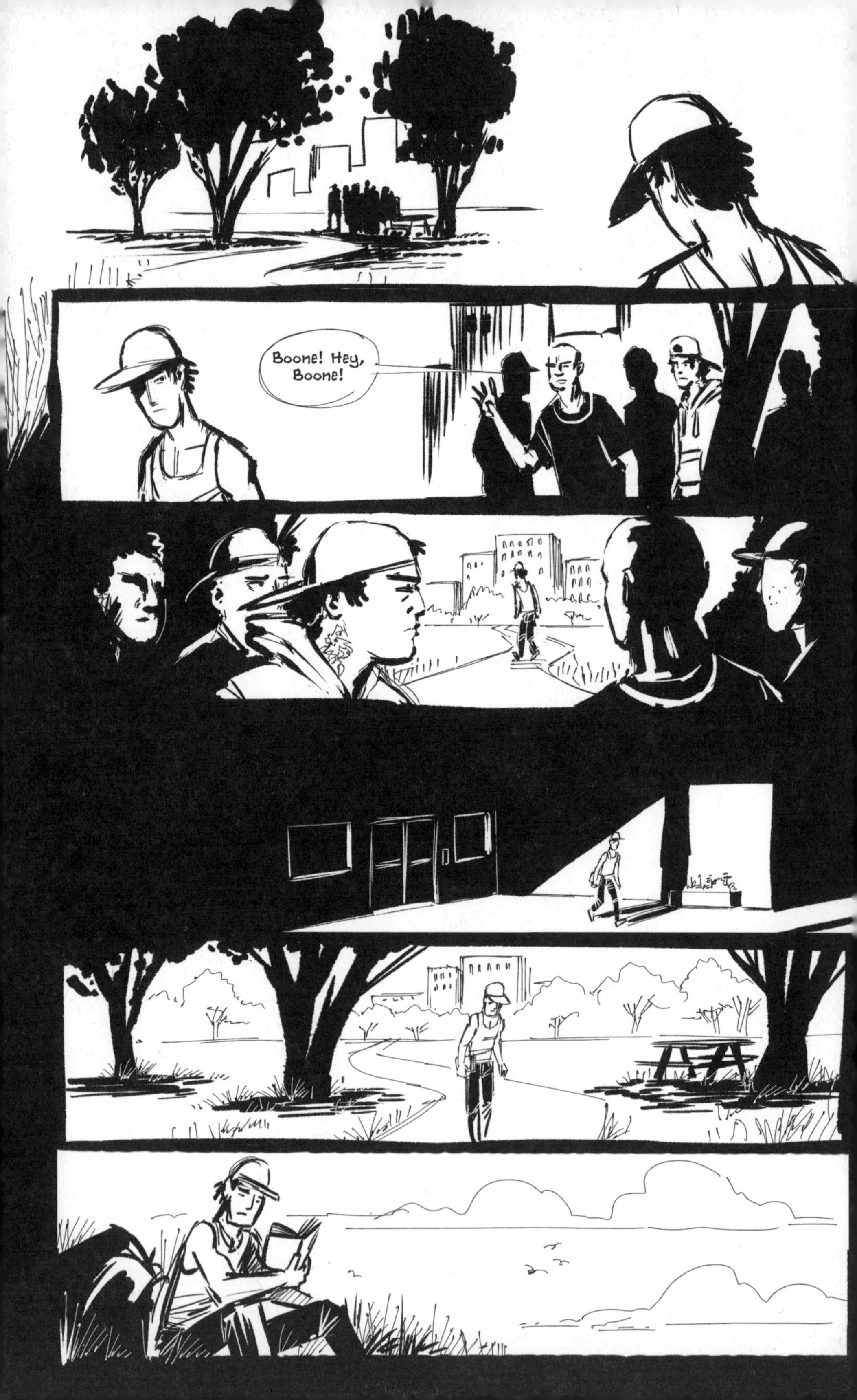
Boone! Hey, Boone!

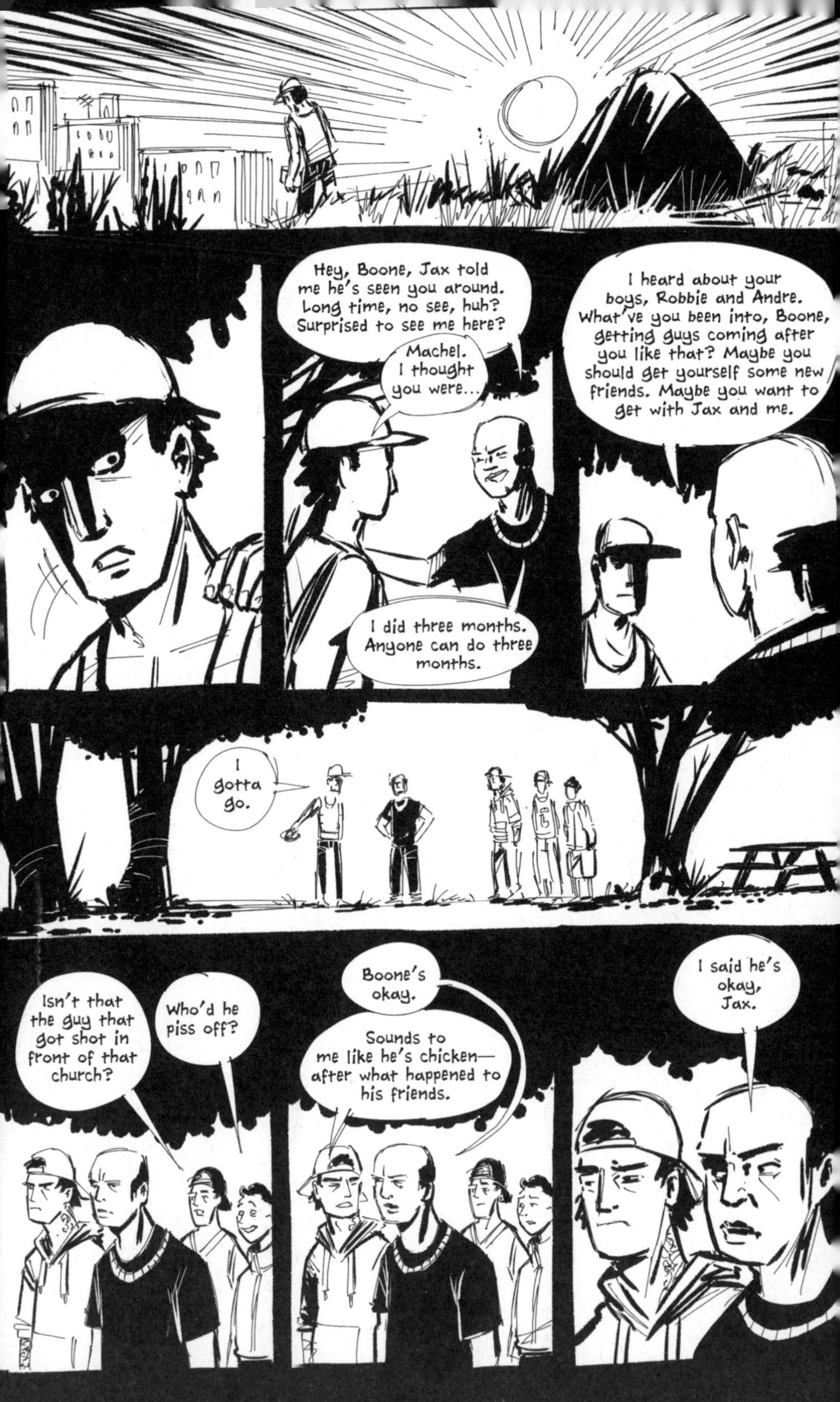
Hey, Boone, Jax told me he's seen you around. Long time, no see, huh? Surprised to see me here?
Machel. I thought you were...
I did three months. Anyone can do three months.
I heard about your boys, Robbie and Andre. What've you been into, Boone, getting guys coming after you like that? Maybe you should get yourself some new friends. Maybe you want to get with Jax and me.
I gotta go.
Isn't that the guy that got shot in front of that church?
Who'd he piss off?
Boone's okay.
Sounds to me like he's chicken— after what happened to his friends.
I said he's okay, Jax.

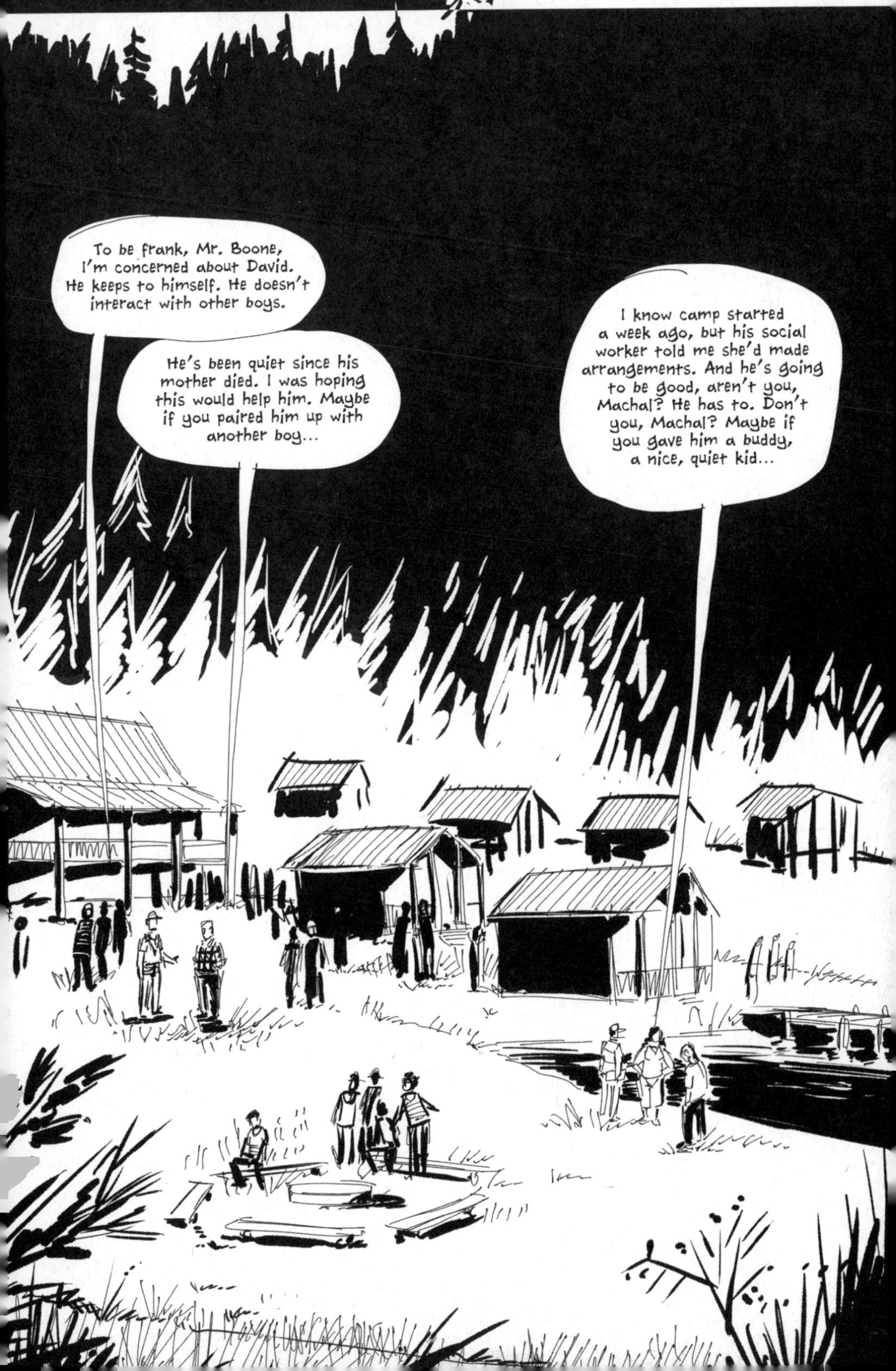
To be frank, Mr. Boone, I'm concerned about David. He keeps to himself. He doesn't interact with other boys.
He's been quiet since his mother died. I was hoping this would help him. Maybe if you paired him up with another boy...
I know camp started a week ago, but his social worker told me she'd made arrangements. And he's going to be good, aren't you, Machal? He has to. Don't you, Machal? Maybe if you gave him a buddy, a nice, quiet kid...

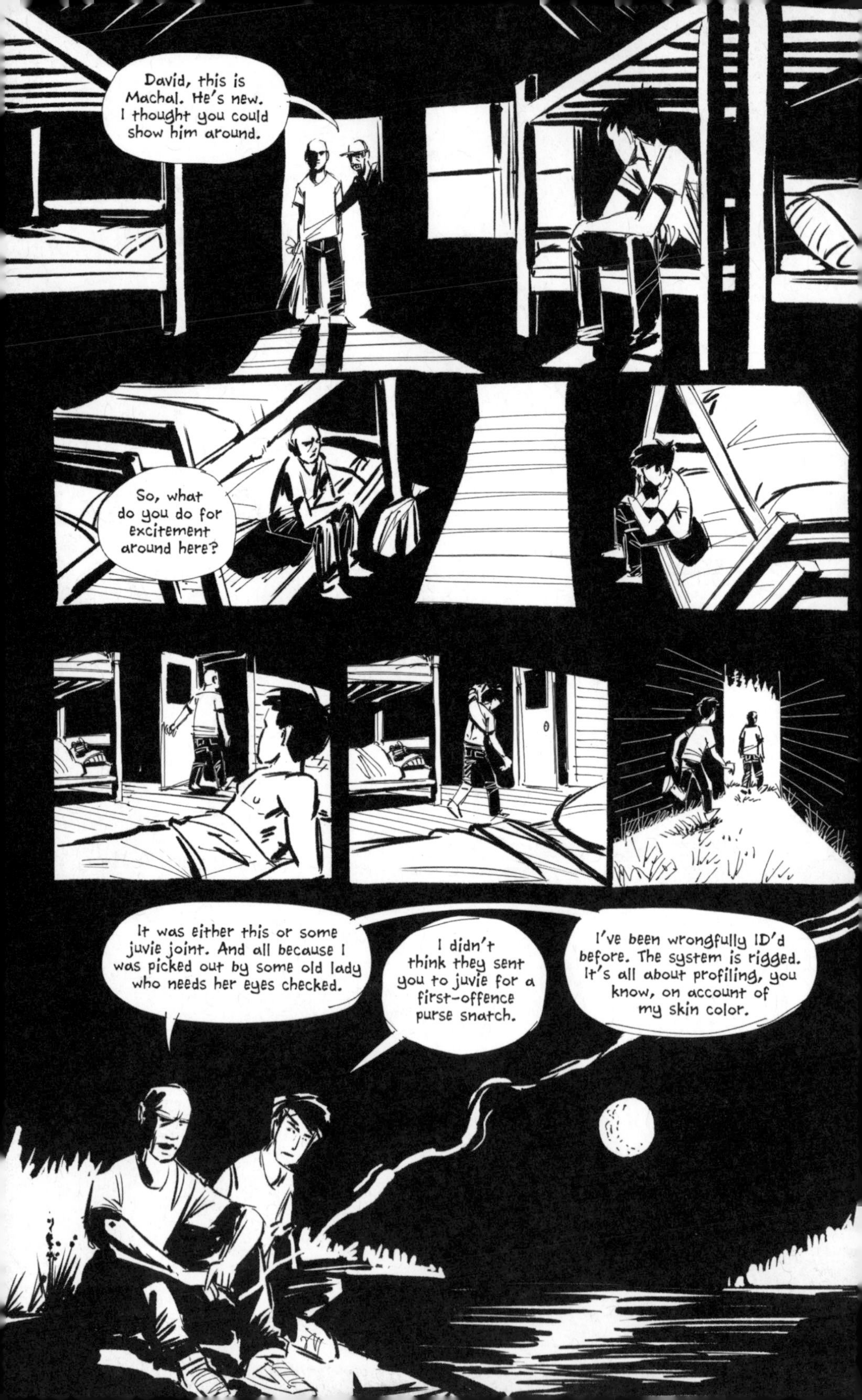
David, this is Machal. He's new. I thought you could show him around.
So, what do you do for excitement around here?
It was either this or some juvie joint. And all because I was picked out by some old lady who needs her eyes checked.
I didn't think they sent you to juvie for a first-offence purse snatch.
I've been wrongfully ID'd before. The system is rigged. It's all about profiling, you know, on account of my skin color.

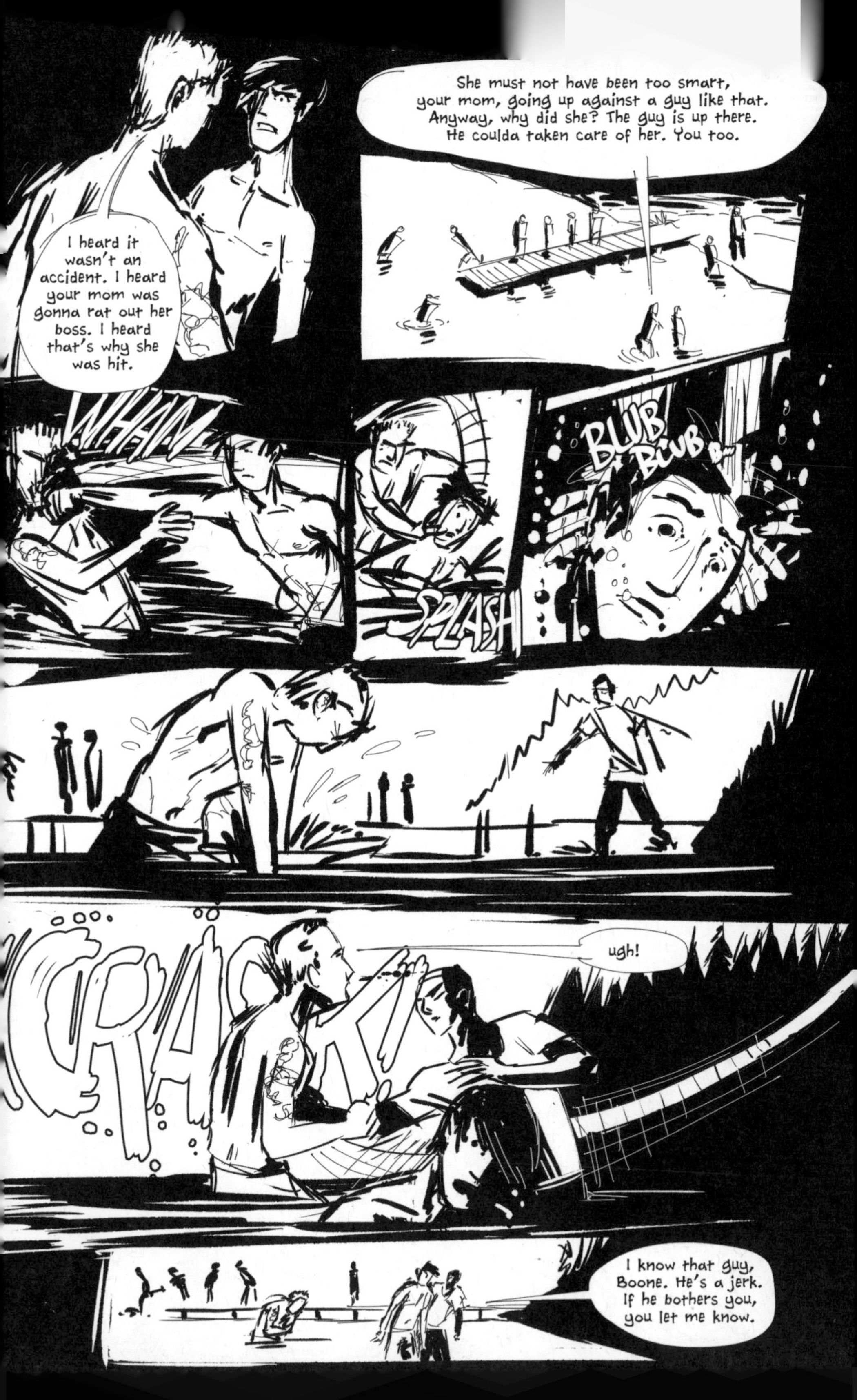
I heard it wasn't an accident. I heard your mom was gonna rat out her boss. I heard that's why she was hit.
She must not have been too smart, your mom, going up against a guy like that. Anyway, why did she? The guy is up there. He coulda taken care of her. You too.
WHAM
SPLASH
BLUB BLUB B...
CRASH
ugh!
I know that guy, Boone. He's a jerk. If he bothers you, you let me know.

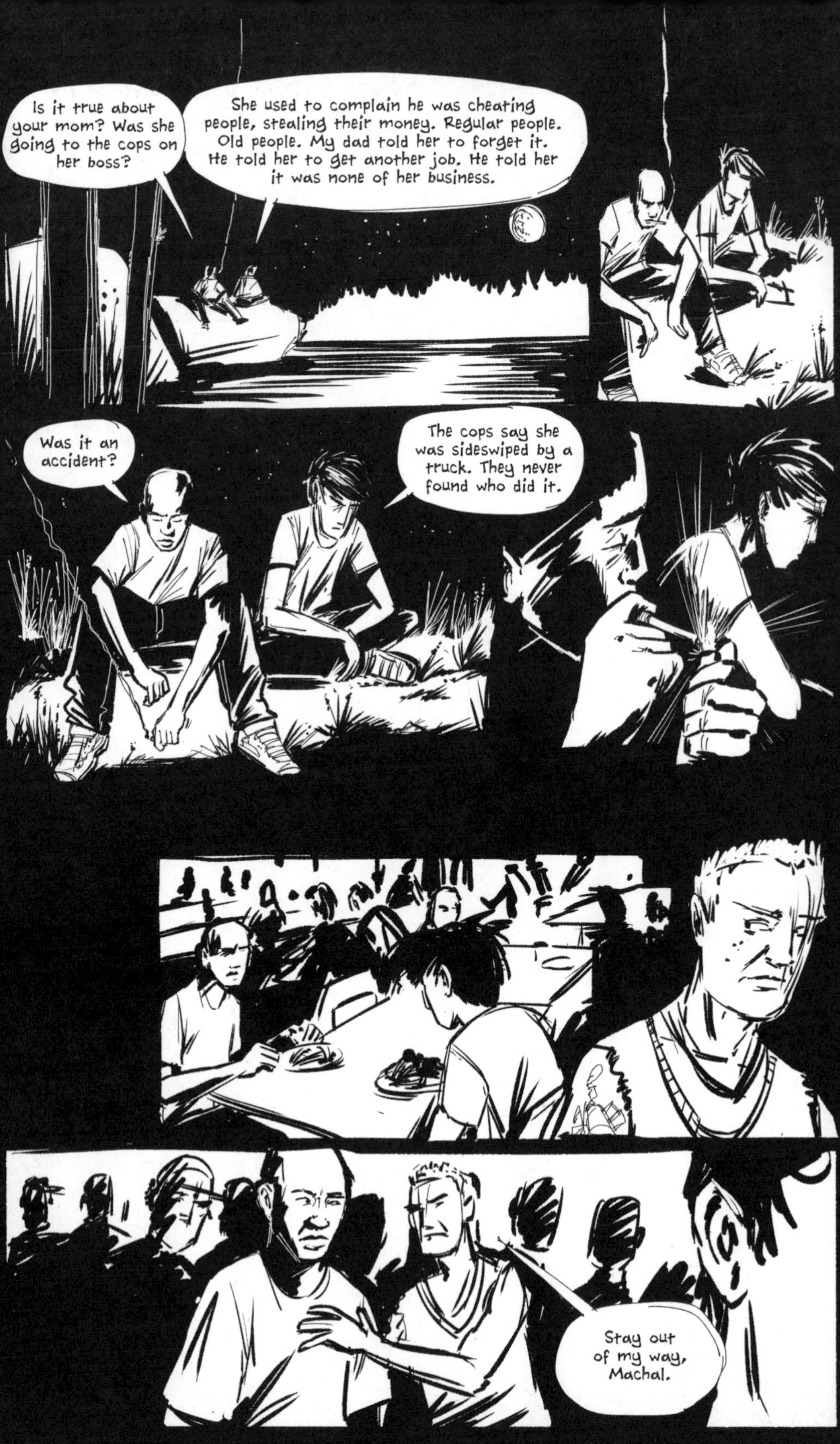
Is it true about your mom? Was she going to the cops on her boss?
She used to complain he was cheating people, stealing their money. Regular people. Old people. My dad told her to forget it. He told her to get another job. He told her it was none of her business.
Was it an accident?
The cops say she was sideswiped by a truck. They never found who did it.
Stay out of my way, Machal.

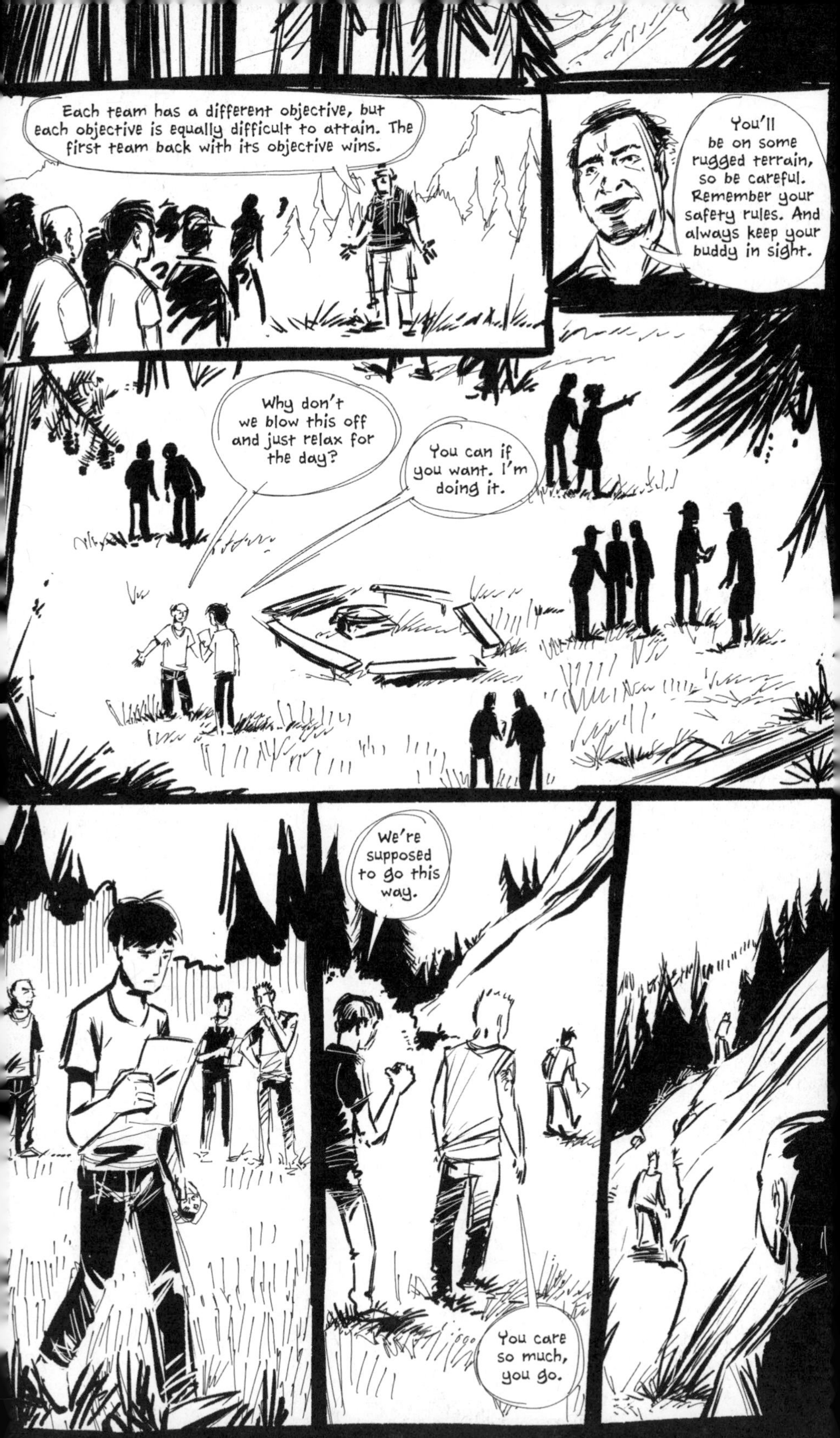
Each team has a different objective, but each objective is equally difficult to attain. The first team back with its objective wins.
You'll be on some rugged terrain, so be careful. Remember your safety rules. And always keep your buddy in sight.
Why don't we blow this off and just relax for the day?
You can if you want. I'm doing it.
We're supposed to go this way.
You care so much, you go.

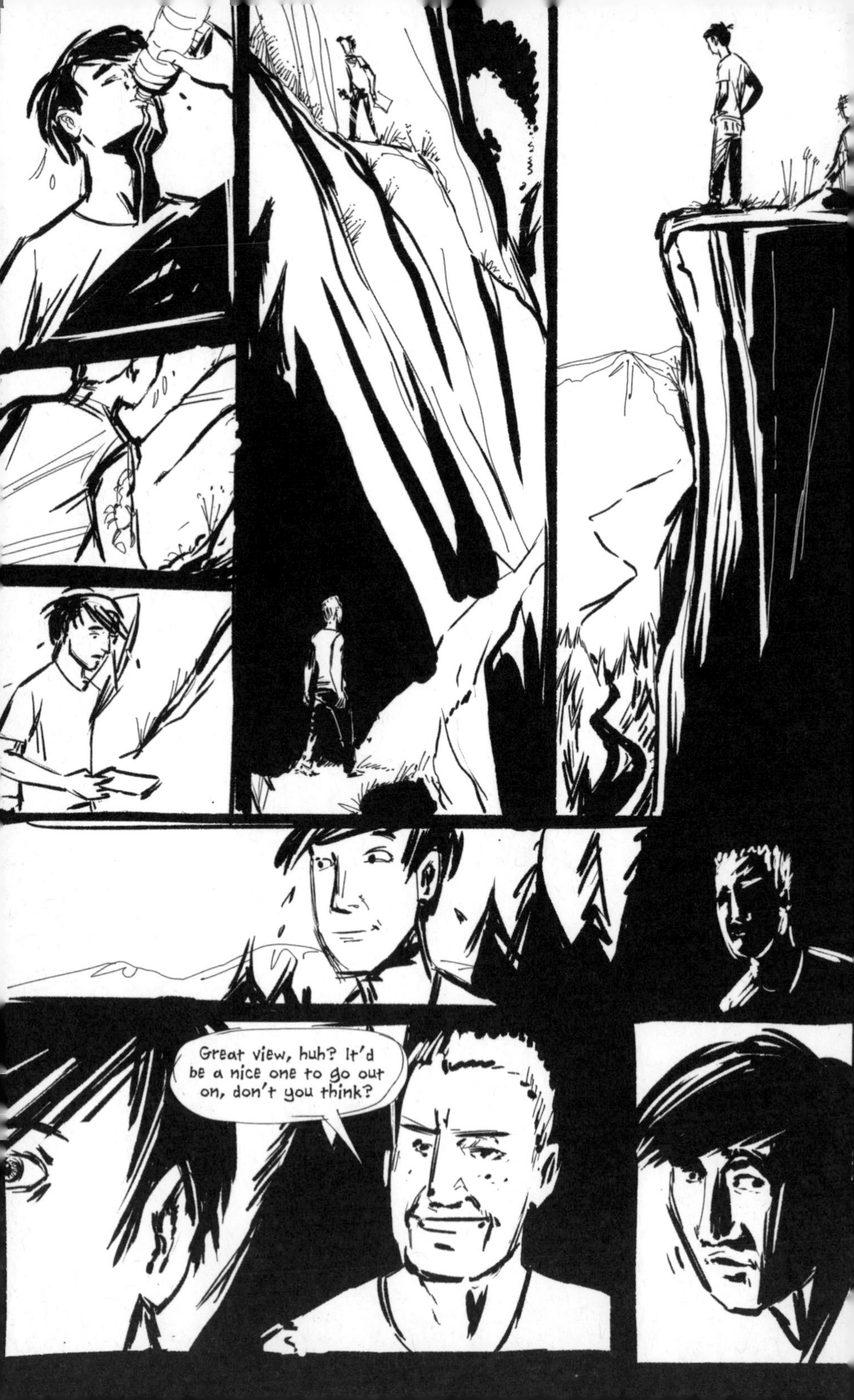
Great view, huh? It'd be a nice one to go out on, don't you think?

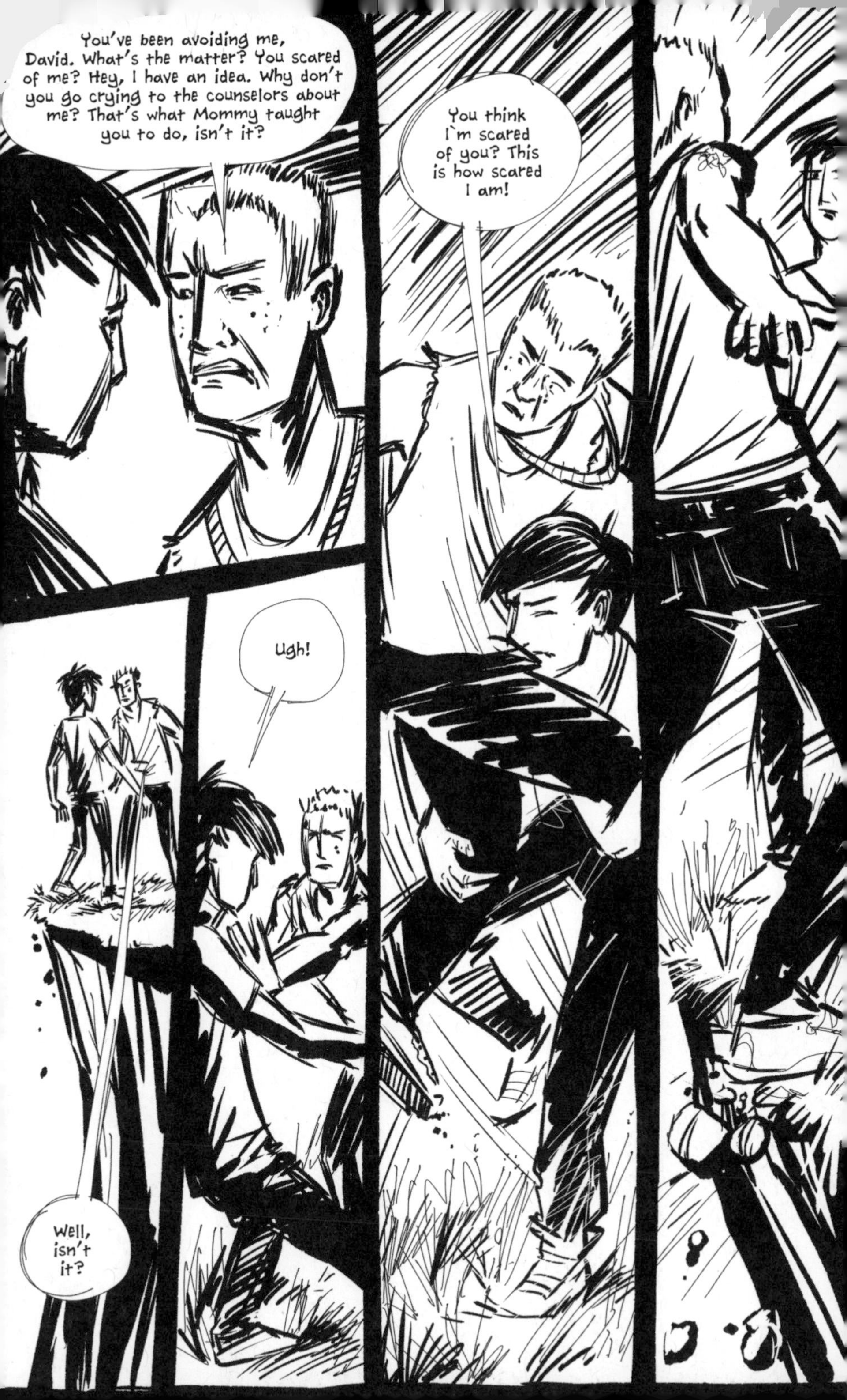
You've been avoiding me, David. What's the matter? You scared of me? Hey, I have an idea. Why don't you go crying to the counselors about me? That's what Mommy taught you to do, isn't it?
Well, isn't it?
Ugh!
You think I'm scared of you? This is how scared I am!

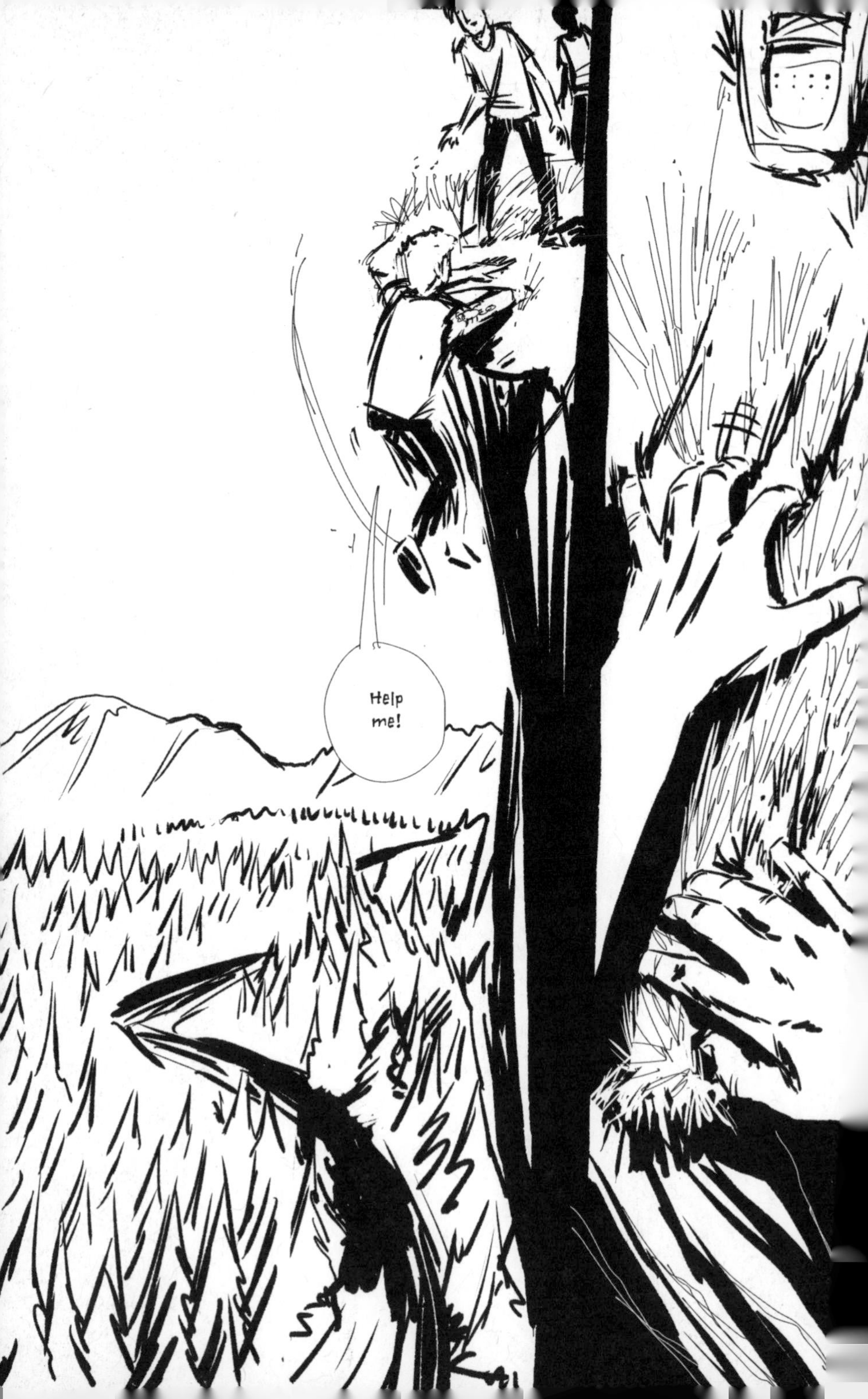
Help me!

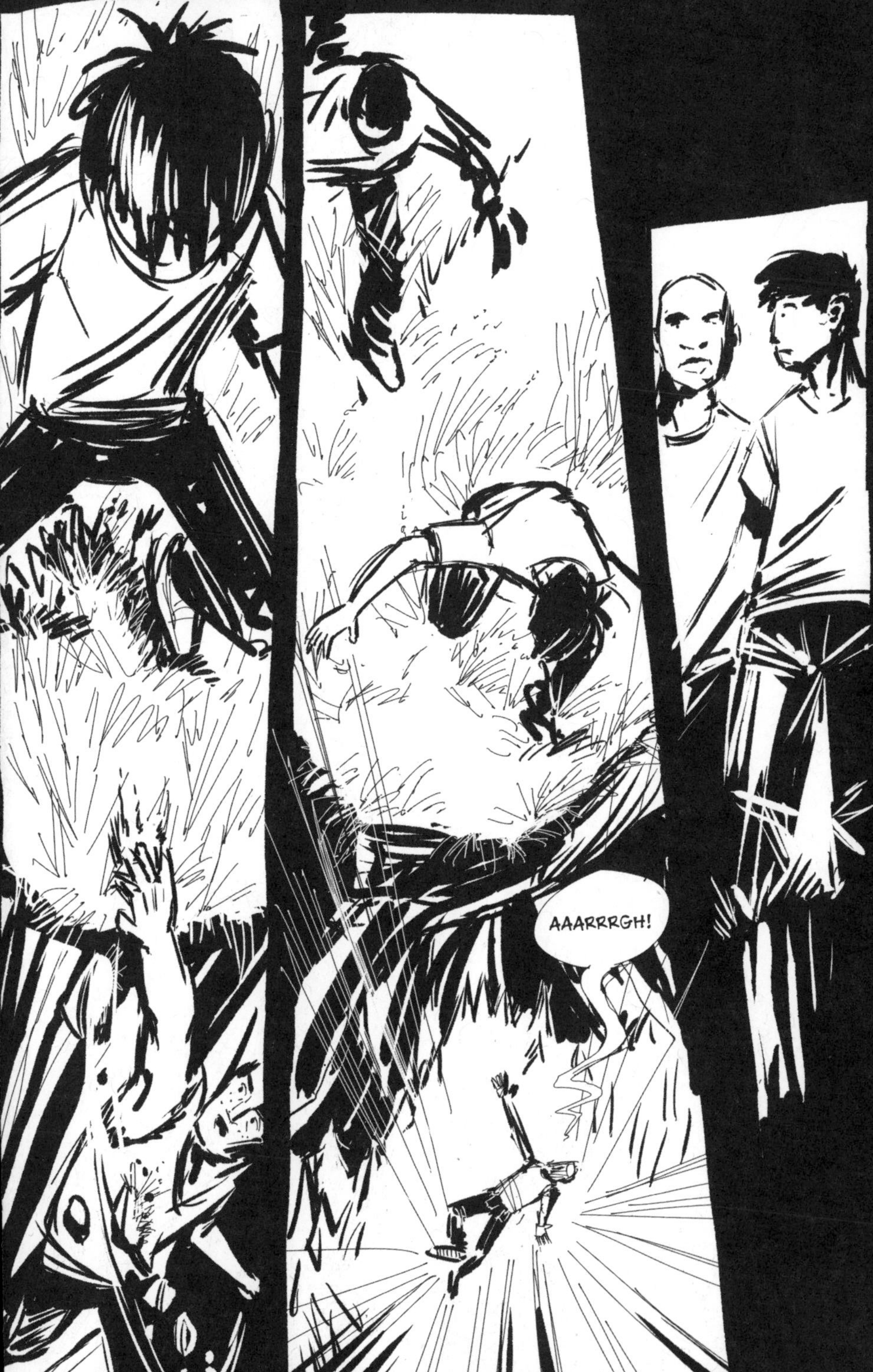
AAARRRGH!

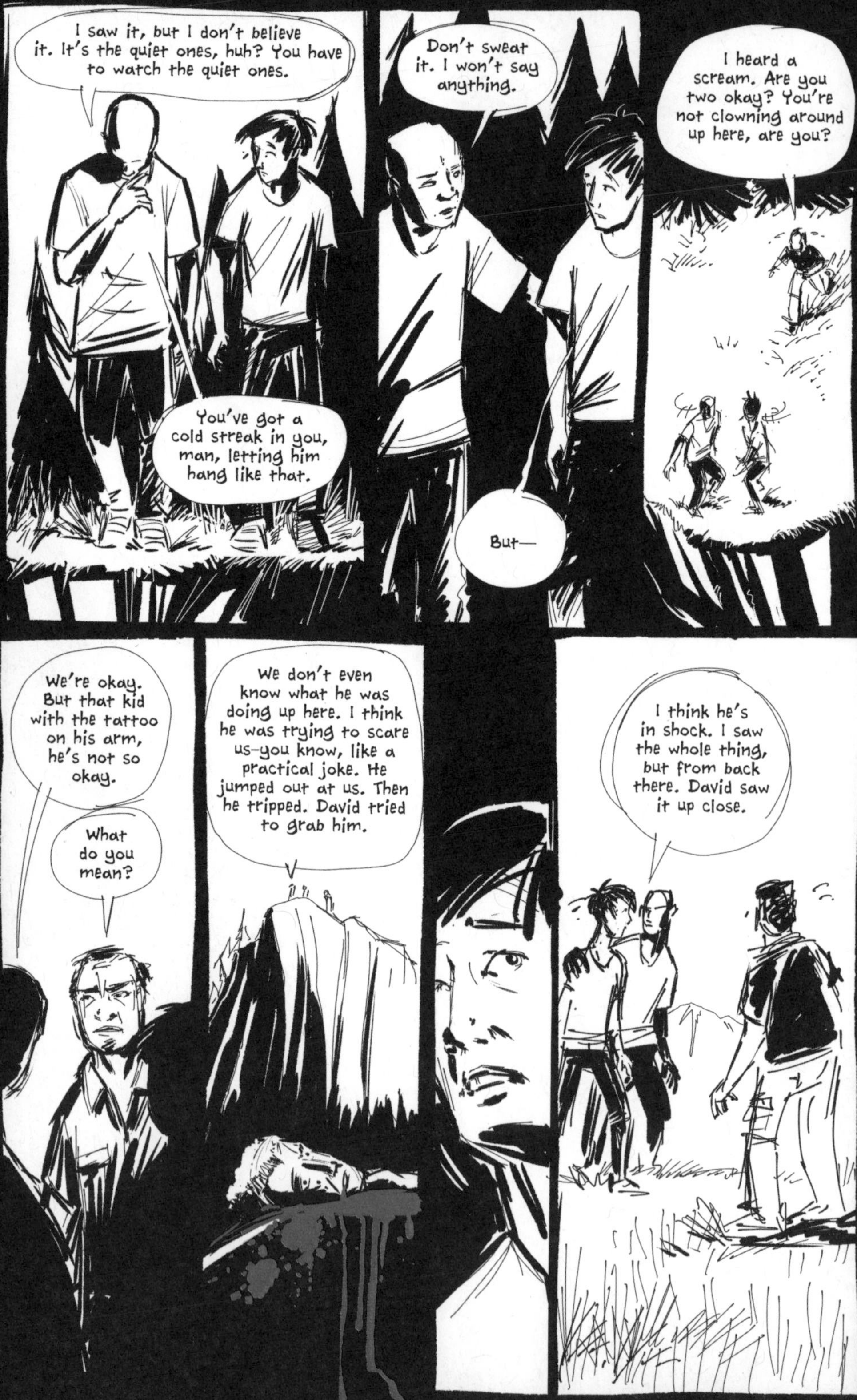
I saw it, but I don't believe it. It's the quiet ones, huh? You have to watch the quiet ones.
You've got a cold streak in you, man, letting him hang like that.
Don't sweat it. I won't say anything.
But—
I heard a scream. Are you two okay? You're not clowning around up here, are you?
We're okay. But that kid with the tattoo on his arm, he's not so okay.
What do you mean?
We don't even know what he was doing up here. I think he was trying to scare us–you know, like a practical joke. He jumped out at us. Then he tripped. David tried to grab him.
I think he's in shock. I saw the whole thing, but from back there. David saw it up close.

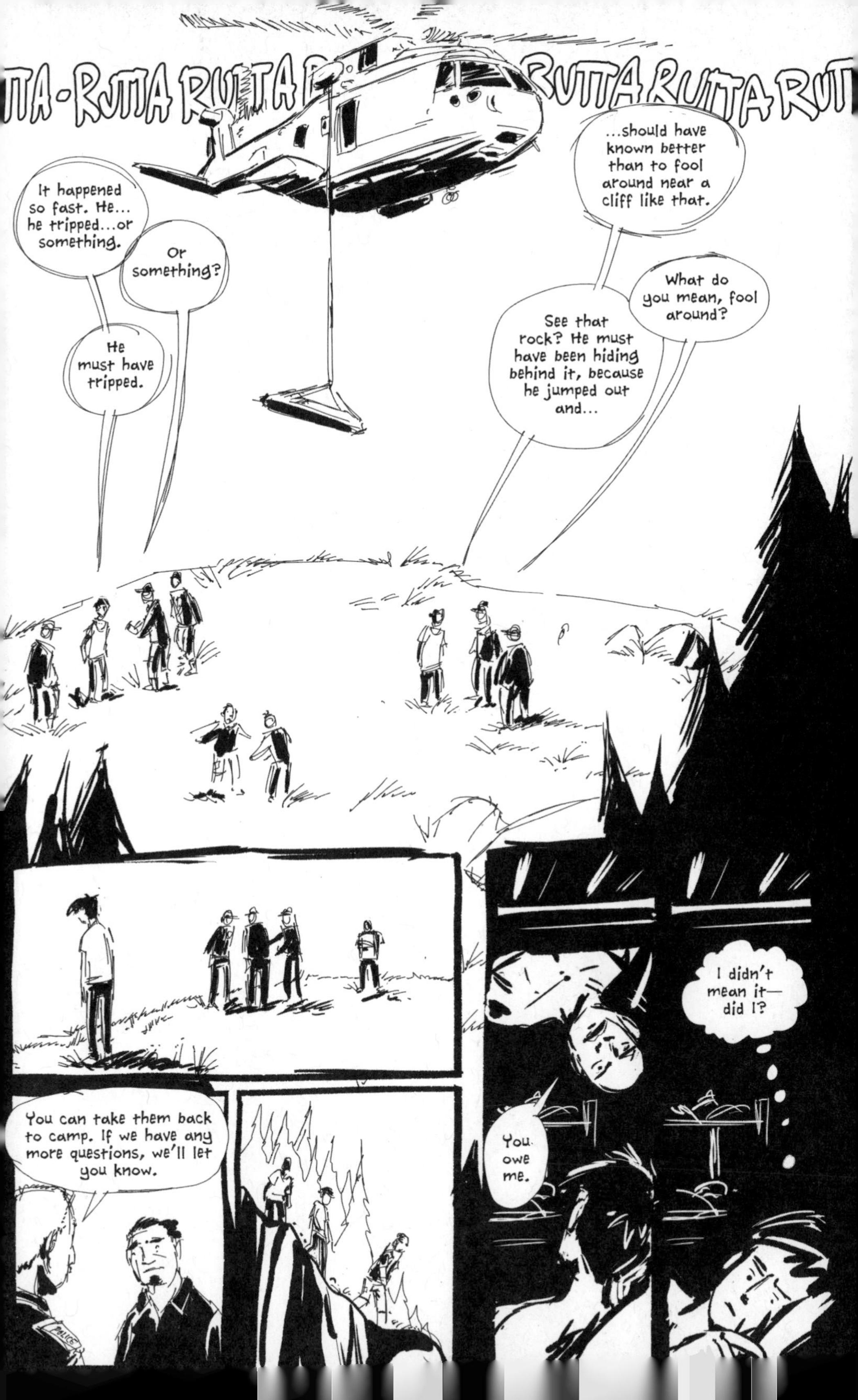

TTA-RUTTA RUTTA R
RUTTA RUTTA RUT
It happened so fast. He... he tripped...or something.
Or something?
He must have tripped.
...should have known better than to fool around near a cliff like that.
What do you mean, fool around?
See that rock? He must have been hiding behind it, because he jumped out and...
You can take them back to camp. If we have any more questions, we'll let you know.
POLICE
I didn't mean it—did I?
You owe me.

the train

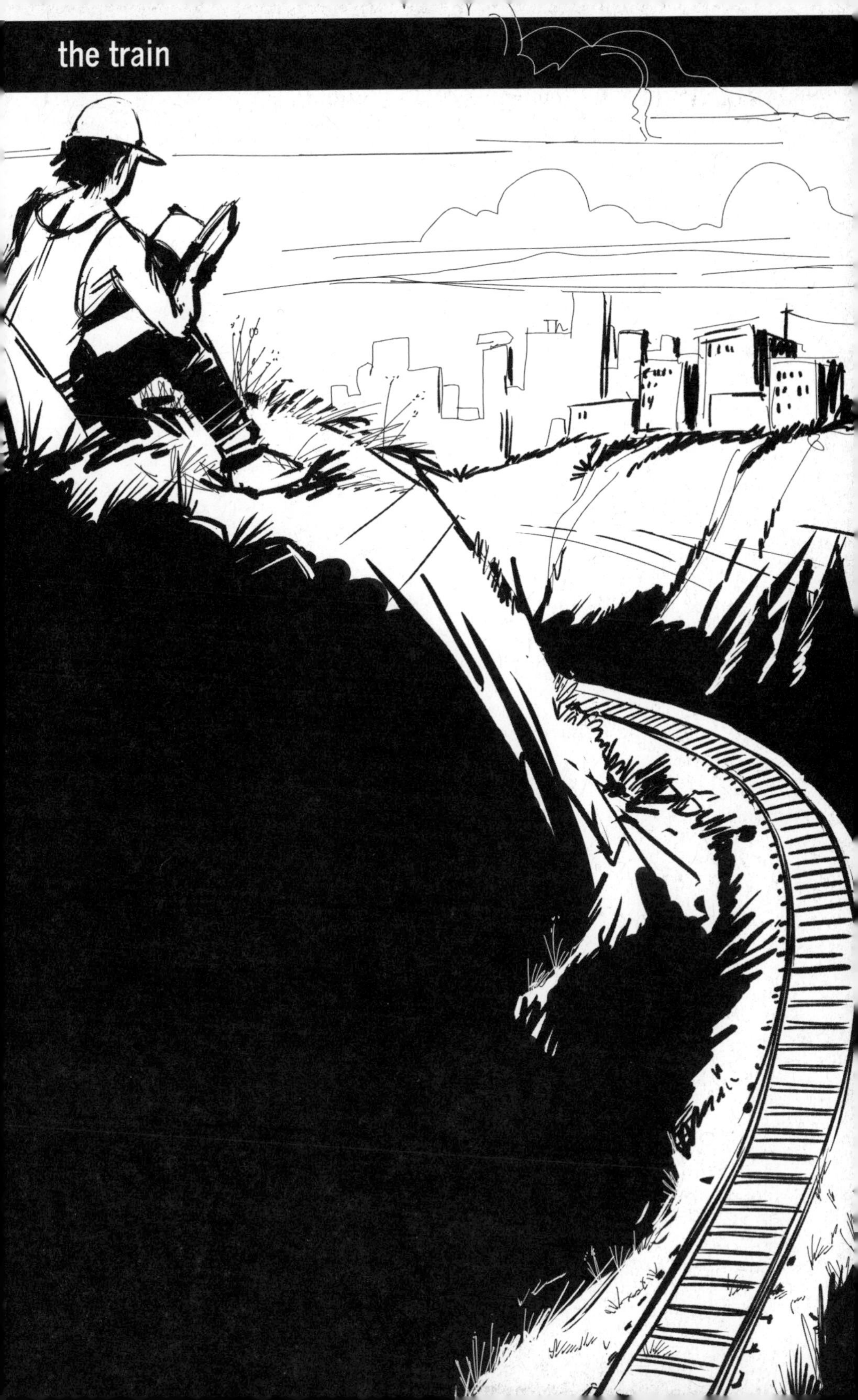

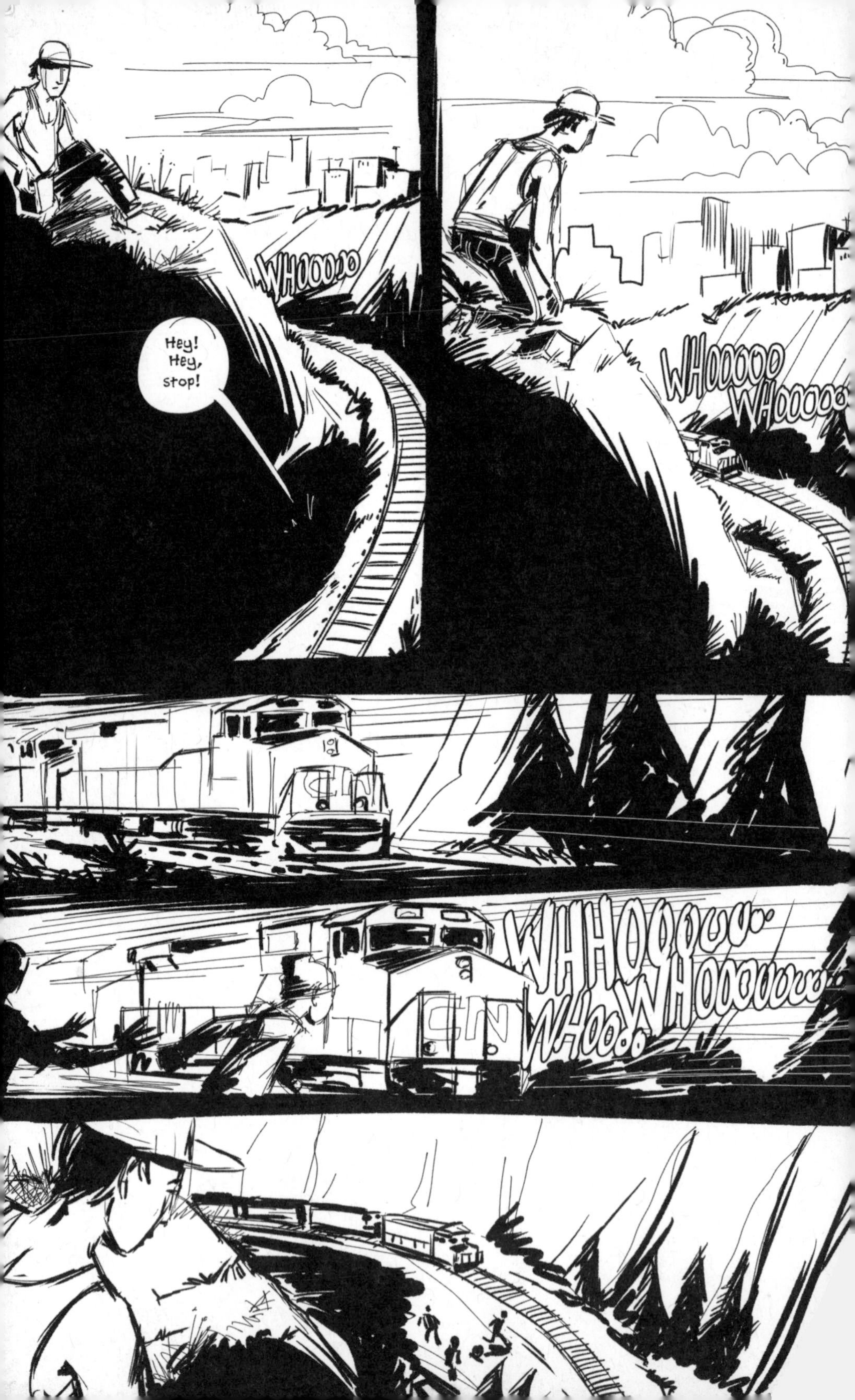
WHOOOOO
Hey! Hey, stop!
WHOOOOO
WHOOOOO
WHOOOUU..
WHOO..WHOOOUUU..

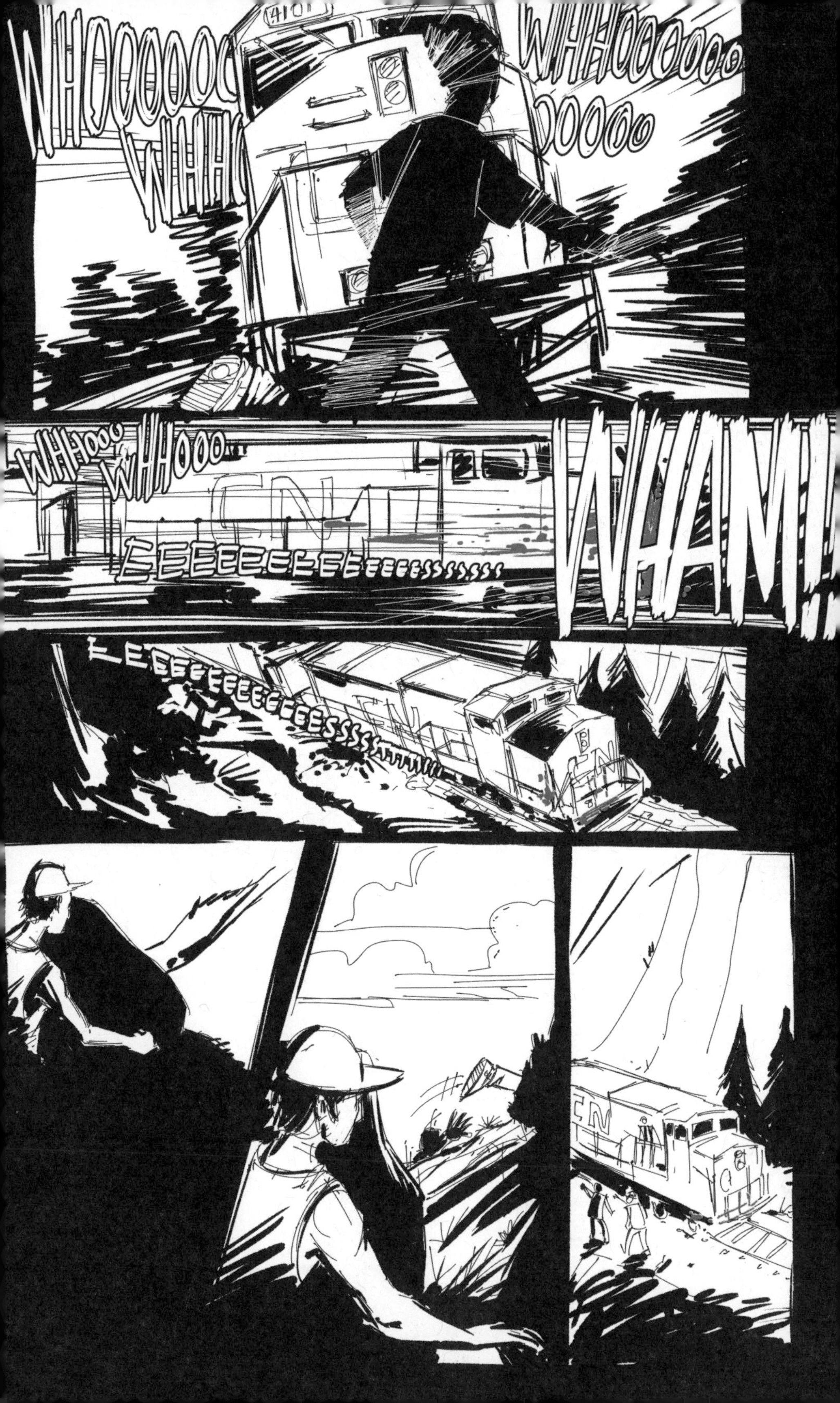
WHOOOOOO
WHHOOOOOoo
OOOOOo
WHHOOO
WHHOOO...
EEEEEEEEEEEeeeessssss
WHAM!!
EEEEEEEEEEEEEEEEESSSSSSS

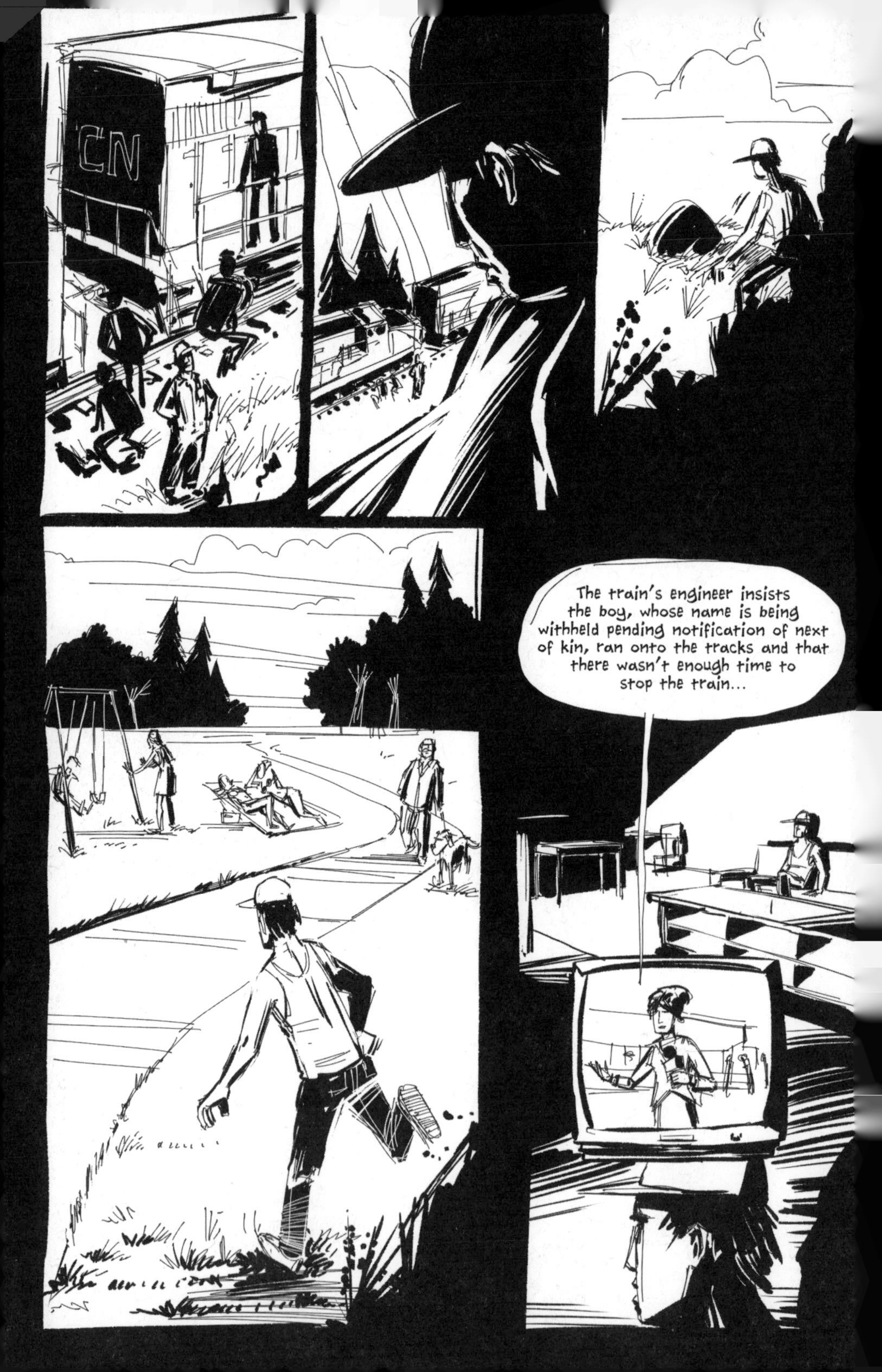
The train's engineer insists the boy, whose name is being withheld pending notification of next of kin, ran onto the tracks and that there wasn't enough time to stop the train...
CN

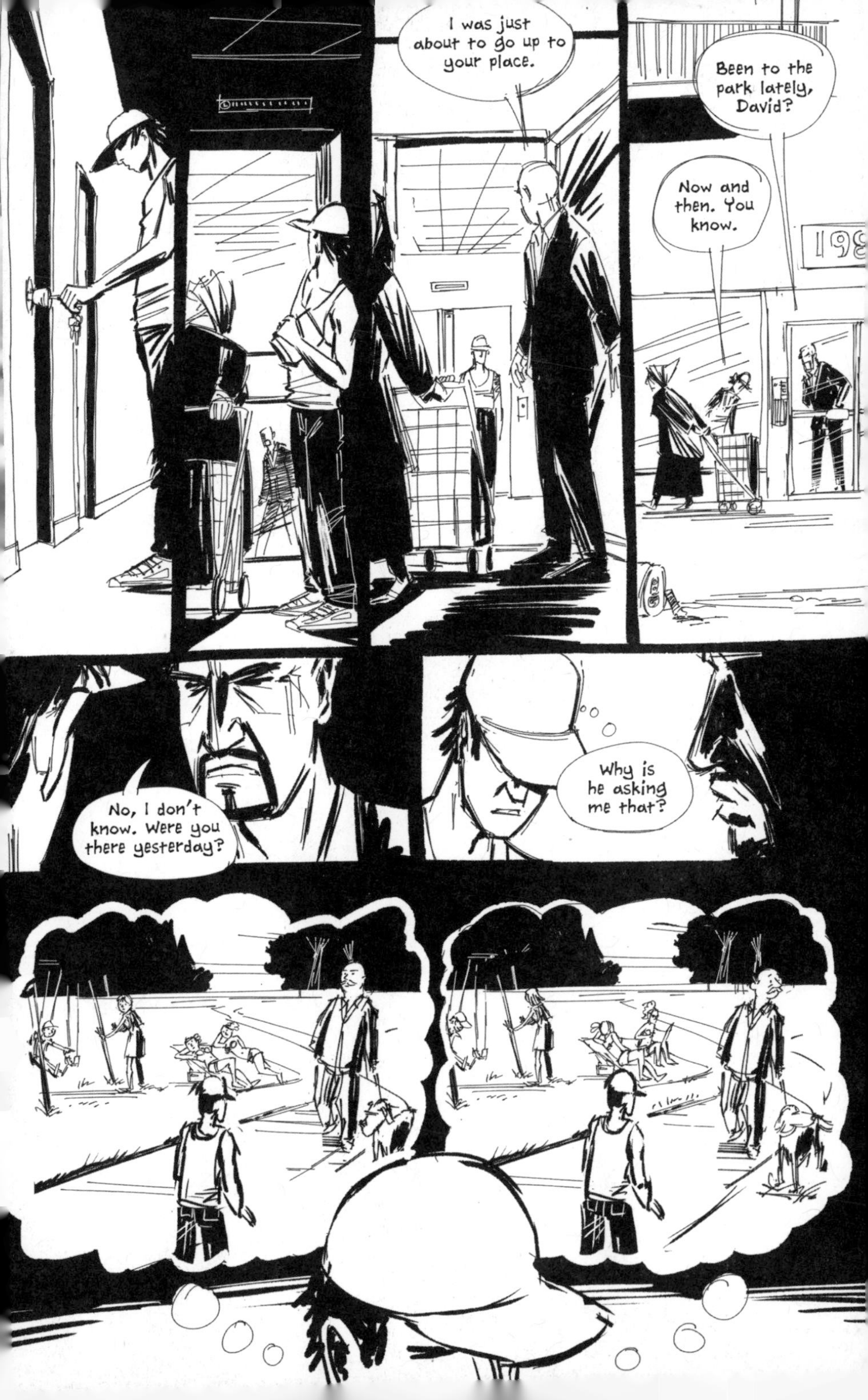
I was just about to go up to your place.
Been to the park lately, David?
Now and then. You know.
No, I don't know. Were you there yesterday?
Why is he asking me that?

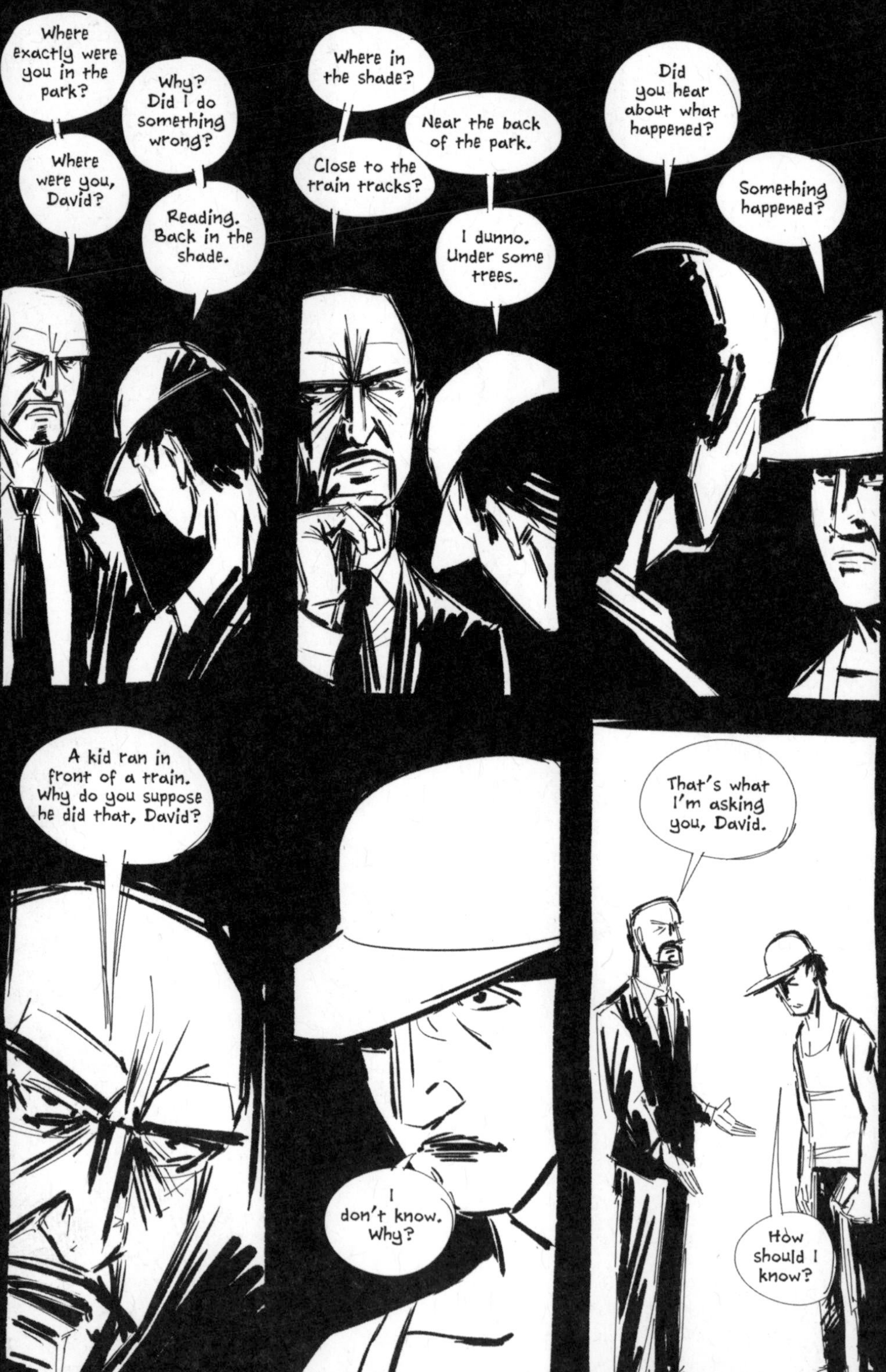
Where exactly were you in the park?
Where were you, David?
Why? Did I do something wrong?
Reading. Back in the shade.
Where in the shade?
Close to the train tracks?
Near the back of the park.
I dunno. Under some trees.
Did you hear about what happened?
Something happened?
A kid ran in front of a train. Why do you suppose he did that, David?
I don't know. Why?
That's what I'm asking you, David.
How should I know?

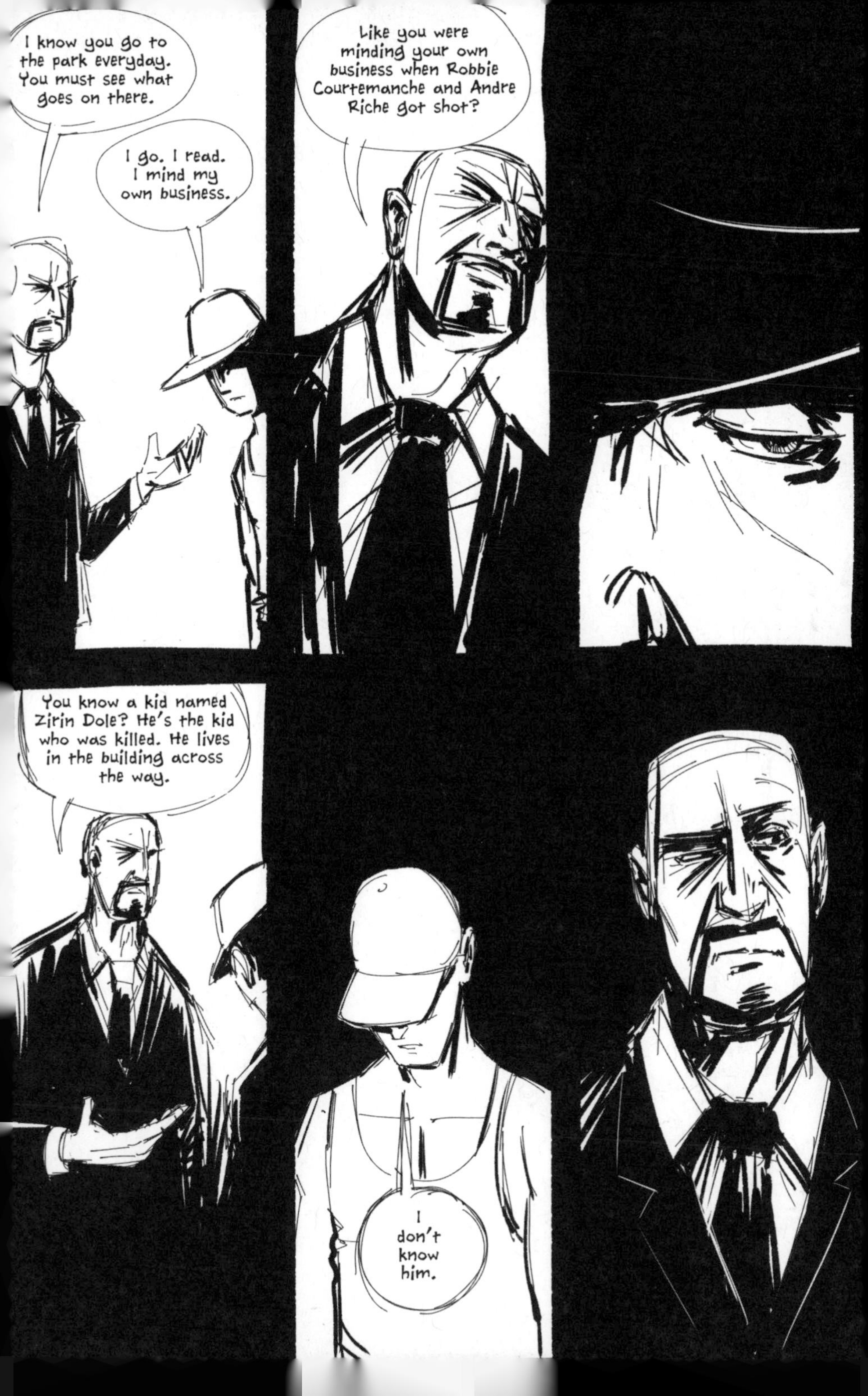
I know you go to the park everyday. You must see what goes on there.
I go. I read. I mind my own business.
Like you were minding your own business when Robbie Courtemanche and Andre Riche got shot?
You know a kid named Zirin Dole? He's the kid who was killed. He lives in the building across the way.
I don't know him.

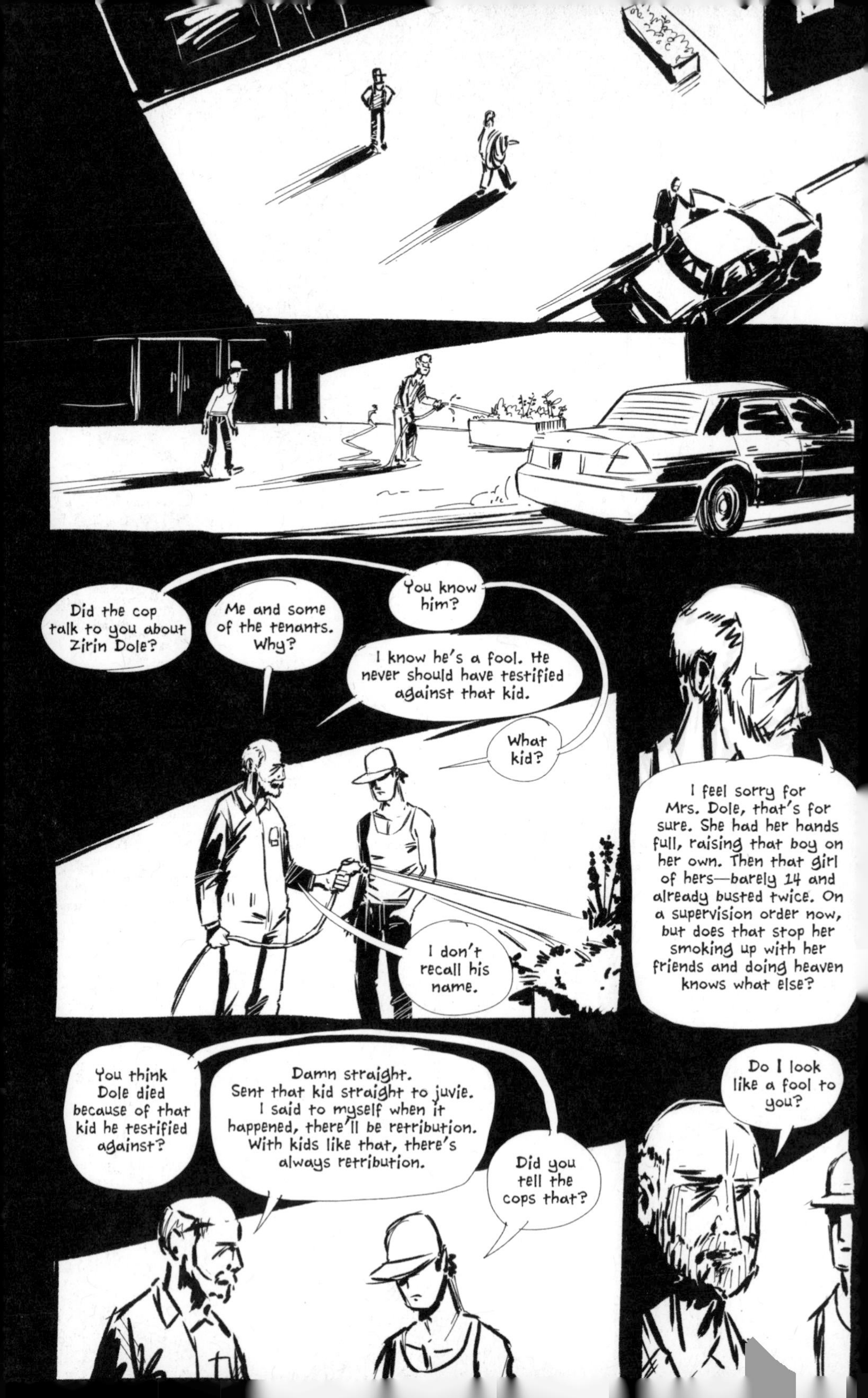
Did the cop talk to you about Zirin Dole?
Me and some of the tenants. Why?
You know him?
I know he's a fool. He never should have testified against that kid.
What kid?
I don't recall his name.
I feel sorry for Mrs. Dole, that's for sure. She had her hands full, raising that boy on her own. Then that girl of hers—barely 14 and already busted twice. On a supervision order now, but does that stop her smoking up with her friends and doing heaven knows what else?
You think Dole died because of that kid he testified against?
Damn straight. Sent that kid straight to juvie. I said to myself when it happened, there'll be retribution. With kids like that, there's always retribution.
Did you tell the cops that?
Do I look like a fool to you?

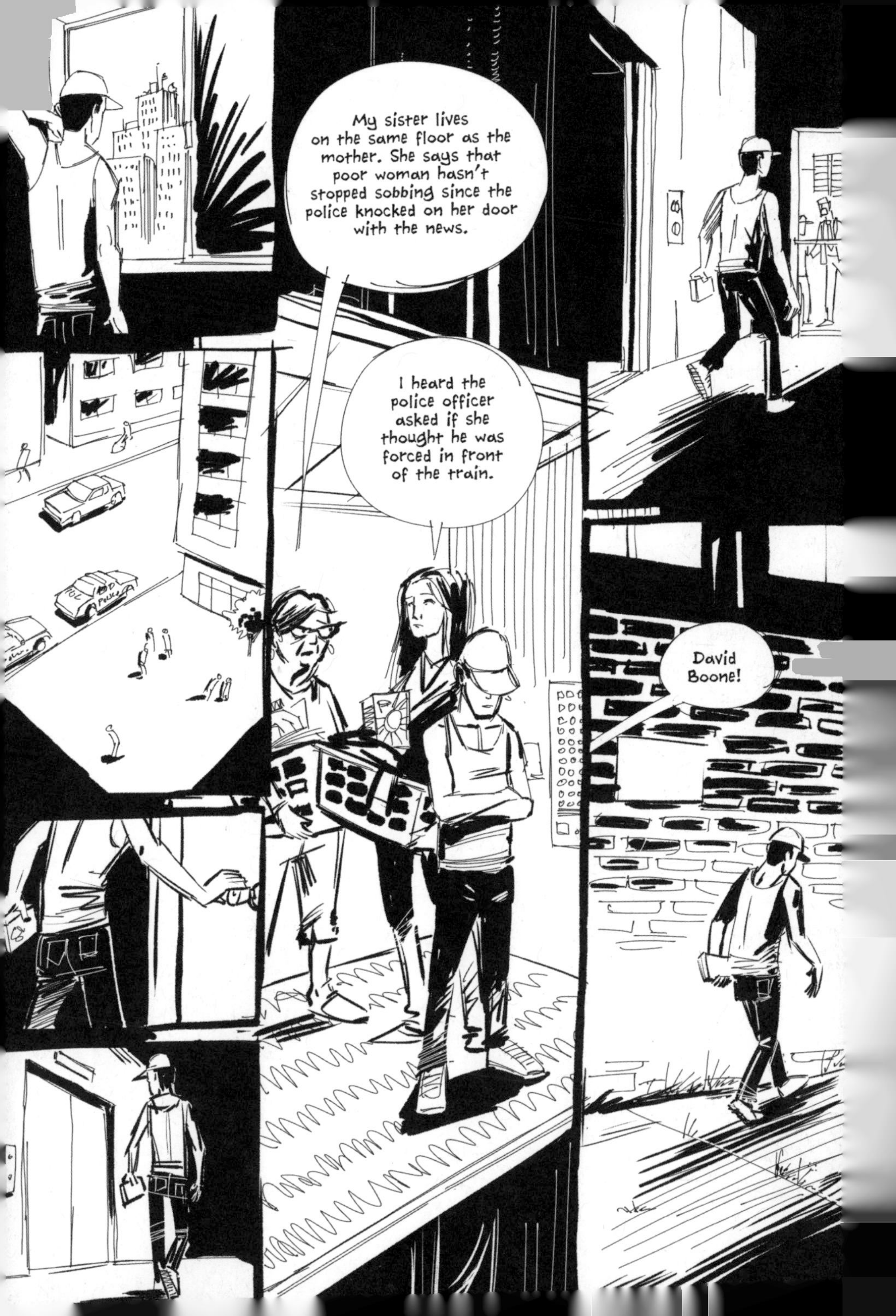
My sister lives on the same floor as the mother. She says that poor woman hasn't stopped sobbing since the police knocked on her door with the news.
I heard the police officer asked if she thought he was forced in front of the train.
David Boone!

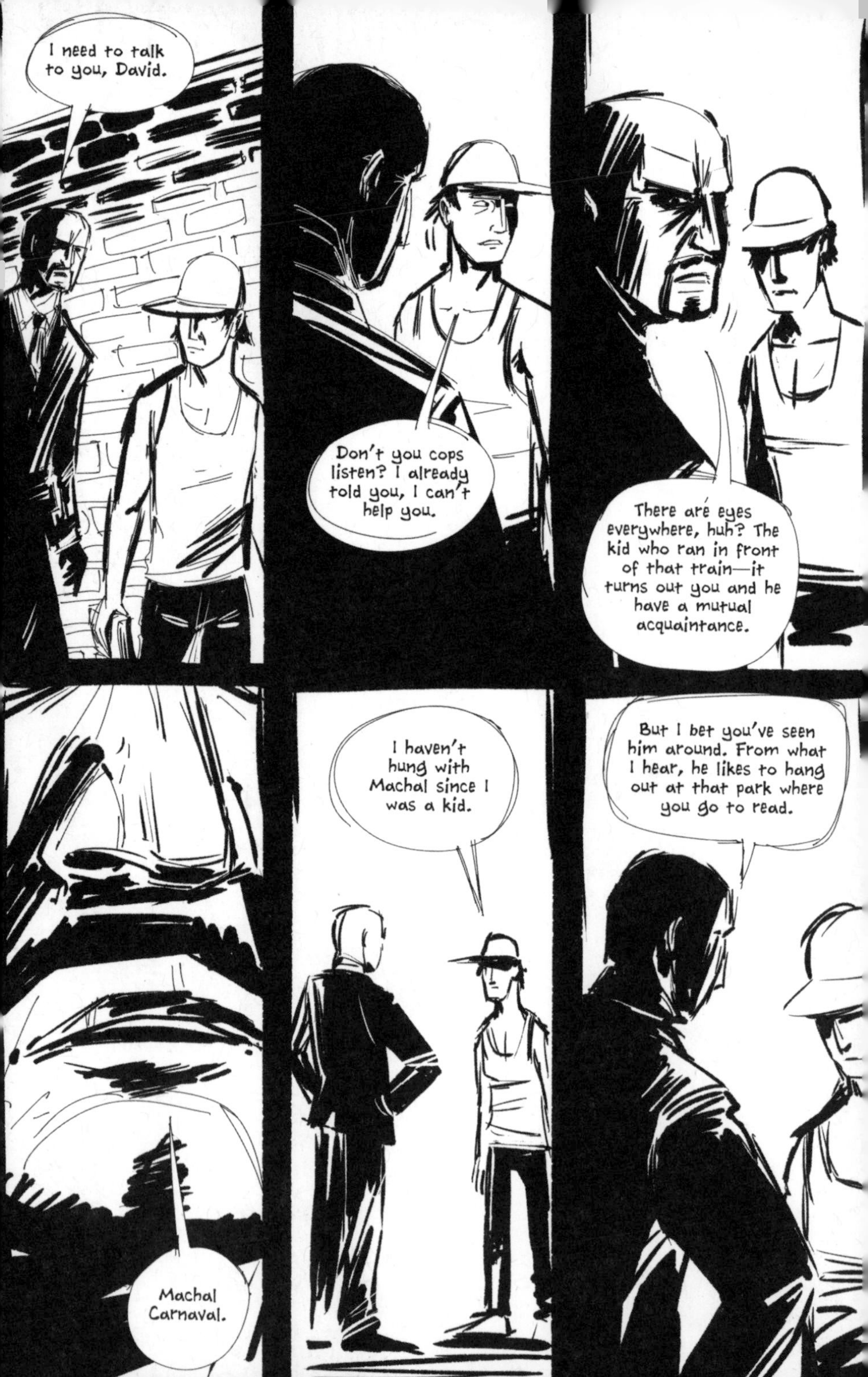
I need to talk to you, David.
Don't you cops listen? I already told you, I can't help you.
There are eyes everywhere, huh? The kid who ran in front of that train—it turns out you and he have a mutual acquaintance.
Machal Carnaval.
I haven't hung with Machal since I was a kid.
But I bet you've seen him around. From what I hear, he likes to hang out at that park where you go to read.

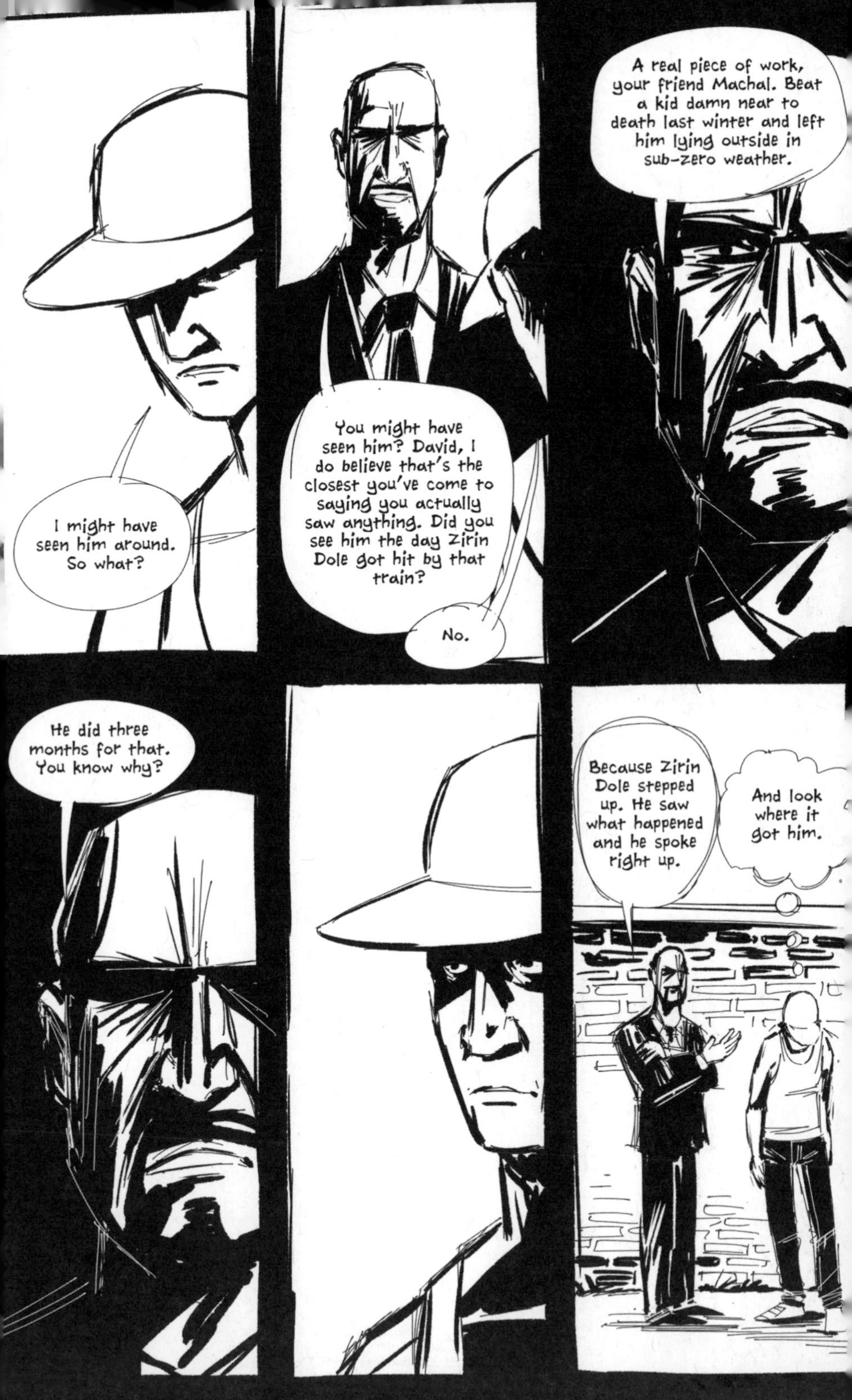
I might have seen him around. So what?
You might have seen him? David, I do believe that's the closest you've come to saying you actually saw anything. Did you see him the day Zirin Dole got hit by that train?
No.
A real piece of work, your friend Machal. Beat a kid damn near to death last winter and left him lying outside in sub-zero weather.
He did three months for that. You know why?
Because Zirin Dole stepped up. He saw what happened and he spoke right up.
And look where it got him.

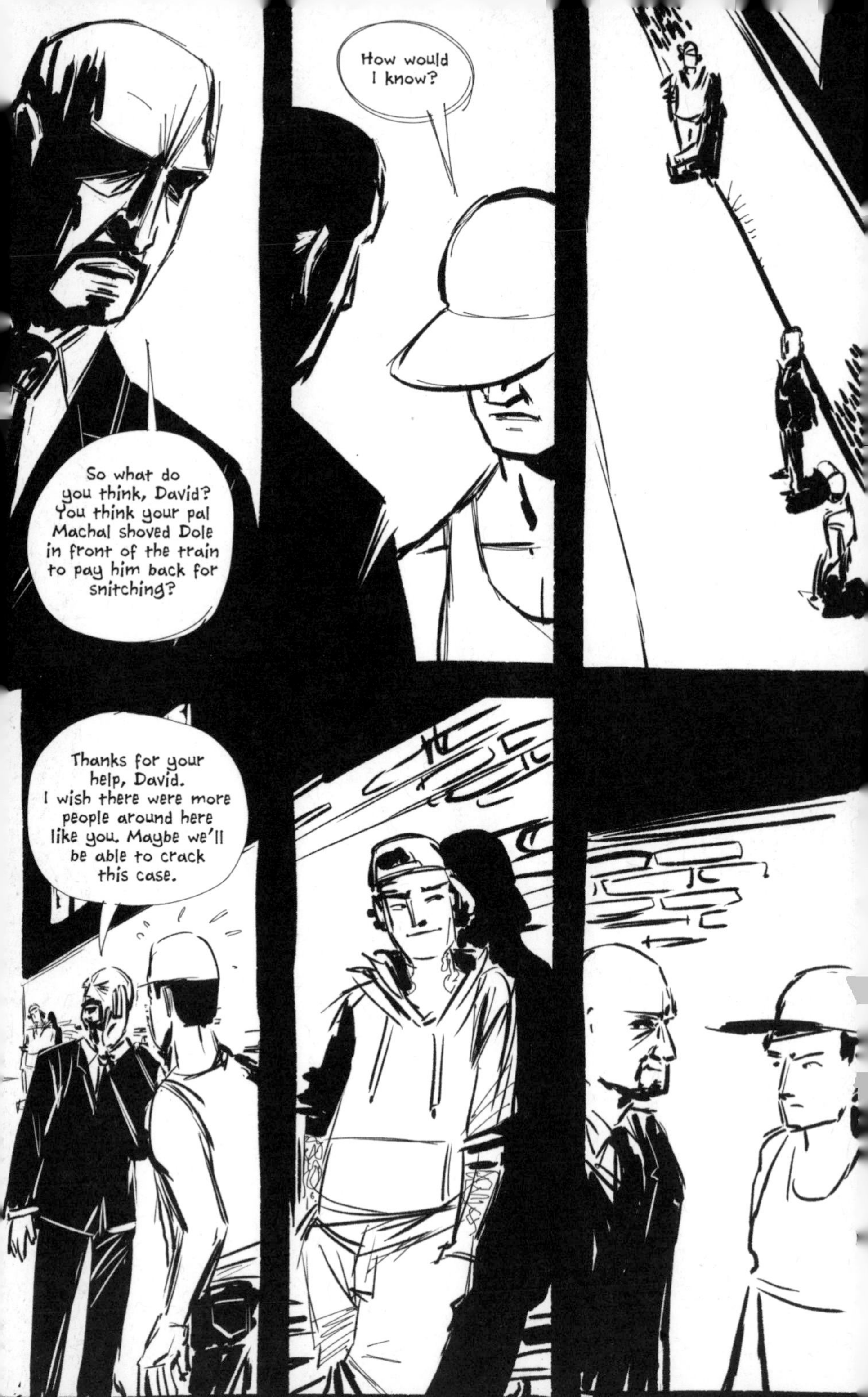
So what do you think, David? You think your pal Machal shoved Dole in front of the train to pay him back for snitching?
How would I know?
Thanks for your help, David. I wish there were more people around here like you. Maybe we'll be able to crack this case.

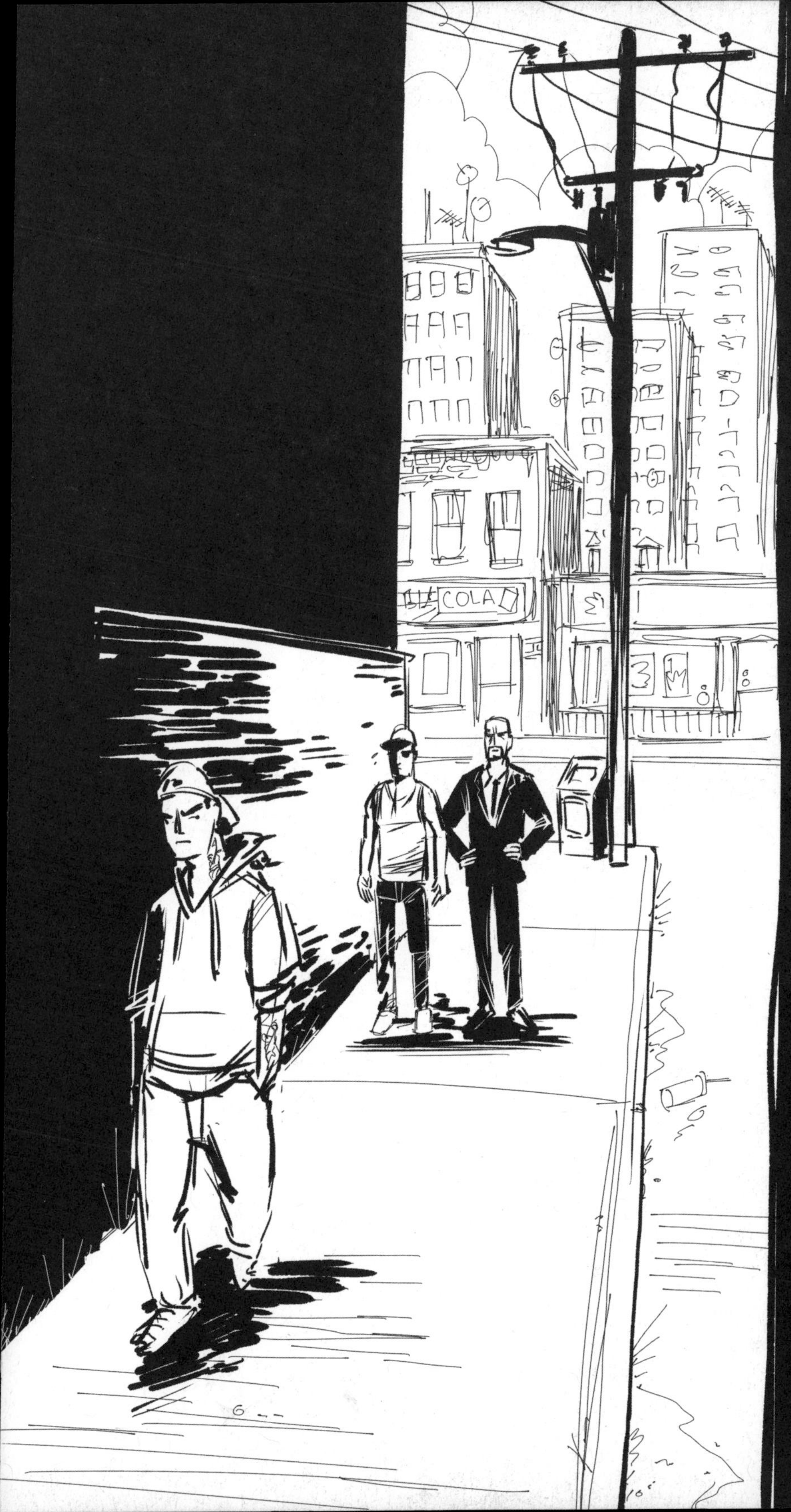
COLA

school

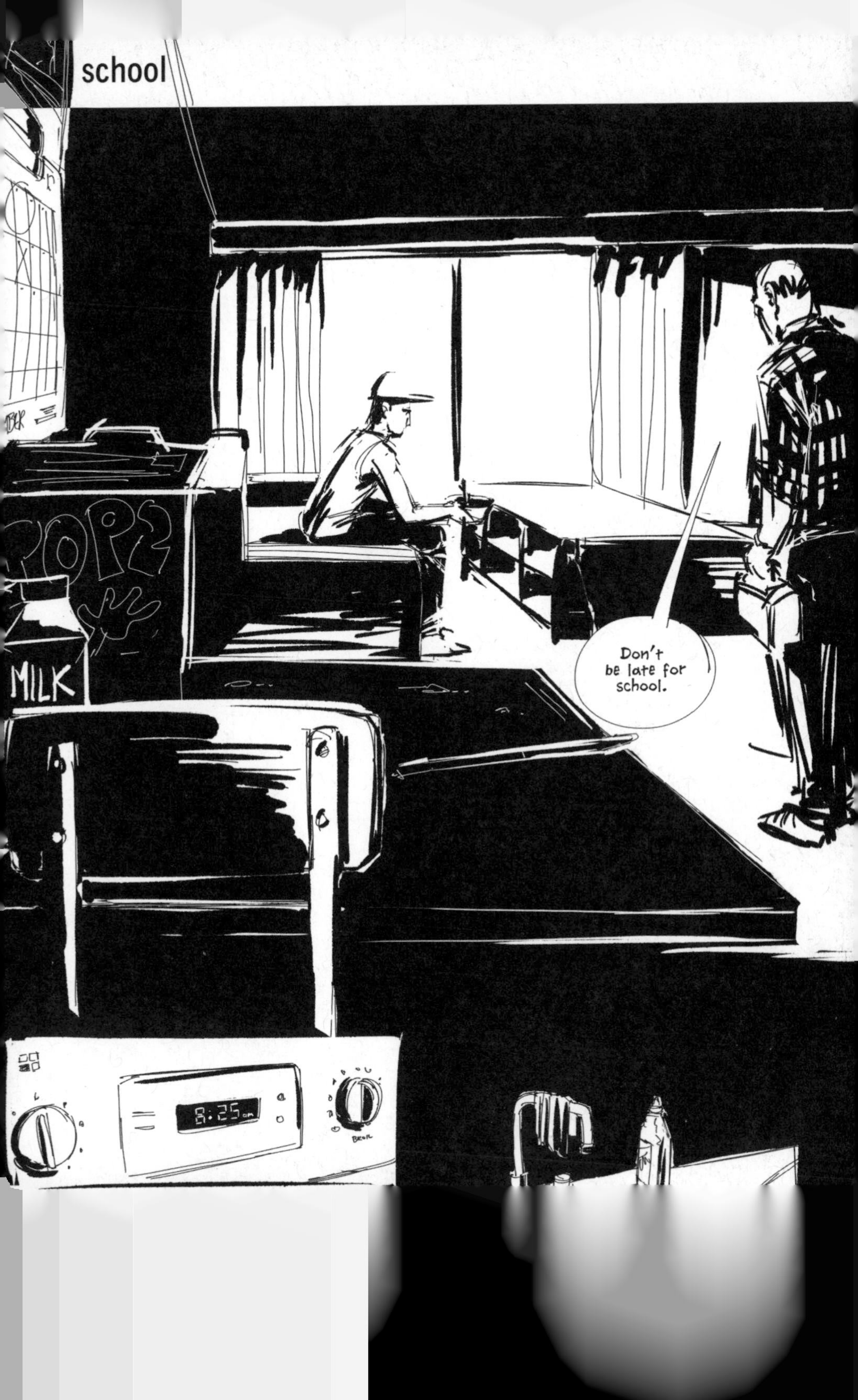
MILK
Don't be late for school.
8:25

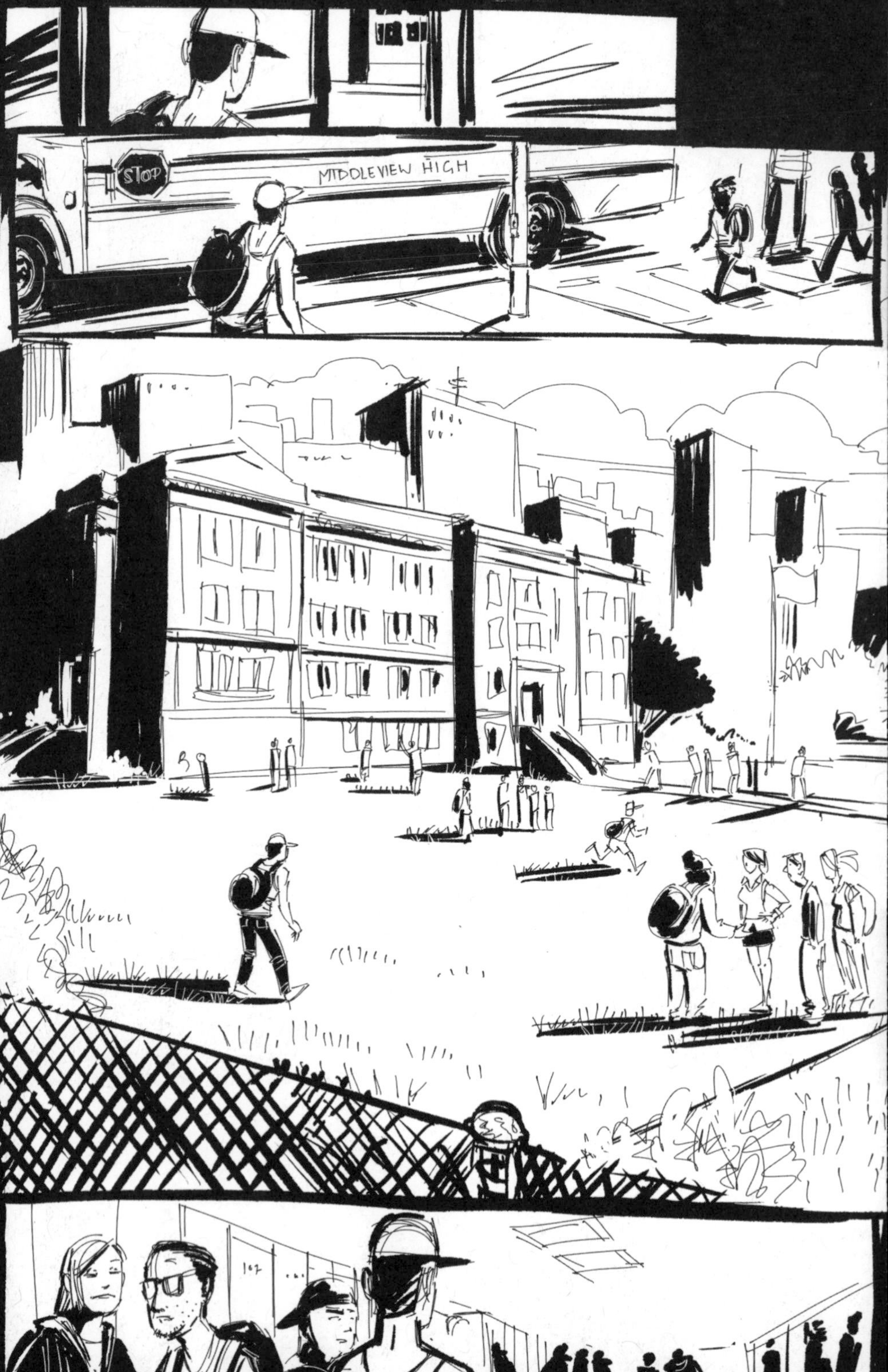
STOP
MIDDLEVIEW HIGH

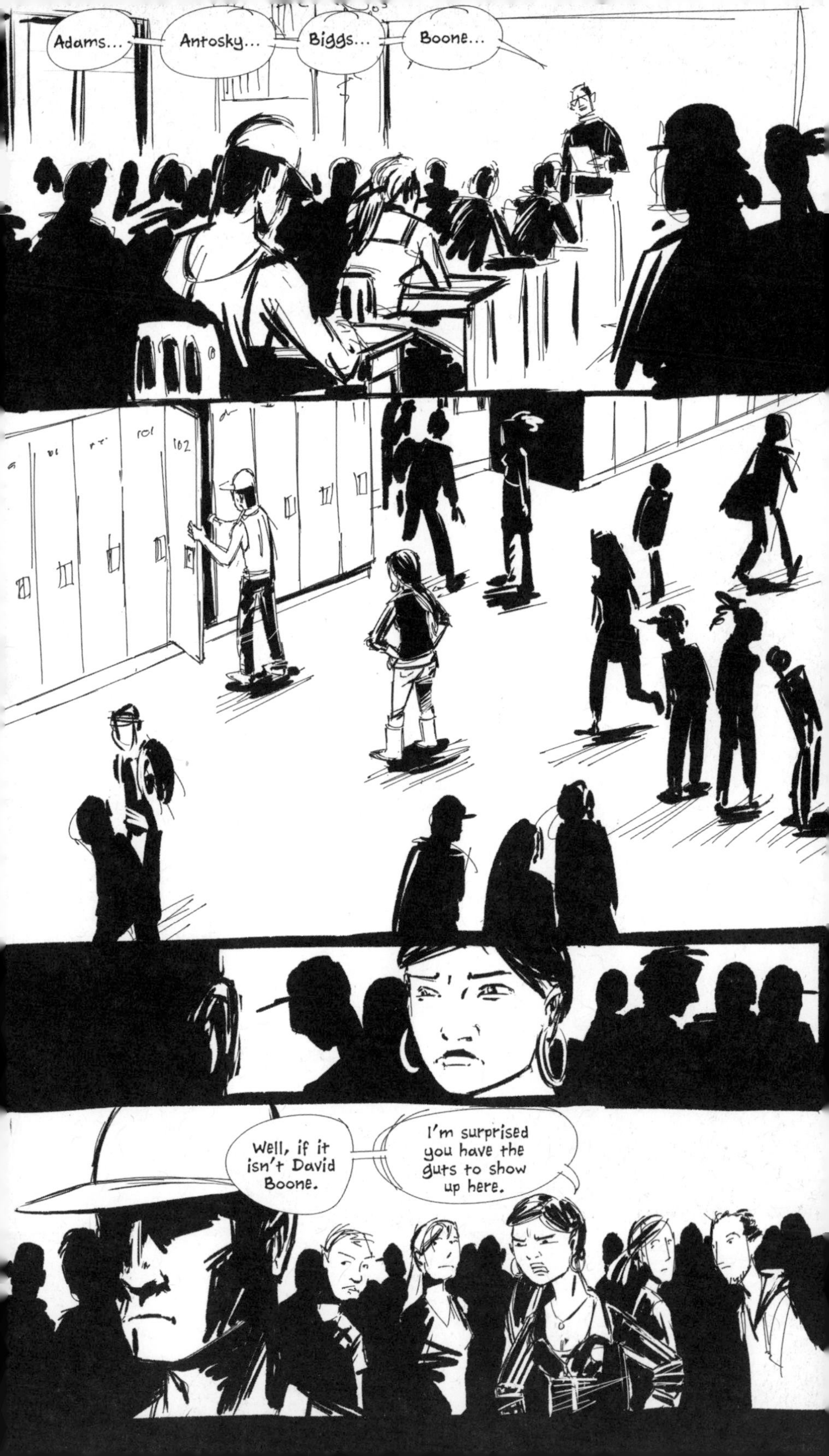
Adams...
Antosky...
Biggs...
Boone...
Well, if it isn't David Boone.
I'm surprised you have the guts to show up here.

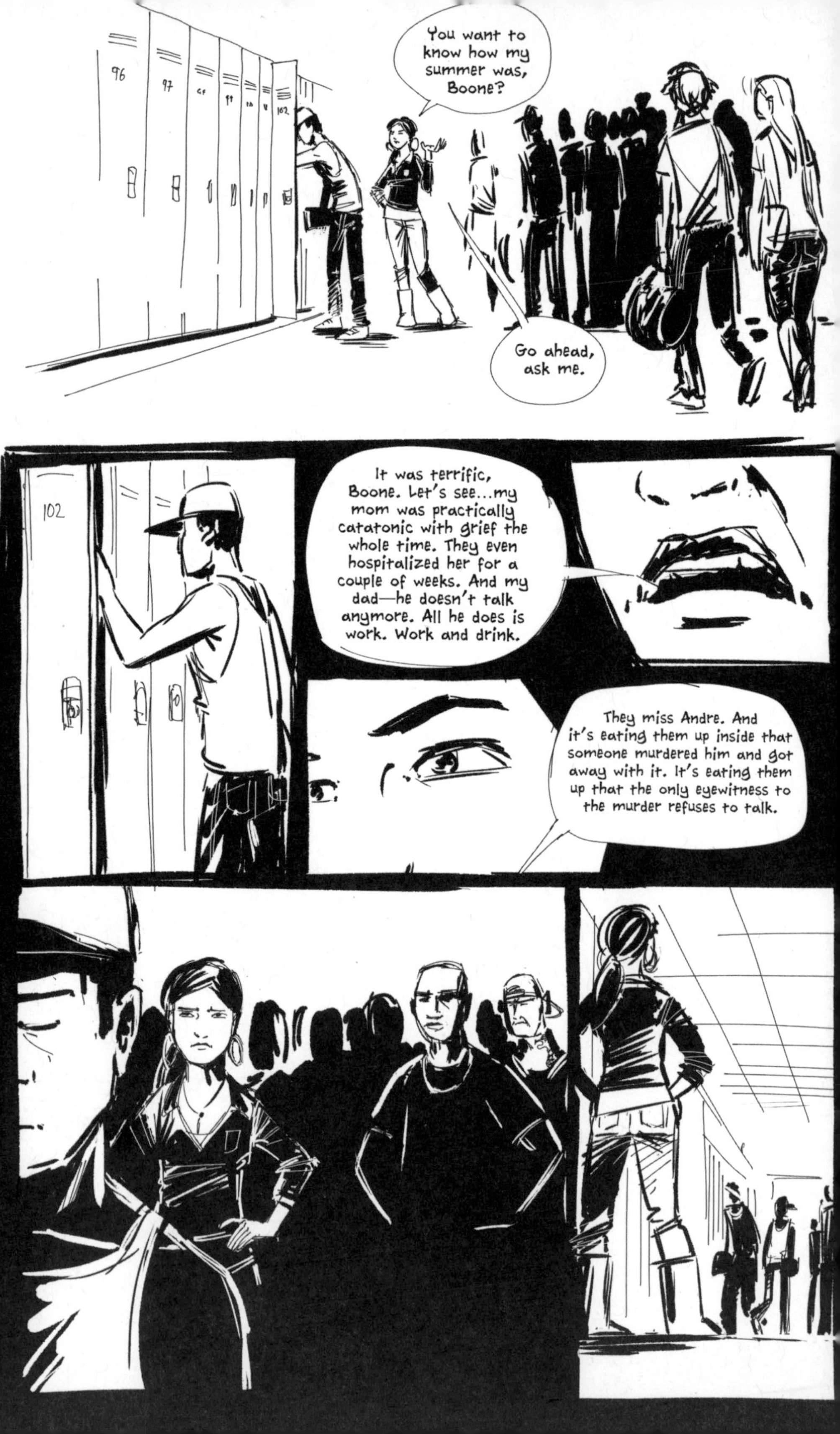
96
97
102
You want to know how my summer was, Boone?
Go ahead, ask me.
102
It was terrific, Boone. Let's see...my mom was practically catatonic with grief the whole time. They even hospitalized her for a couple of weeks. And my dad—he doesn't talk anymore. All he does is work. Work and drink.
They miss Andre. And it's eating them up inside that someone murdered him and got away with it. It's eating them up that the only eyewitness to the murder refuses to talk.

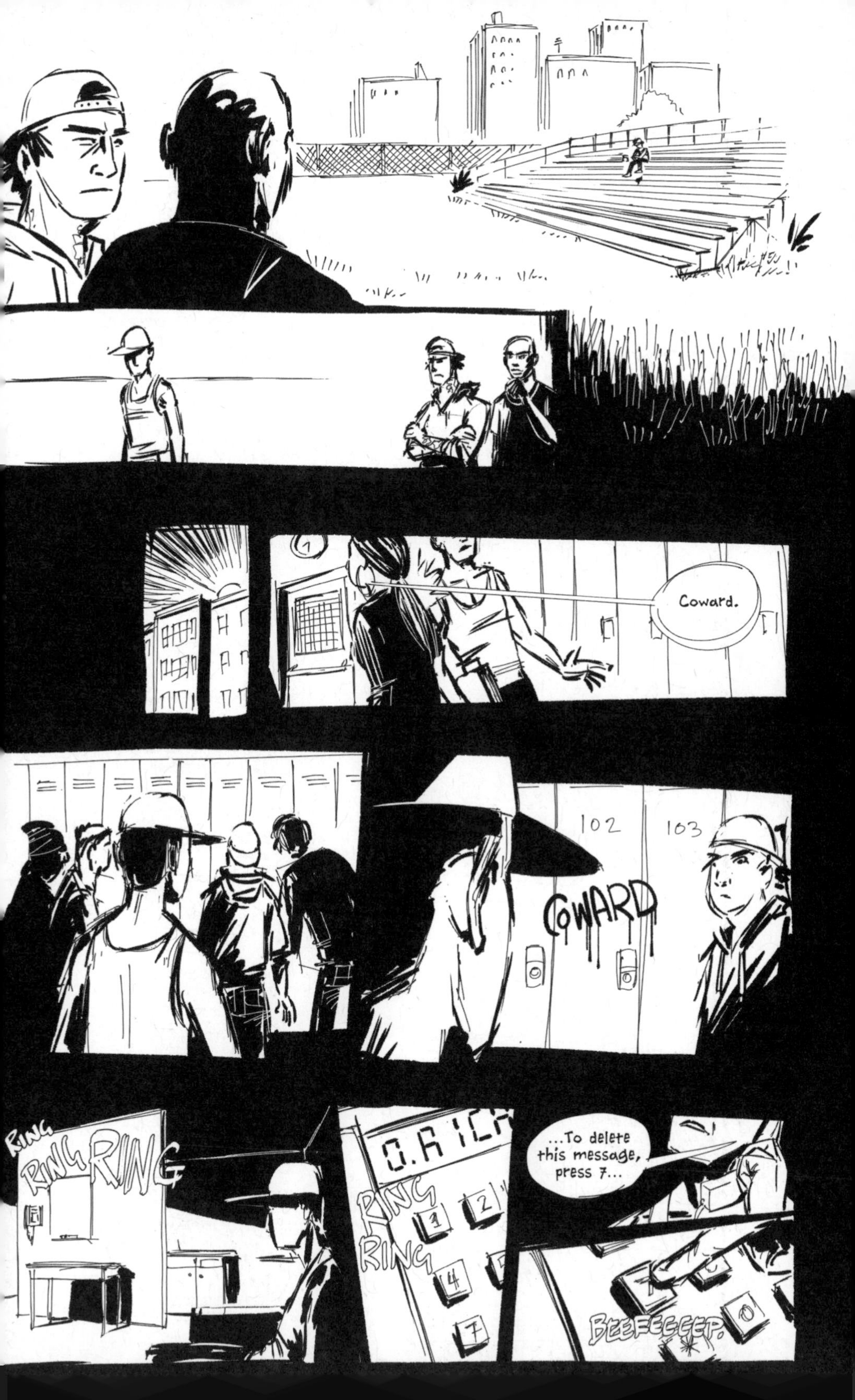
Coward.
102
103
COWARD
RING
RING RING
RING
O.R ICH
RING
RING
1
2
4
7
...To delete this message, press 7...
BEEEEEEP.
0

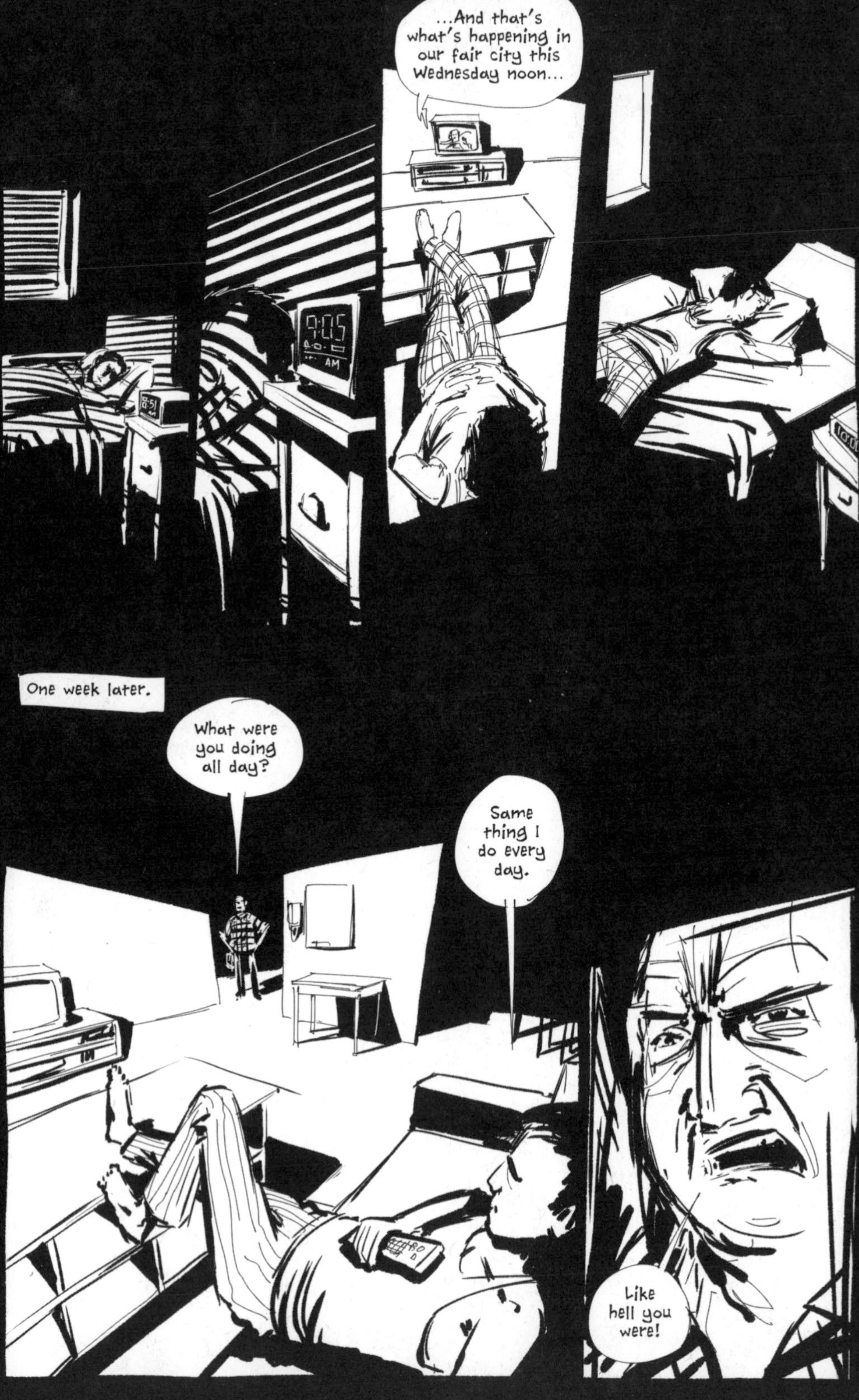
...And that's what's happening in our fair city this Wednesday noon...
One week later.
What were you doing all day?
Same thing I do every day.
Like hell you were!

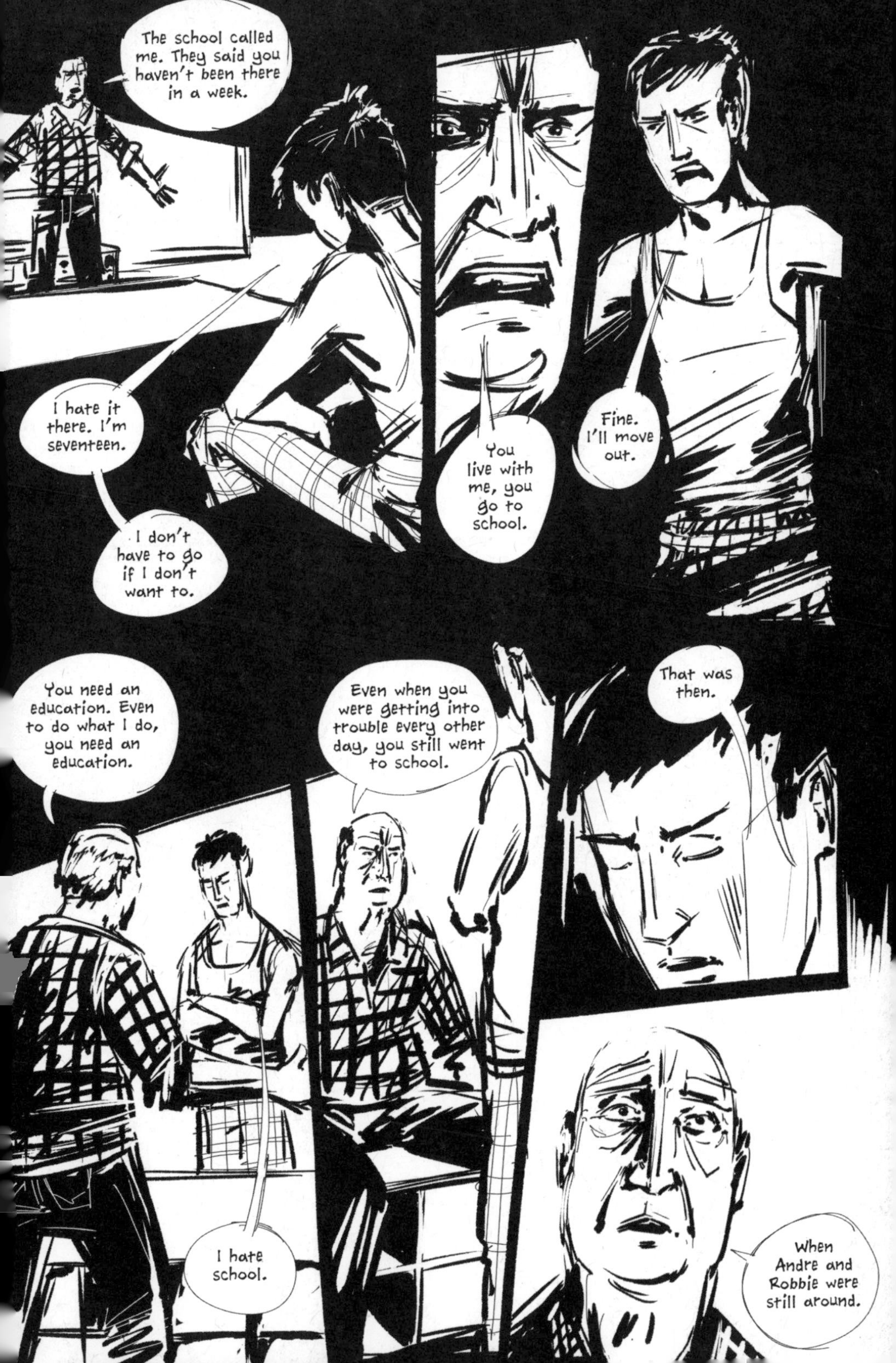
The school called me. They said you haven't been there in a week.
I hate it there. I'm seventeen.
I don't have to go if I don't want to.
You live with me, you go to school.
Fine. I'll move out.
You need an education. Even to do what I do, you need an education.
I hate school.
Even when you were getting into trouble every other day, you still went to school.
That was then.
When Andre and Robbie were still around.

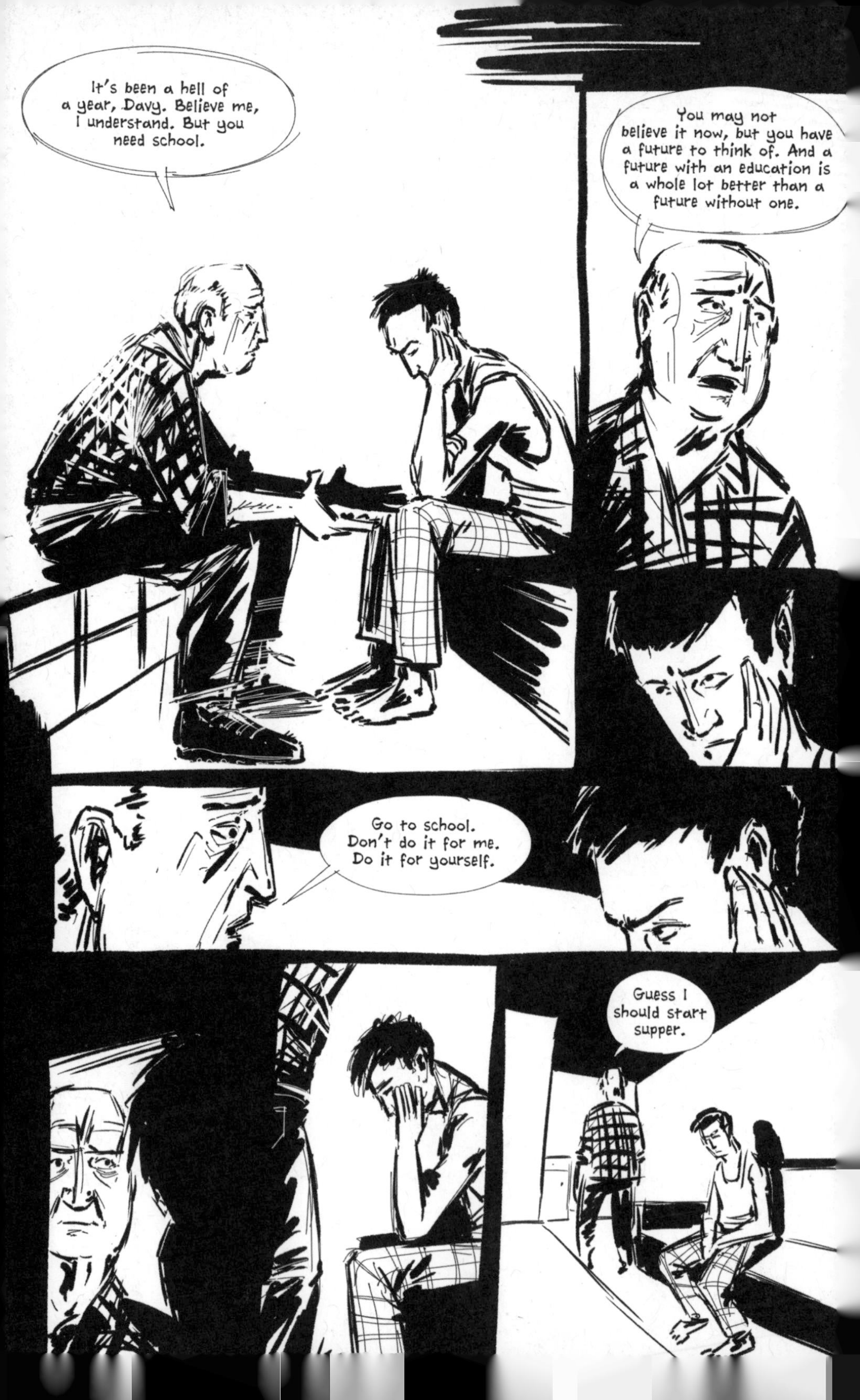
It's been a hell of a year, Davy. Believe me, I understand. But you need school.
You may not believe it now, but you have a future to think of. And a future with an education is a whole lot better than a future without one.
Go to school. Don't do it for me. Do it for yourself.
Guess I should start supper.

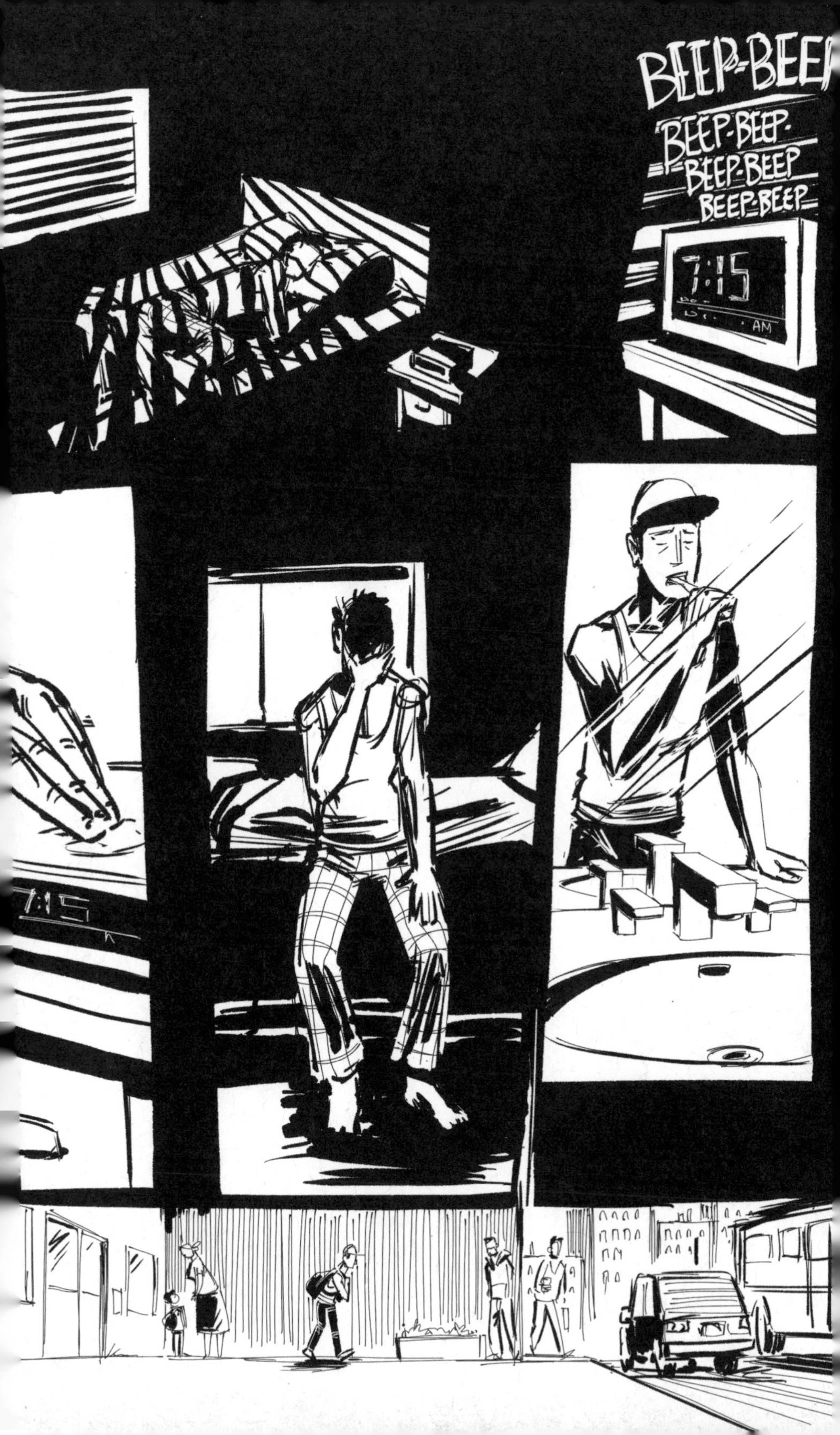
BEEP-BEEP
BEEP-BEEP-
BEEP-BEEP
BEEP-BEEP
7:15
AM

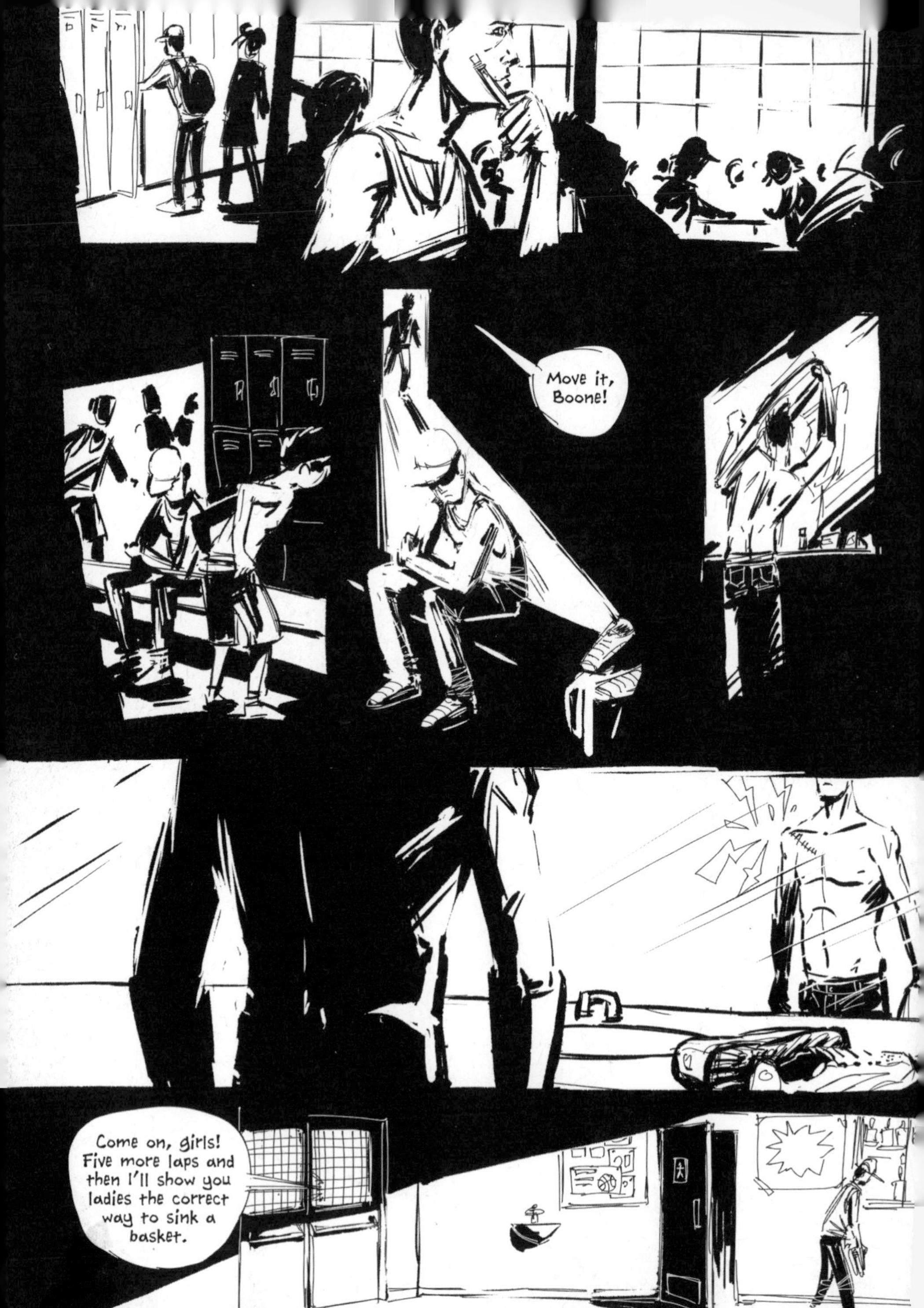
Move it, Boone!
Come on, girls! Five more laps and then I'll show you ladies the correct way to sink a basket.

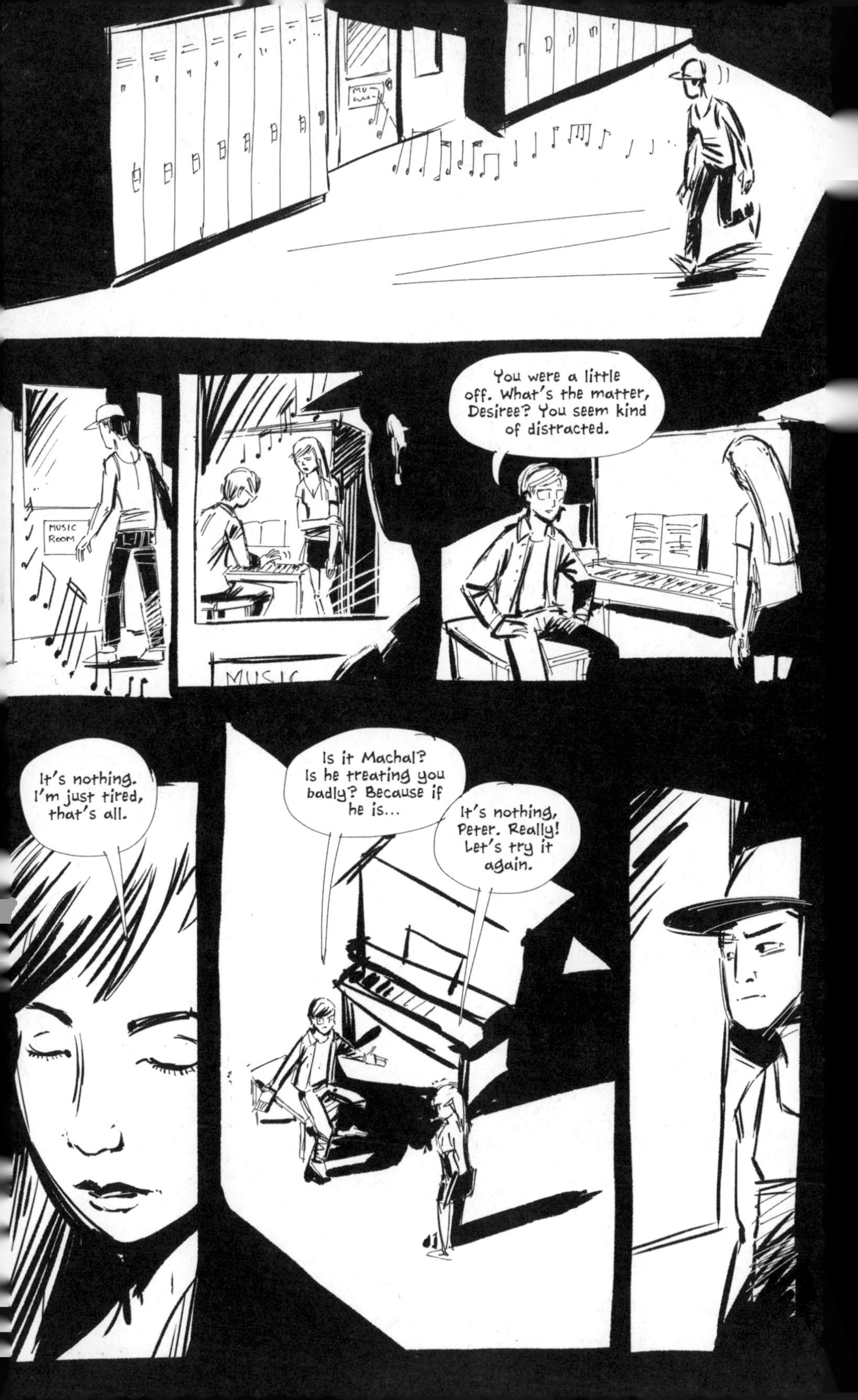
MUSIC ROOM
You were a little off. What's the matter, Desiree? You seem kind of distracted.
It's nothing. I'm just tired, that's all.
Is it Machal? Is he treating you badly? Because if he is...
It's nothing, Peter. Really! Let's try it again.

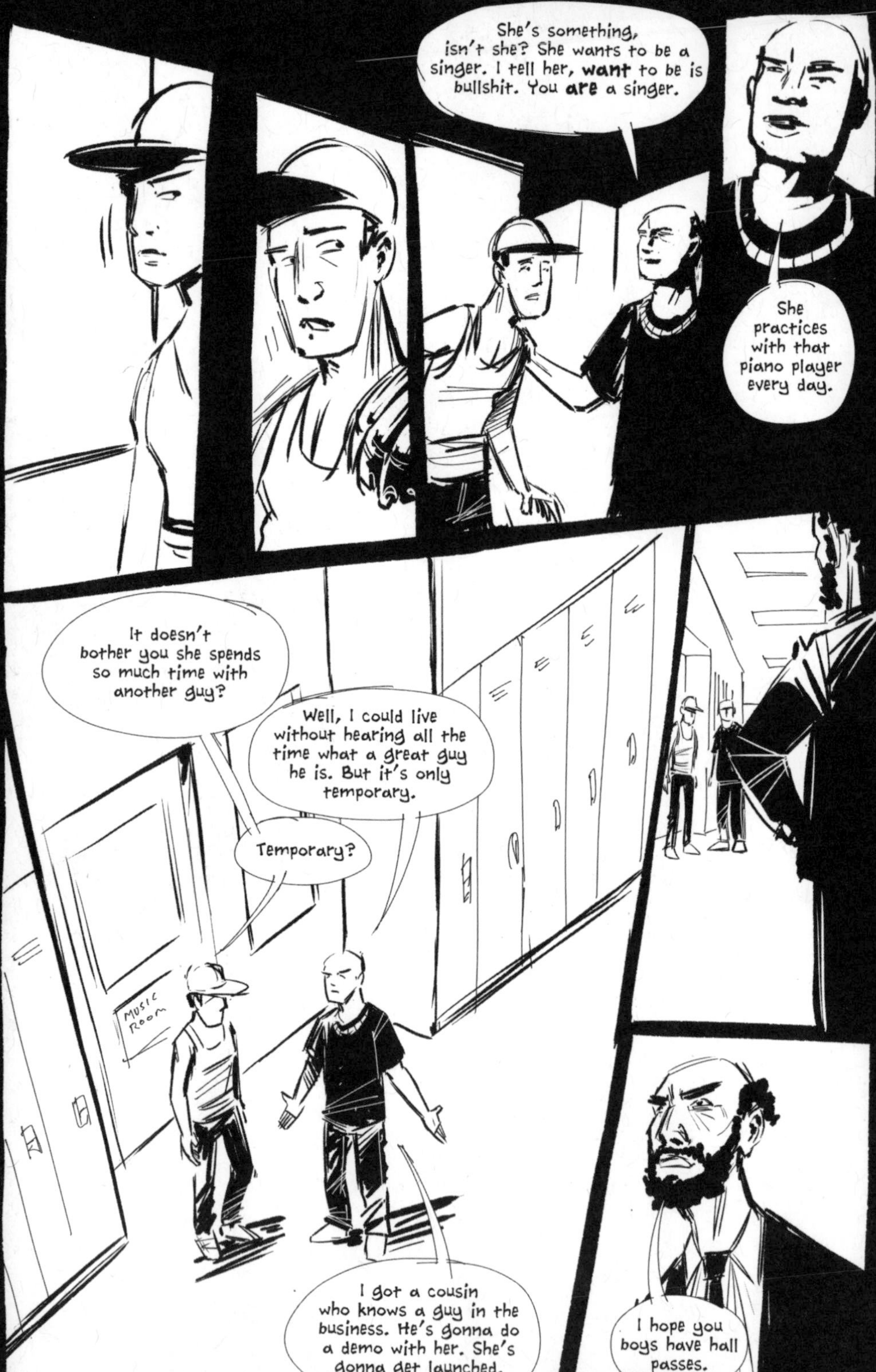
She's something, isn't she? She wants to be a singer. I tell her, **want** to be is bullshit. You **are** a singer.
She practices with that piano player every day.
It doesn't bother you she spends so much time with another guy?
Well, I could live without hearing all the time what a great guy he is. But it's only temporary.
Temporary?
MUSIC ROOM
I got a cousin who knows a guy in the business. He's gonna do a demo with her. She's gonna get launched.
I hope you boys have hall passes.

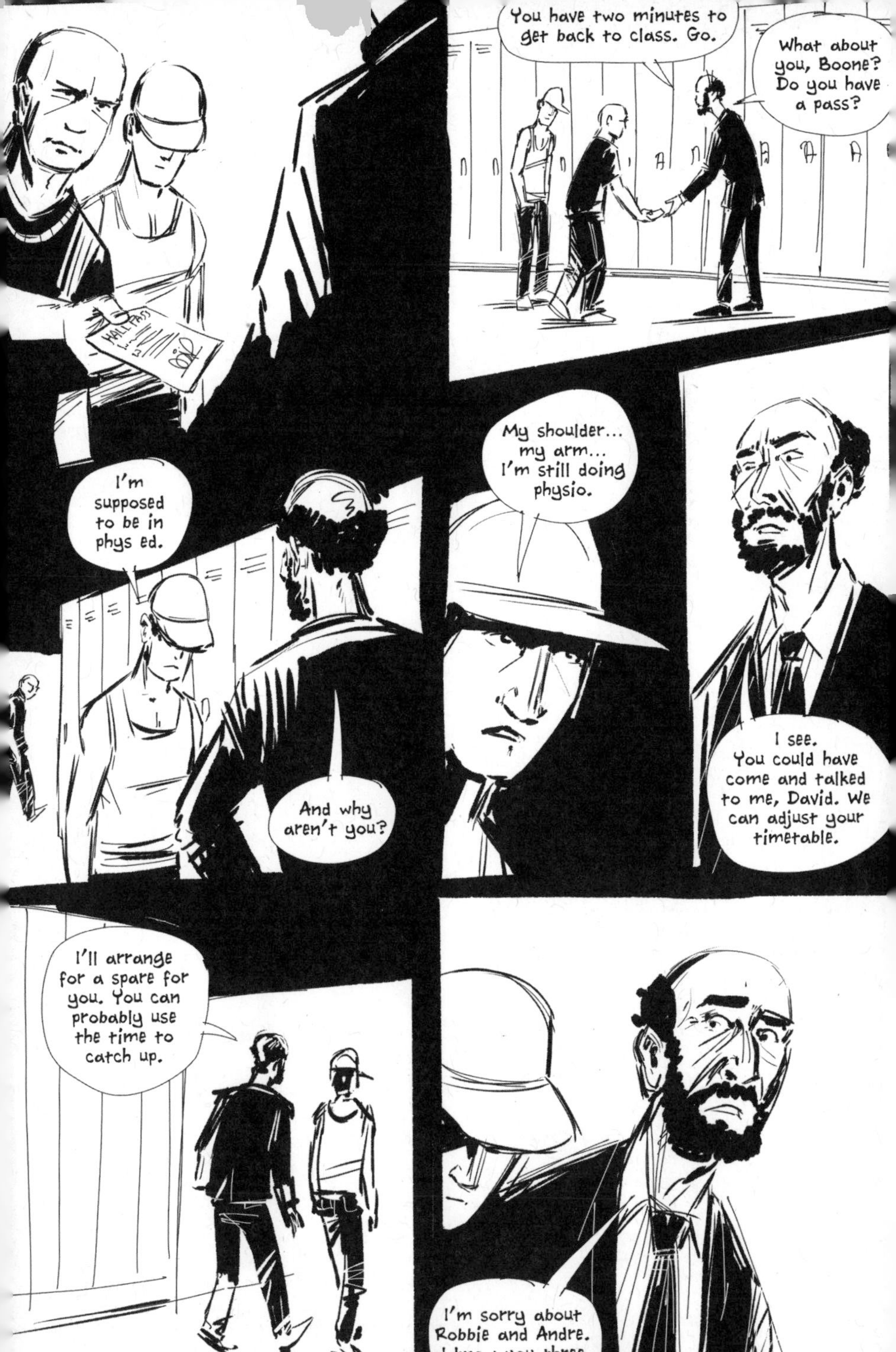
HALL PASS
You have two minutes to get back to class. Go.
What about you, Boone? Do you have a pass?
I'm supposed to be in phys ed.
And why aren't you?
My shoulder... my arm... I'm still doing physio.
I see. You could have come and talked to me, David. We can adjust your timetable.
I'll arrange for a spare for you. You can probably use the time to catch up.
I'm sorry about Robbie and Andre. I know you three were close.

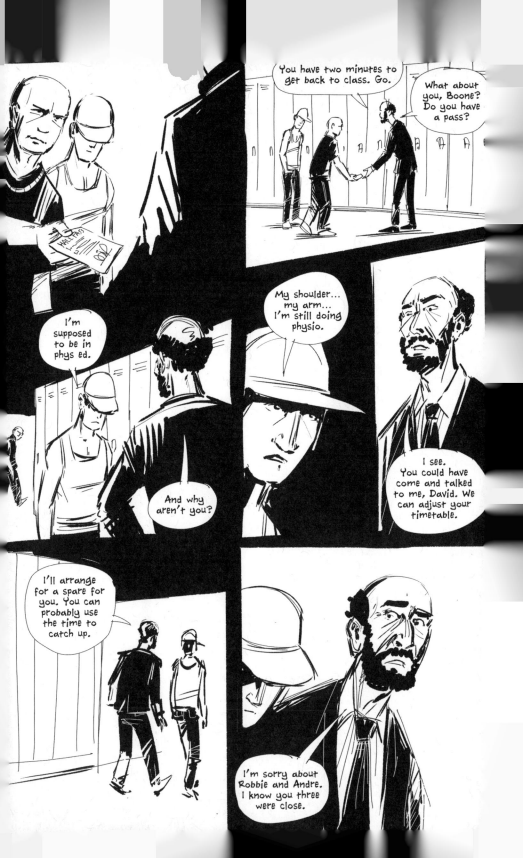

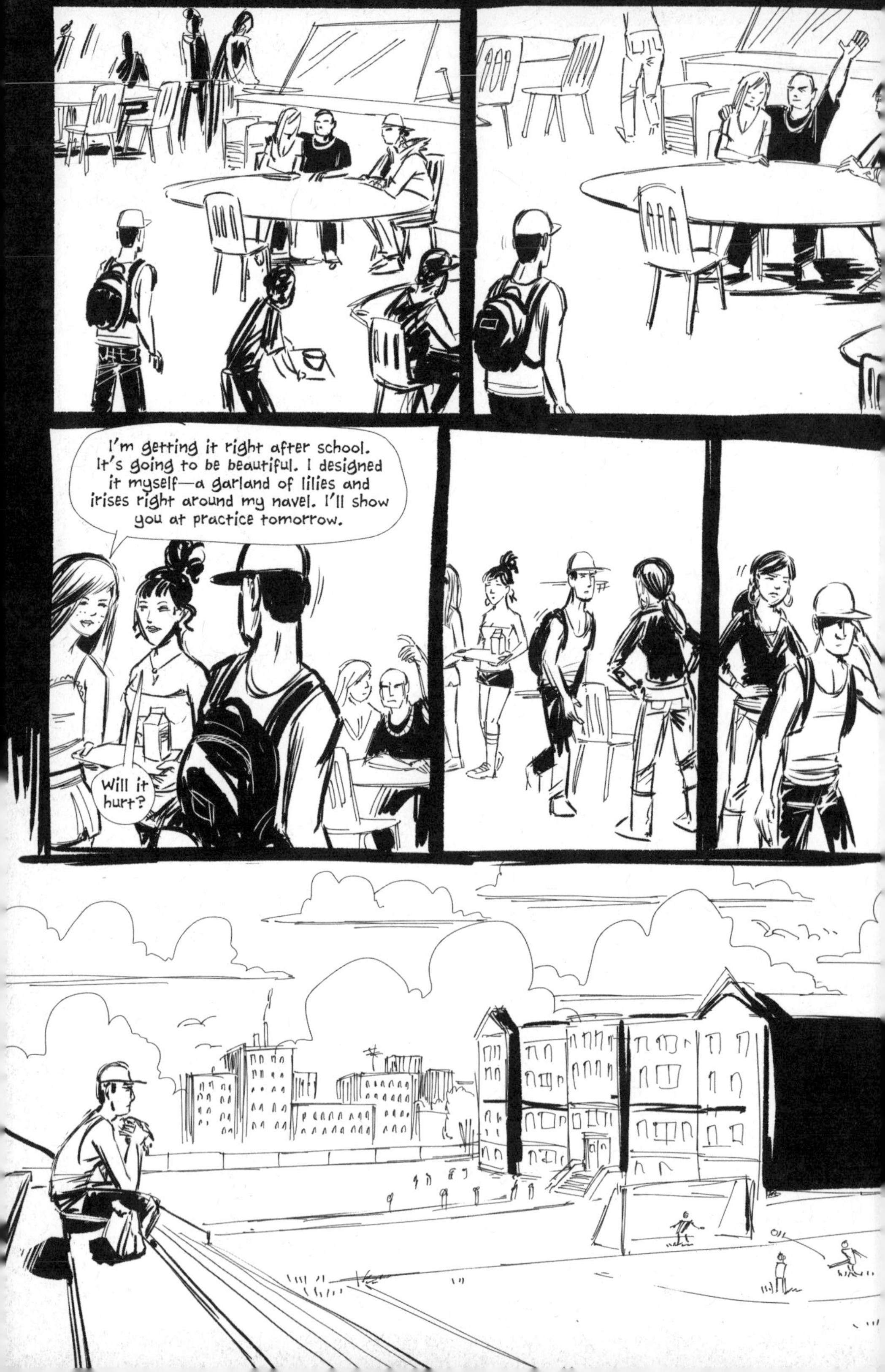
I'm getting it right after school. It's going to be beautiful. I designed it myself—a garland of lilies and irises right around my navel. I'll show you at practice tomorrow.
Will it hurt?

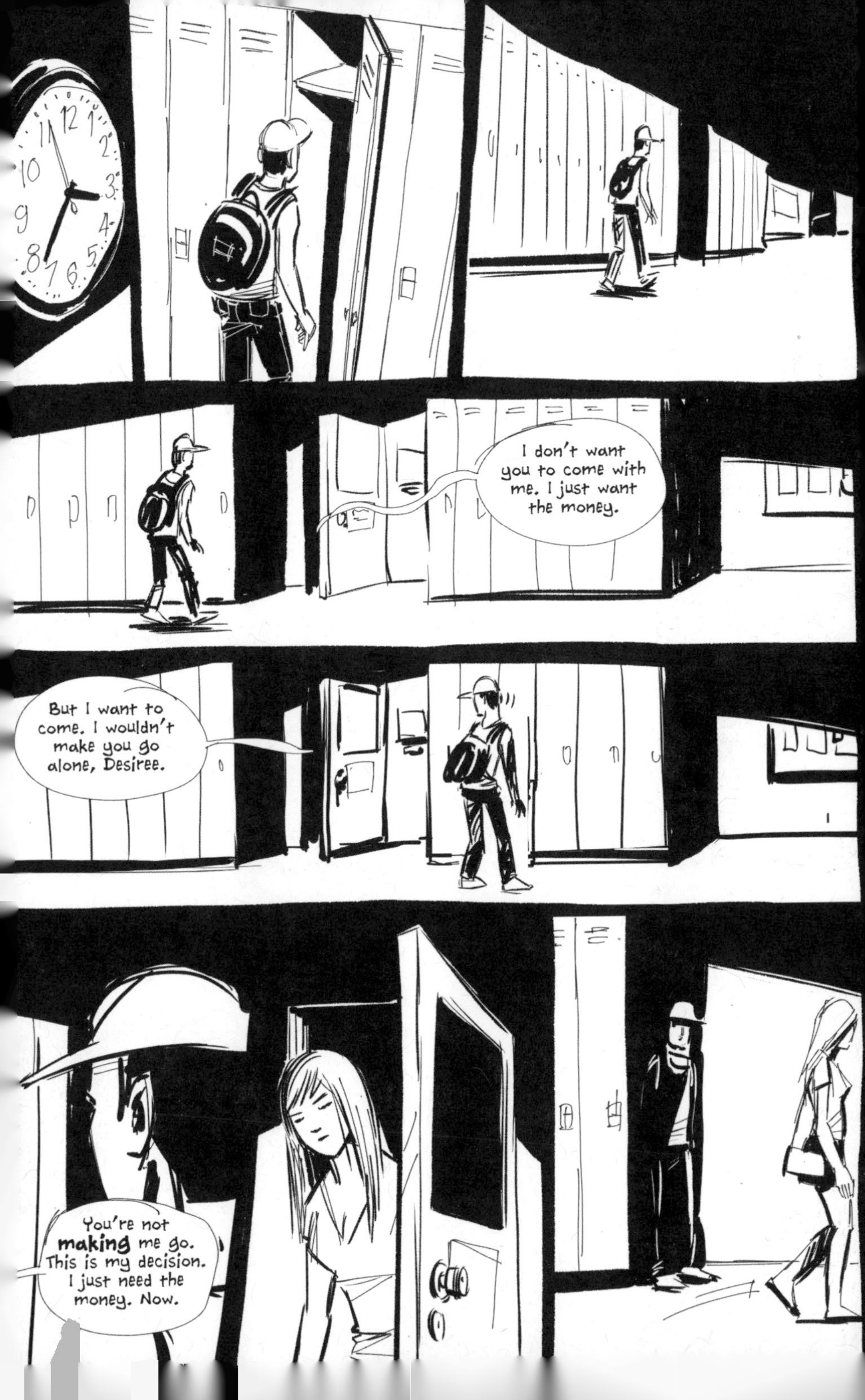
I don't want you to come with me. I just want the money.
But I want to come. I wouldn't make you go alone, Desiree.
You're not **making** me go. This is my decision. I just need the money. Now.

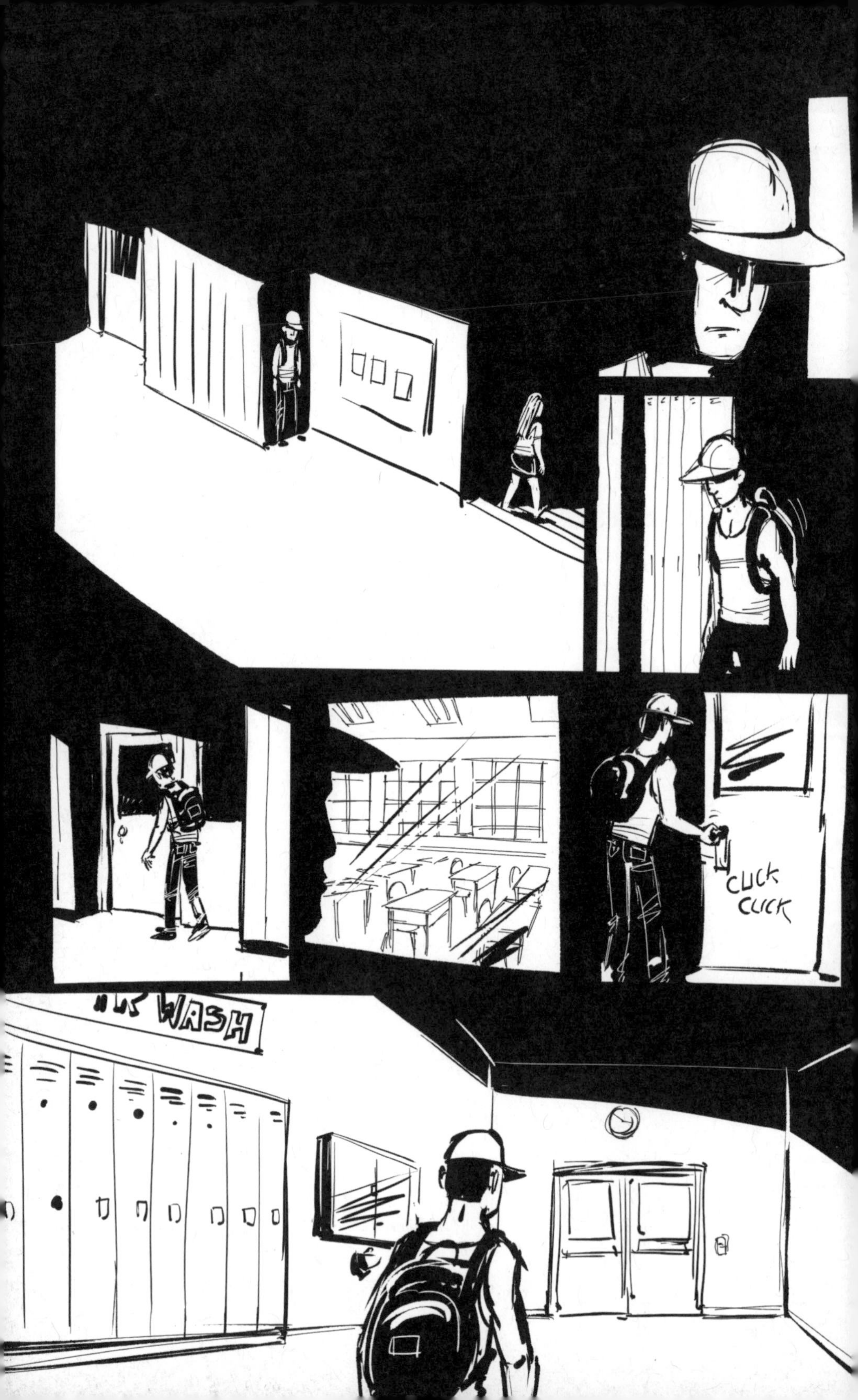
CLICK
CLICK
WASH

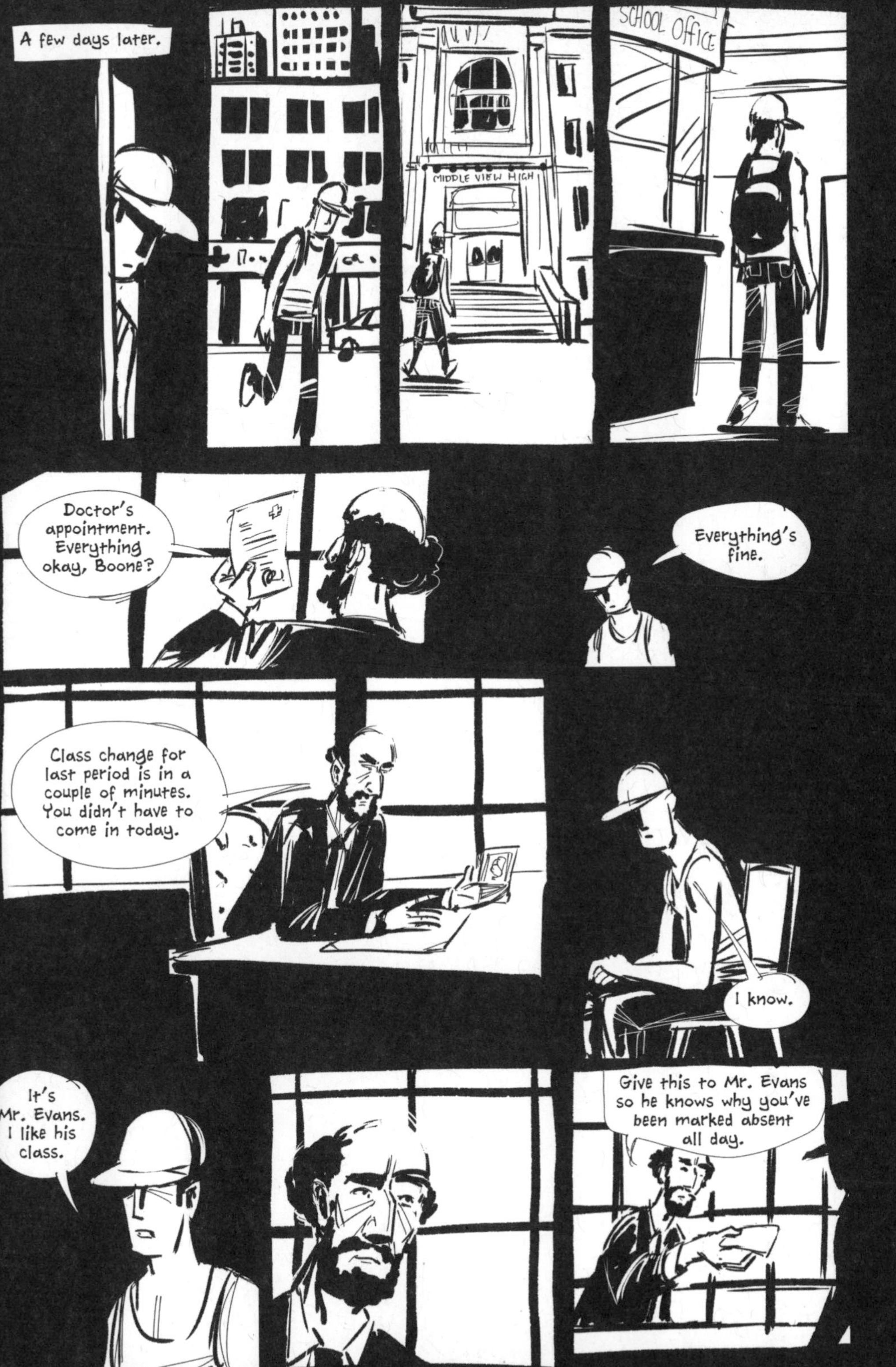
A few days later.
SCHOOL OFFICE
MIDDLE VIEW HIGH
Doctor's appointment. Everything okay, Boone?
Everything's fine.
Class change for last period is in a couple of minutes. You didn't have to come in today.
I know.
It's Mr. Evans. I like his class.
Give this to Mr. Evans so he knows why you've been marked absent all day.

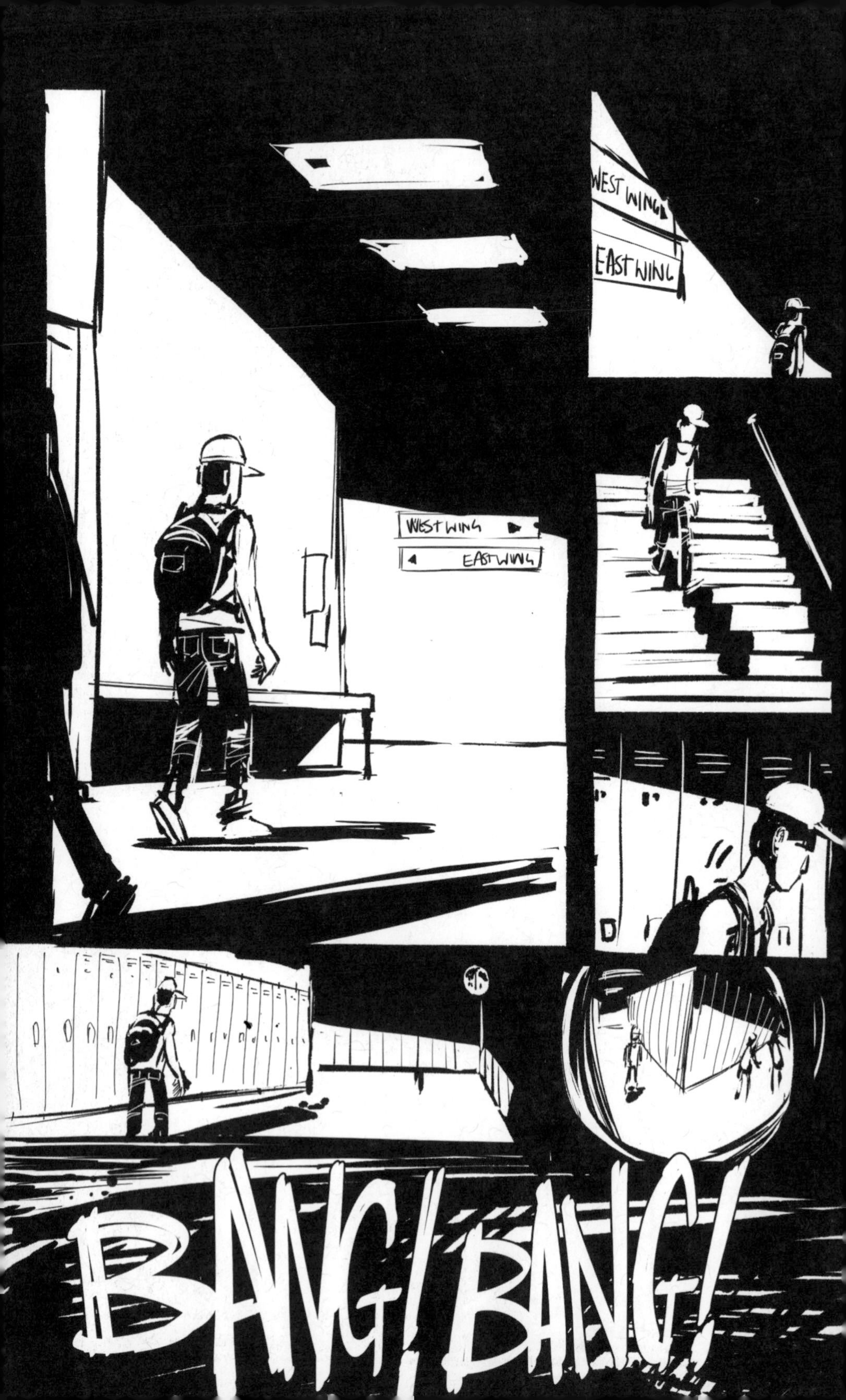

WEST WING
EAST WING
WEST WING
EAST WING
BANG! BANG!

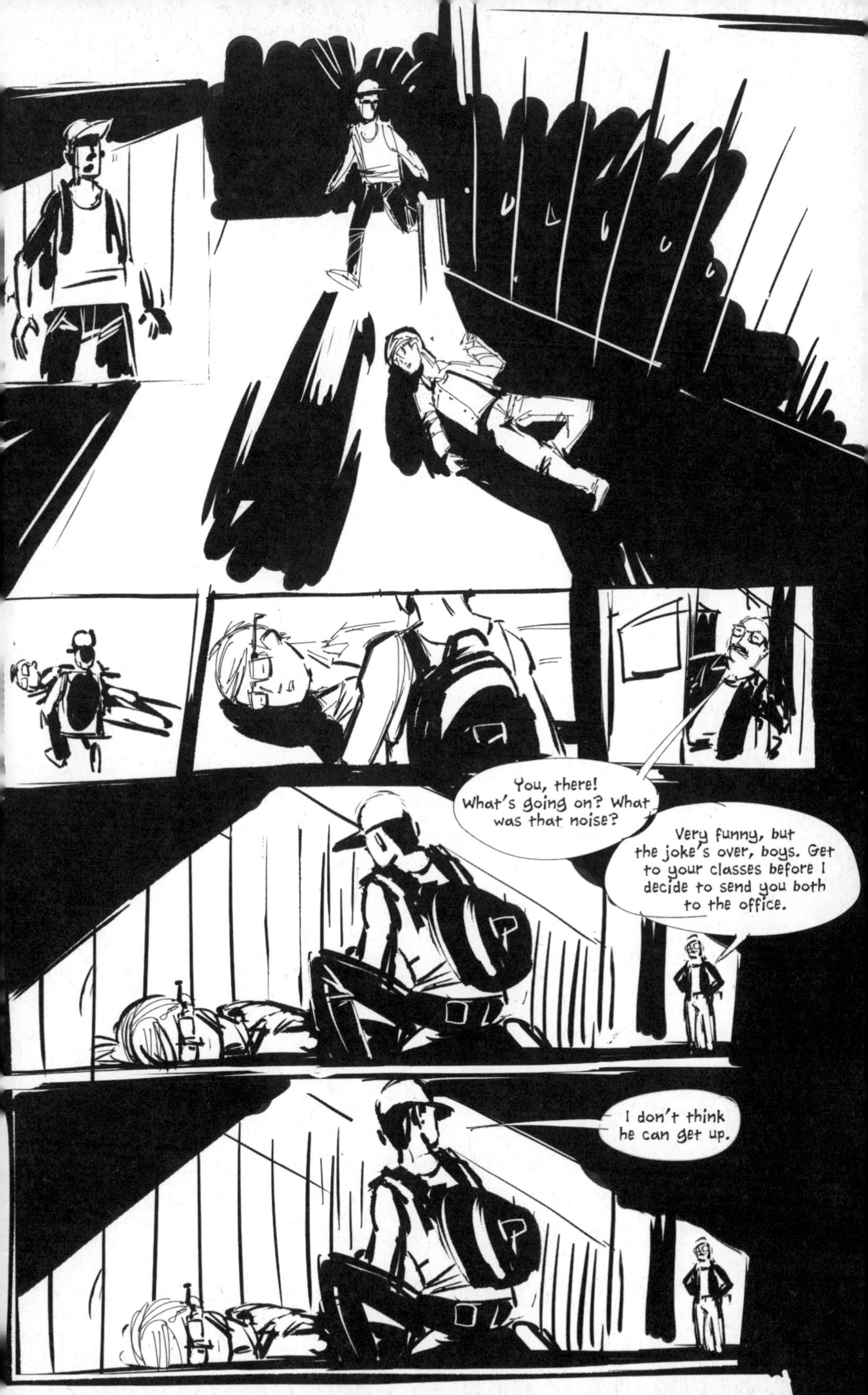
You, there! What's going on? What was that noise?
Very funny, but the joke's over, boys. Get to your classes before I decide to send you both to the office.
I don't think he can get up.

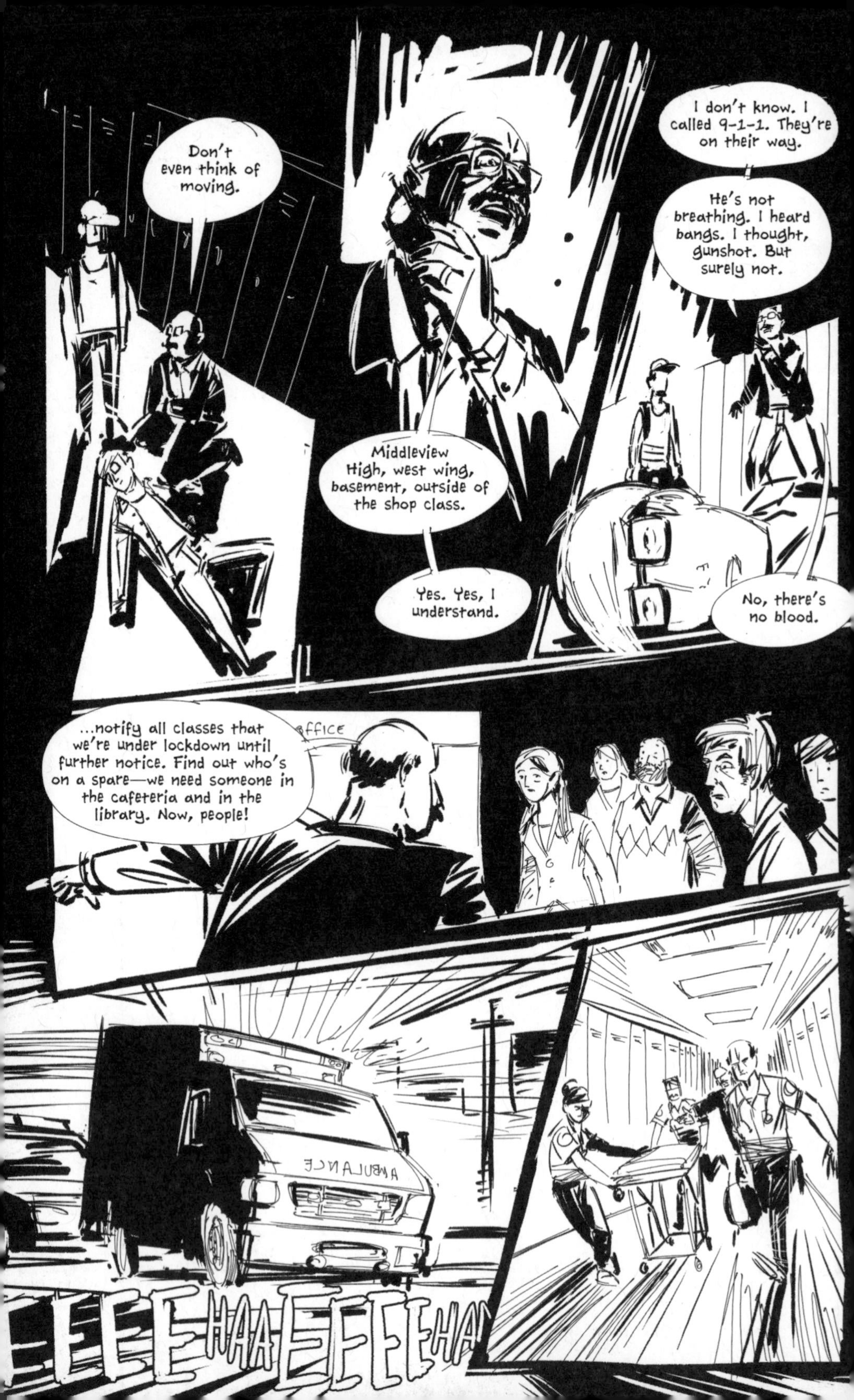
Don't even think of moving.
Middleview High, west wing, basement, outside of the shop class.
Yes. Yes, I understand.
I don't know. I called 9-1-1. They're on their way.
He's not breathing. I heard bangs. I thought, gunshot. But surely not.
No, there's no blood.
OFFICE
...notify all classes that we're under lockdown until further notice. Find out who's on a spare—we need someone in the cafeteria and in the library. Now, people!
AMBULANCE
EEEE HAA EEEE HA

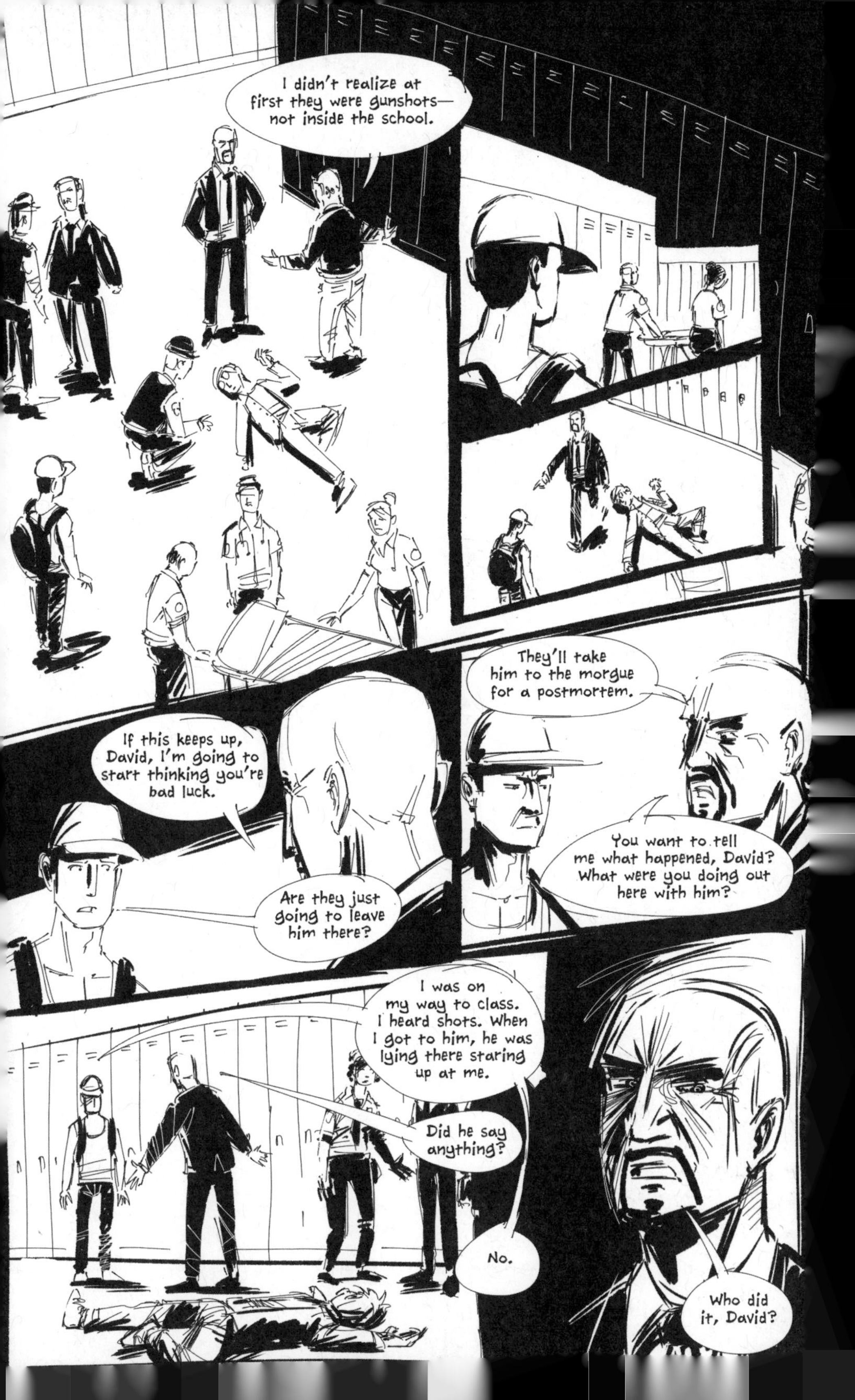
I didn't realize at first they were gunshots— not inside the school.
They'll take him to the morgue for a postmortem.
If this keeps up, David, I'm going to start thinking you're bad luck.
Are they just going to leave him there?
You want to tell me what happened, David? What were you doing out here with him?
I was on my way to class. I heard shots. When I got to him, he was lying there staring up at me.
Did he say anything?
No.
Who did it, David?

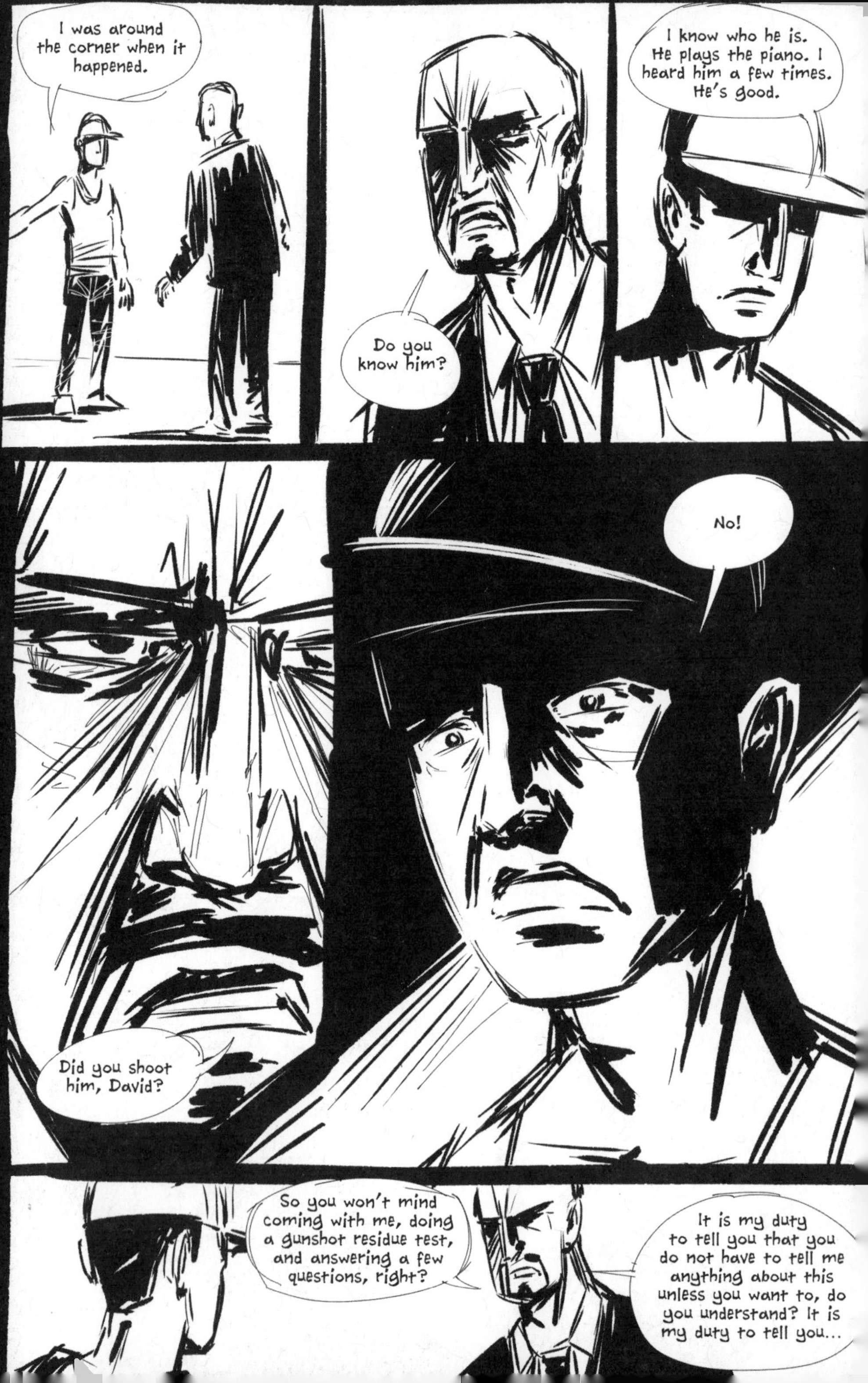
I was around the corner when it happened.
Do you know him?
I know who he is. He plays the piano. I heard him a few times. He's good.
Did you shoot him, David?
No!
So you won't mind coming with me, doing a gunshot residue test, and answering a few questions, right?
It is my duty to tell you that you do not have to tell me anything about this unless you want to, do you understand? It is my duty to tell you...

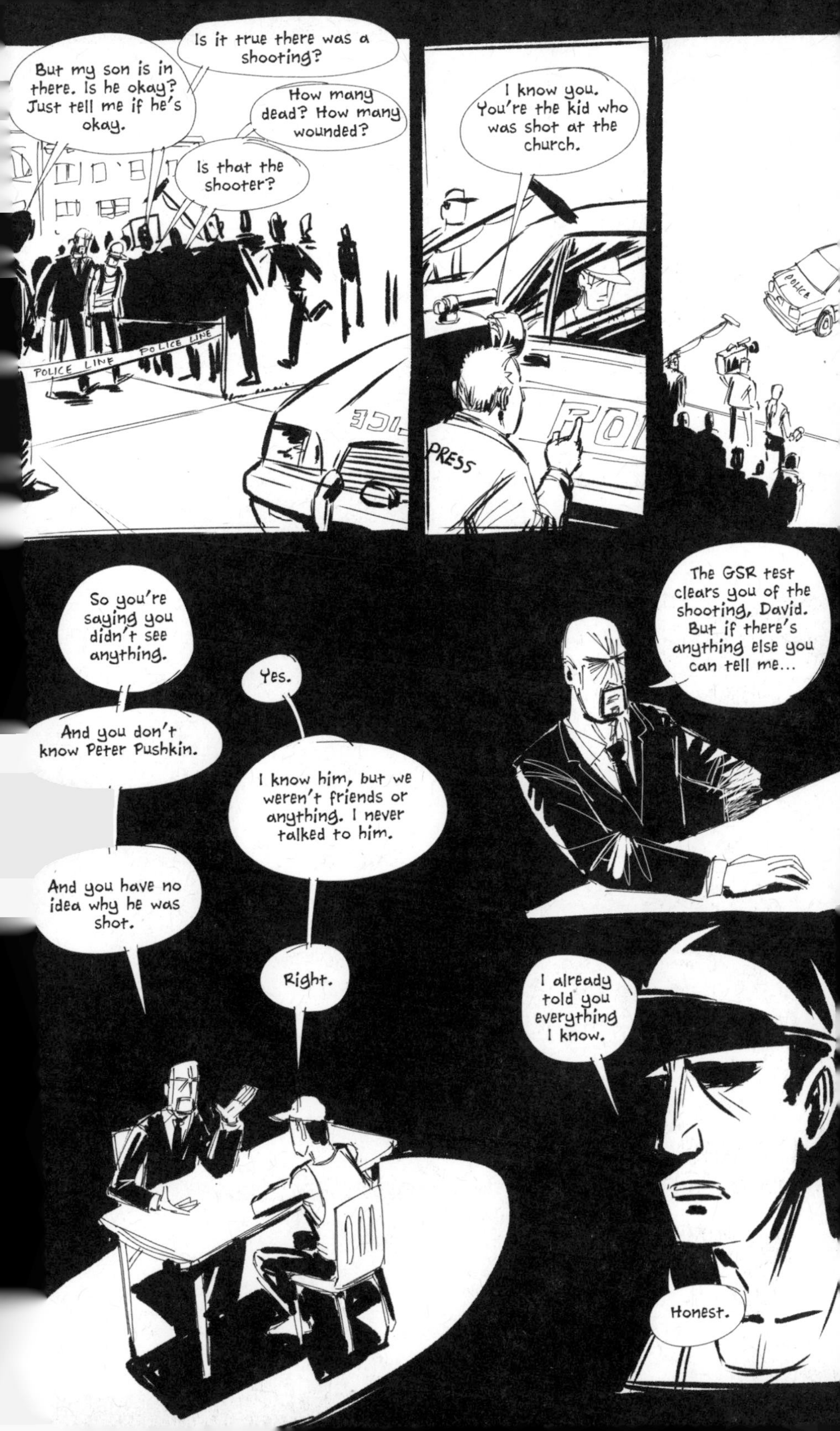
But my son is in there. Is he okay? Just tell me if he's okay.
Is it true there was a shooting?
How many dead? How many wounded?
Is that the shooter?
POLICE LINE
POLICE LINE
I know you. You're the kid who was shot at the church.
PRESS
POLICE
So you're saying you didn't see anything.
Yes.
And you don't know Peter Pushkin.
I know him, but we weren't friends or anything. I never talked to him.
And you have no idea why he was shot.
Right.
The GSR test clears you of the shooting, David. But if there's anything else you can tell me...
I already told you everything I know.
Honest.

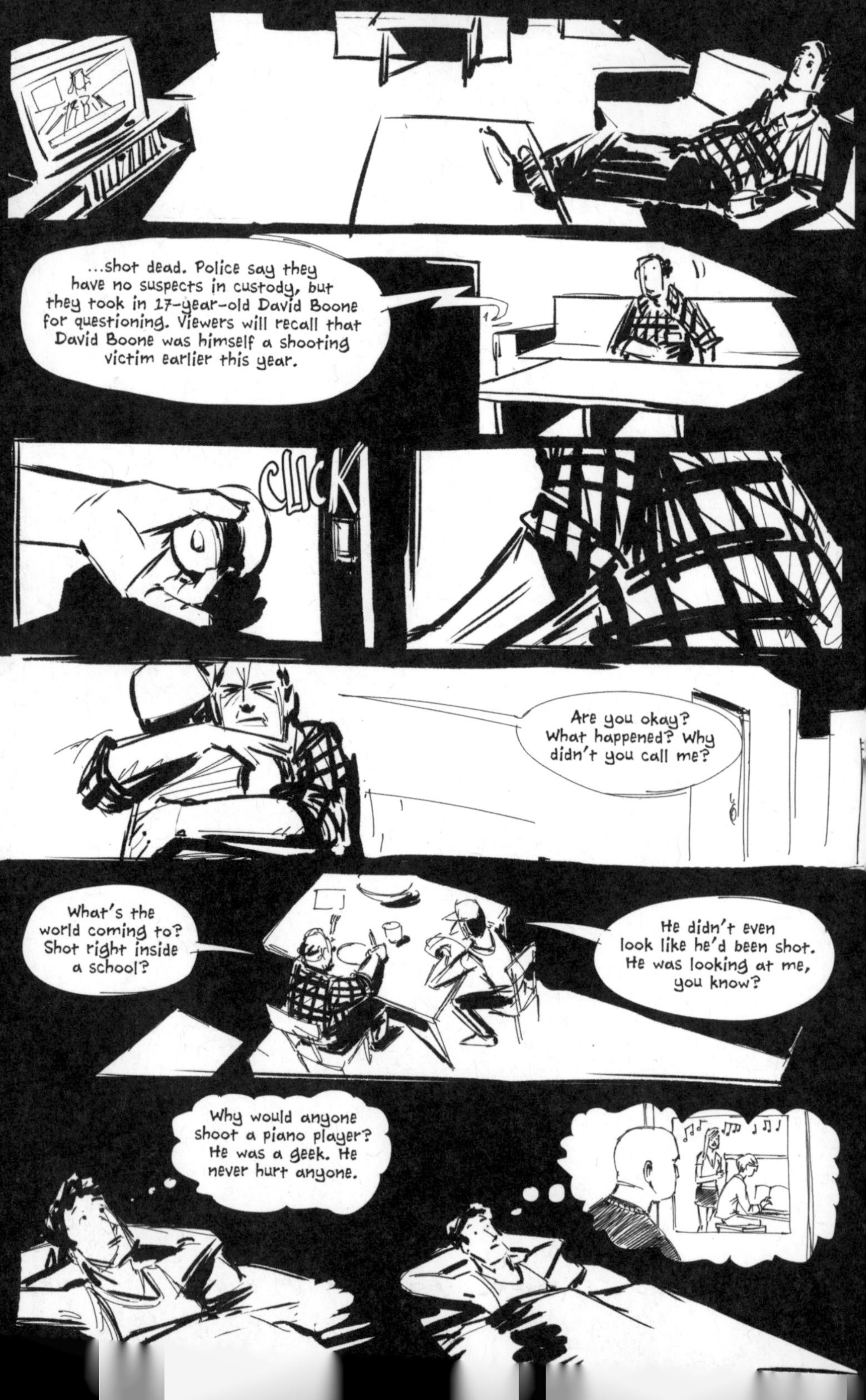
...shot dead. Police say they have no suspects in custody, but they took in 17-year-old David Boone for questioning. Viewers will recall that David Boone was himself a shooting victim earlier this year.
CLICK
Are you okay? What happened? Why didn't you call me?
What's the world coming to? Shot right inside a school?
He didn't even look like he'd been shot. He was looking at me, you know?
Why would anyone shoot a piano player? He was a geek. He never hurt anyone.

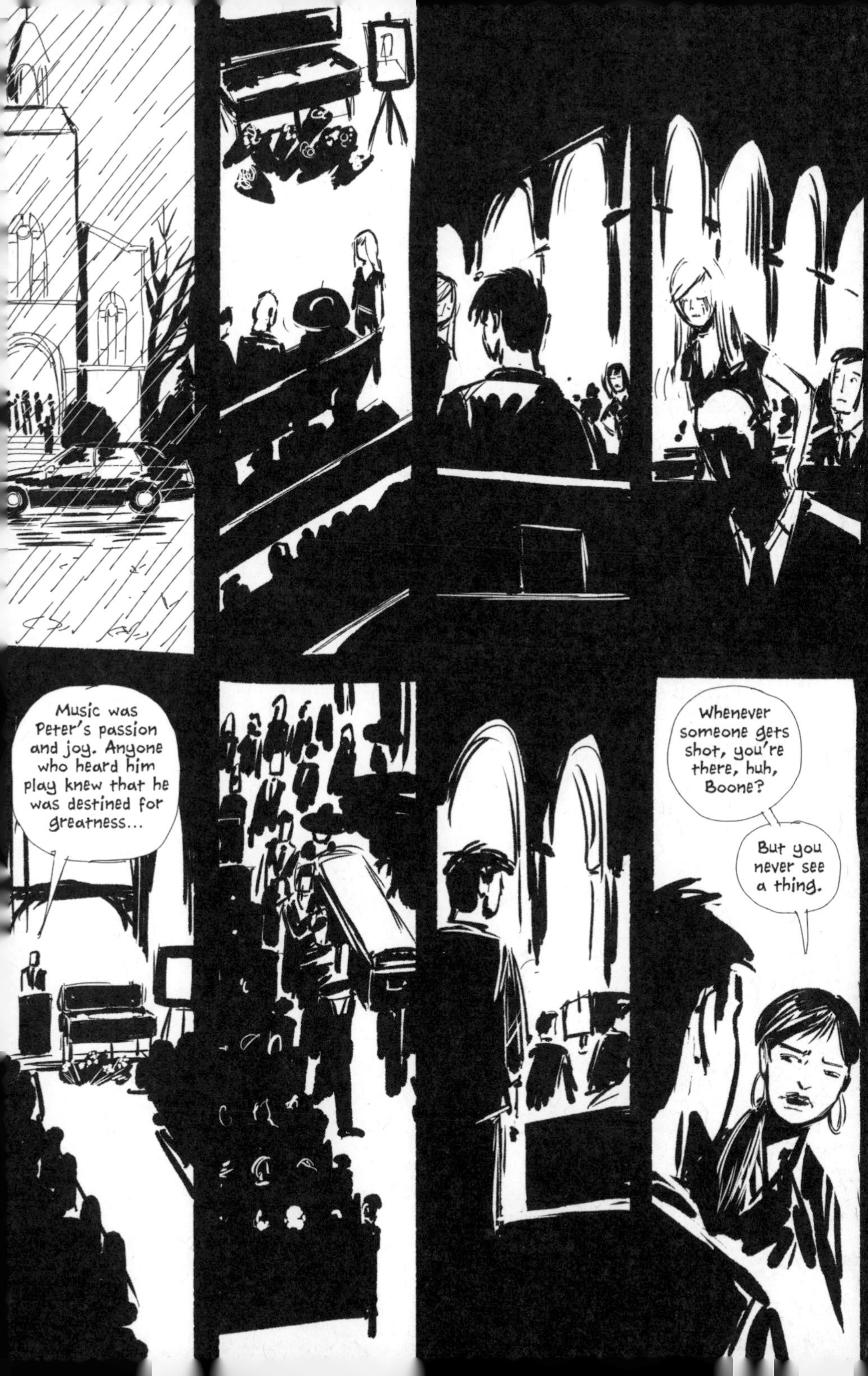
Music was Peter's passion and joy. Anyone who heard him play knew that he was destined for greatness...
Whenever someone gets shot, you're there, huh, Boone?
But you never see a thing.

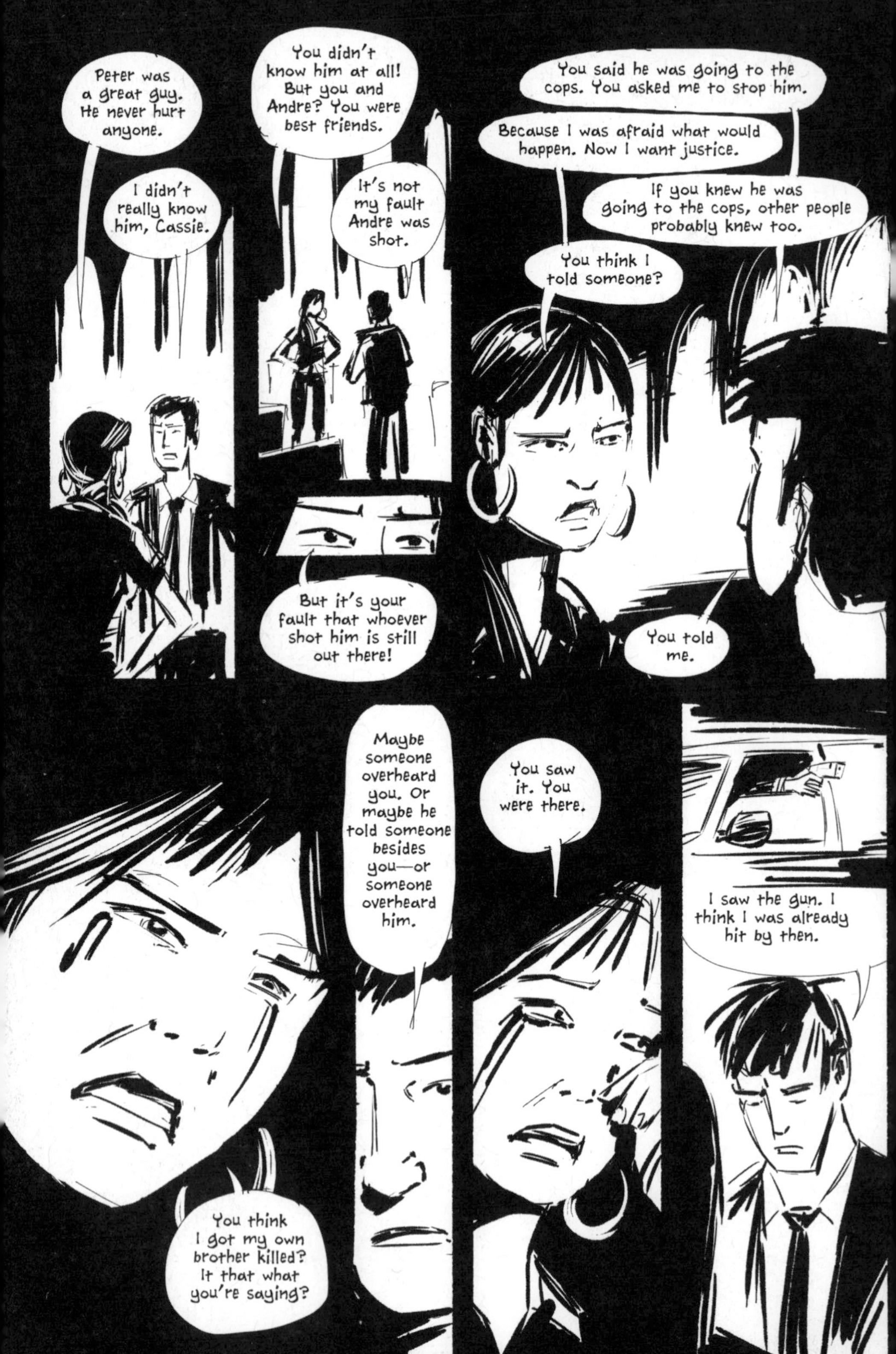
Peter was a great guy. He never hurt anyone.
I didn't really know him, Cassie.
You didn't know him at all! But you and Andre? You were best friends.
It's not my fault Andre was shot.
But it's your fault that whoever shot him is still out there!
You said he was going to the cops. You asked me to stop him.
Because I was afraid what would happen. Now I want justice.
If you knew he was going to the cops, other people probably knew too.
You think I told someone?
You told me.
You think I got my own brother killed? It that what you're saying?
Maybe someone overheard you. Or maybe he told someone besides you—or someone overheard him.
You saw it. You were there.
I saw the gun. I think I was already hit by then.

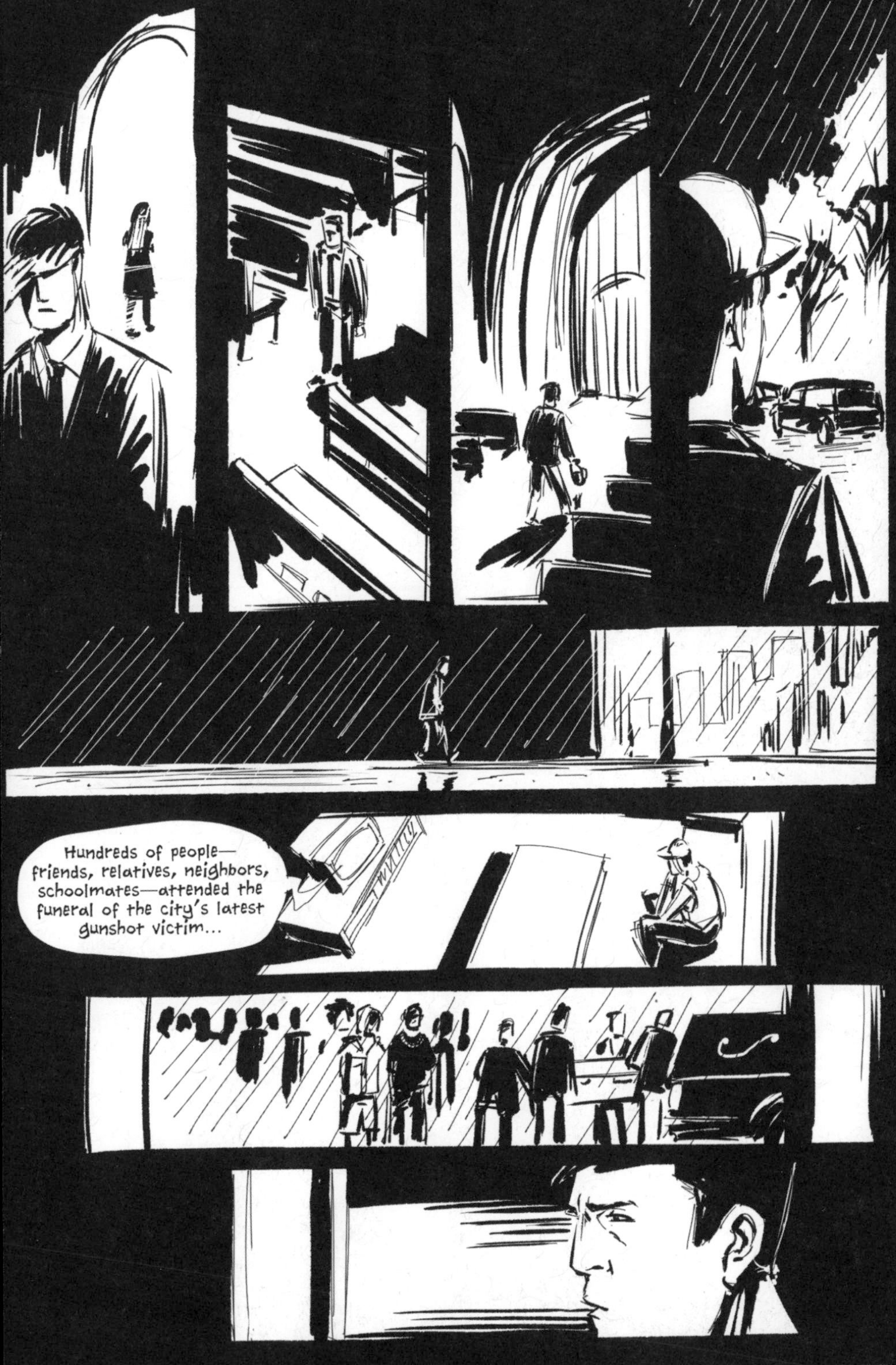
Hundreds of people—friends, relatives, neighbors, schoolmates—attended the funeral of the city's latest gunshot victim...

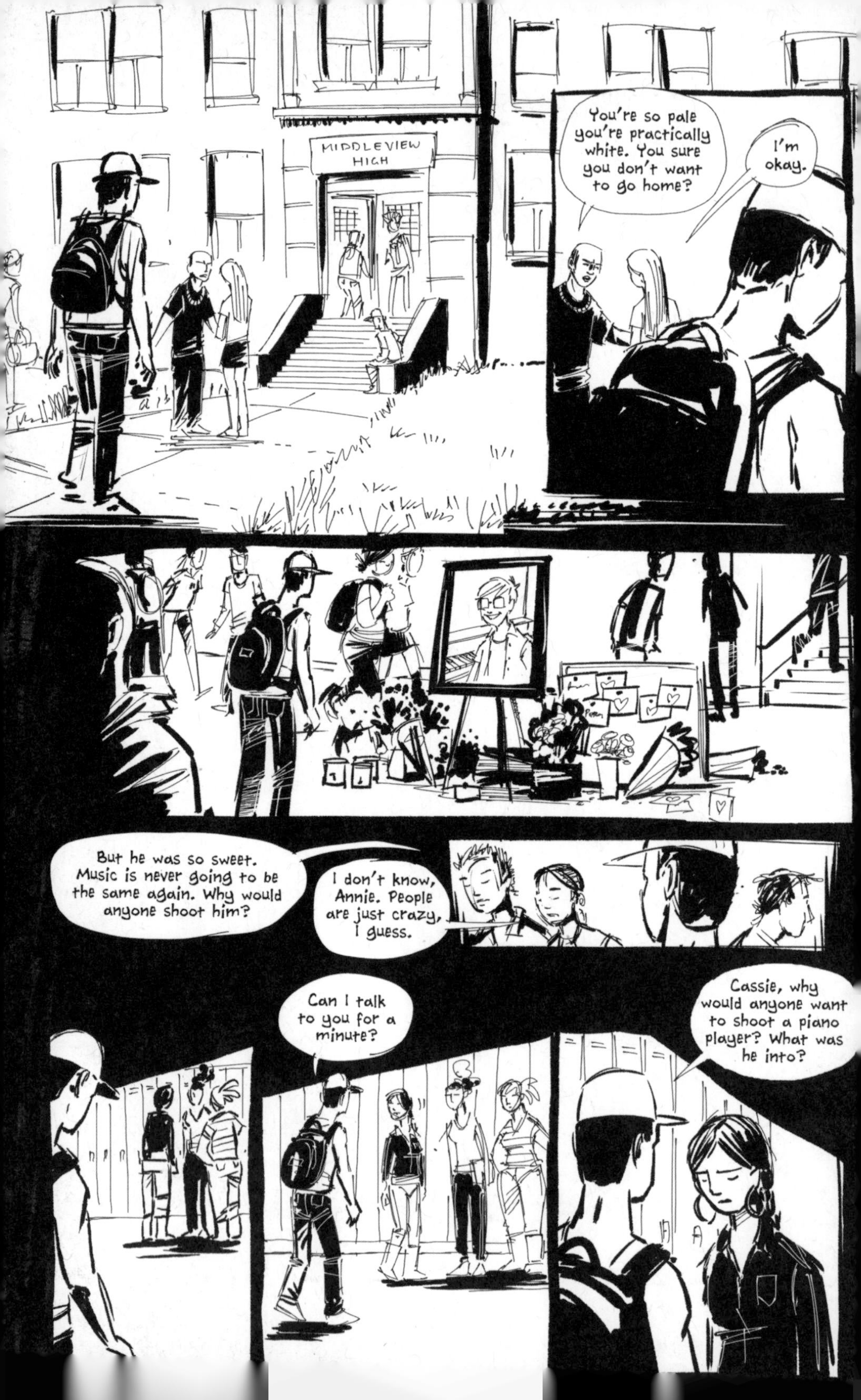
MIDDLEVIEW HIGH
You're so pale you're practically white. You sure you don't want to go home?
I'm okay.
But he was so sweet. Music is never going to be the same again. Why would anyone shoot him?
I don't know, Annie. People are just crazy, I guess.
Can I talk to you for a minute?
Cassie, why would anyone want to shoot a piano player? What was he into?

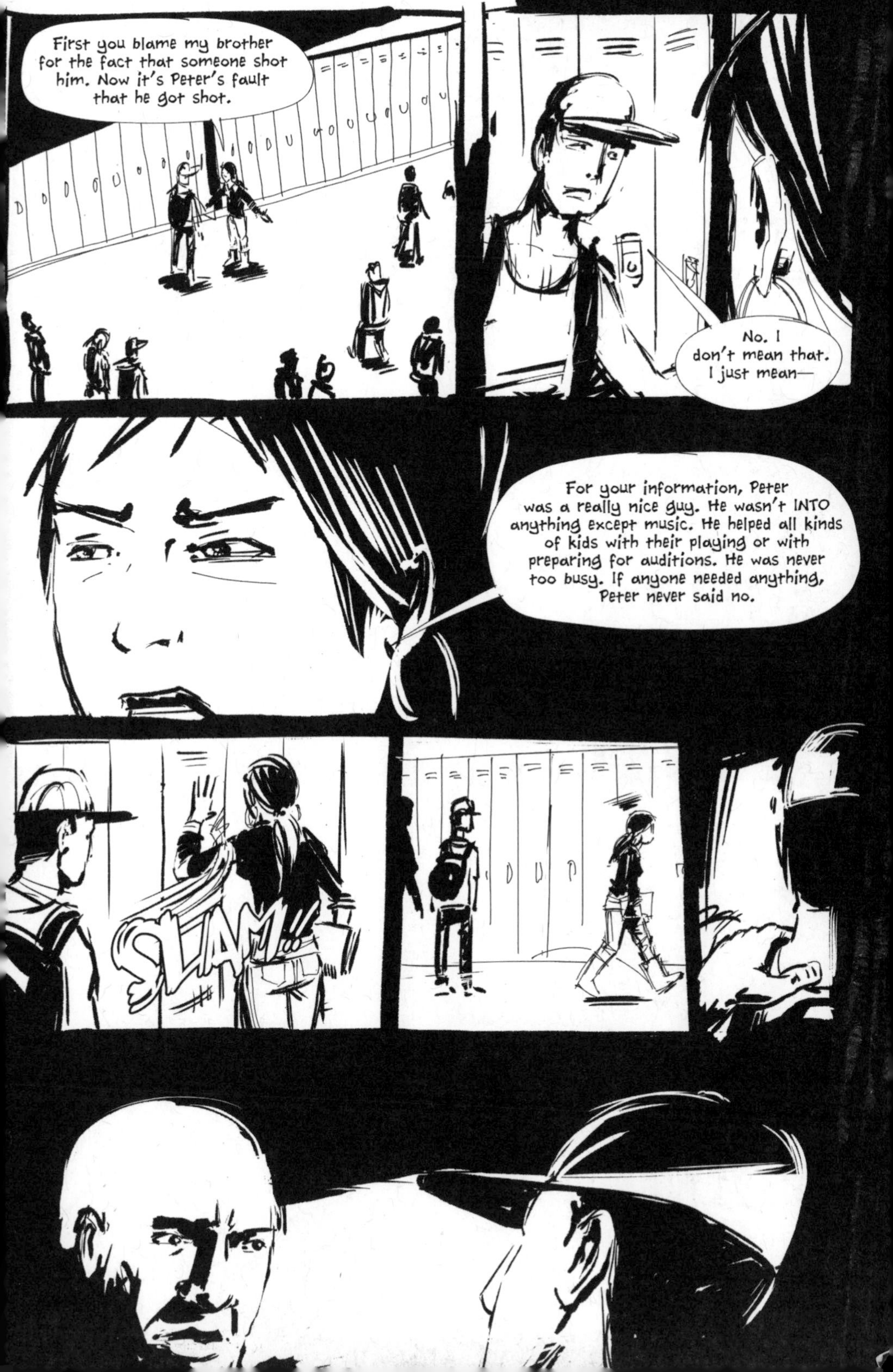

First you blame my brother for the fact that someone shot him. Now it's Peter's fault that he got shot.
No. I don't mean that. I just mean—
For your information, Peter was a really nice guy. He wasn't INTO anything except music. He helped all kinds of kids with their playing or with preparing for auditions. He was never too busy. If anyone needed anything, Peter never said no.
SLAM!!

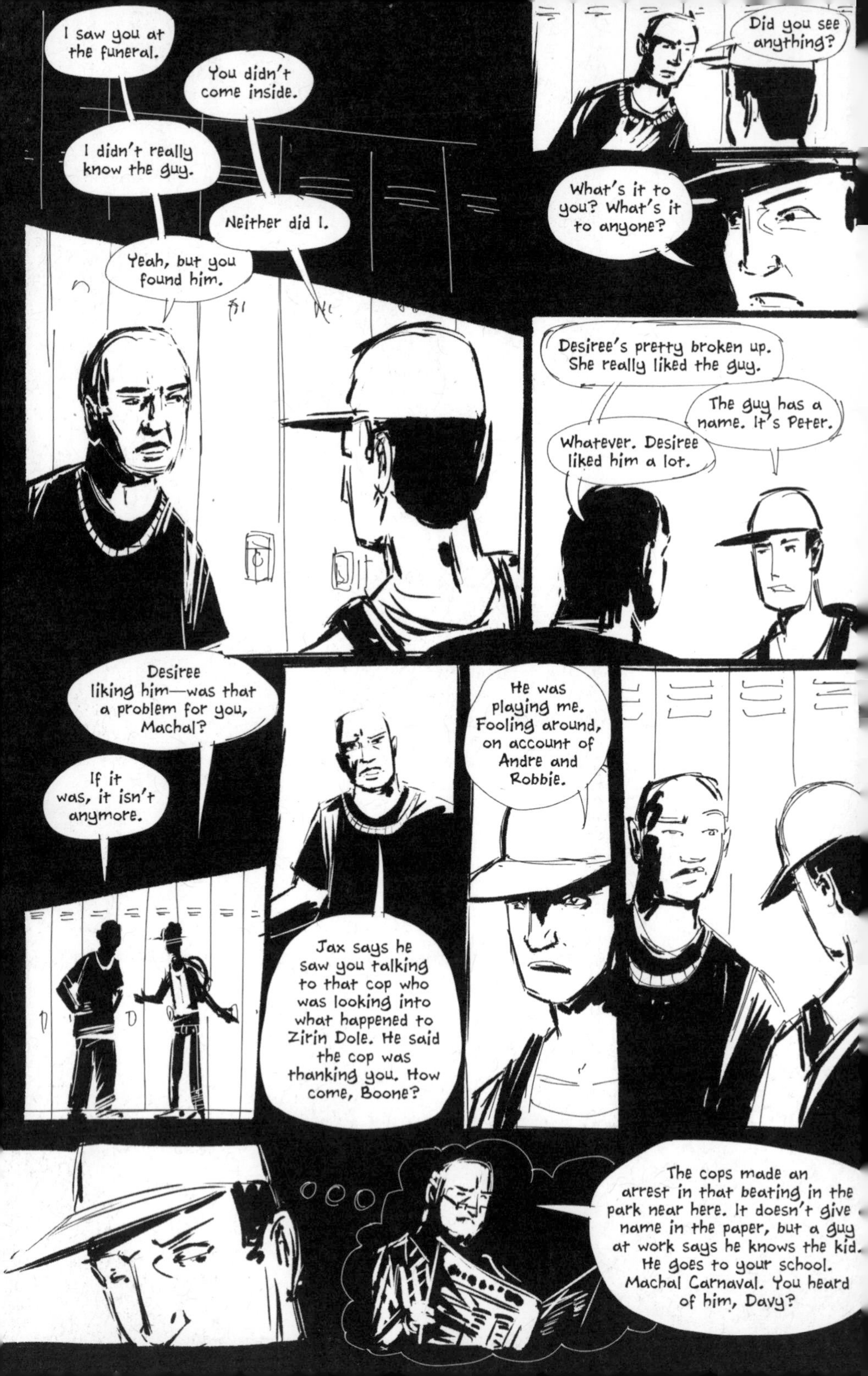
I saw you at the funeral.
You didn't come inside.
I didn't really know the guy.
Neither did I.
Yeah, but you found him.
Did you see anything?
What's it to you? What's it to anyone?
Desiree's pretty broken up. She really liked the guy.
The guy has a name. It's Peter.
Whatever. Desiree liked him a lot.
Desiree liking him—was that a problem for you, Machal?
If it was, it isn't anymore.
Jax says he saw you talking to that cop who was looking into what happened to Zirin Dole. He said the cop was thanking you. How come, Boone?
He was playing me. Fooling around, on account of Andre and Robbie.
The cops made an arrest in that beating in the park near here. It doesn't give name in the paper, but a guy at work says he knows the kid. He goes to your school. Machal Carnaval. You heard of him, Davy?

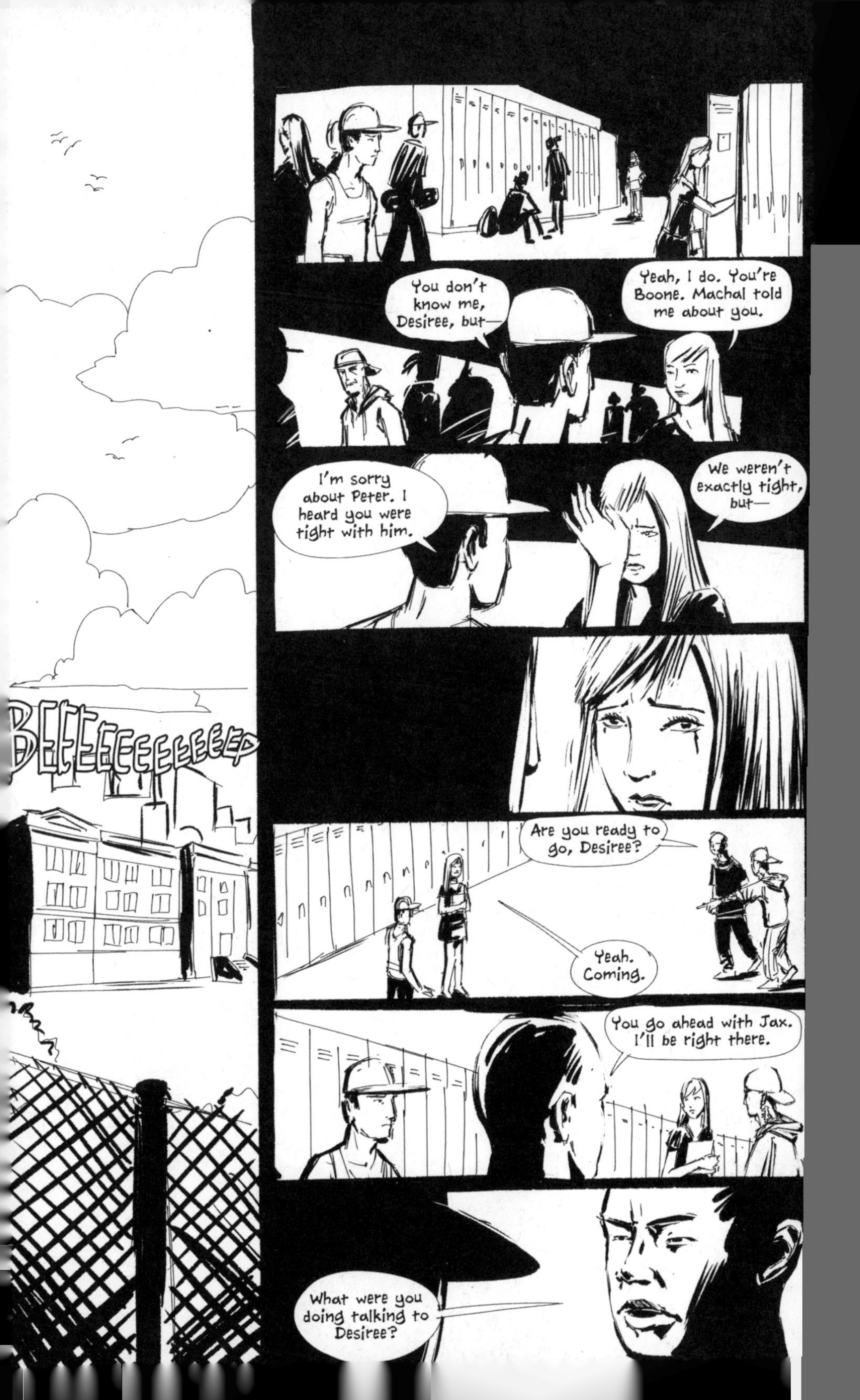
BEEEEEEEEEEEEP
You don't know me, Desiree, but—
Yeah, I do. You're Boone. Machal told me about you.
I'm sorry about Peter. I heard you were tight with him.
We weren't exactly tight, but—
Are you ready to go, Desiree?
Yeah. Coming.
You go ahead with Jax. I'll be right there.
What were you doing talking to Desiree?

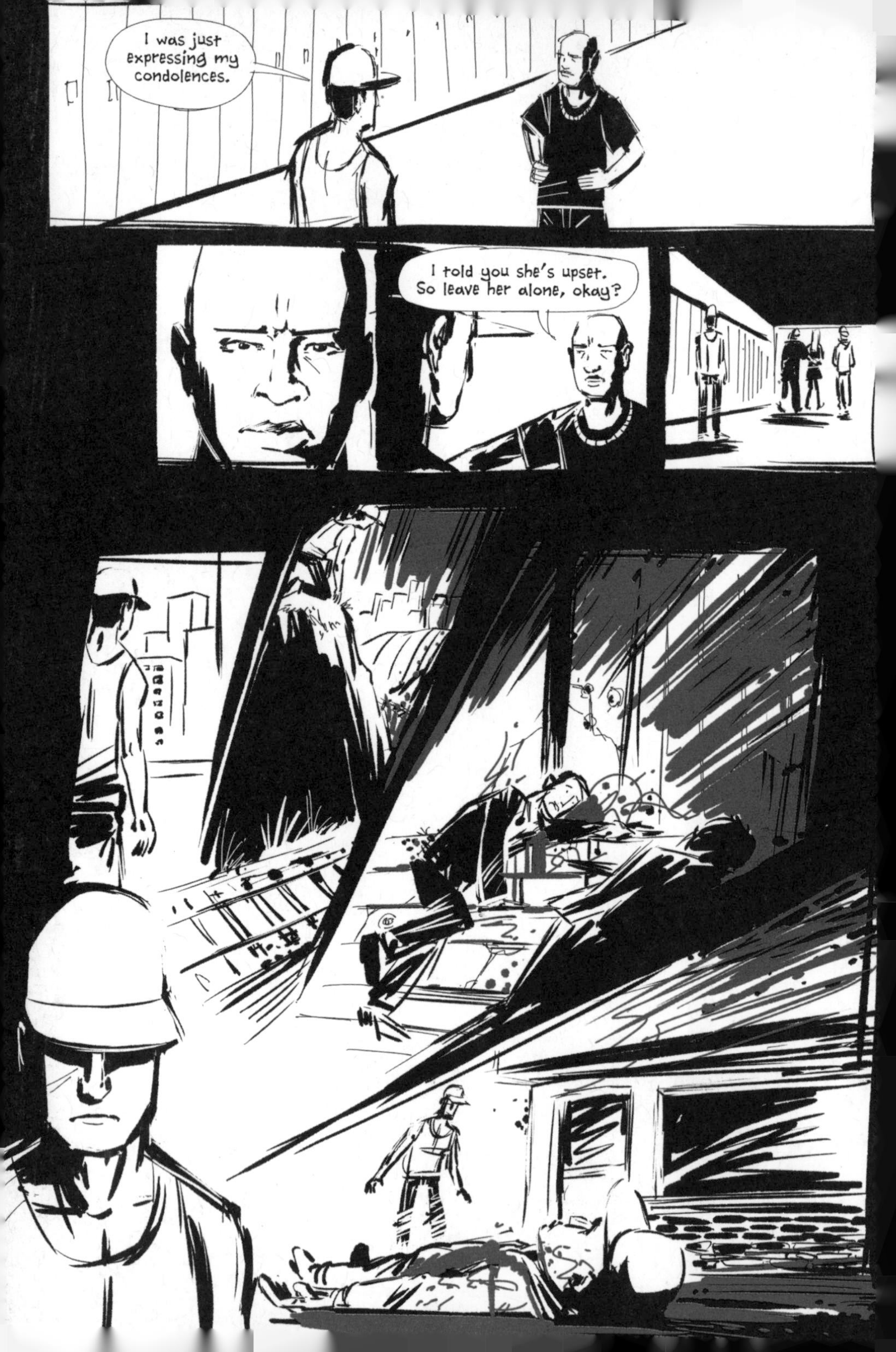
I was just expressing my condolences.
I told you she's upset. So leave her alone, okay?

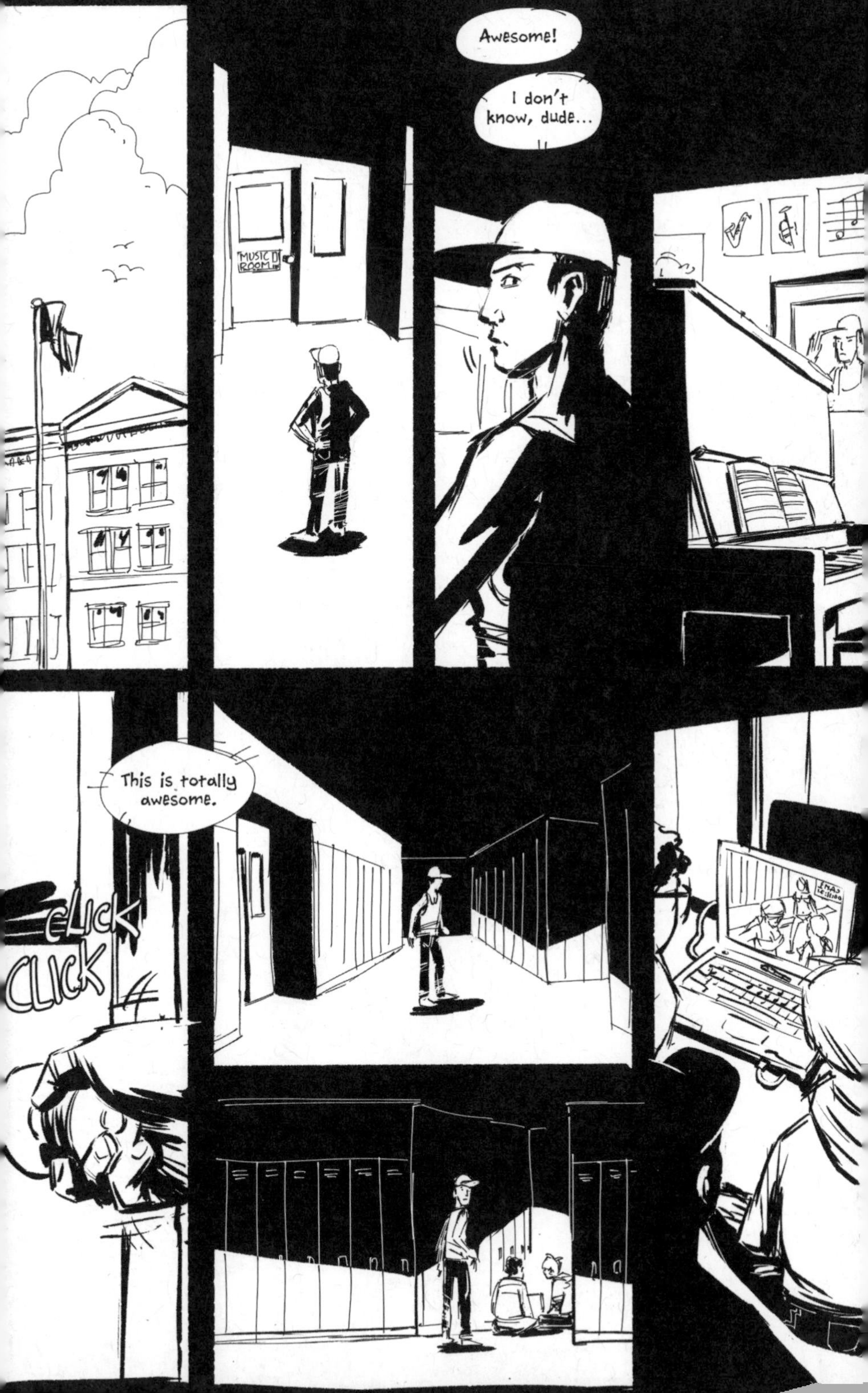
MUSIC ROOM
Awesome!
I don't know, dude...
This is totally awesome.
CLICK
CLICK

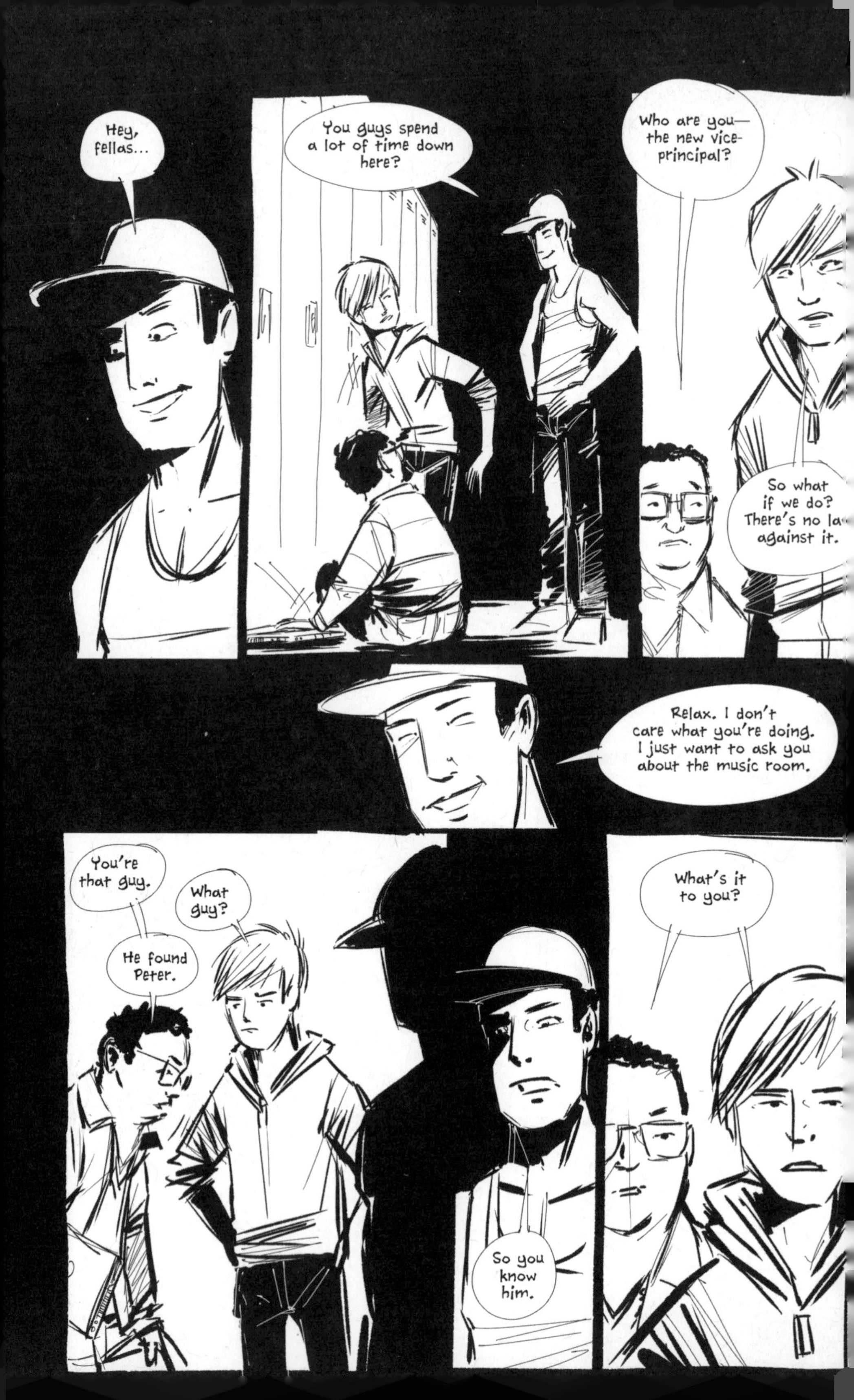
Hey, fellas...
You guys spend a lot of time down here?
Who are you— the new vice-principal?
So what if we do? There's no la against it.
Relax. I don't care what you're doing. I just want to ask you about the music room.
You're that guy.
What guy?
He found Peter.
So you know him.
What's it to you?

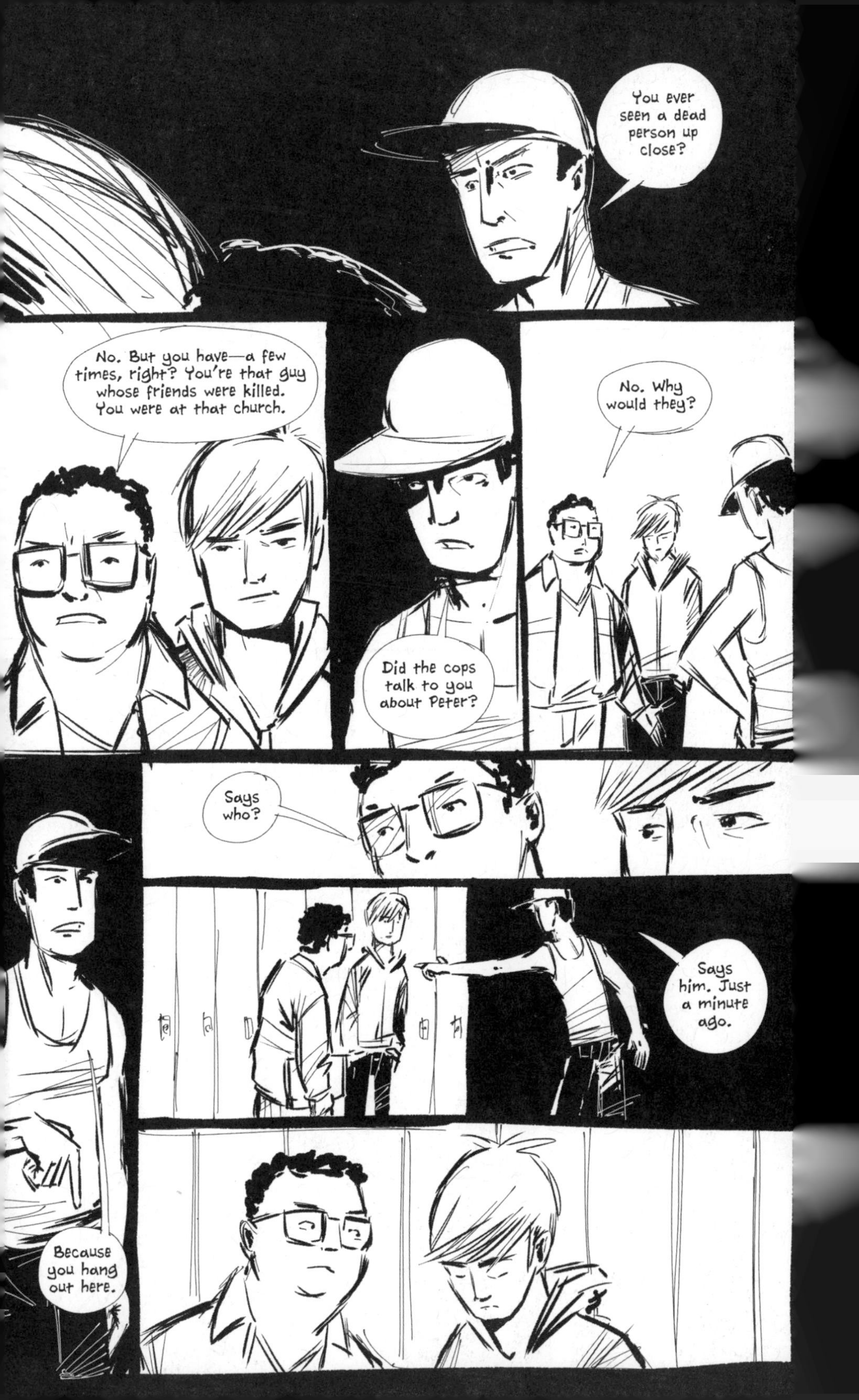
You ever seen a dead person up close?
No. But you have—a few times, right? You're that guy whose friends were killed. You were at that church.
Did the cops talk to you about Peter?
No. Why would they?
Because you hang out here.
Says who?
Says him. Just a minute ago.

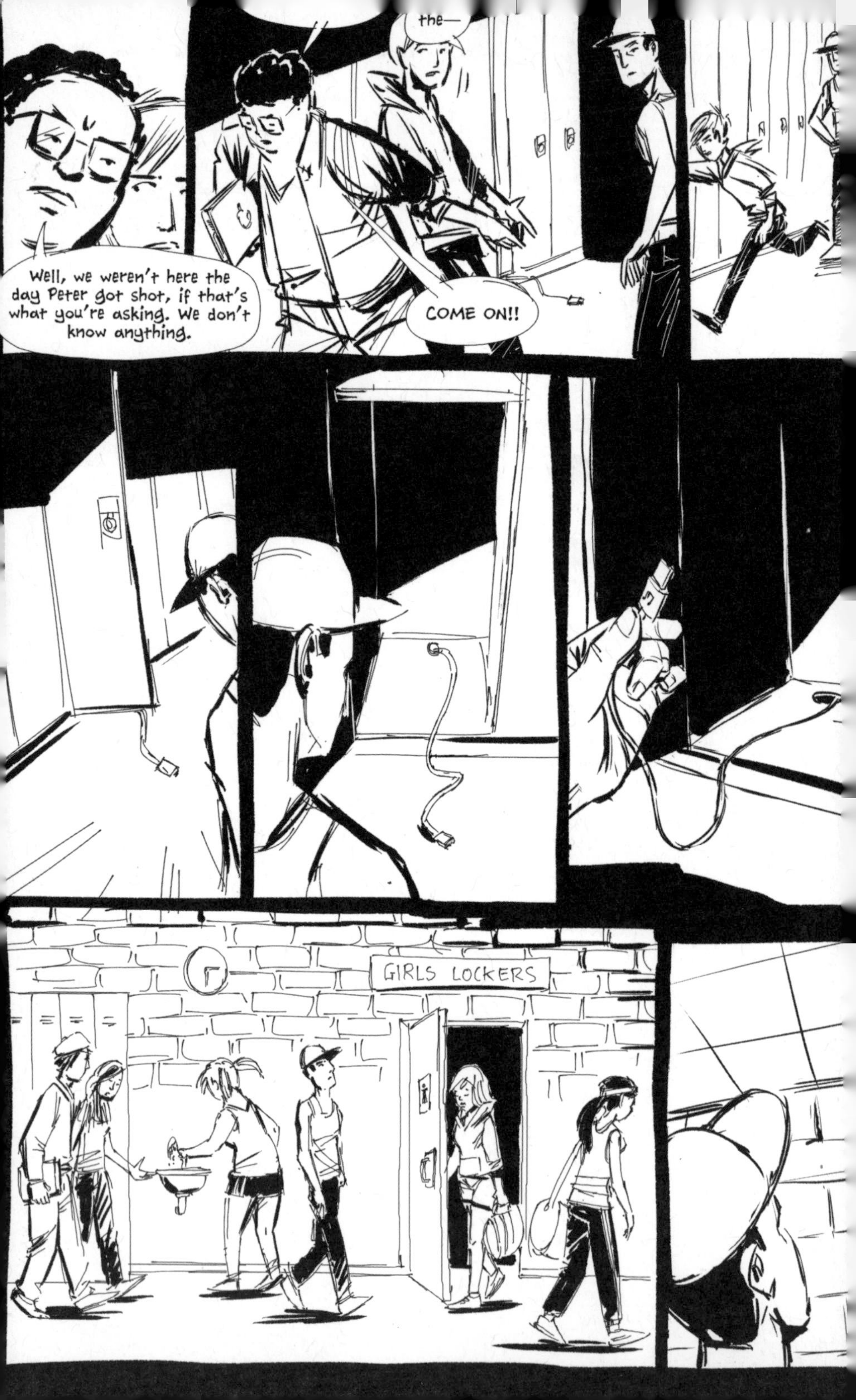
the—
Well, we weren't here the day Peter got shot, if that's what you're asking. We don't know anything.
COME ON!!
GIRLS LOCKERS

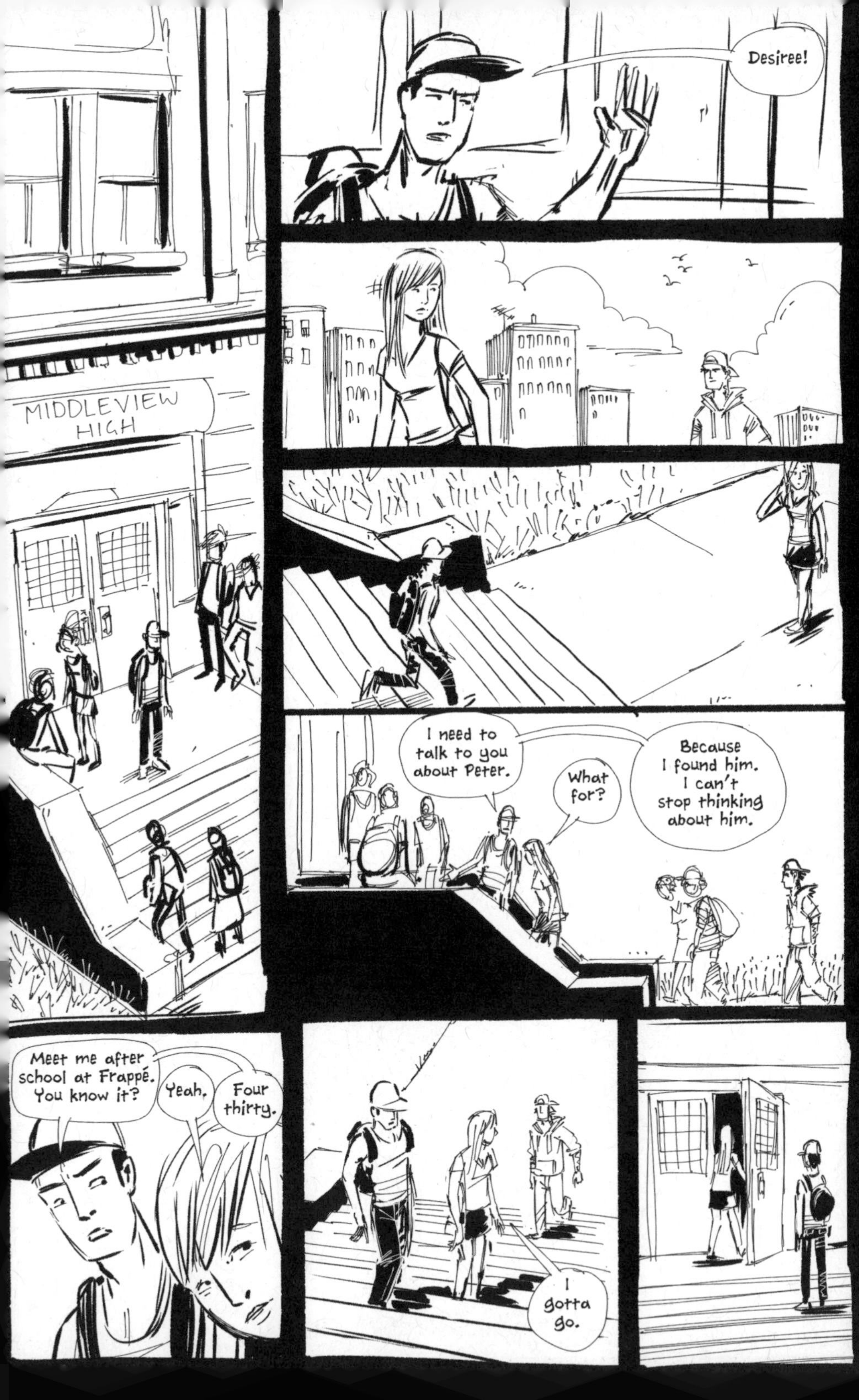
MIDDLEVIEW HIGH
Desiree!
I need to talk to you about Peter.
What for?
Because I found him. I can't stop thinking about him.
Meet me after school at Frappé. You know it?
Yeah.
Four thirty.
I gotta go.

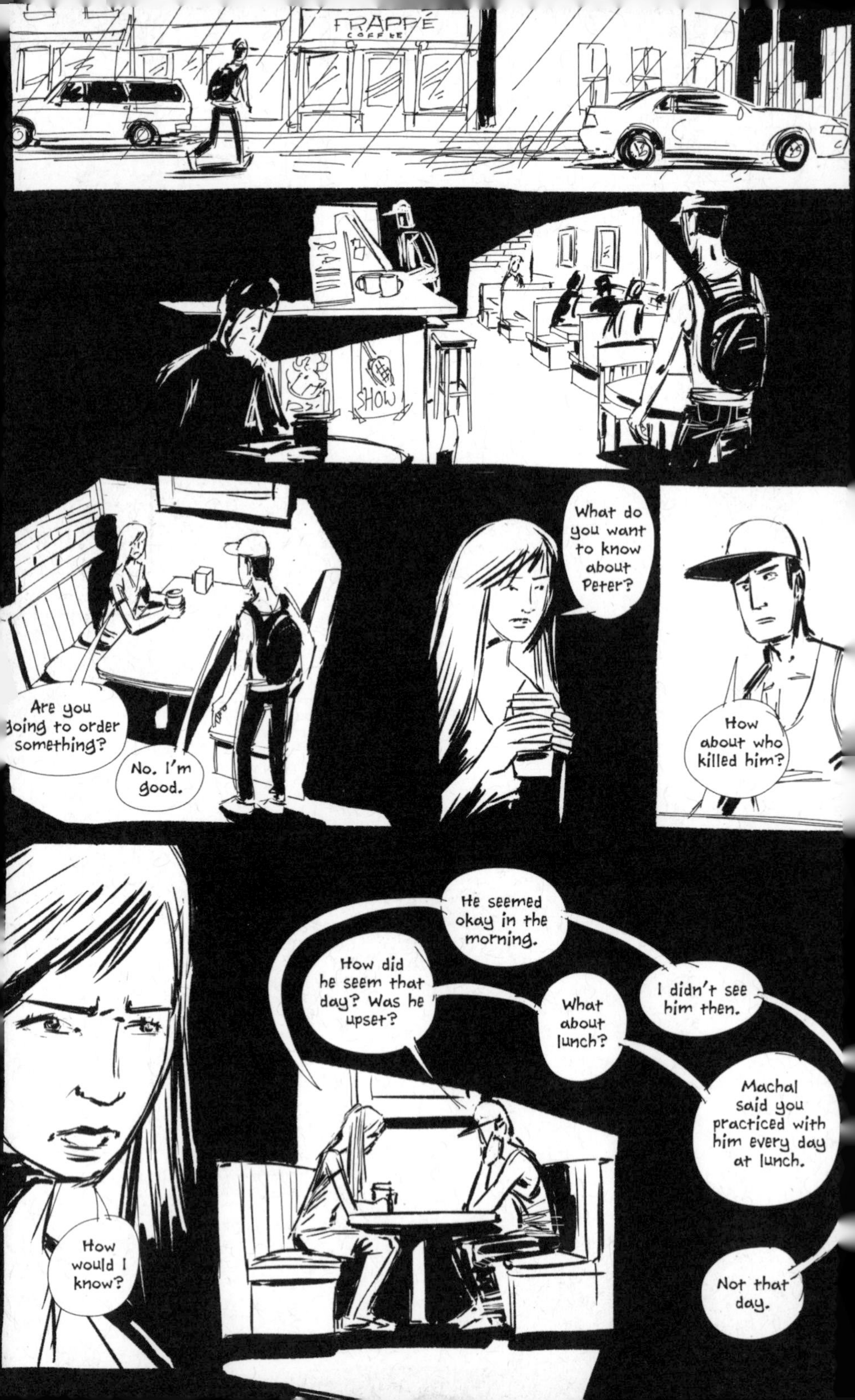
FRAPPÉ
COFFEE
SHOW
Are you going to order something?
No. I'm good.
What do you want to know about Peter?
How about who killed him?
How would I know?
How did he seem that day? Was he upset?
He seemed okay in the morning.
What about lunch?
I didn't see him then.
Machal said you practiced with him every day at lunch.
Not that day.

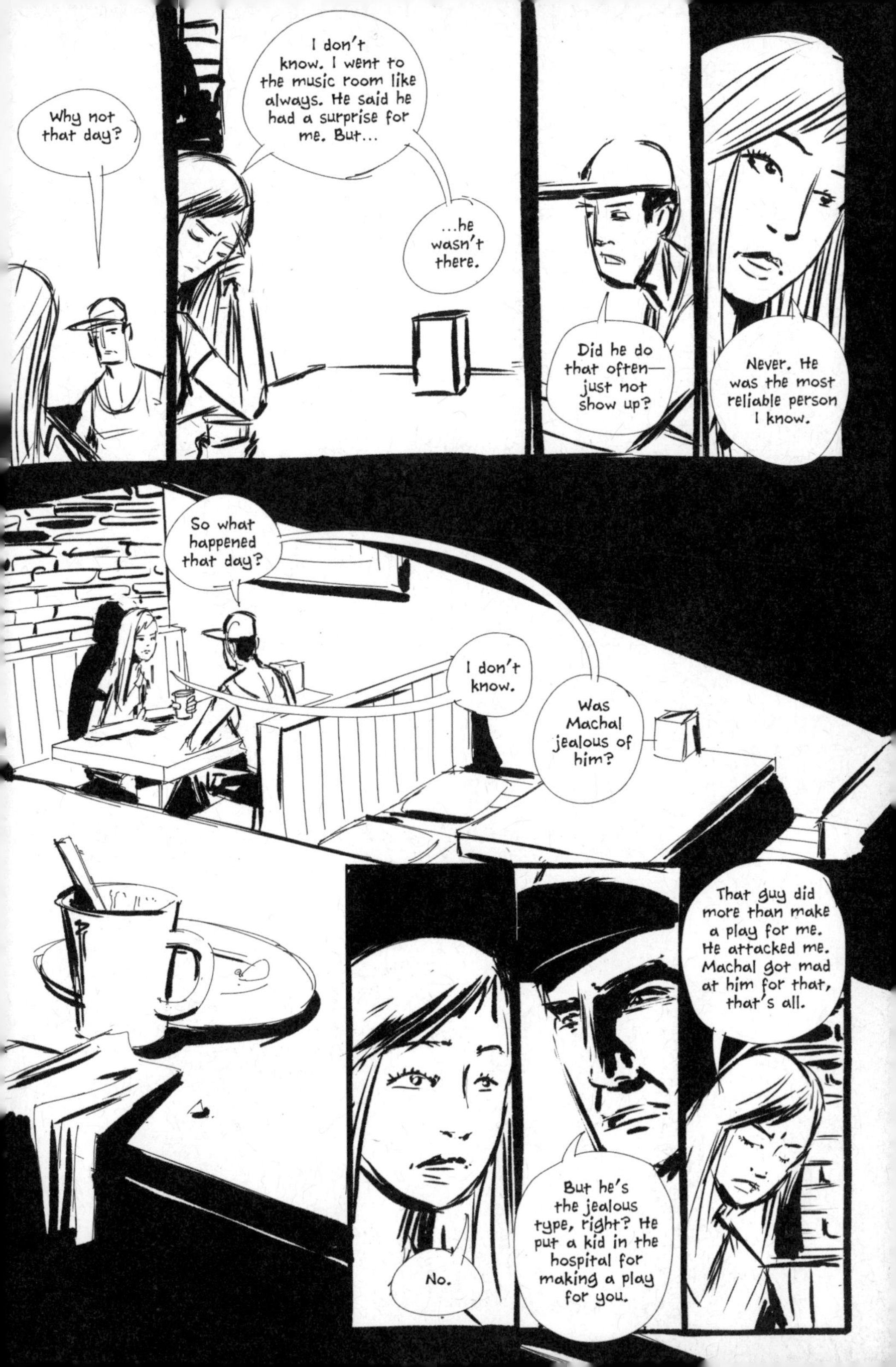
Why not that day?
I don't know. I went to the music room like always. He said he had a surprise for me. But...
...he wasn't there.
Did he do that often—just not show up?
Never. He was the most reliable person I know.
So what happened that day?
I don't know.
Was Machal jealous of him?
No.
But he's the jealous type, right? He put a kid in the hospital for making a play for you.
That guy did more than make a play for me. He attacked me. Machal got mad at him for that, that's all.

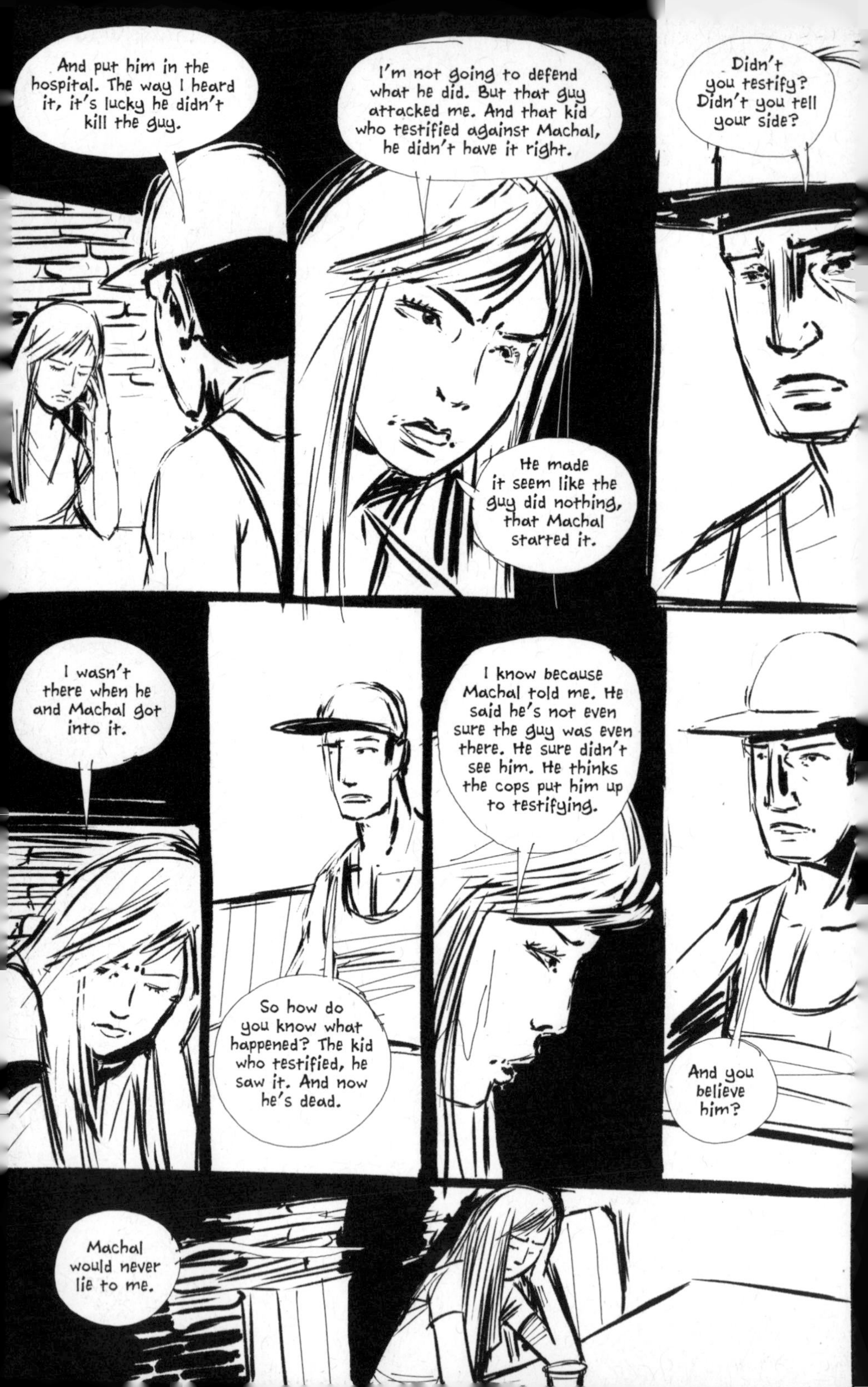
And put him in the hospital. The way I heard it, it's lucky he didn't kill the guy.
I'm not going to defend what he did. But that guy attacked me. And that kid who testified against Machal, he didn't have it right.
He made it seem like the guy did nothing, that Machal started it.
Didn't you testify? Didn't you tell your side?
I wasn't there when he and Machal got into it.
So how do you know what happened? The kid who testified, he saw it. And now he's dead.
I know because Machal told me. He said he's not even sure the guy was even there. He sure didn't see him. He thinks the cops put him up to testifying.
And you believe him?
Machal would never lie to me.

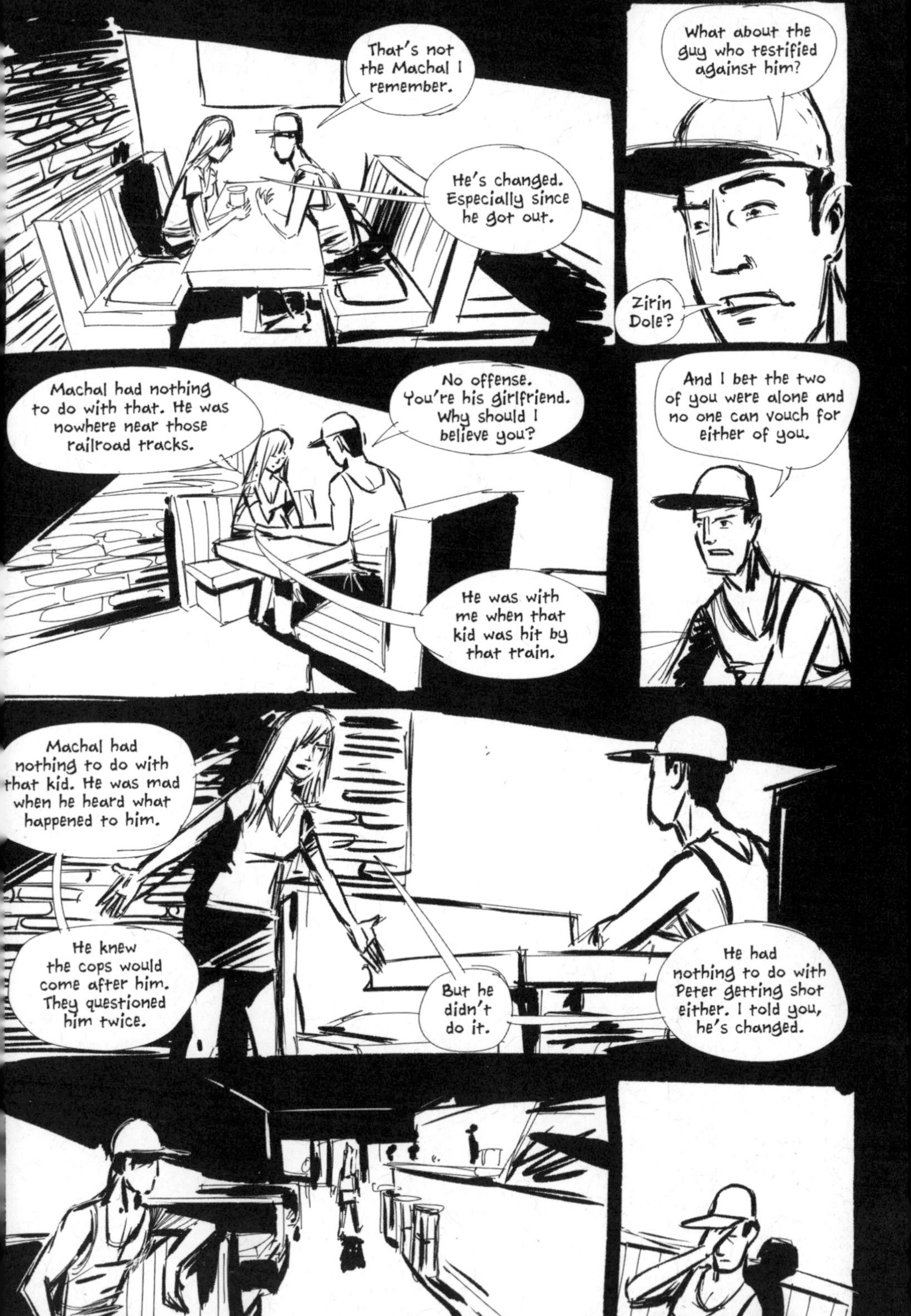
That's not the Machal I remember.
He's changed. Especially since he got out.
What about the guy who testified against him?
Zirin Dole?
Machal had nothing to do with that. He was nowhere near those railroad tracks.
No offense. You're his girlfriend. Why should I believe you?
He was with me when that kid was hit by that train.
And I bet the two of you were alone and no one can vouch for either of you.
Machal had nothing to do with that kid. He was mad when he heard what happened to him.
He knew the cops would come after him. They questioned him twice.
But he didn't do it.
He had nothing to do with Peter getting shot either. I told you, he's changed.

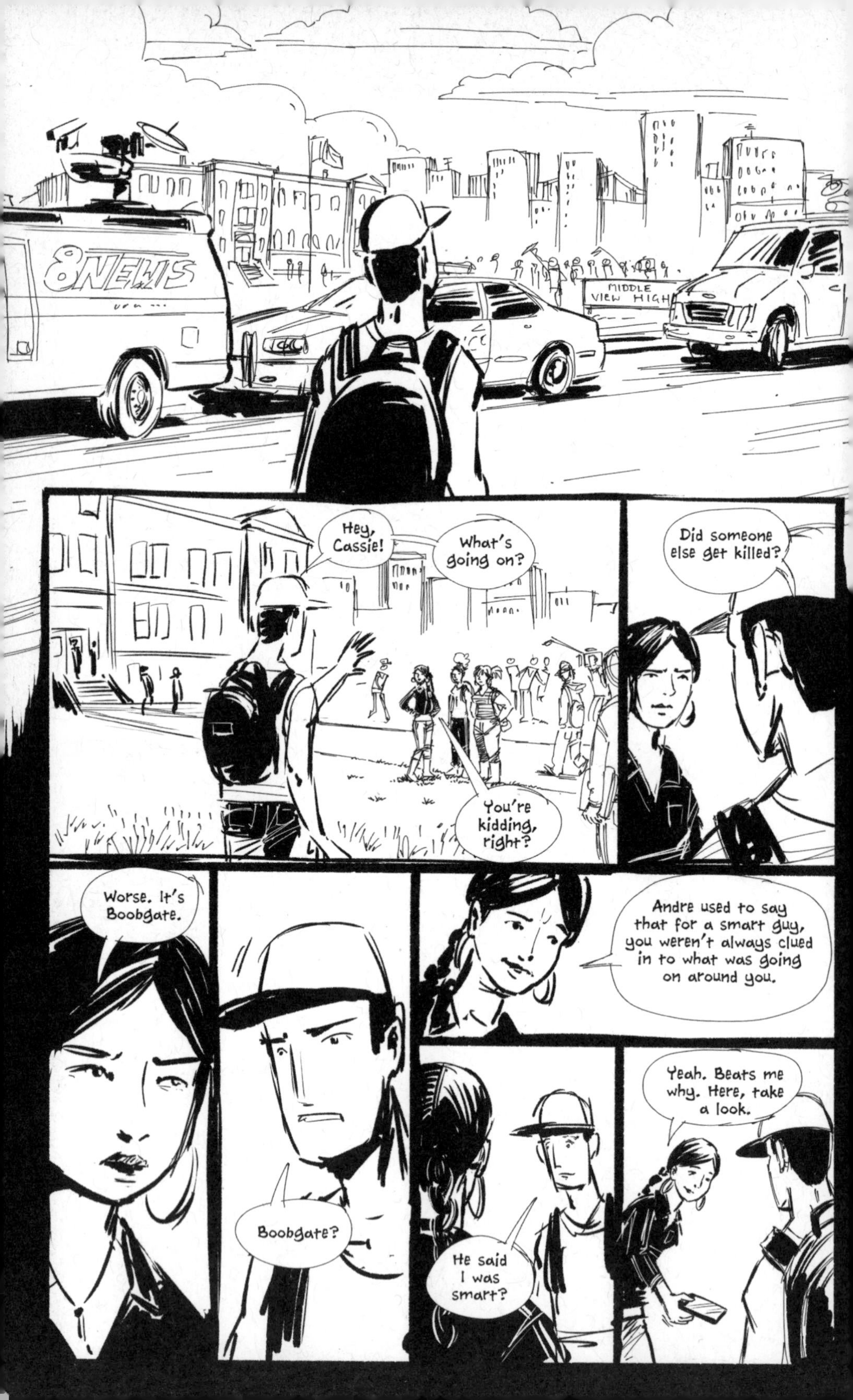
8NEWS
MIDDLE VIEW HIGH
Hey, Cassie!
What's going on?
You're kidding, right?
Did someone else get killed?
Worse. It's Boobgate.
Boobgate?
Andre used to say that for a smart guy, you weren't always clued in to what was going on around you.
He said I was smart?
Yeah. Beats me why. Here, take a look.

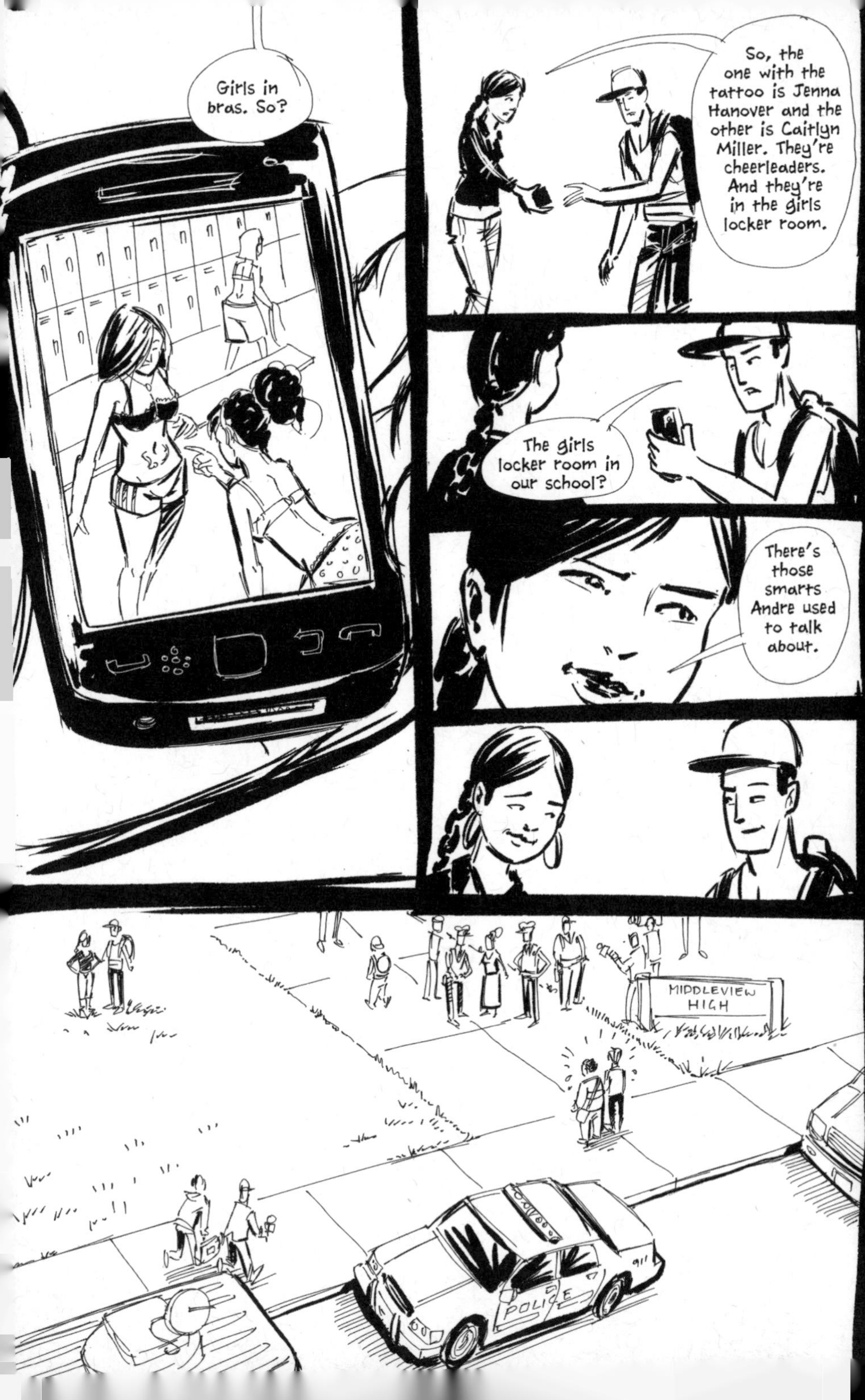
Girls in bras. So?
So, the one with the tattoo is Jenna Hanover and the other is Caitlyn Miller. They're cheerleaders. And they're in the girls locker room.
The girls locker room in our school?
There's those smarts Andre used to talk about.
MIDDLEVIEW HIGH
POLICE

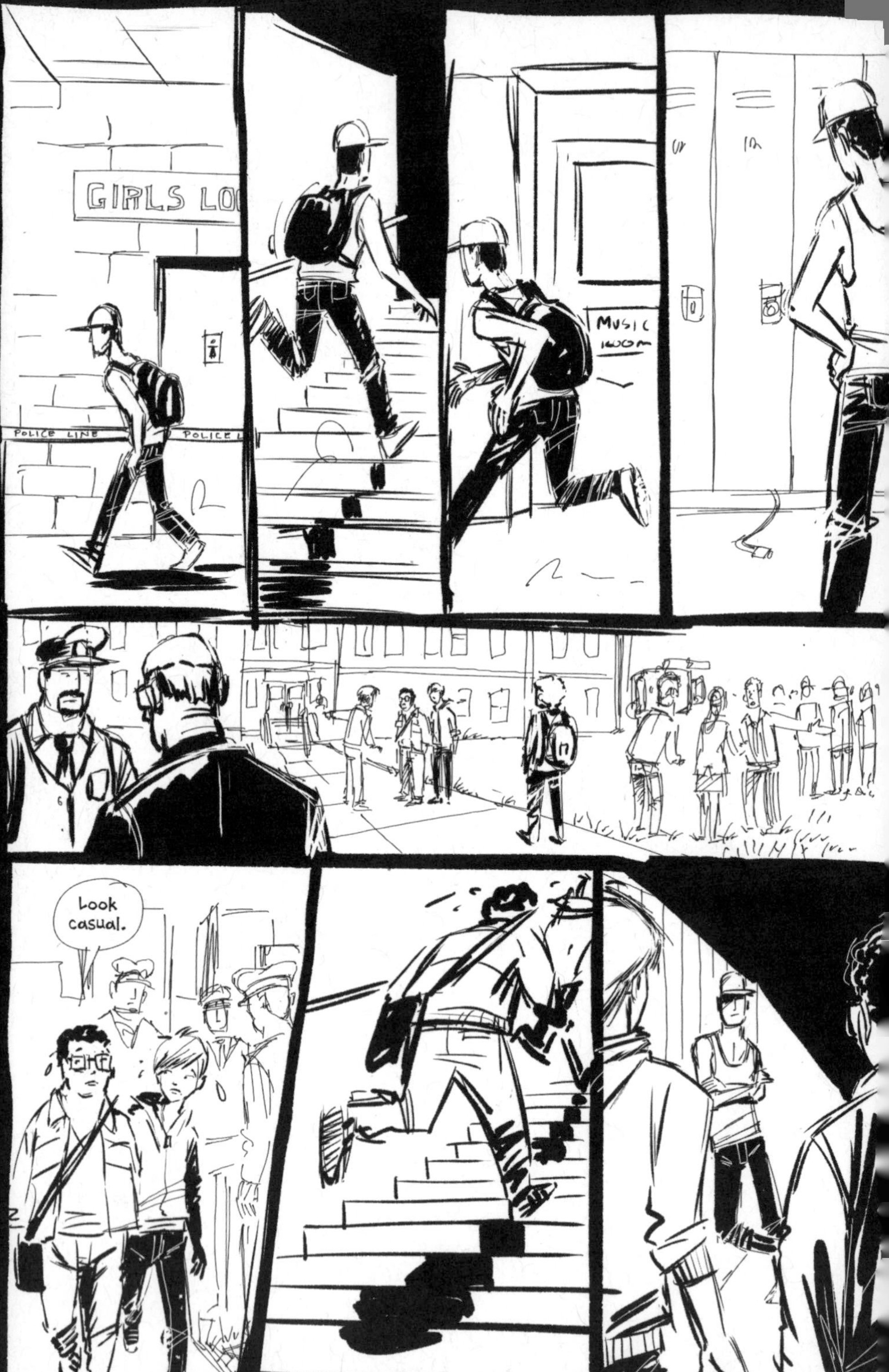
GIRLS LOC
POLICE LINE
POLICE L
MUSIC ROOM
Look casual.

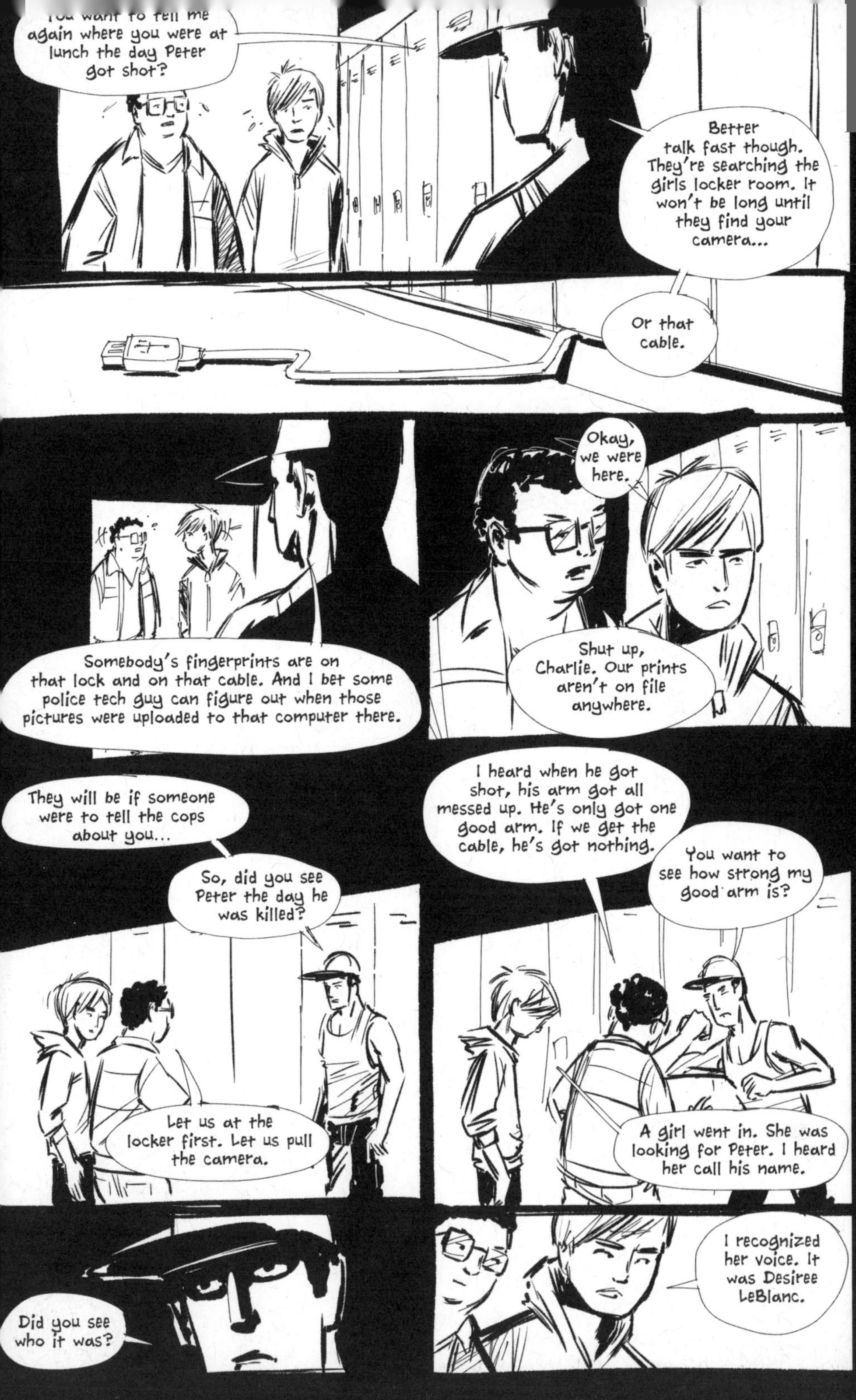
again where you were at lunch the day Peter got shot?
Better talk fast though. They're searching the girls locker room. It won't be long until they find your camera...
Or that cable.
Okay, we were here.
Somebody's fingerprints are on that lock and on that cable. And I bet some police tech guy can figure out when those pictures were uploaded to that computer there.
Shut up, Charlie. Our prints aren't on file anywhere.
They will be if someone were to tell the cops about you...
So, did you see Peter the day he was killed?
Let us at the locker first. Let us pull the camera.
I heard when he got shot, his arm got all messed up. He's only got one good arm. If we get the cable, he's got nothing.
You want to see how strong my good arm is?
A girl went in. She was looking for Peter. I heard her call his name.
Did you see who it was?
I recognized her voice. It was Desiree LeBlanc.

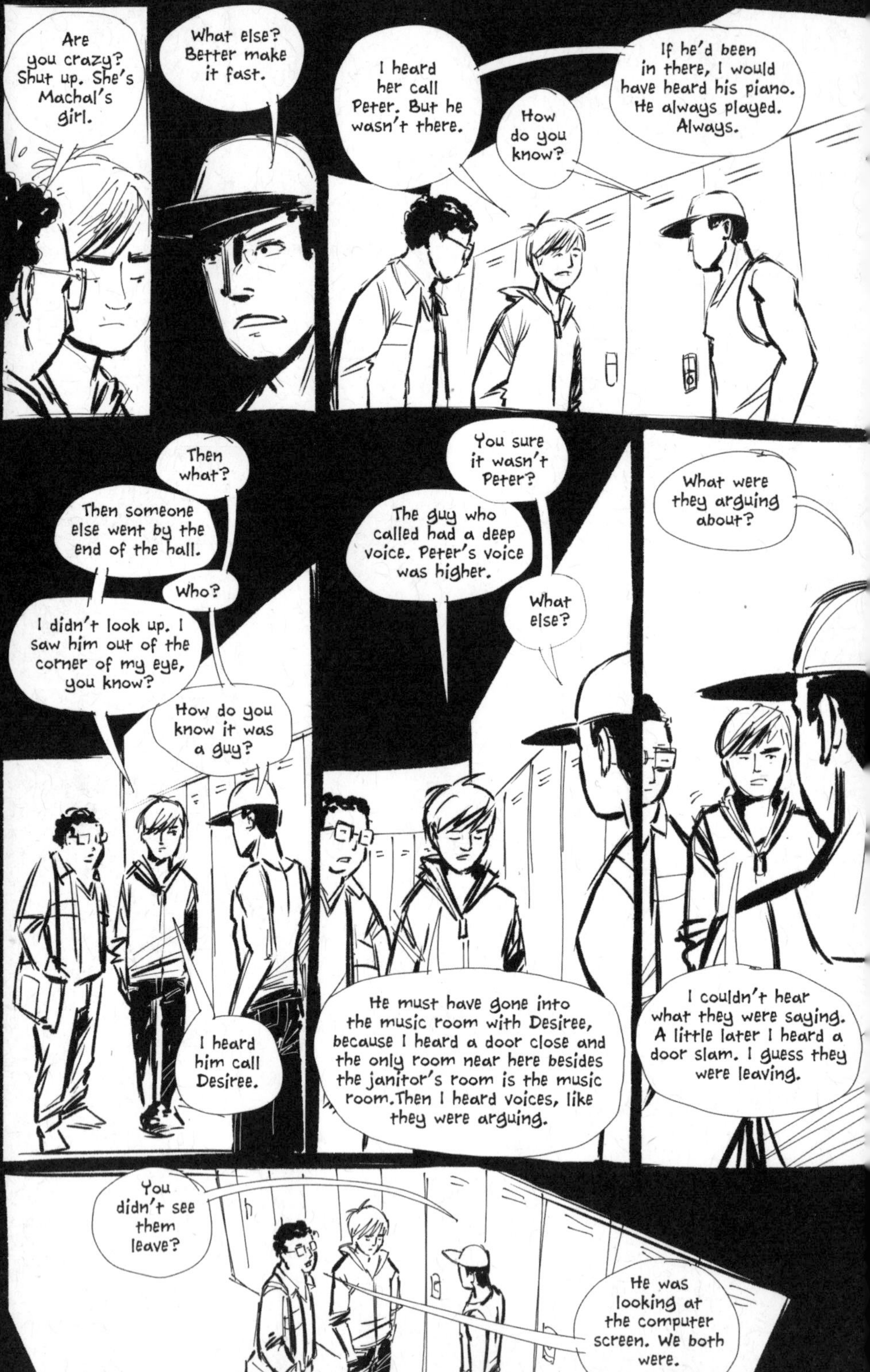
Are you crazy? Shut up. She's Machal's girl.
What else? Better make it fast.
I heard her call Peter. But he wasn't there.
How do you know?
If he'd been in there, I would have heard his piano. He always played. Always.
Then what?
Then someone else went by the end of the hall.
Who?
I didn't look up. I saw him out of the corner of my eye, you know?
How do you know it was a guy?
I heard him call Desiree.
You sure it wasn't Peter?
The guy who called had a deep voice. Peter's voice was higher.
What else?
He must have gone into the music room with Desiree, because I heard a door close and the only room near here besides the janitor's room is the music room. Then I heard voices, like they were arguing.
What were they arguing about?
I couldn't hear what they were saying. A little later I heard a door slam. I guess they were leaving.
You didn't see them leave?
He was looking at the computer screen. We both were.

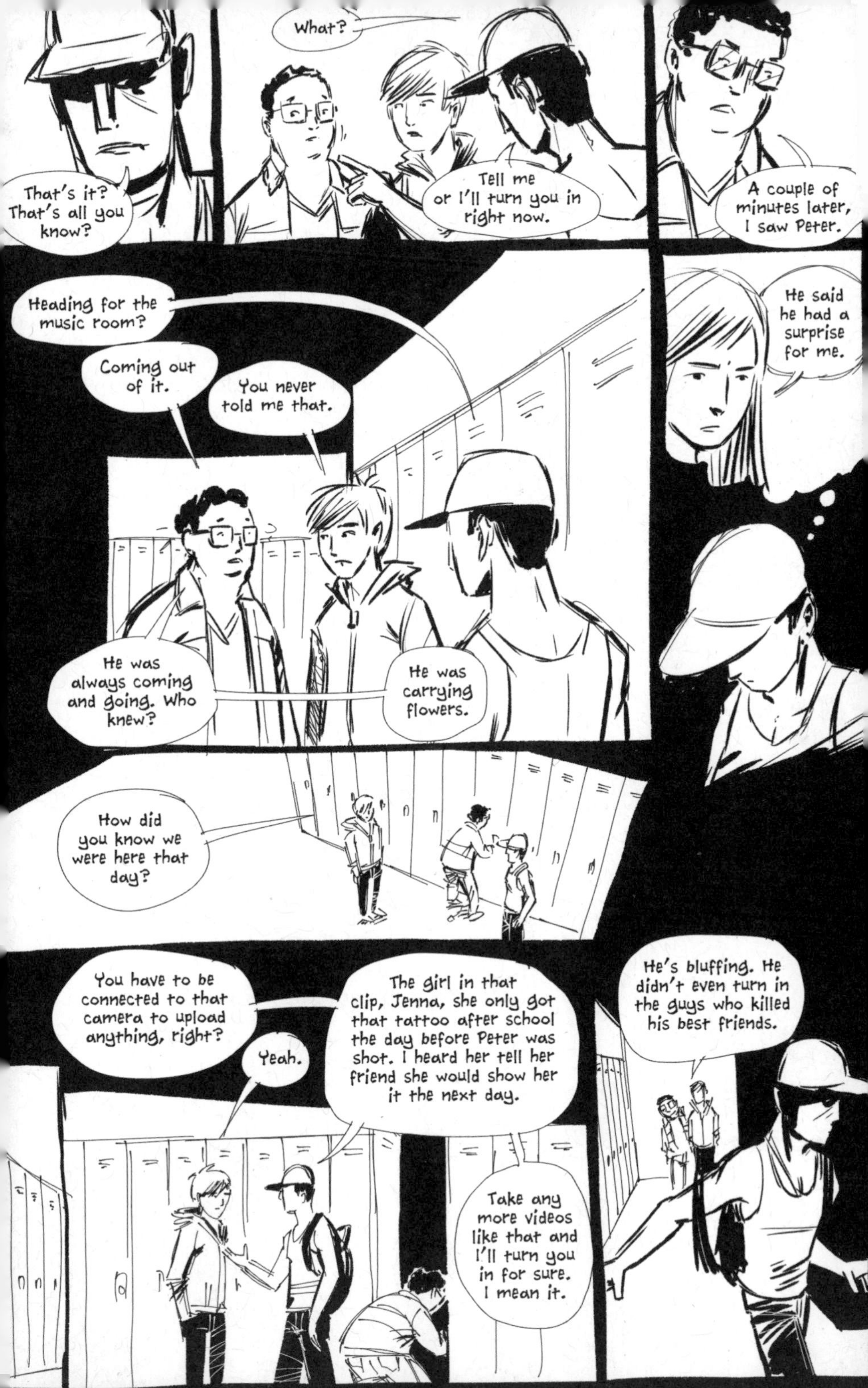
That's it? That's all you know?
What?
Tell me or I'll turn you in right now.
A couple of minutes later, I saw Peter.
Heading for the music room?
Coming out of it.
You never told me that.
He said he had a surprise for me.
He was always coming and going. Who knew?
He was carrying flowers.
How did you know we were here that day?
You have to be connected to that camera to upload anything, right?
Yeah.
The girl in that clip, Jenna, she only got that tattoo after school the day before Peter was shot. I heard her tell her friend she would show her it the next day.
Take any more videos like that and I'll turn you in for sure. I mean it.
He's bluffing. He didn't even turn in the guys who killed his best friends.

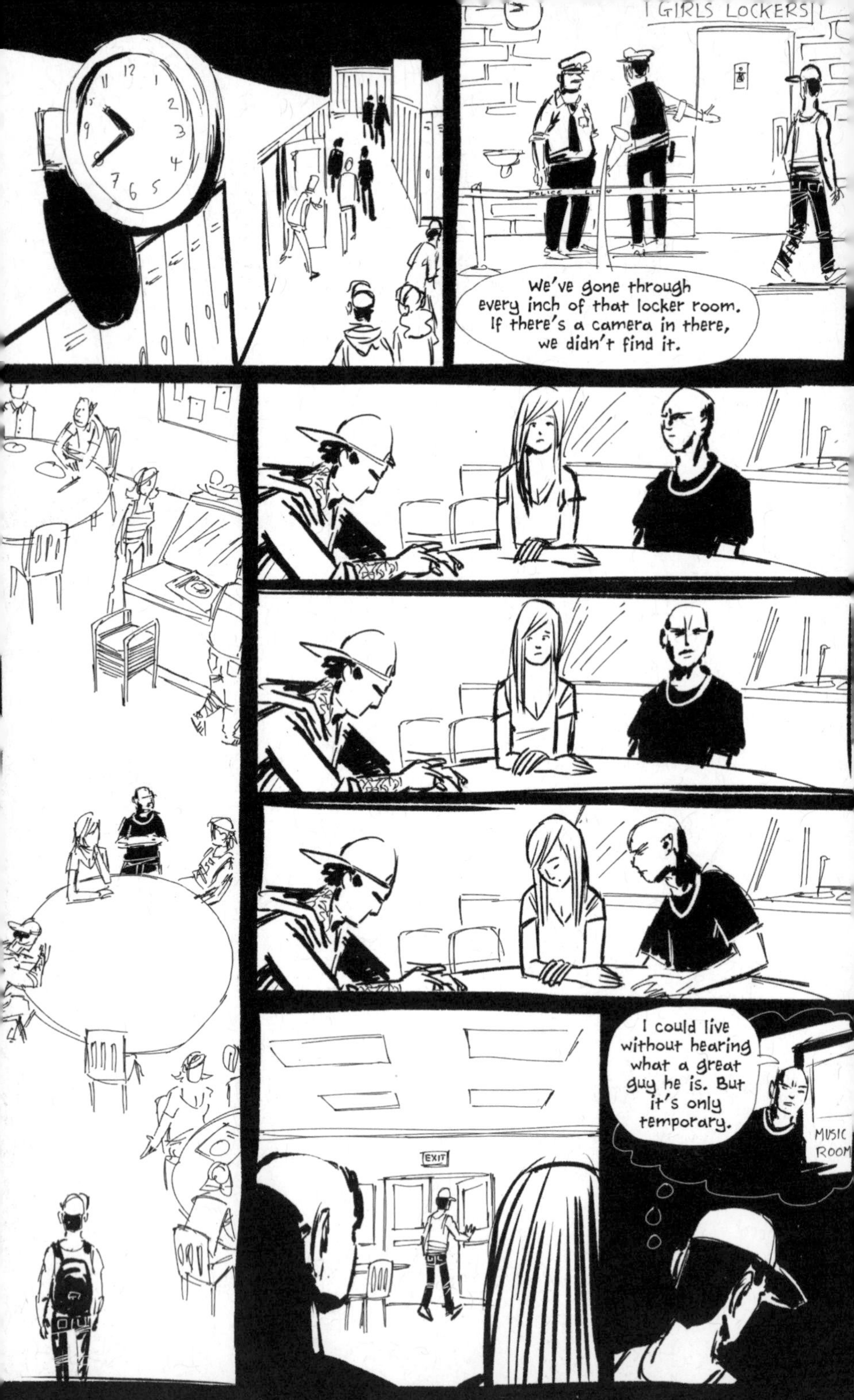
GIRLS LOCKERS
We've gone through every inch of that locker room. If there's a camera in there, we didn't find it.
EXIT
I could live without hearing what a great guy he is. But it's only temporary.
MUSIC ROOM

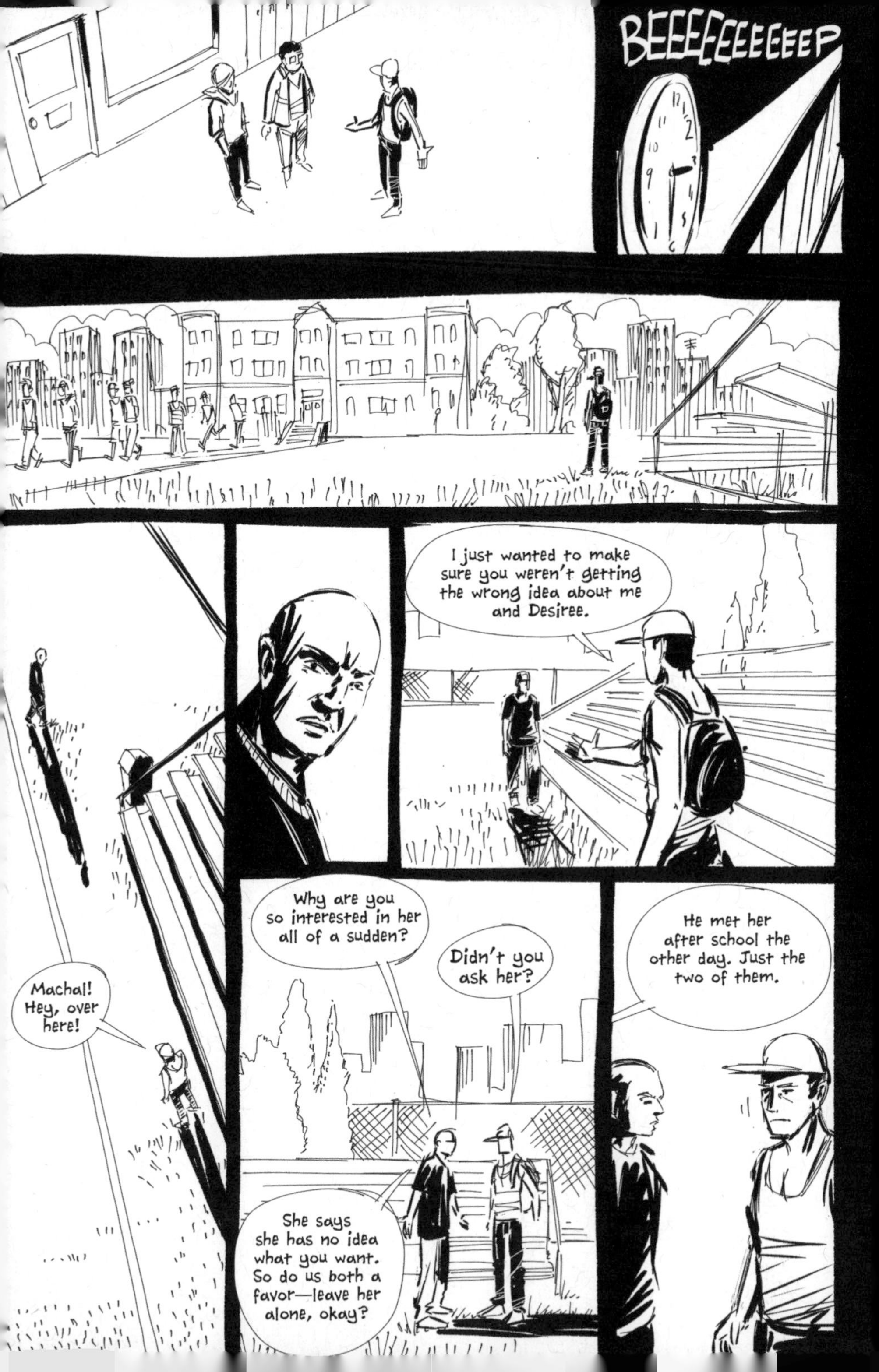
BEEEEEEEEEEP
Machal! Hey, over here!
I just wanted to make sure you weren't getting the wrong idea about me and Desiree.
Why are you so interested in her all of a sudden?
Didn't you ask her?
He met her after school the other day. Just the two of them.
She says she has no idea what you want. So do us both a favor—leave her alone, okay?

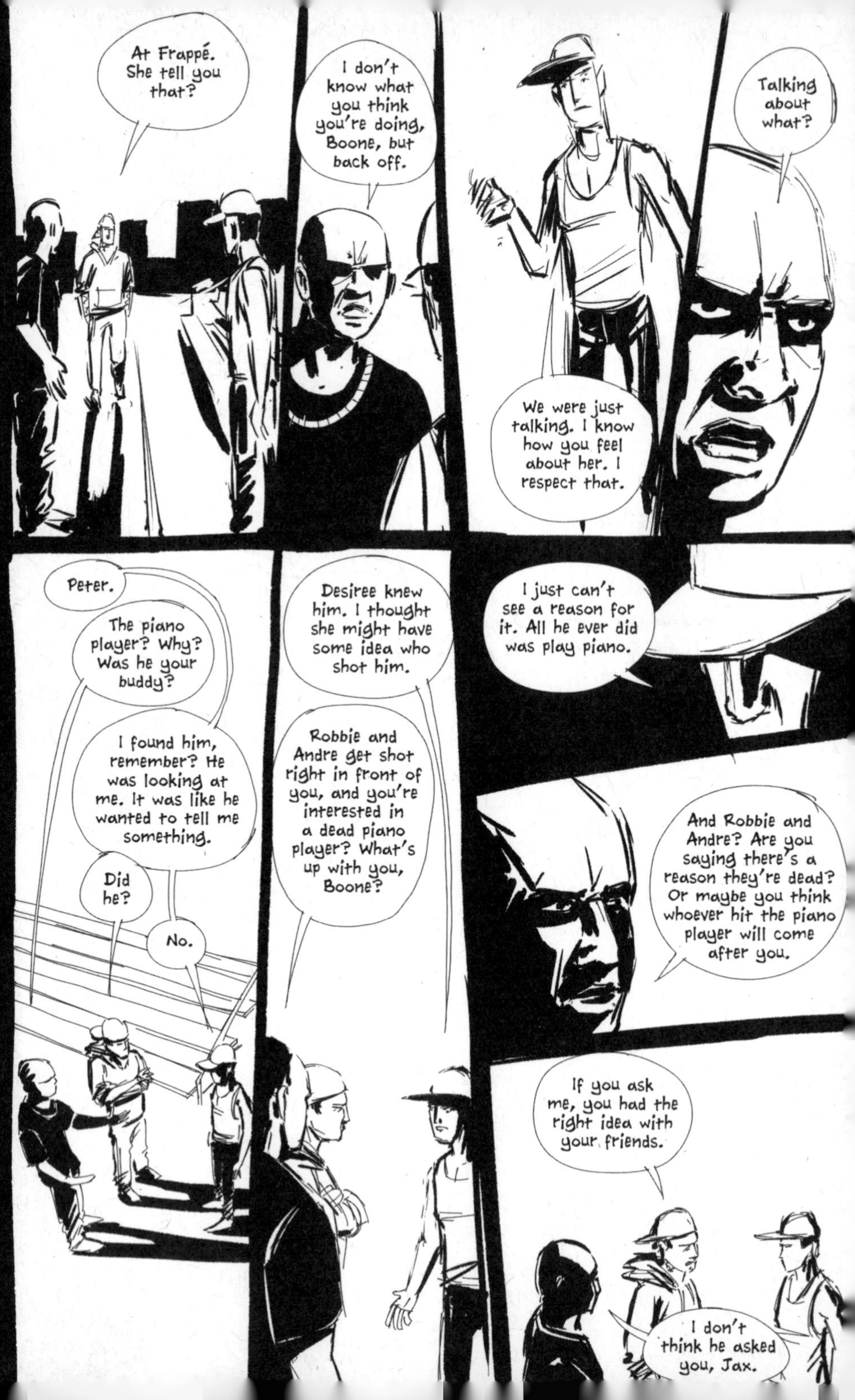
At Frappé. She tell you that?
I don't know what you think you're doing, Boone, but back off.
Talking about what?
We were just talking. I know how you feel about her. I respect that.
Peter.
The piano player? Why? Was he your buddy?
I found him, remember? He was looking at me. It was like he wanted to tell me something.
Did he?
No.
Desiree knew him. I thought she might have some idea who shot him.
Robbie and Andre get shot right in front of you, and you're interested in a dead piano player? What's up with you, Boone?
I just can't see a reason for it. All he ever did was play piano.
And Robbie and Andre? Are you saying there's a reason they're dead? Or maybe you think whoever hit the piano player will come after you.
If you ask me, you had the right idea with your friends.
I don't think he asked you, Jax.

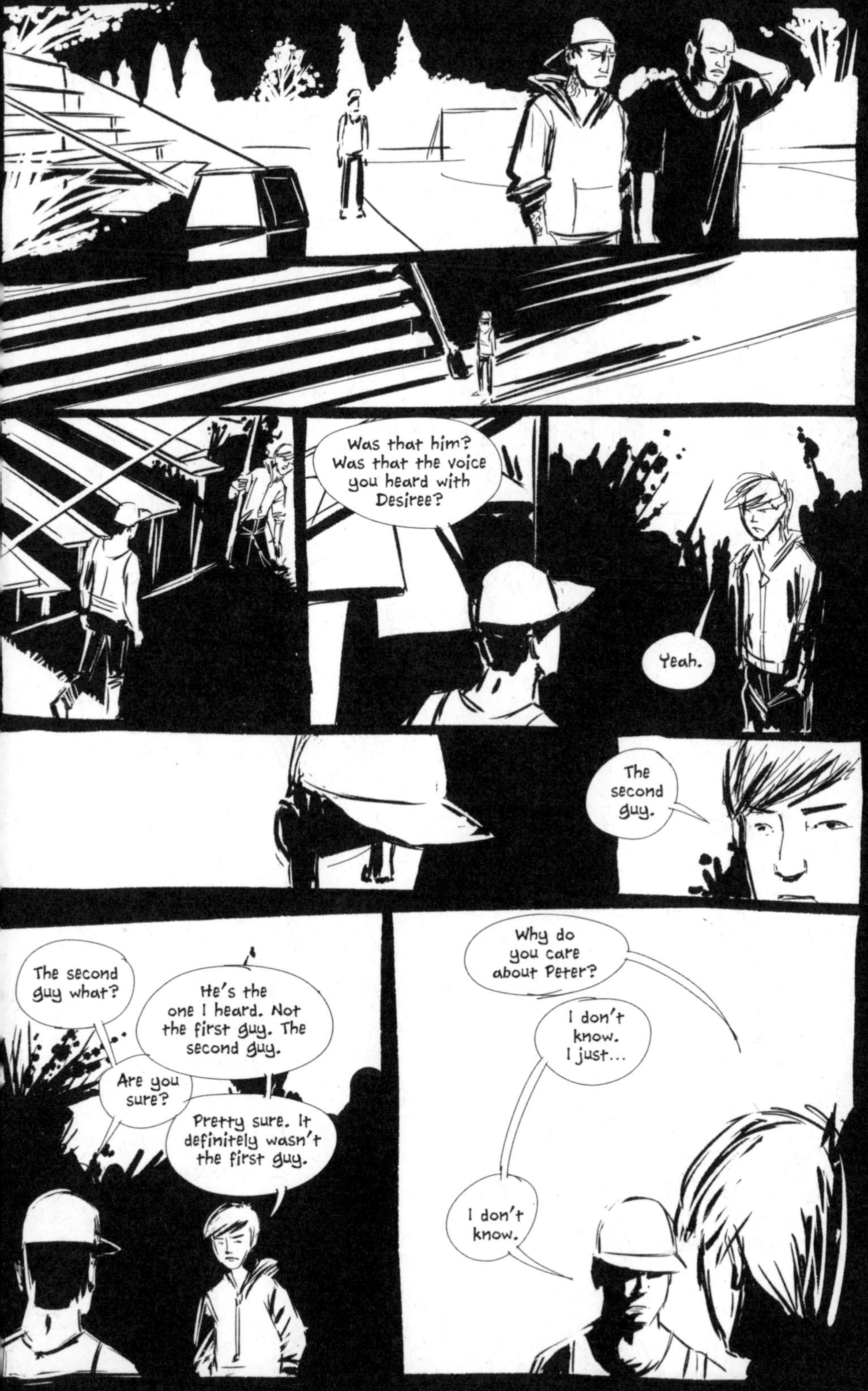
Was that him? Was that the voice you heard with Desiree?
Yeah.
The second guy.
The second guy what?
He's the one I heard. Not the first guy. The second guy.
Are you sure?
Pretty sure. It definitely wasn't the first guy.
Why do you care about Peter?
I don't know. I just...
I don't know.

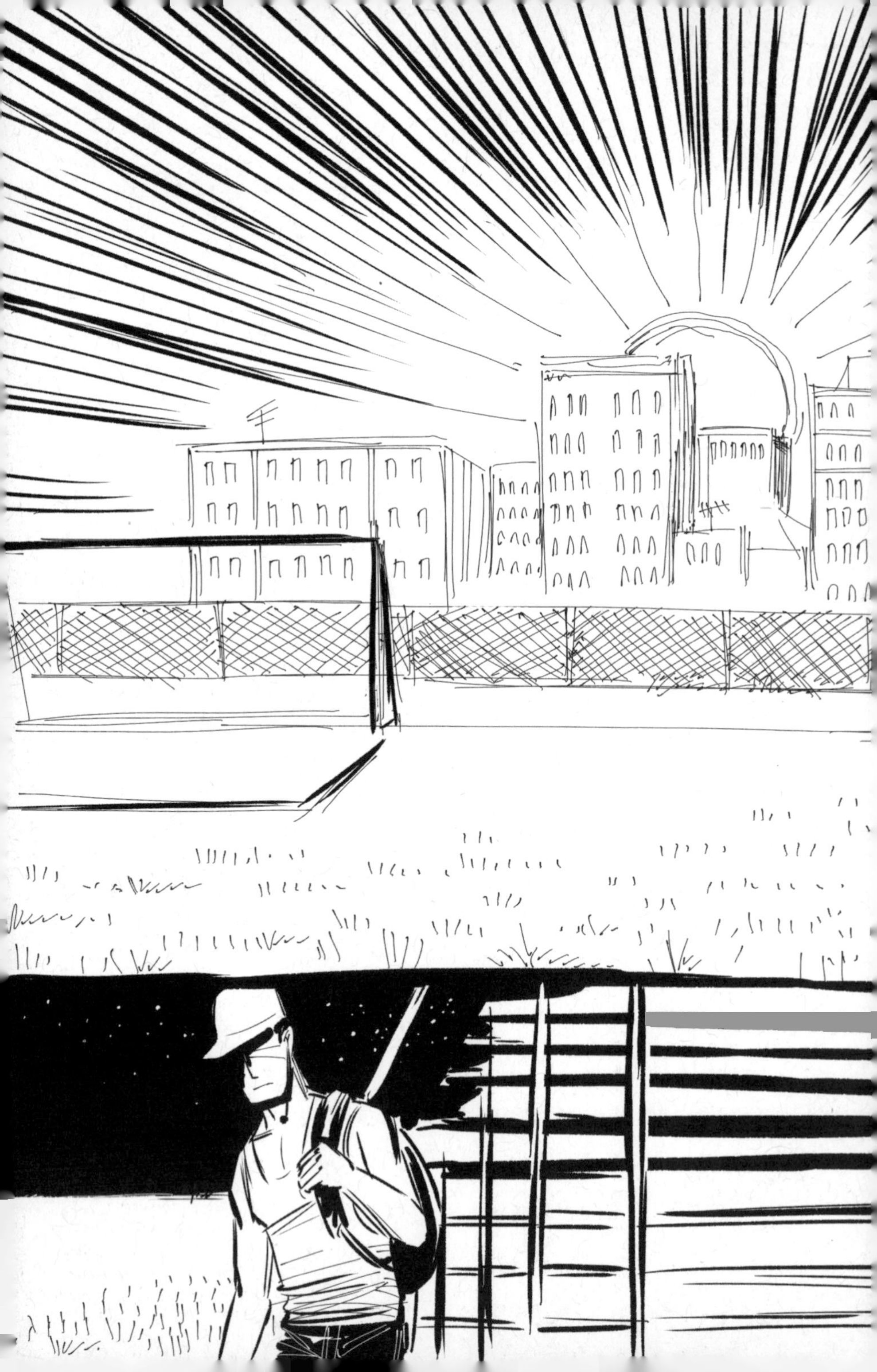

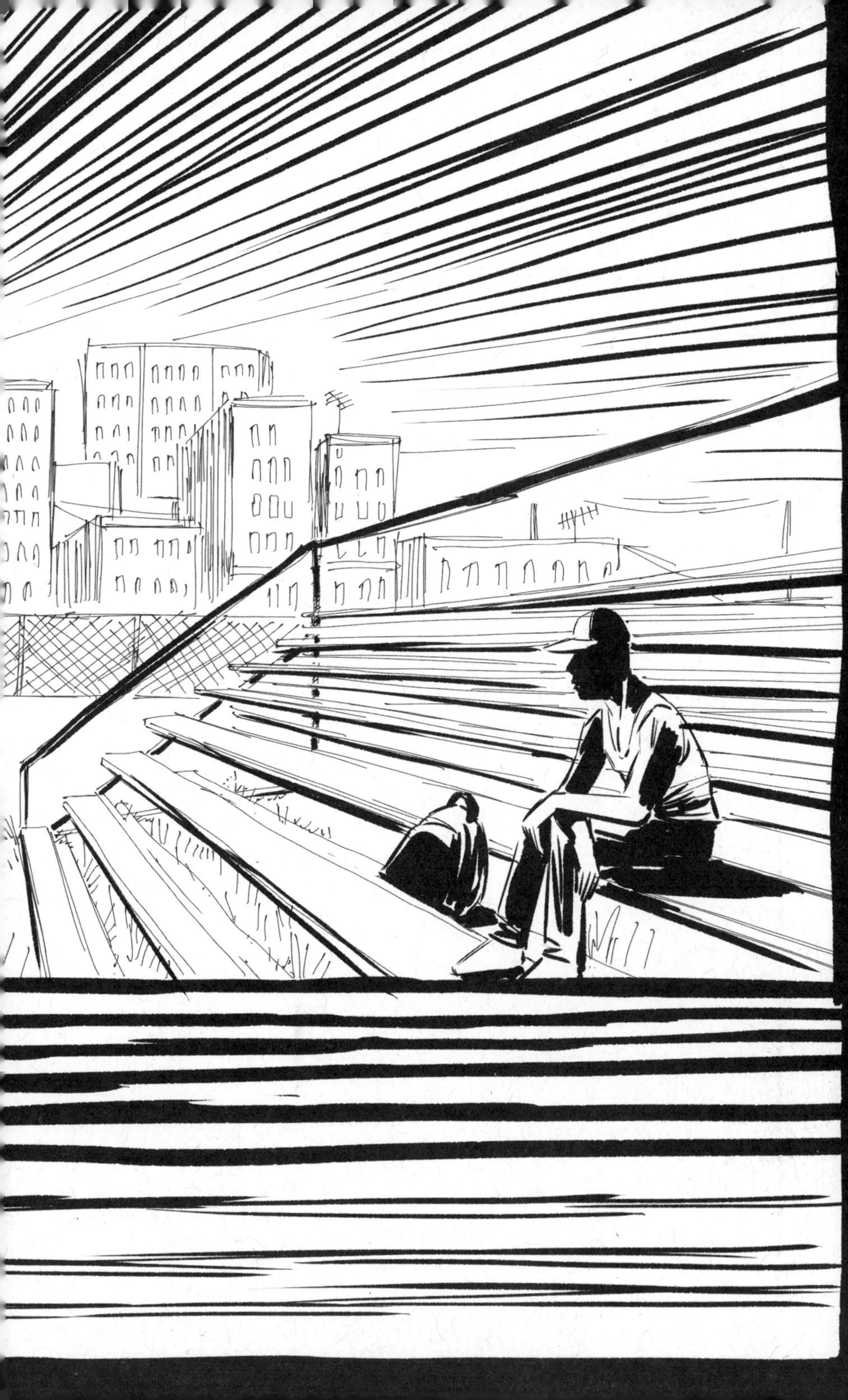

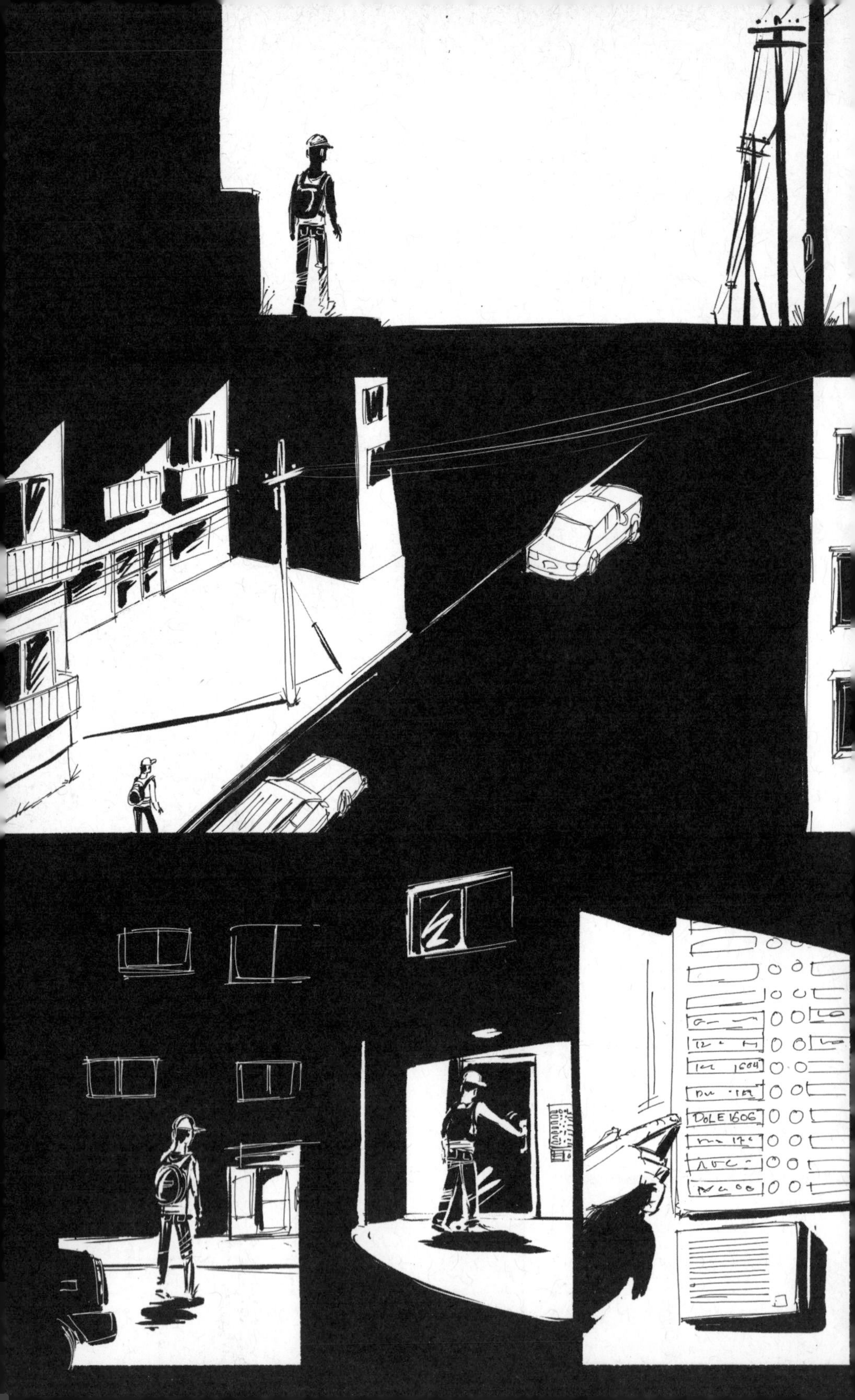
DoLE 1606

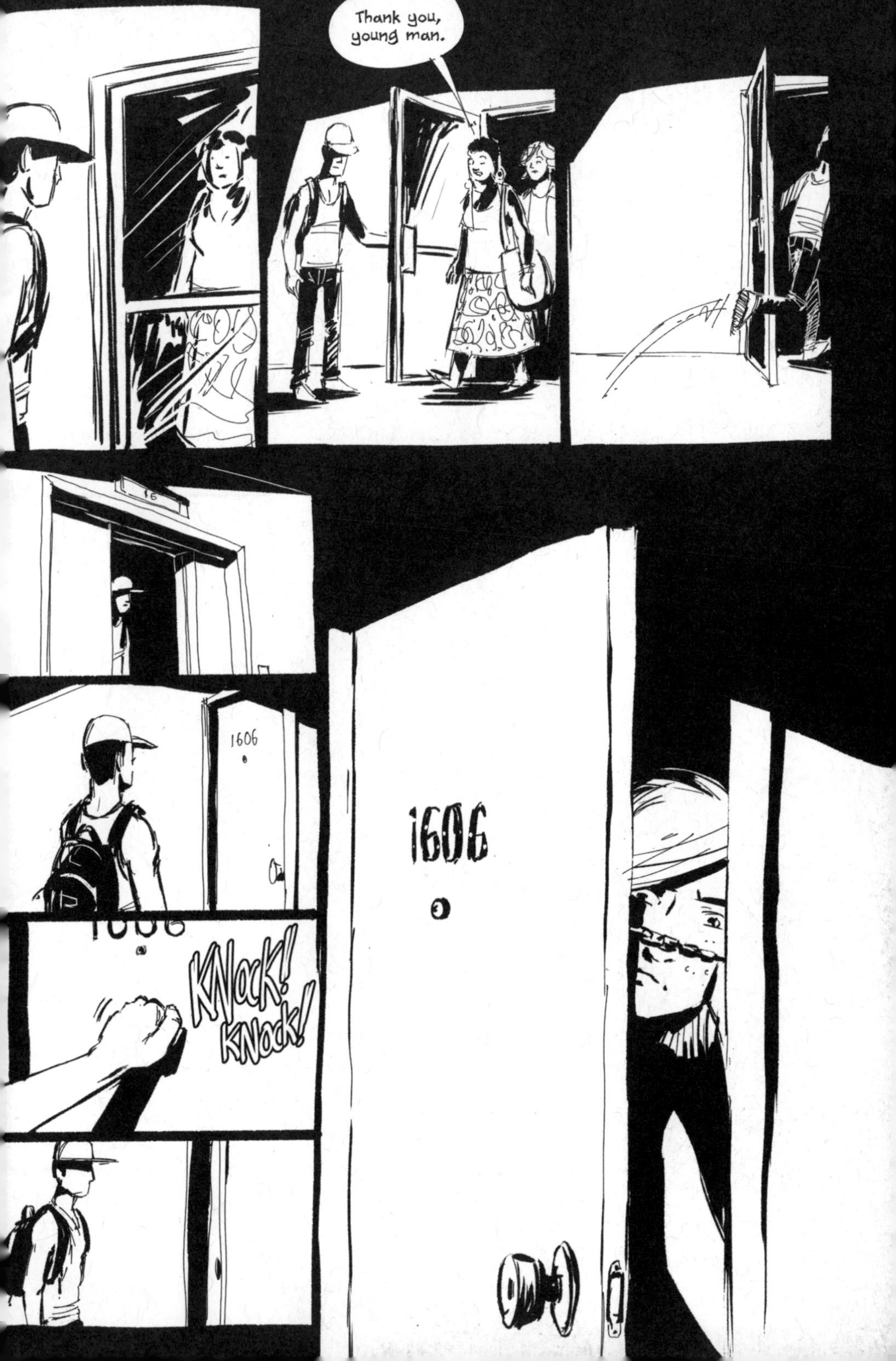
Thank you, young man.
1606
KNOCK! KNOCK!
1606

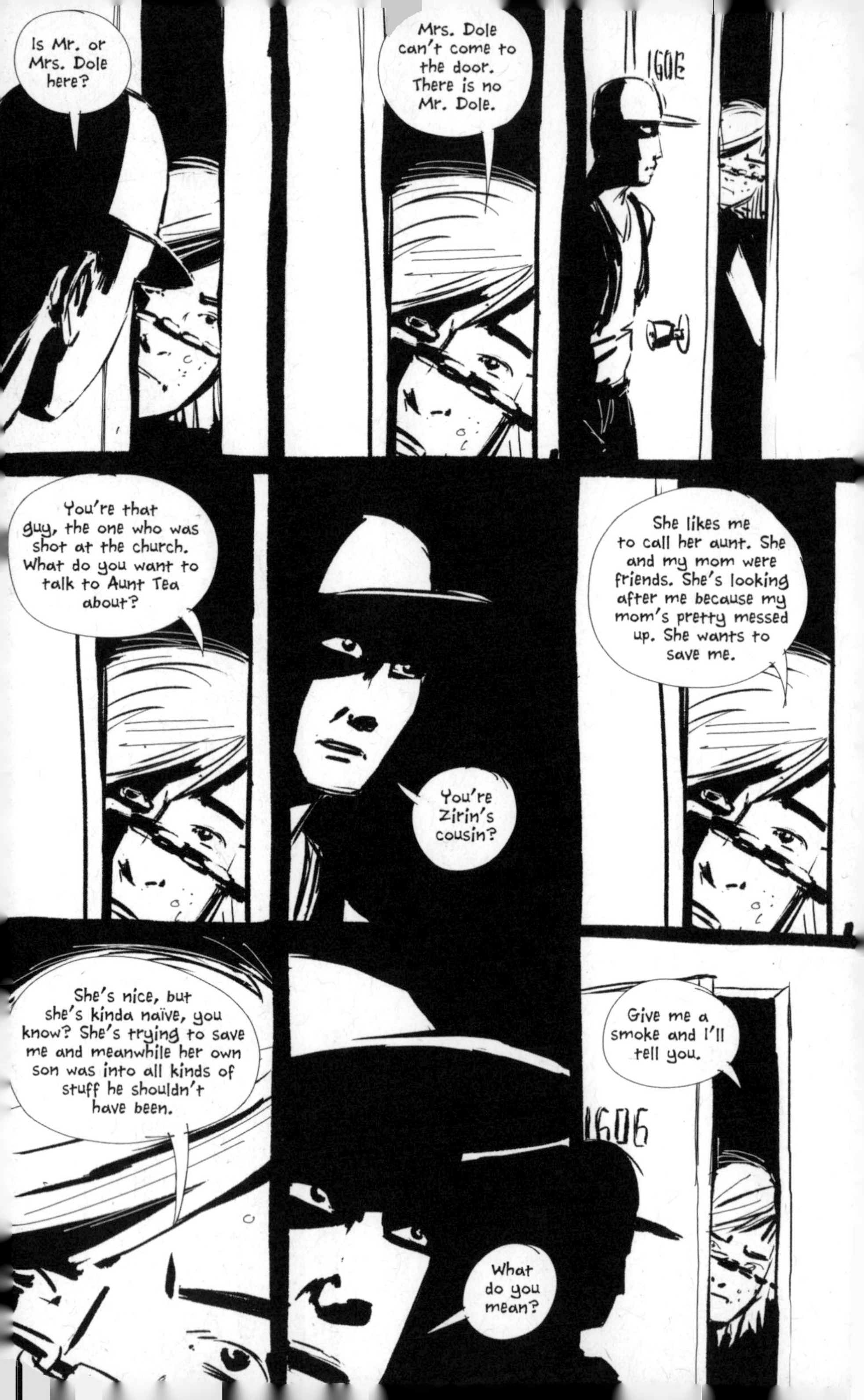
Is Mr. or Mrs. Dole here?
Mrs. Dole can't come to the door. There is no Mr. Dole.
1606
You're that guy, the one who was shot at the church. What do you want to talk to Aunt Tea about?
You're Zirin's cousin?
She likes me to call her aunt. She and my mom were friends. She's looking after me because my mom's pretty messed up. She wants to save me.
She's nice, but she's kinda naïve, you know? She's trying to save me and meanwhile her own son was into all kinds of stuff he shouldn't have been.
What do you mean?
Give me a smoke and I'll tell you.
1606

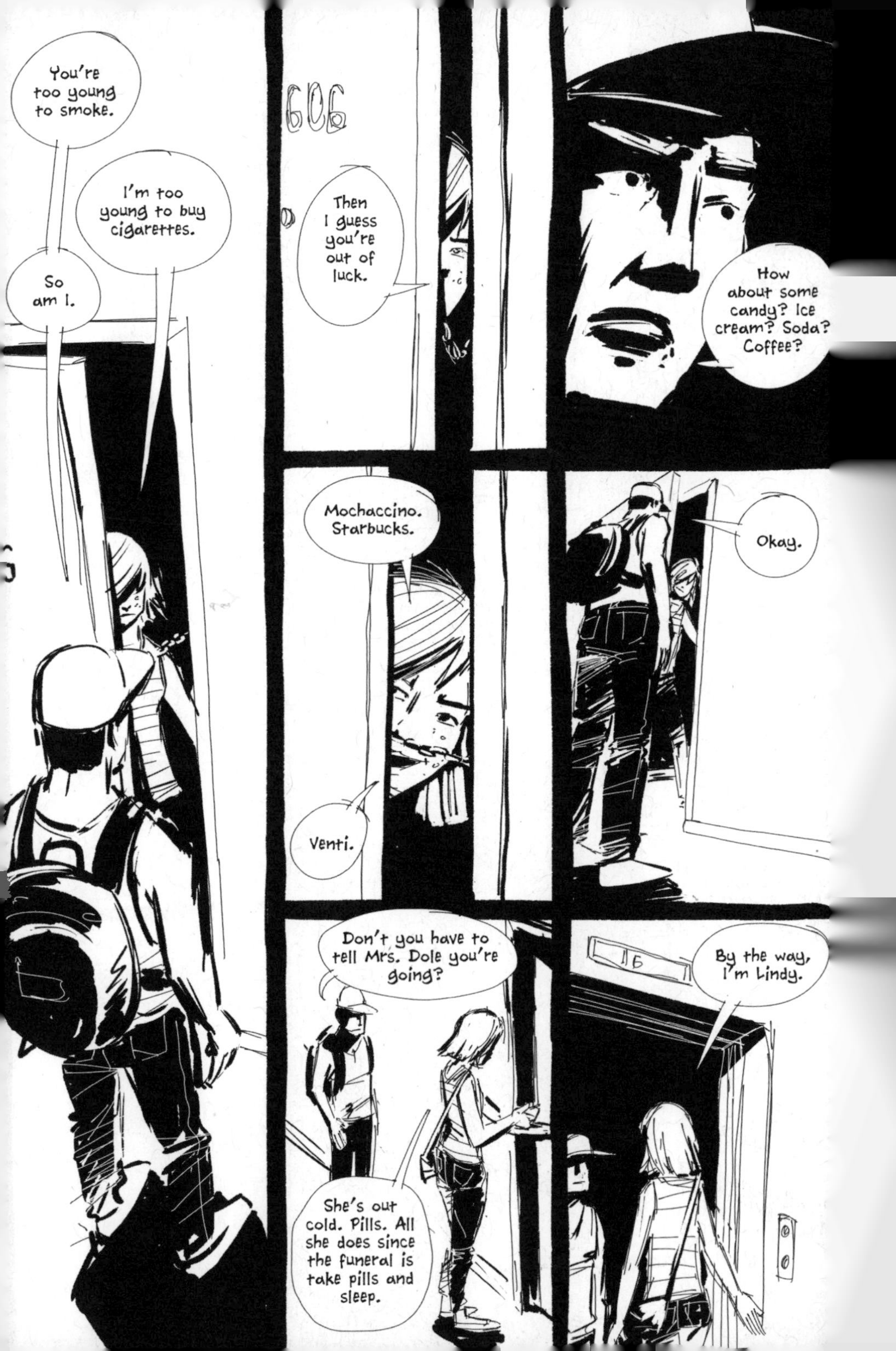
You're too young to smoke.
I'm too young to buy cigarettes.
So am I.
606
Then I guess you're out of luck.
How about some candy? Ice cream? Soda? Coffee?
Mochaccino. Starbucks.
Venti.
Okay.
Don't you have to tell Mrs. Dole you're going?
She's out cold. Pills. All she does since the funeral is take pills and sleep.
By the way, I'm Lindy.

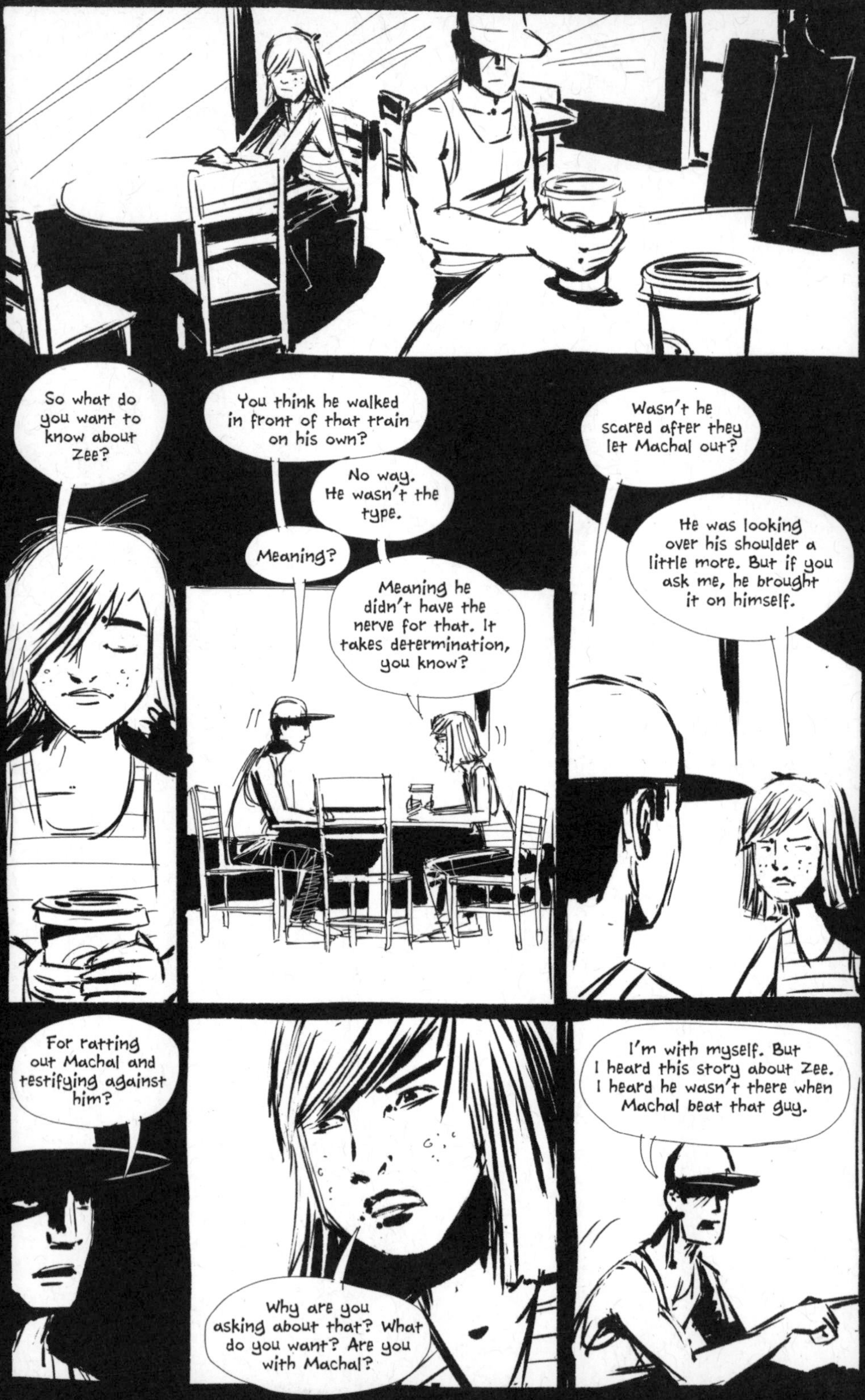

So what do you want to know about Zee?
You think he walked in front of that train on his own?
No way. He wasn't the type.
Meaning?
Meaning he didn't have the nerve for that. It takes determination, you know?
Wasn't he scared after they let Machal out?
He was looking over his shoulder a little more. But if you ask me, he brought it on himself.
For ratting out Machal and testifying against him?
Why are you asking about that? What do you want? Are you with Machal?
I'm with myself. But I heard this story about Zee. I heard he wasn't there when Machal beat that guy.

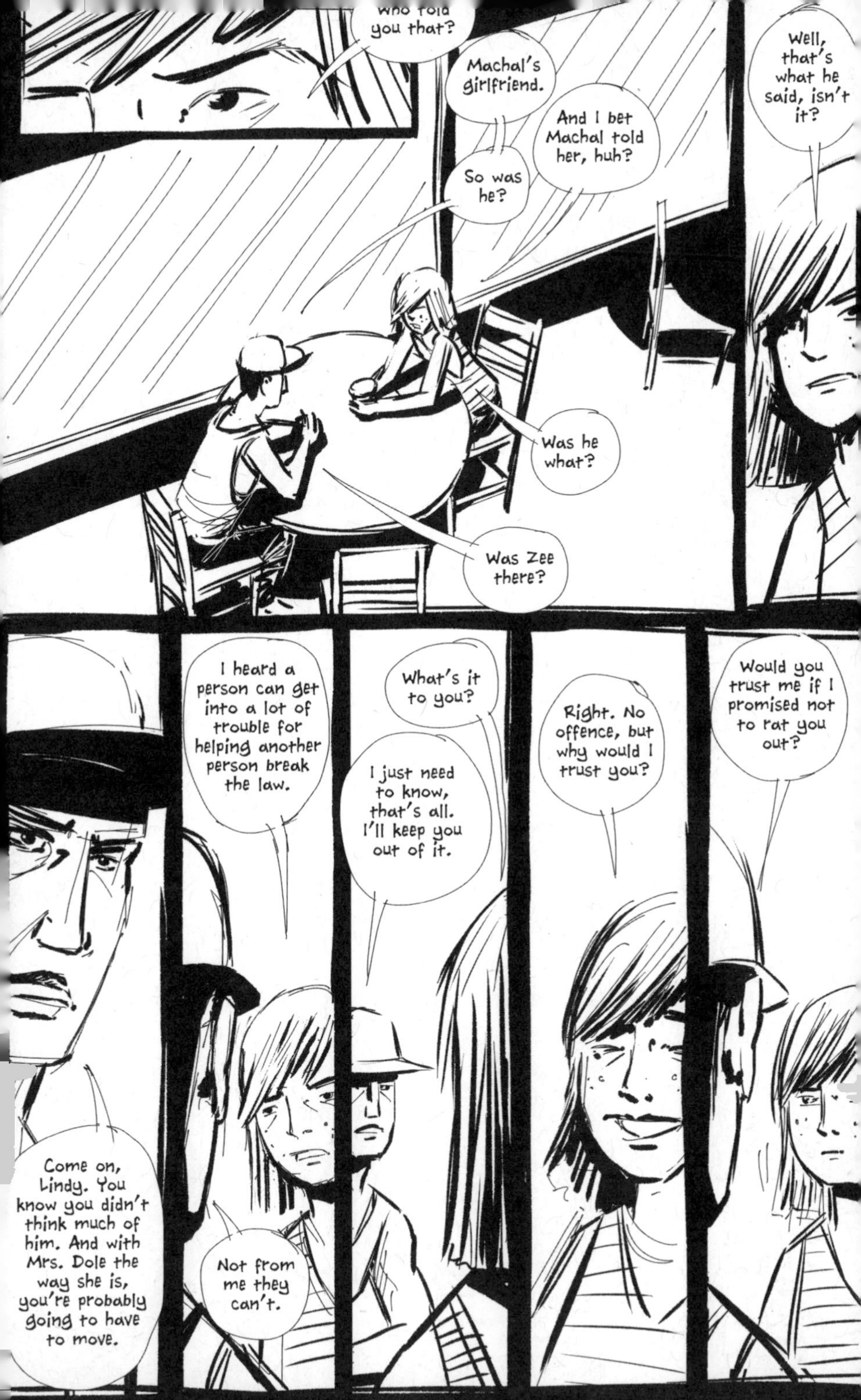
Who told you that?
Machal's girlfriend.
And I bet Machal told her, huh?
So was he?
Well, that's what he said, isn't it?
Was he what?
Was Zee there?
Come on, Lindy. You know you didn't think much of him. And with Mrs. Dole the way she is, you're probably going to have to move.
I heard a person can get into a lot of trouble for helping another person break the law.
Not from me they can't.
What's it to you?
I just need to know, that's all. I'll keep you out of it.
Right. No offence, but why would I trust you?
Would you trust me if I promised not to rat you out?

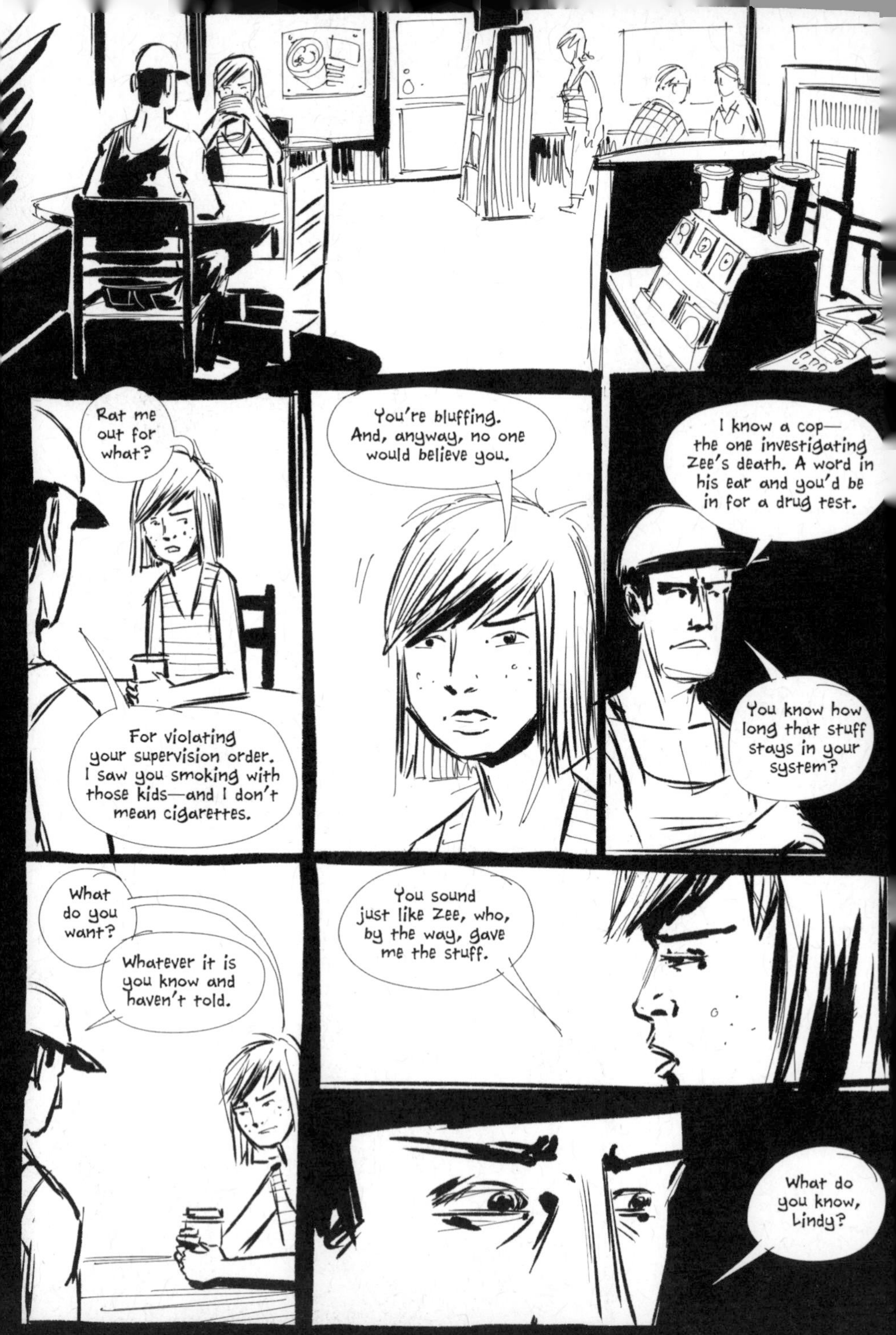

Rat me out for what?
For violating your supervision order. I saw you smoking with those kids—and I don't mean cigarettes.
You're bluffing. And, anyway, no one would believe you.
I know a cop—the one investigating Zee's death. A word in his ear and you'd be in for a drug test.
You know how long that stuff stays in your system?
What do you want?
Whatever it is you know and haven't told.
You sound just like Zee, who, by the way, gave me the stuff.
What do you know, Lindy?

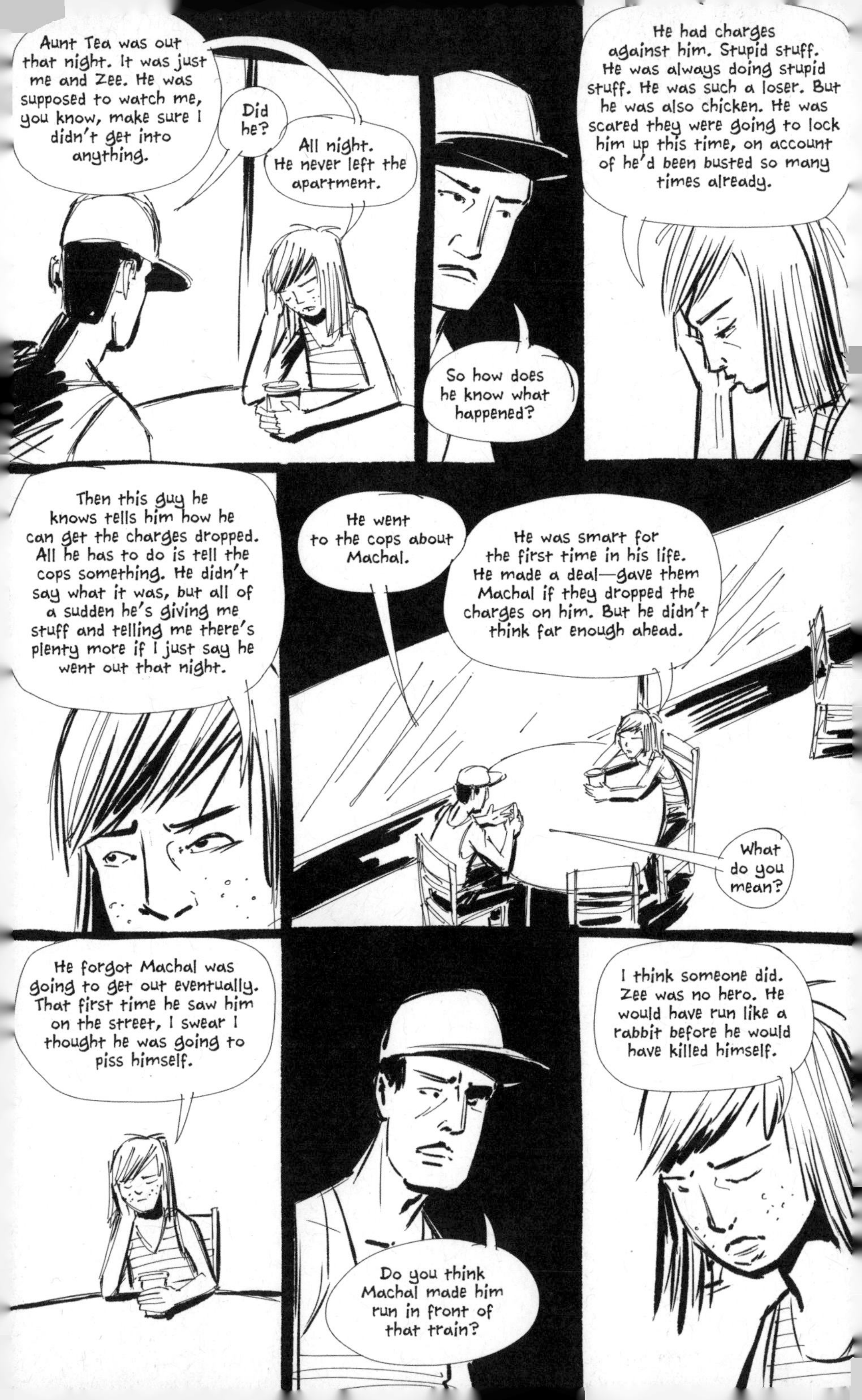
Aunt Tea was out that night. It was just me and Zee. He was supposed to watch me, you know, make sure I didn't get into anything.
Did he?
All night. He never left the apartment.
So how does he know what happened?
He had charges against him. Stupid stuff. He was always doing stupid stuff. He was such a loser. But he was also chicken. He was scared they were going to lock him up this time, on account of he'd been busted so many times already.
Then this guy he knows tells him how he can get the charges dropped. All he has to do is tell the cops something. He didn't say what it was, but all of a sudden he's giving me stuff and telling me there's plenty more if I just say he went out that night.
He went to the cops about Machal.
He was smart for the first time in his life. He made a deal—gave them Machal if they dropped the charges on him. But he didn't think far enough ahead.
What do you mean?
He forgot Machal was going to get out eventually. That first time he saw him on the street, I swear I thought he was going to piss himself.
Do you think Machal made him run in front of that train?
I think someone did. Zee was no hero. He would have run like a rabbit before he would have killed himself.

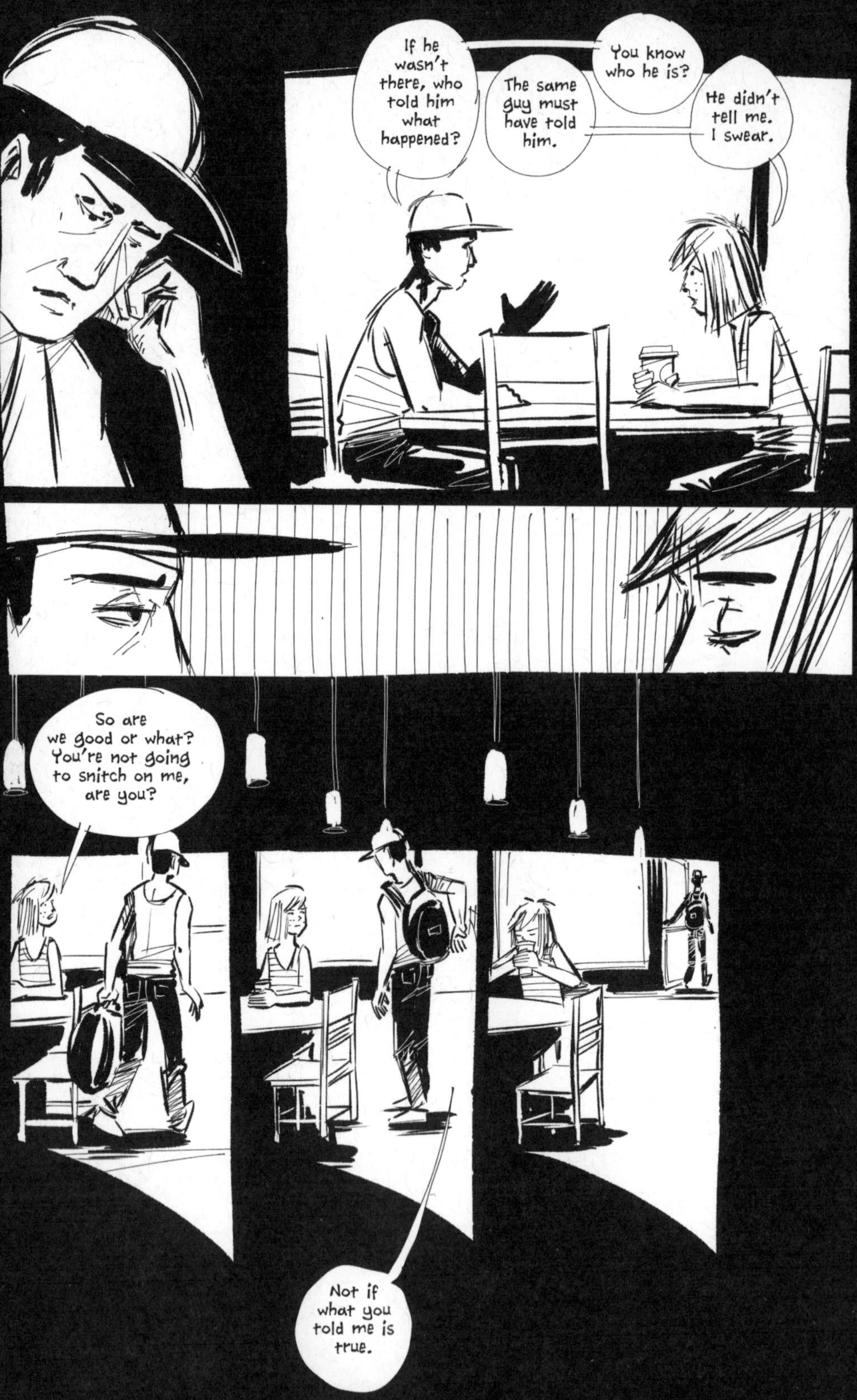
If he wasn't there, who told him what happened?
The same guy must have told him.
You know who he is?
He didn't tell me. I swear.
So are we good or what? You're not going to snitch on me, are you?
Not if what you told me is true.

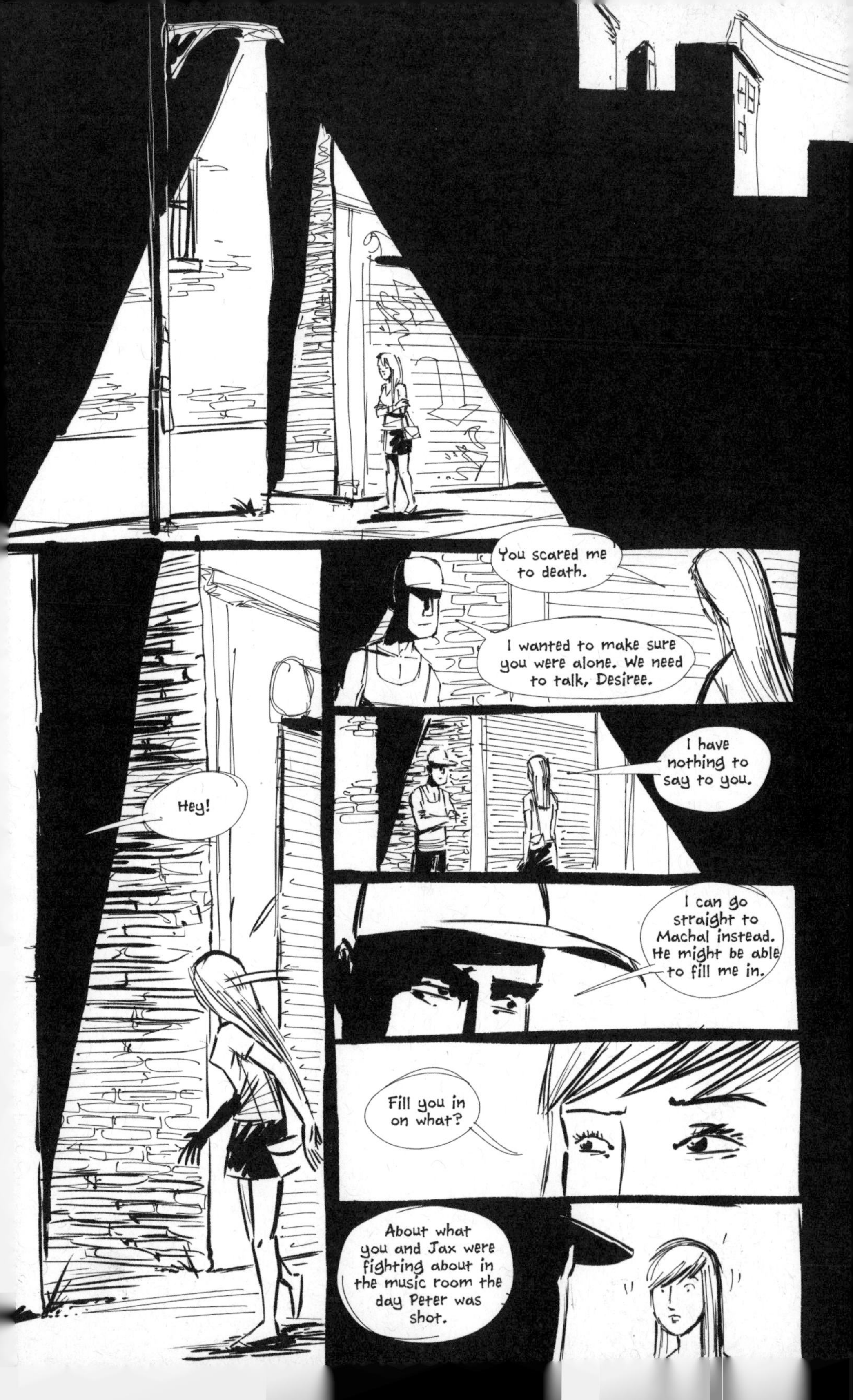
Hey!
You scared me to death.
I wanted to make sure you were alone. We need to talk, Desiree.
I have nothing to say to you.
I can go straight to Machal instead. He might be able to fill me in.
Fill you in on what?
About what you and Jax were fighting about in the music room the day Peter was shot.

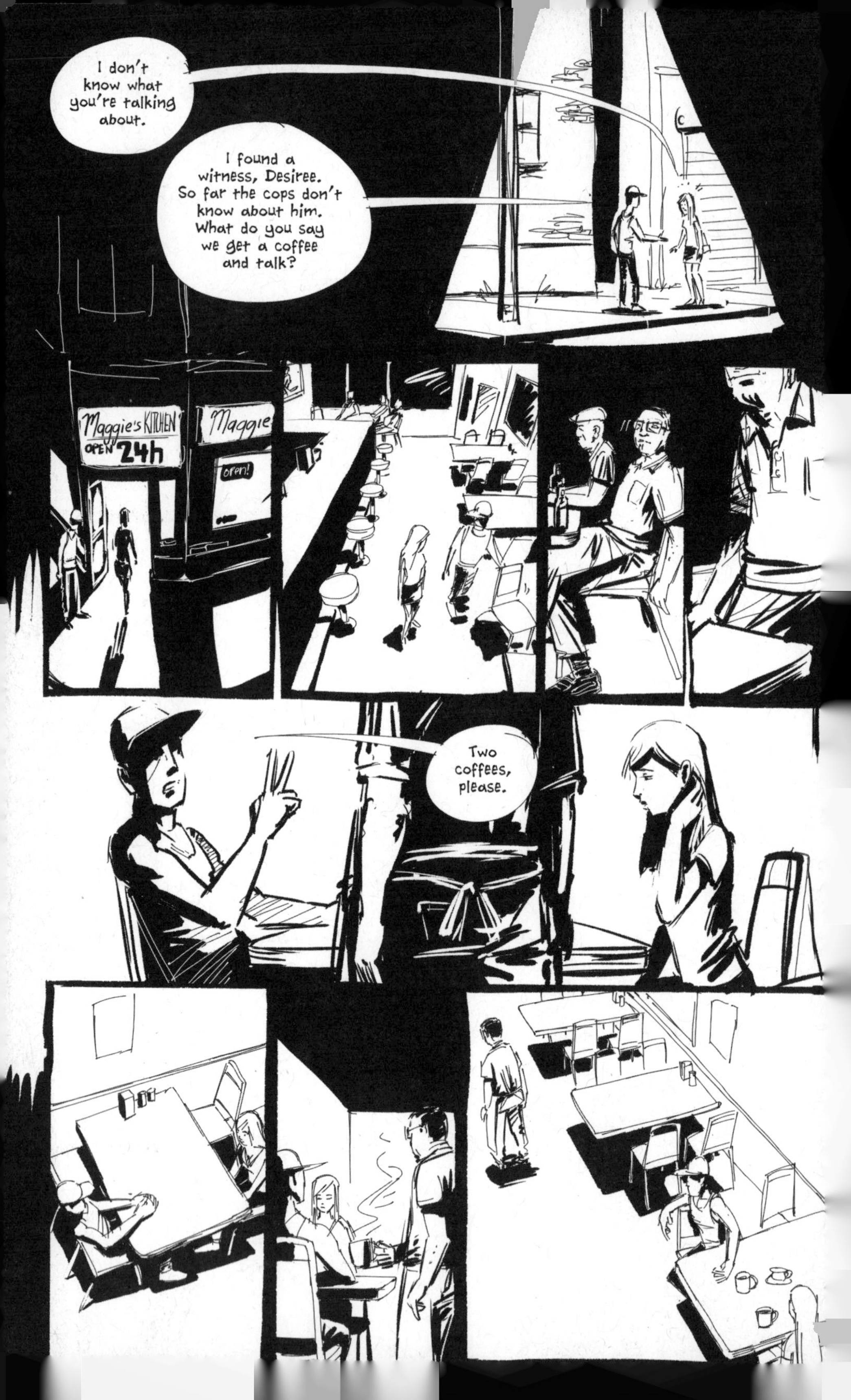
I don't know what you're talking about.
I found a witness, Desiree. So far the cops don't know about him. What do you say we get a coffee and talk?
Maggie's KITCHEN
OPEN 24h
Maggie
open!
Two coffees, please.

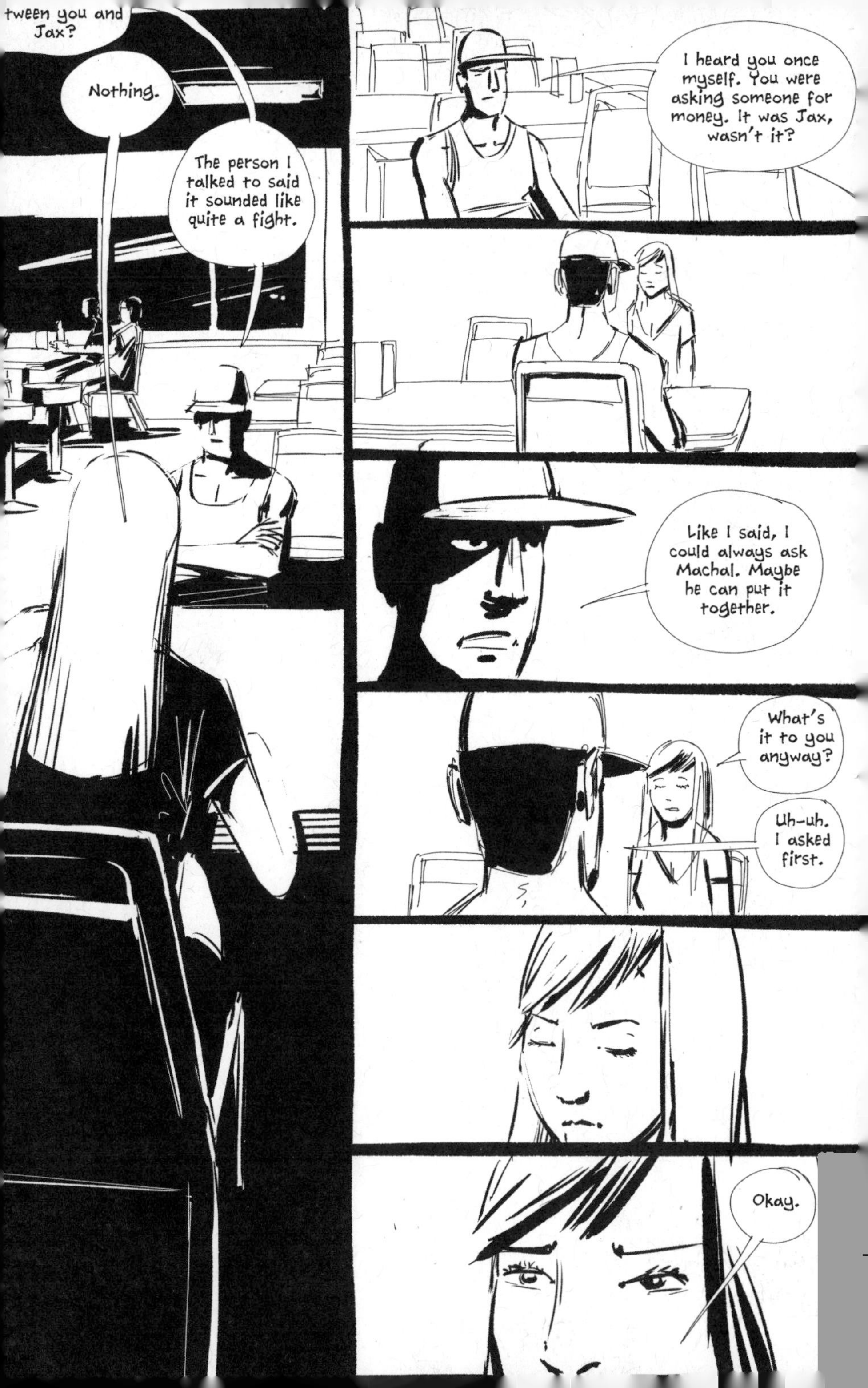
tween you and Jax?
Nothing.
The person I talked to said it sounded like quite a fight.
I heard you once myself. You were asking someone for money. It was Jax, wasn't it?
Like I said, I could always ask Machal. Maybe he can put it together.
What's it to you anyway?
Uh-uh. I asked first.
Okay.

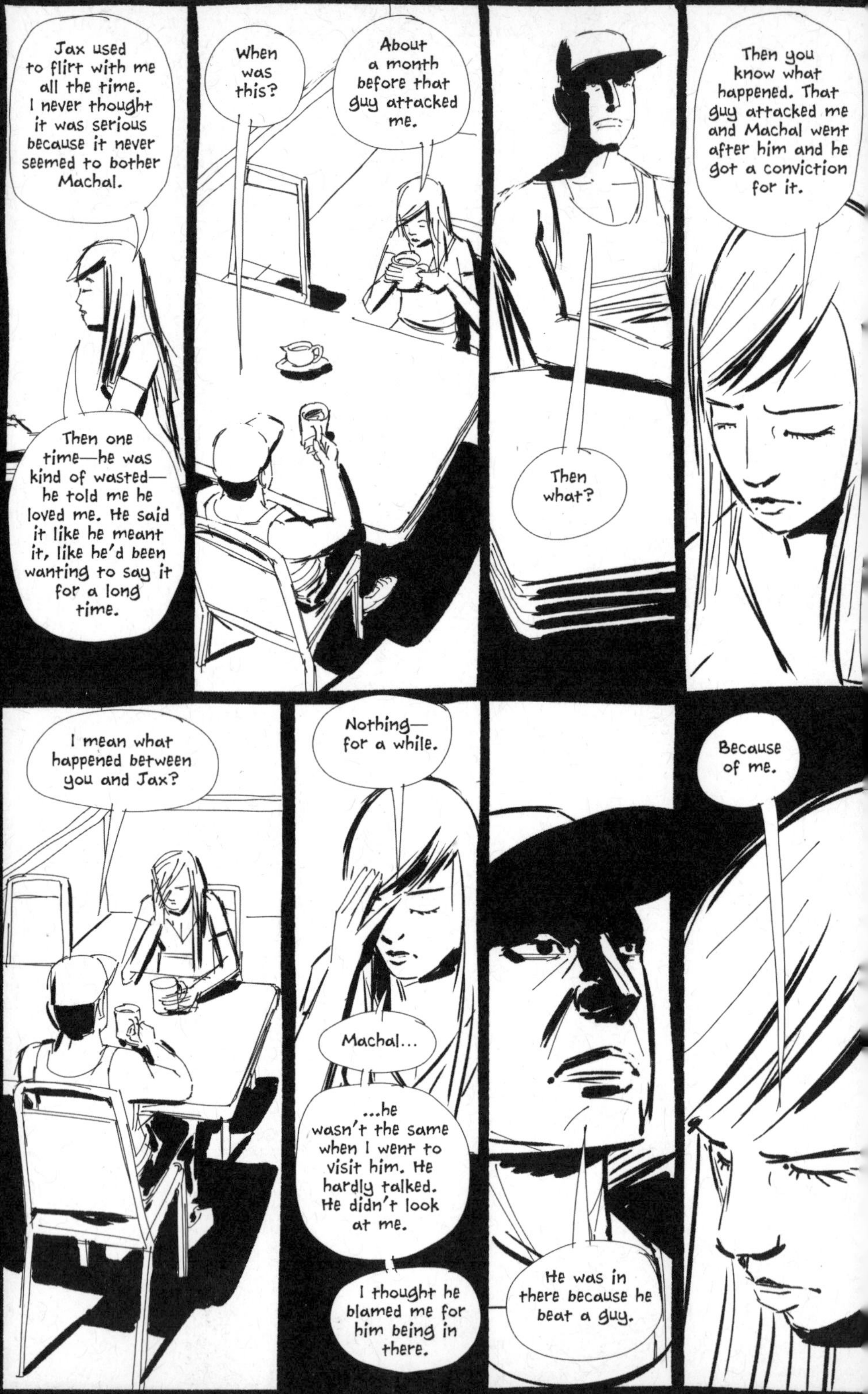
Jax used to flirt with me all the time. I never thought it was serious because it never seemed to bother Machal.
Then one time—he was kind of wasted—he told me he loved me. He said it like he meant it, like he'd been wanting to say it for a long time.
When was this?
About a month before that guy attacked me.
Then what?
Then you know what happened. That guy attacked me and Machal went after him and he got a conviction for it.
I mean what happened between you and Jax?
Nothing—for a while.
Machal...
...he wasn't the same when I went to visit him. He hardly talked. He didn't look at me.
I thought he blamed me for him being in there.
He was in there because he beat a guy.
Because of me.

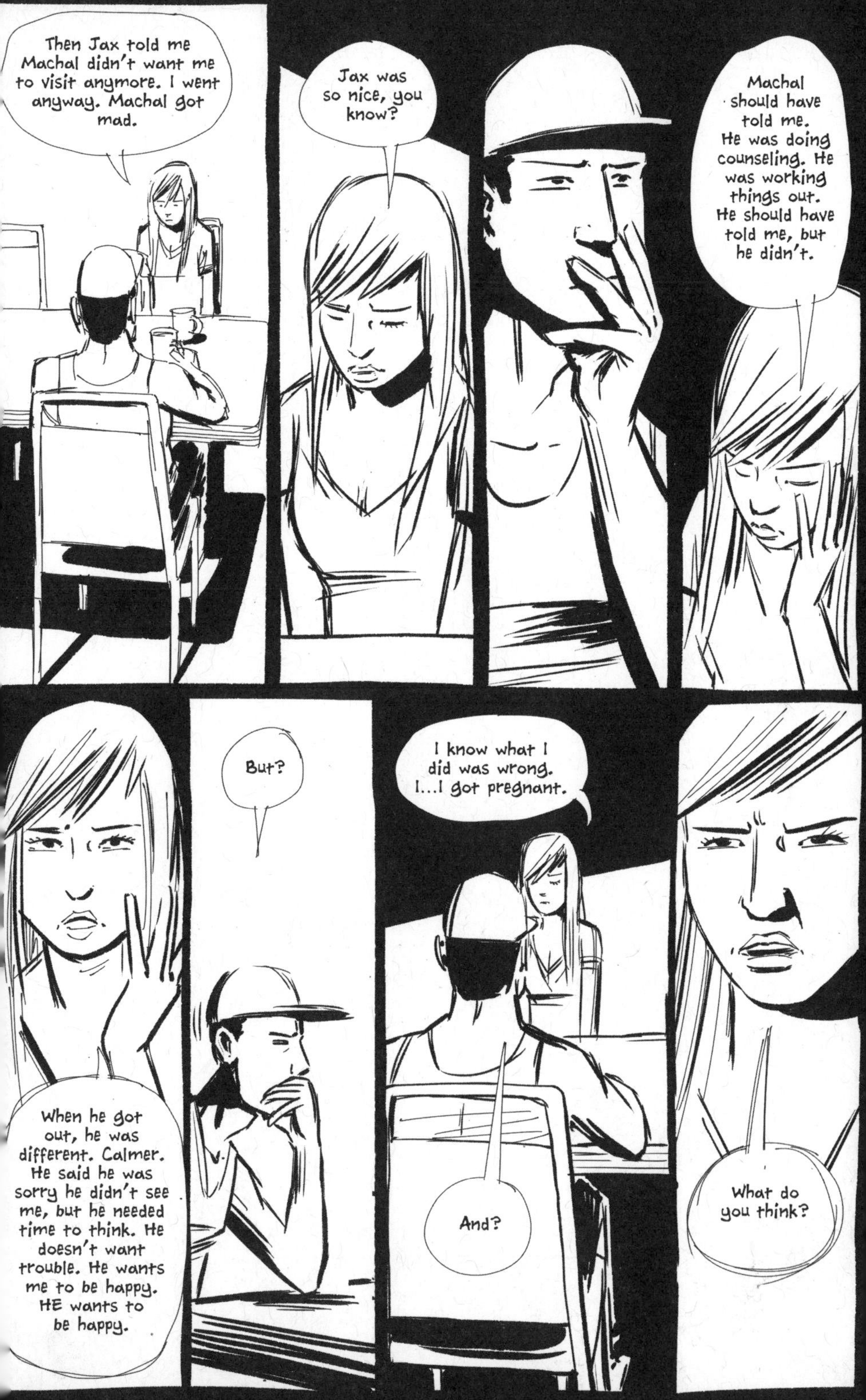
Then Jax told me Machal didn't want me to visit anymore. I went anyway. Machal got mad.
Jax was so nice, you know?
Machal should have told me. He was doing counseling. He was working things out. He should have told me, but he didn't.
When he got out, he was different. Calmer. He said he was sorry he didn't see me, but he needed time to think. He doesn't want trouble. He wants me to be happy. HE wants to be happy.
But?
I know what I did was wrong. I...I got pregnant.
And?
What do you think?

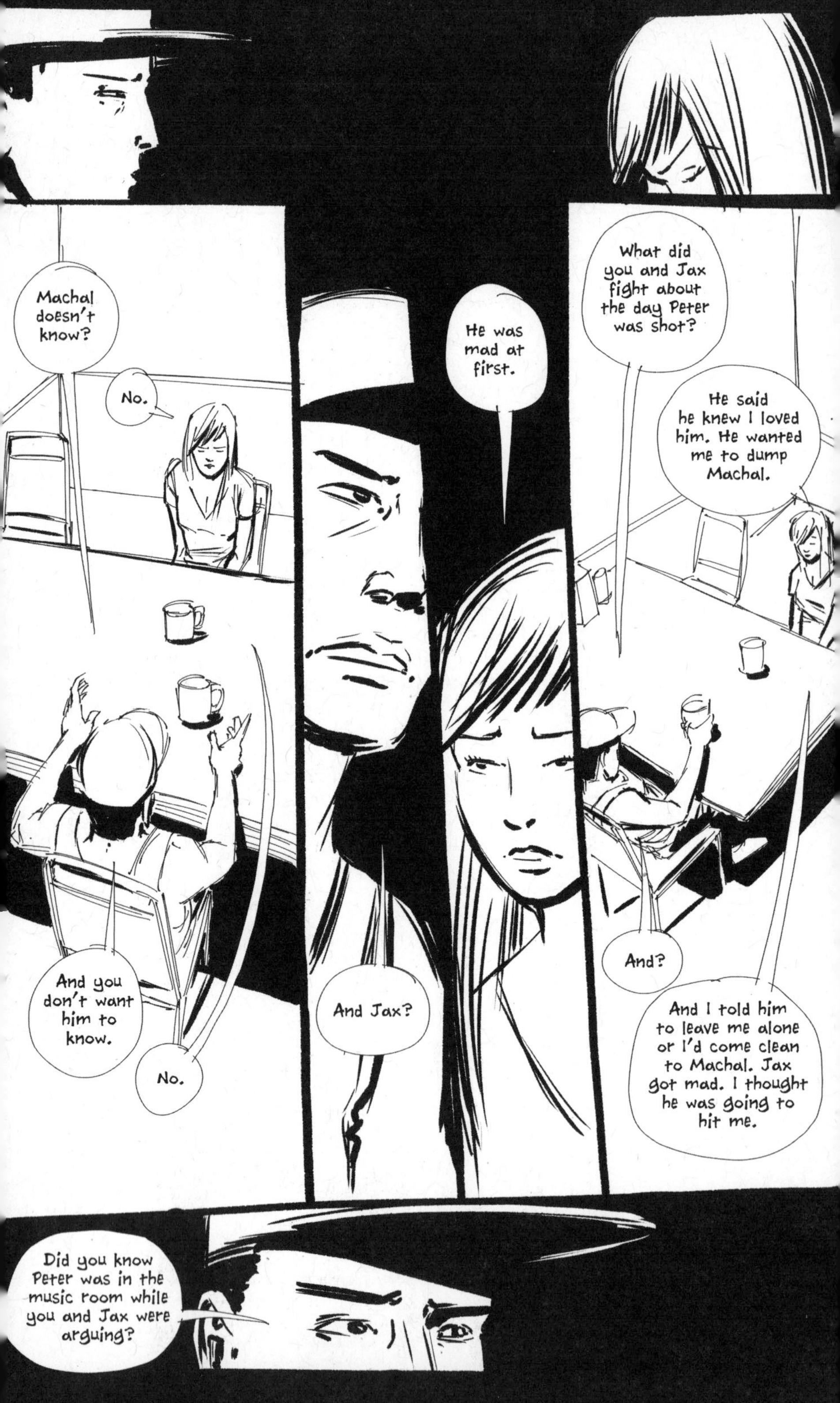
Machal doesn't know?
No.
And you don't want him to know.
No.
He was mad at first.
And Jax?
What did you and Jax fight about the day Peter was shot?
He said he knew I loved him. He wanted me to dump Machal.
And?
And I told him to leave me alone or I'd come clean to Machal. Jax got mad. I thought he was going to hit me.
Did you know Peter was in the music room while you and Jax were arguing?

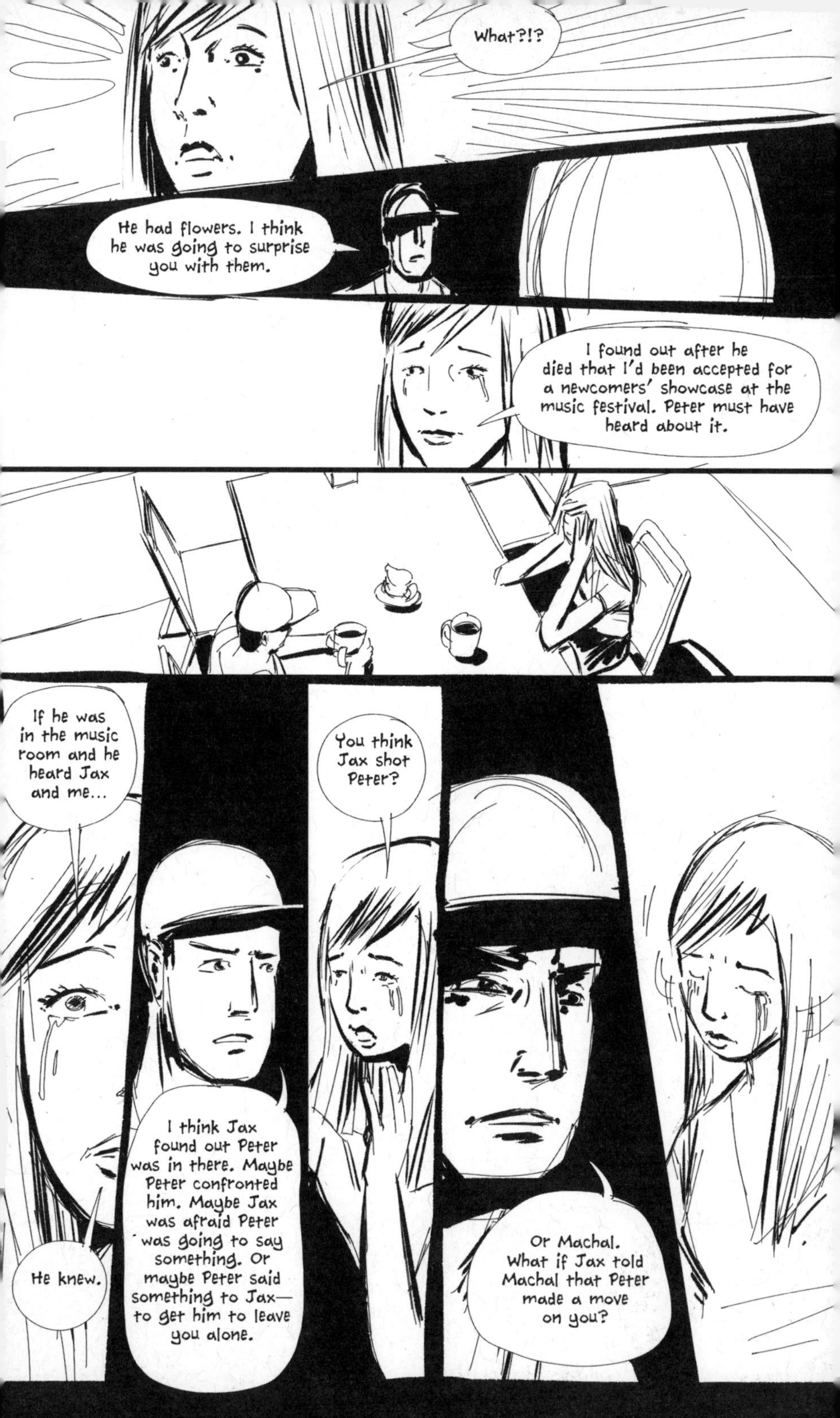
What?!?
He had flowers. I think he was going to surprise you with them.
I found out after he died that I'd been accepted for a newcomers' showcase at the music festival. Peter must have heard about it.
If he was in the music room and he heard Jax and me...
He knew.
I think Jax found out Peter was in there. Maybe Peter confronted him. Maybe Jax was afraid Peter was going to say something. Or maybe Peter said something to Jax—to get him to leave you alone.
You think Jax shot Peter?
Or Machal. What if Jax told Machal that Peter made a move on you?

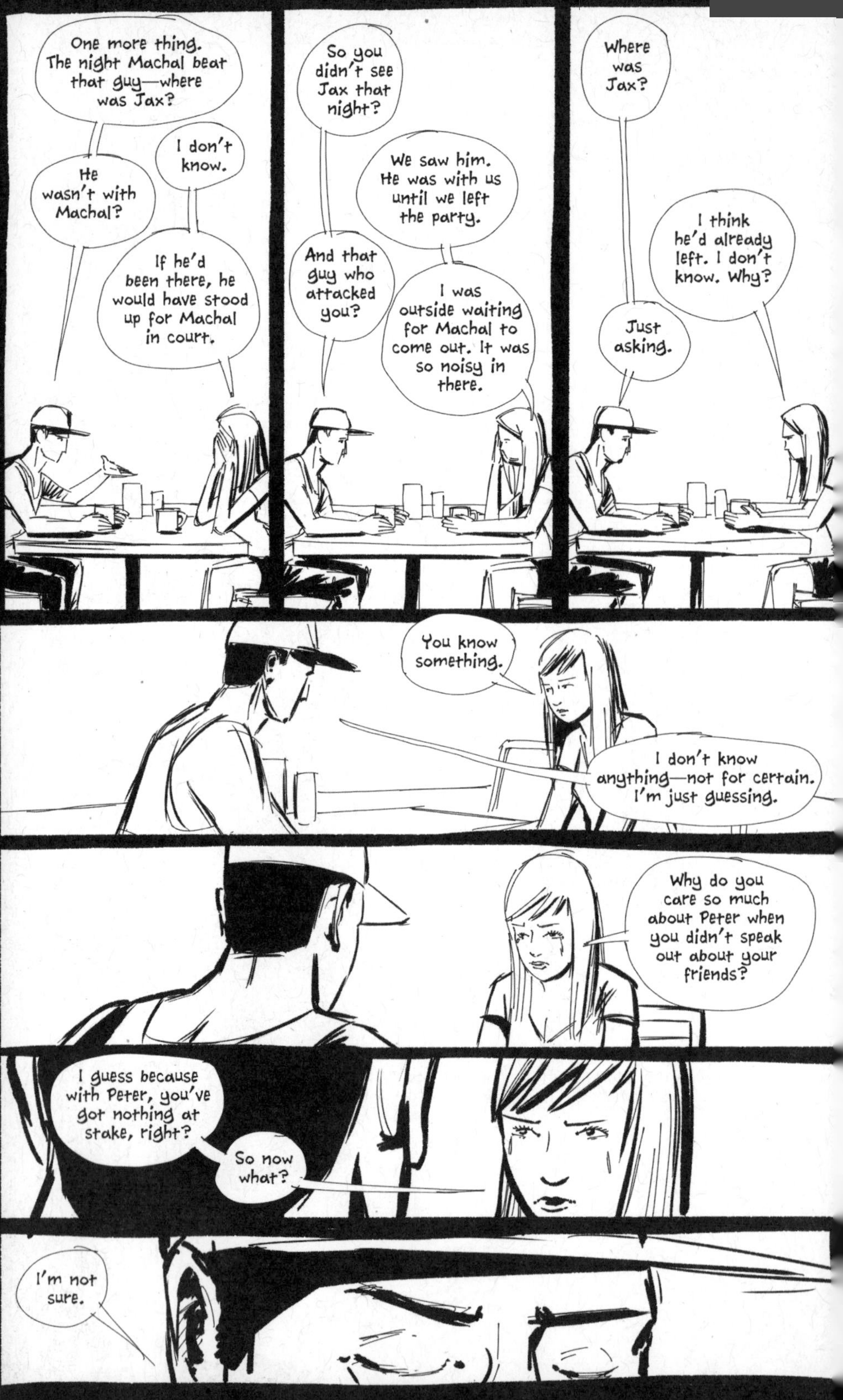

One more thing. The night Machal beat that guy—where was Jax?
He wasn't with Machal?
I don't know.
If he'd been there, he would have stood up for Machal in court.
So you didn't see Jax that night?
We saw him. He was with us until we left the party.
And that guy who attacked you?
I was outside waiting for Machal to come out. It was so noisy in there.
Where was Jax?
I think he'd already left. I don't know. Why?
Just asking.
You know something.
I don't know anything—not for certain. I'm just guessing.
Why do you care so much about Peter when you didn't speak out about your friends?
I guess because with Peter, you've got nothing at stake, right?
So now what?
I'm not sure.

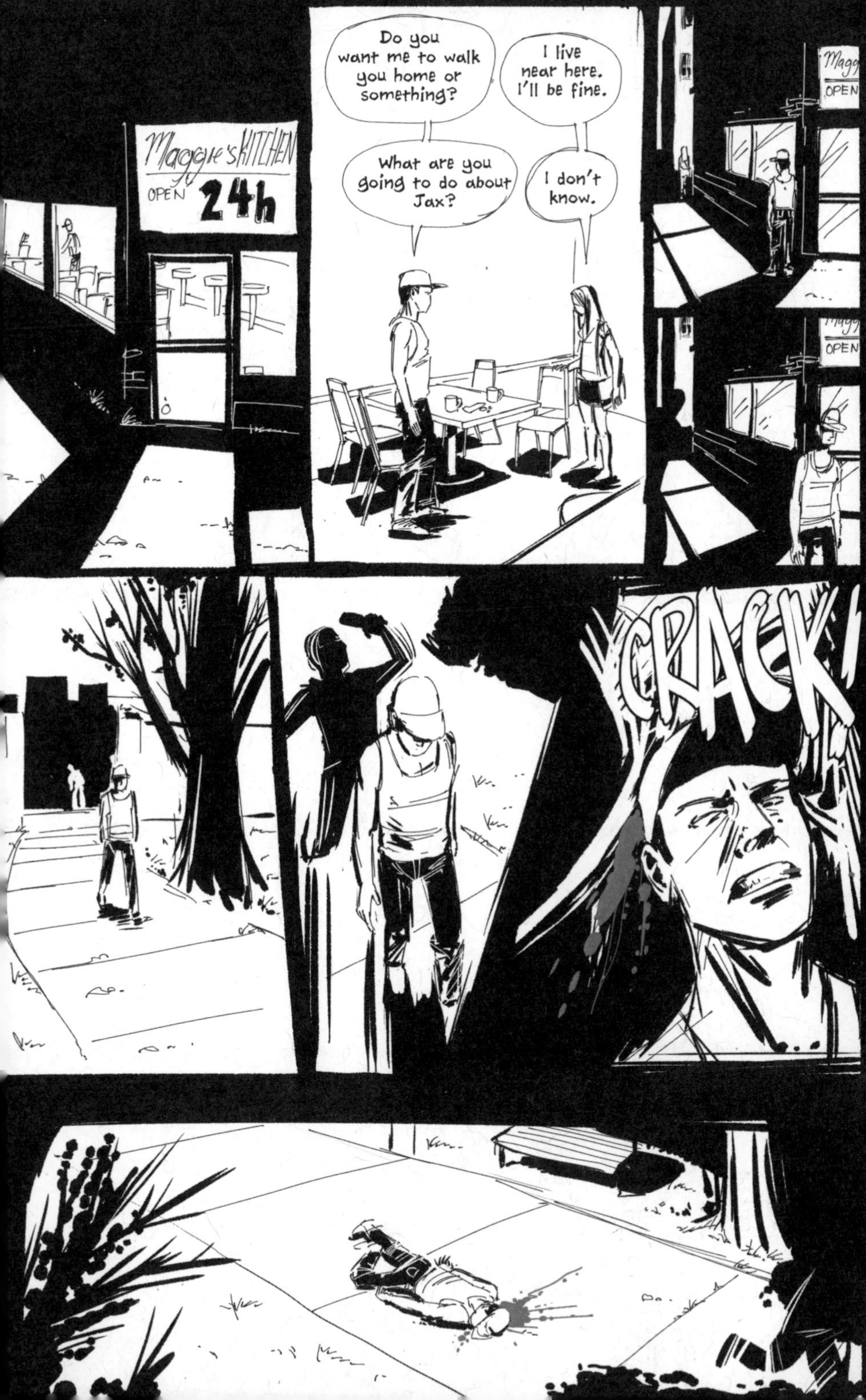
Maggie's KITCHEN
OPEN 24h
Do you want me to walk you home or something?
I live near here. I'll be fine.
What are you going to do about Jax?
I don't know.
Maggie
OPEN
OPEN
CRACK!

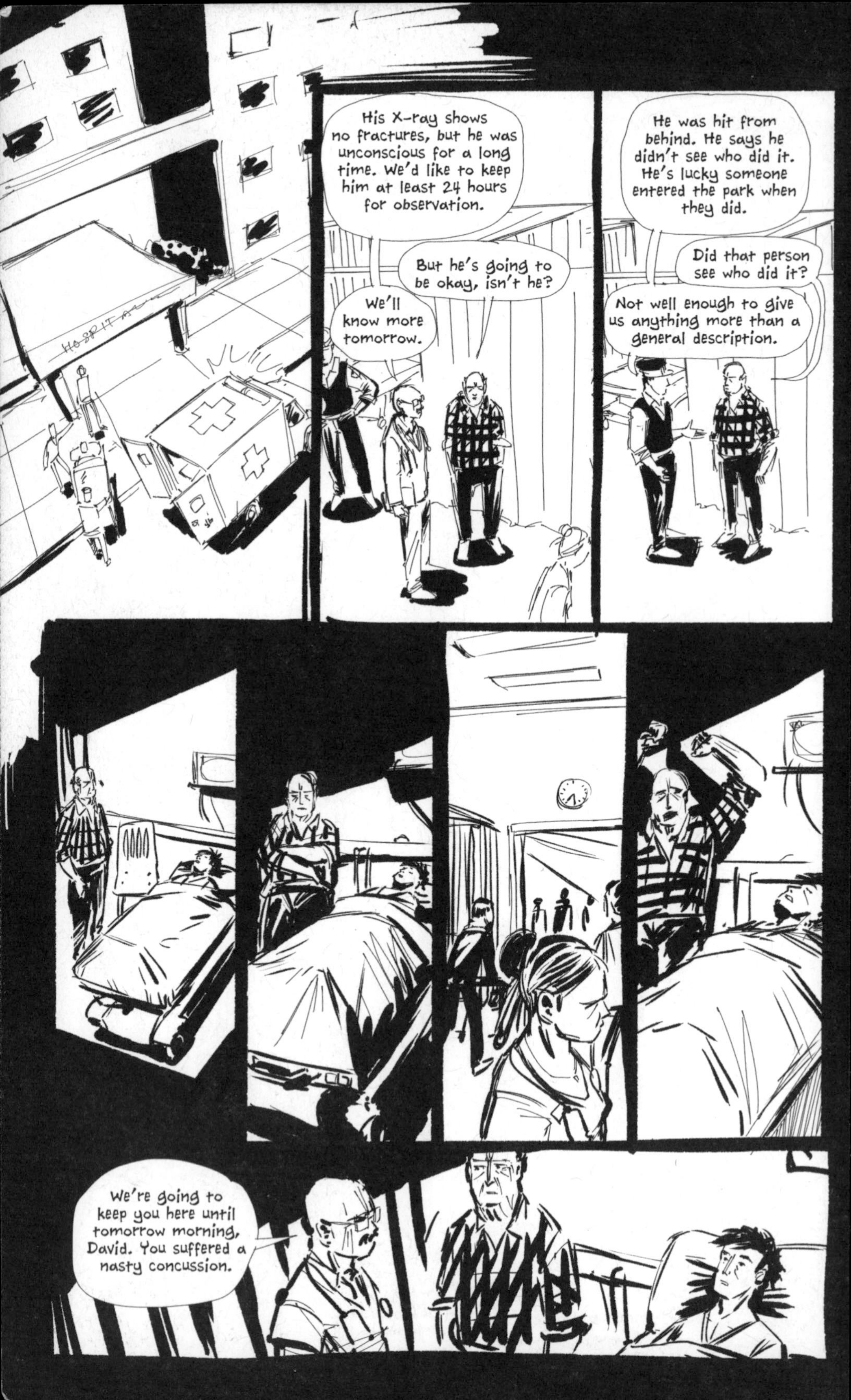

HOSPITAL
His X-ray shows no fractures, but he was unconscious for a long time. We'd like to keep him at least 24 hours for observation.
But he's going to be okay, isn't he?
We'll know more tomorrow.
He was hit from behind. He says he didn't see who did it. He's lucky someone entered the park when they did.
Did that person see who did it?
Not well enough to give us anything more than a general description.
We're going to keep you here until tomorrow morning, David. You suffered a nasty concussion.

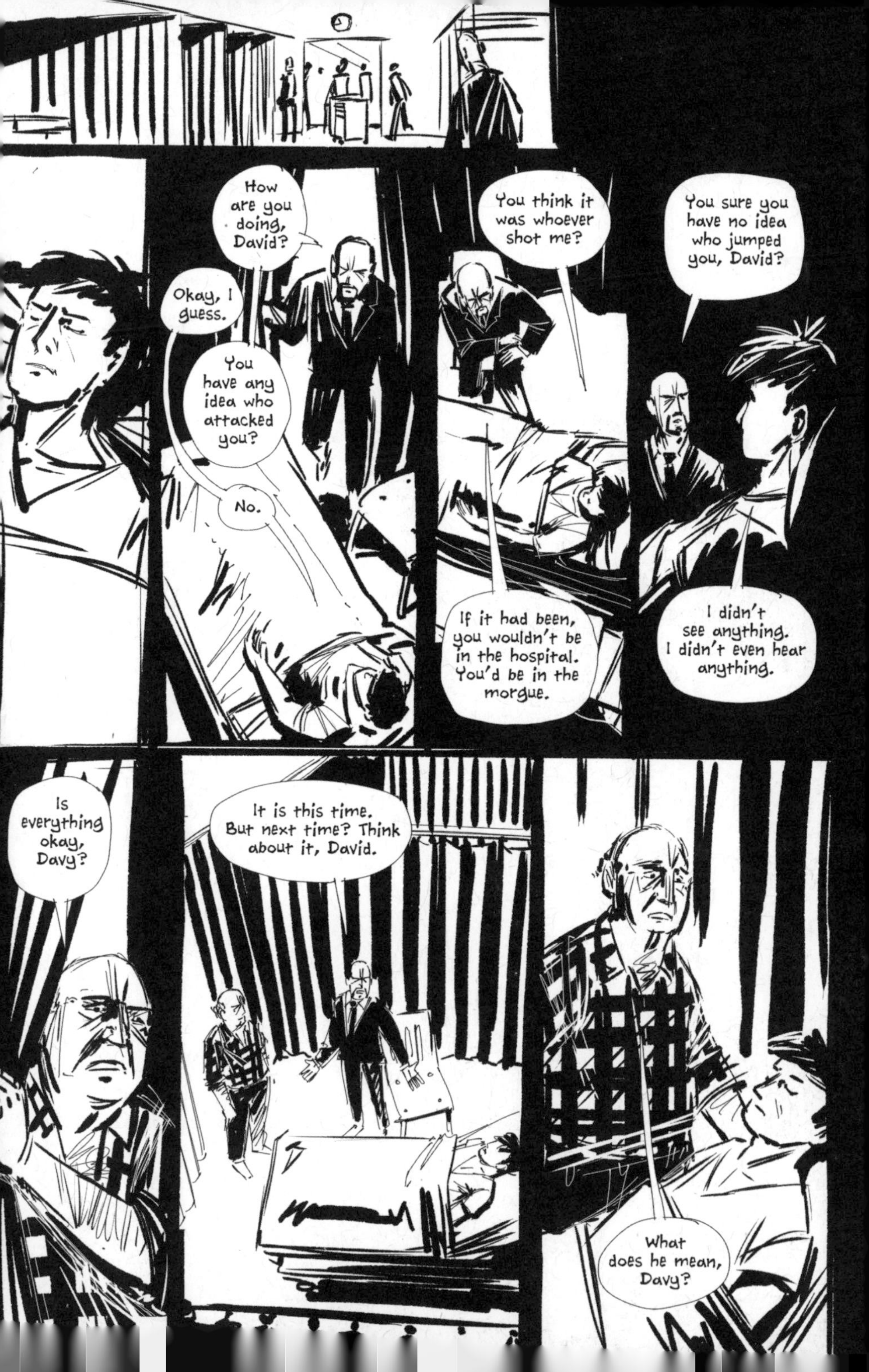
How are you doing, David?
Okay, I guess.
You have any idea who attacked you?
No.
You think it was whoever shot me?
If it had been, you wouldn't be in the hospital. You'd be in the morgue.
You sure you have no idea who jumped you, David?
I didn't see anything. I didn't even hear anything.
Is everything okay, Davy?
It is this time. But next time? Think about it, David.
What does he mean, Davy?

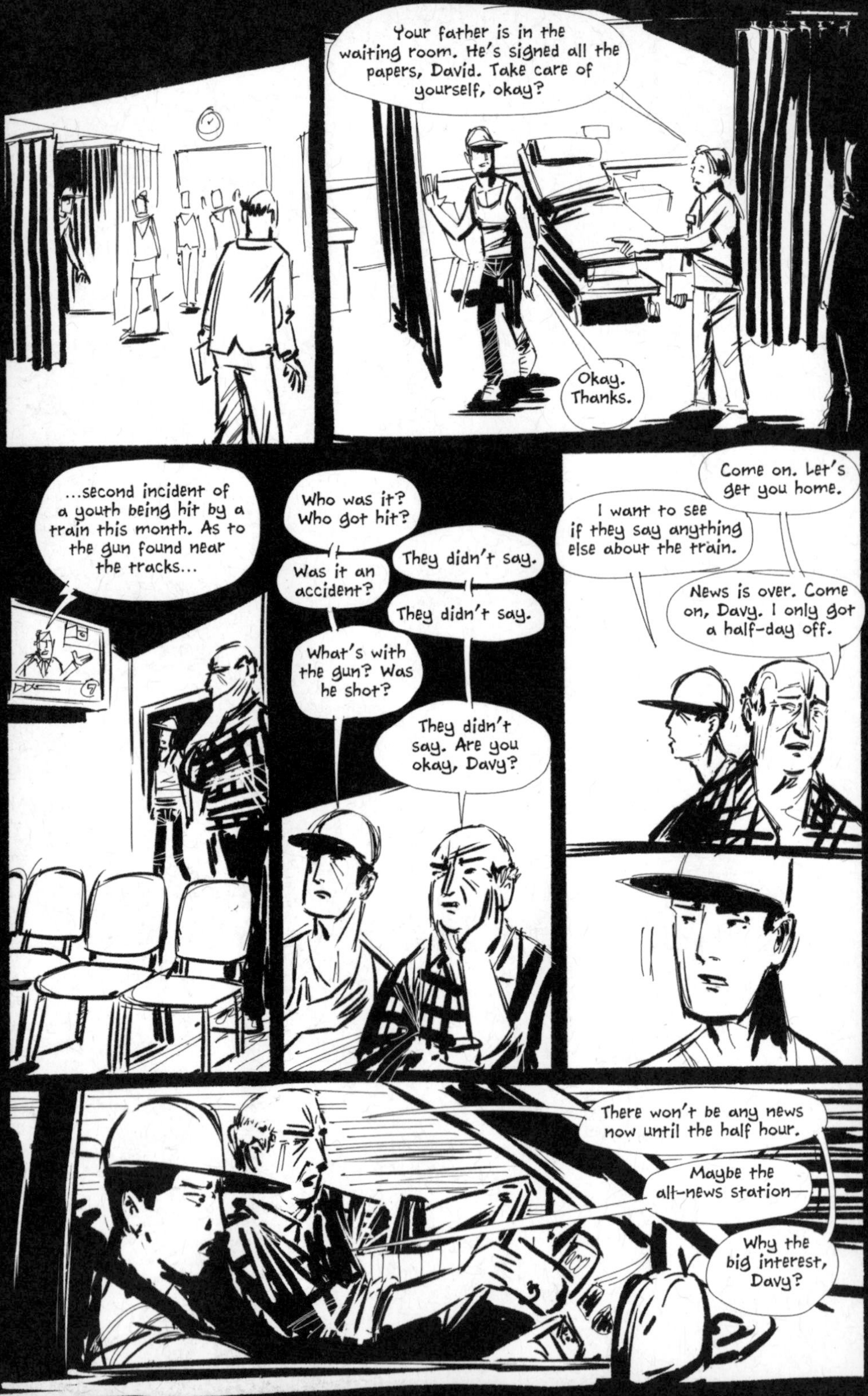
Your father is in the waiting room. He's signed all the papers, David. Take care of yourself, okay?
Okay. Thanks.
...second incident of a youth being hit by a train this month. As to the gun found near the tracks...
Who was it? Who got hit?
They didn't say.
Was it an accident?
They didn't say.
What's with the gun? Was he shot?
They didn't say. Are you okay, Davy?
I want to see if they say anything else about the train.
Come on. Let's get you home.
News is over. Come on, Davy. I only got a half-day off.
There won't be any news now until the half hour.
Maybe the all-news station—
Why the big interest, Davy?

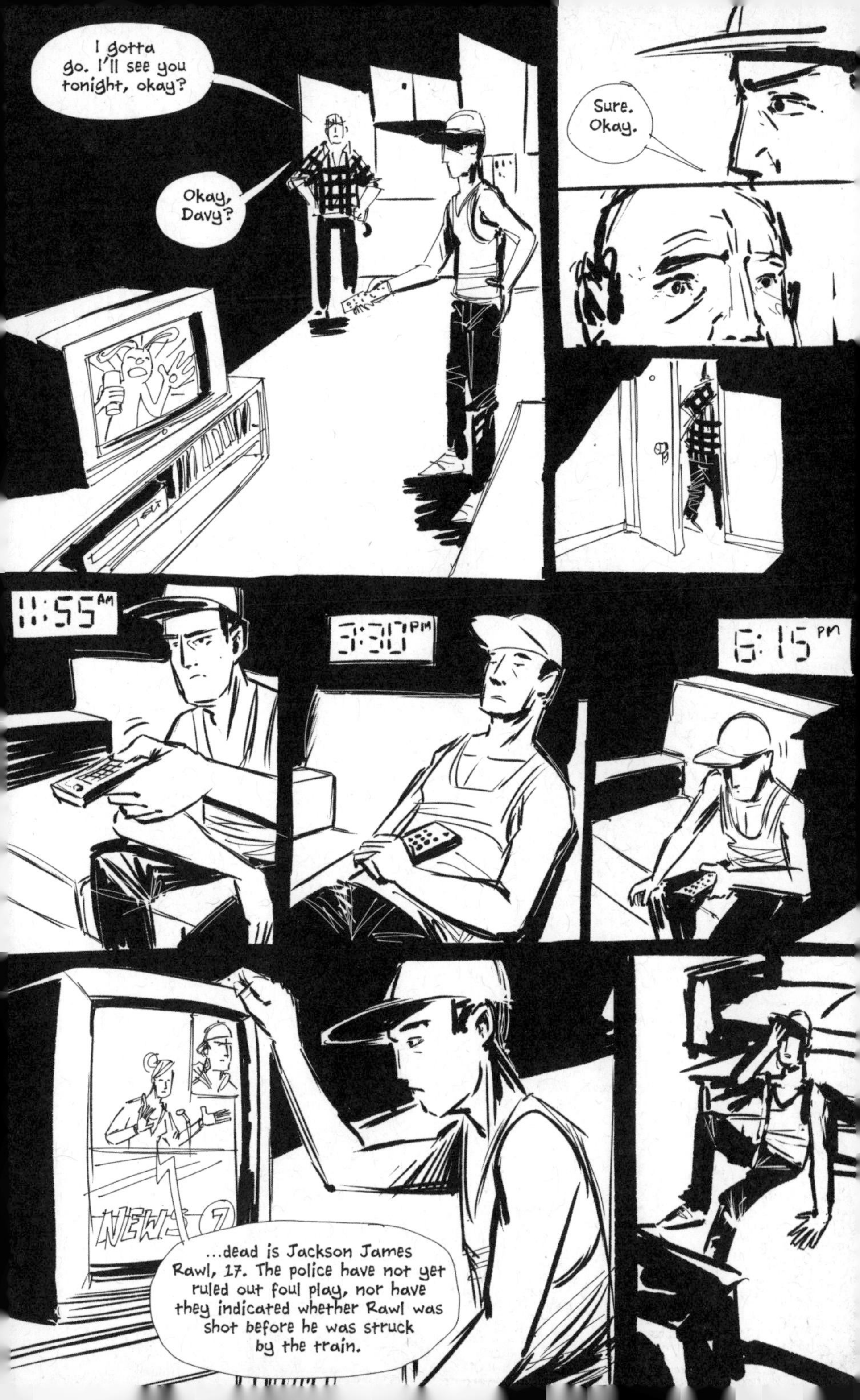
I gotta go. I'll see you tonight, okay?
Okay, Davy?
Sure. Okay.
11:55 AM
3:30 PM
6:15 PM
NEWS 7
...dead is Jackson James Rawl, 17. The police have not yet ruled out foul play, nor have they indicated whether Rawl was shot before he was struck by the train.

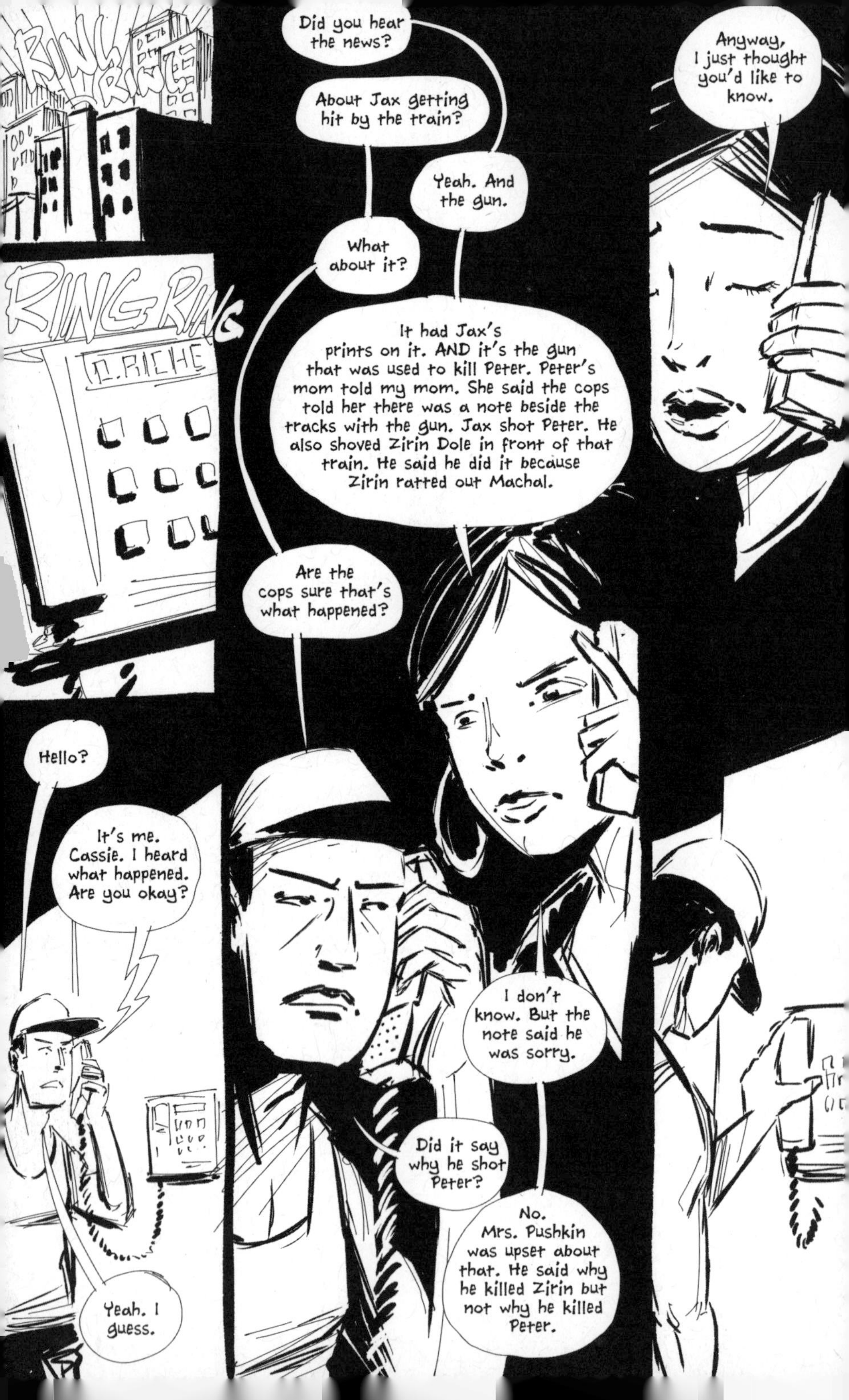
RING RING
RING RING
D. RICHE
Hello?
It's me. Cassie. I heard what happened. Are you okay?
Yeah. I guess.
Did you hear the news?
About Jax getting hit by the train?
Yeah. And the gun.
What about it?
It had Jax's prints on it. AND it's the gun that was used to kill Peter. Peter's mom told my mom. She said the cops told her there was a note beside the tracks with the gun. Jax shot Peter. He also shoved Zirin Dole in front of that train. He said he did it because Zirin ratted out Machal.
Are the cops sure that's what happened?
I don't know. But the note said he was sorry.
Did it say why he shot Peter?
No. Mrs. Pushkin was upset about that. He said why he killed Zirin but not why he killed Peter.
Anyway, I just thought you'd like to know.

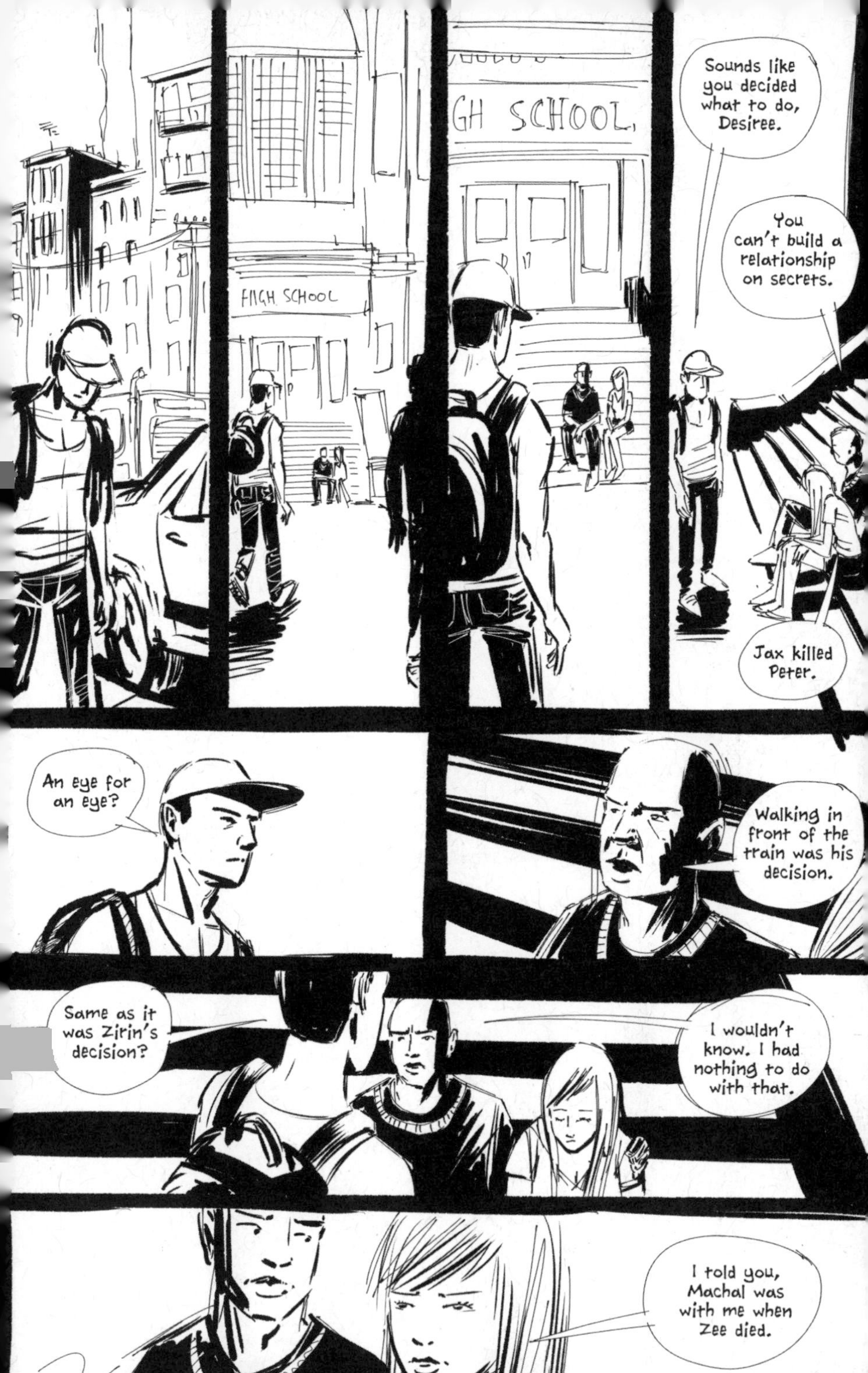

FIGH SCHOOL
GH SCHOOL
Sounds like you decided what to do, Desiree.
You can't build a relationship on secrets.
Jax killed Peter.
An eye for an eye?
Walking in front of the train was his decision.
Same as it was Zirin's decision?
I wouldn't know. I had nothing to do with that.
I told you, Machal was with me when Zee died.

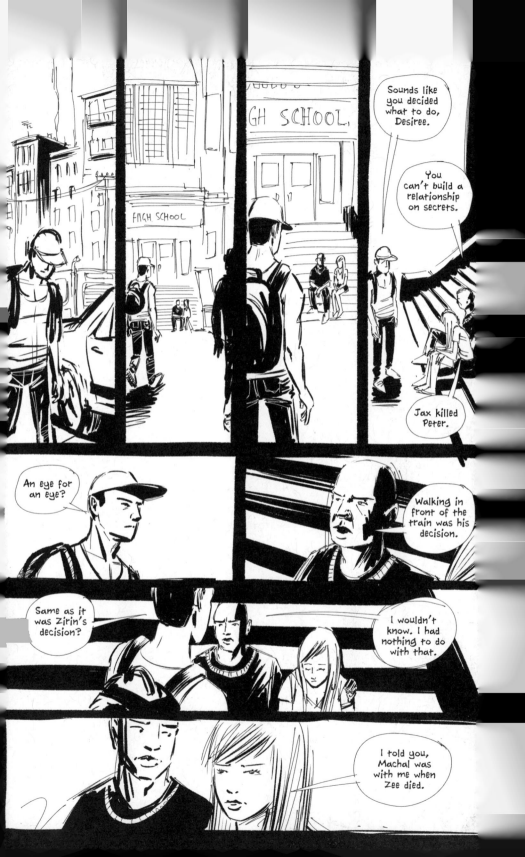

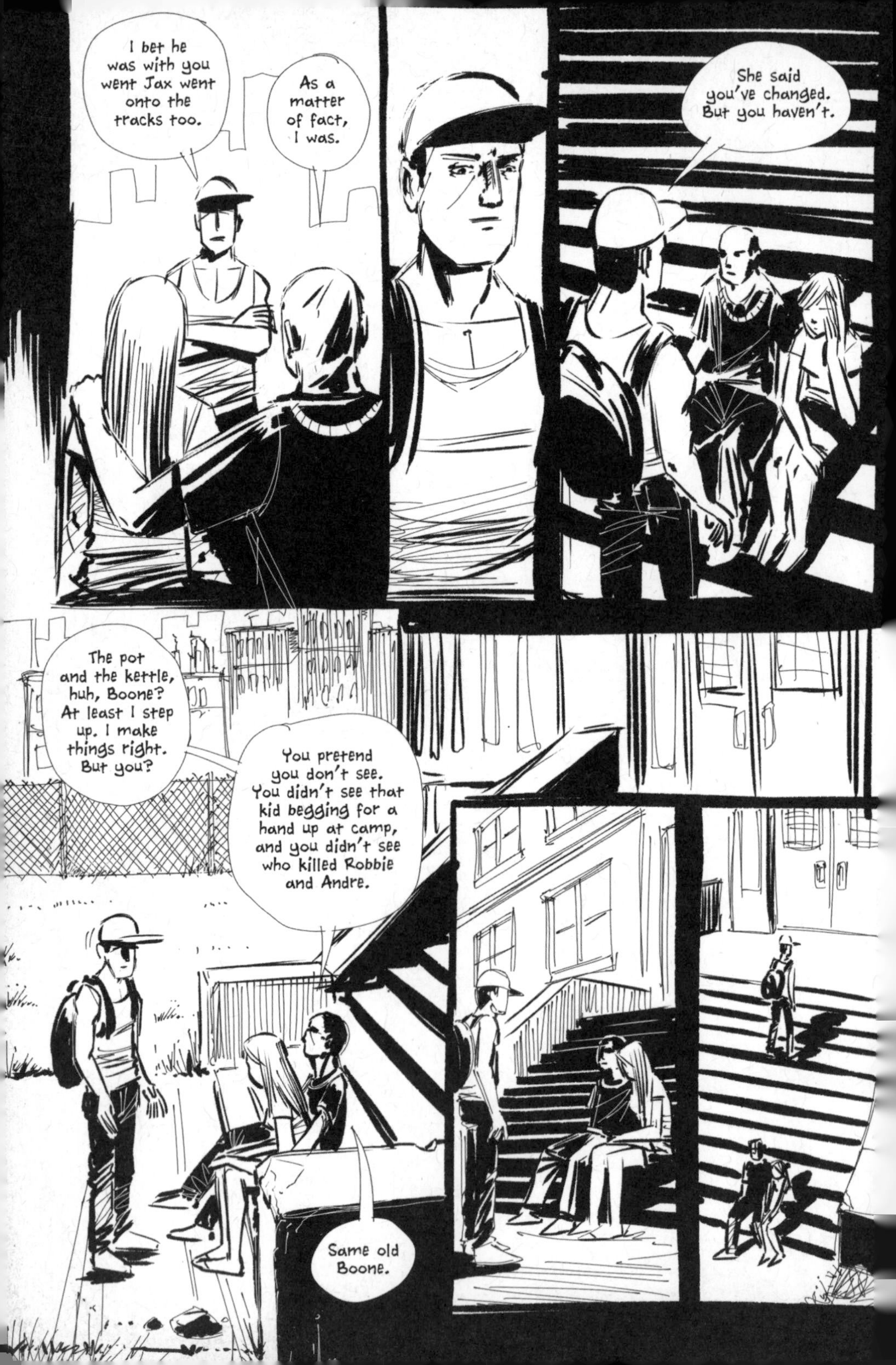
I bet he was with you went Jax went onto the tracks too.
As a matter of fact, I was.
She said you've changed. But you haven't.
The pot and the kettle, huh, Boone? At least I step up. I make things right. But you?
You pretend you don't see. You didn't see that kid begging for a hand up at camp, and you didn't see who killed Robbie and Andre.
Same old Boone.

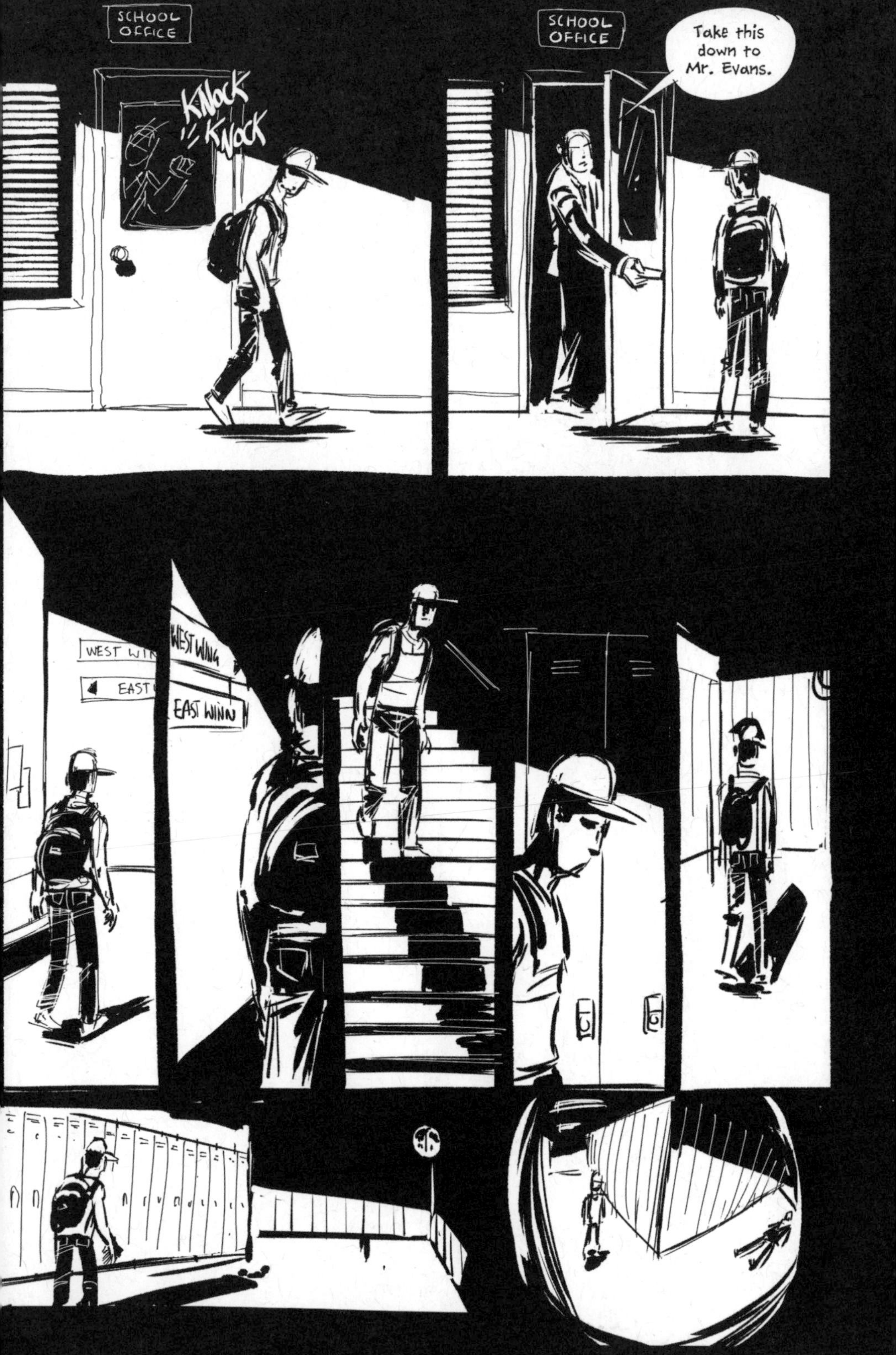
SCHOOL OFFICE
KNOCK KNOCK
SCHOOL OFFICE
Take this down to Mr. Evans.
WEST WIN
EAST
WEST WING
EAST WINN

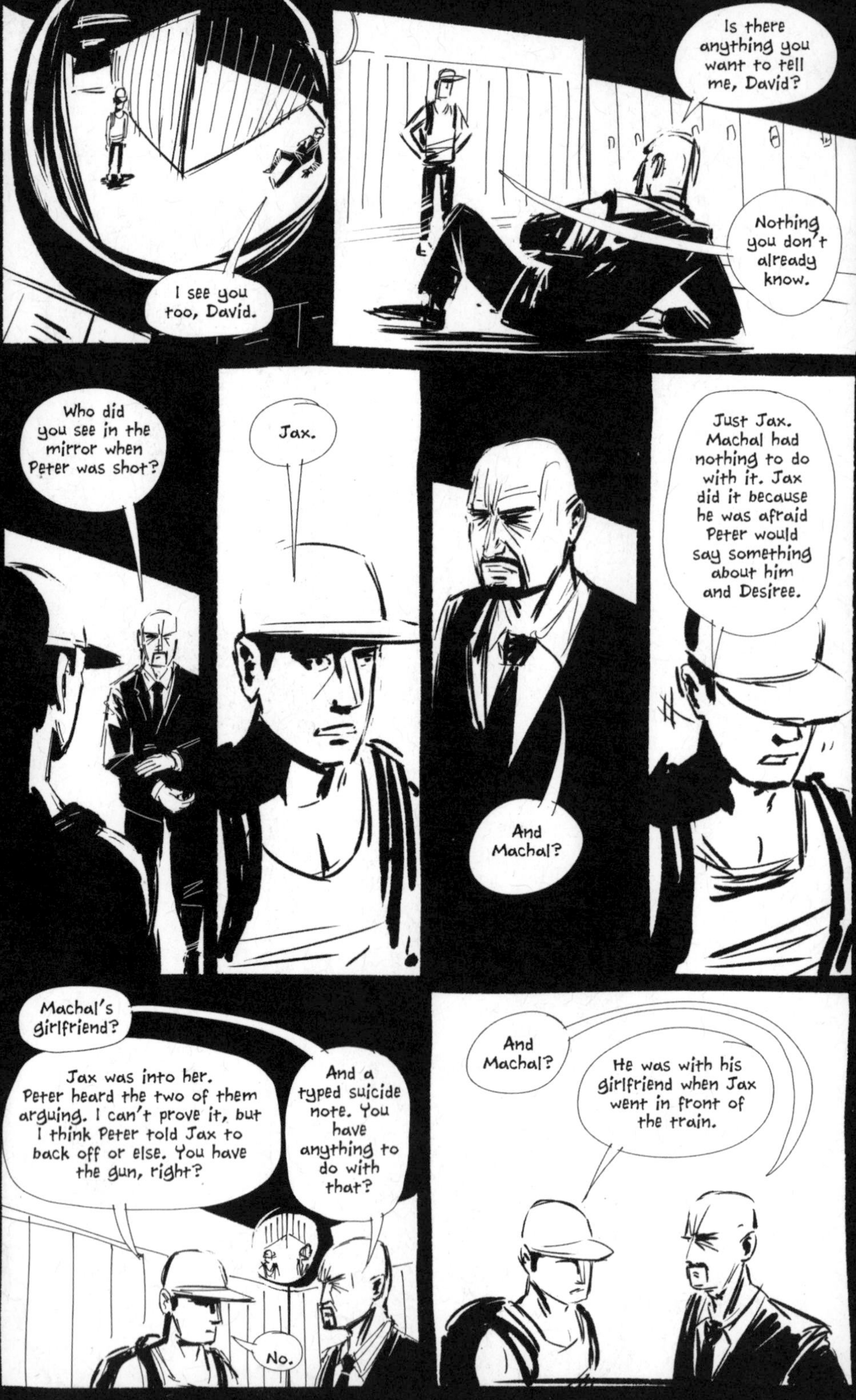
I see you too, David.
Is there anything you want to tell me, David?
Nothing you don't already know.
Who did you see in the mirror when Peter was shot?
Jax.
And Machal?
Just Jax. Machal had nothing to do with it. Jax did it because he was afraid Peter would say something about him and Desiree.
Machal's girlfriend?
Jax was into her. Peter heard the two of them arguing. I can't prove it, but I think Peter told Jax to back off or else. You have the gun, right?
No.
And a typed suicide note. You have anything to do with that?
And Machal?
He was with his girlfriend when Jax went in front of the train.

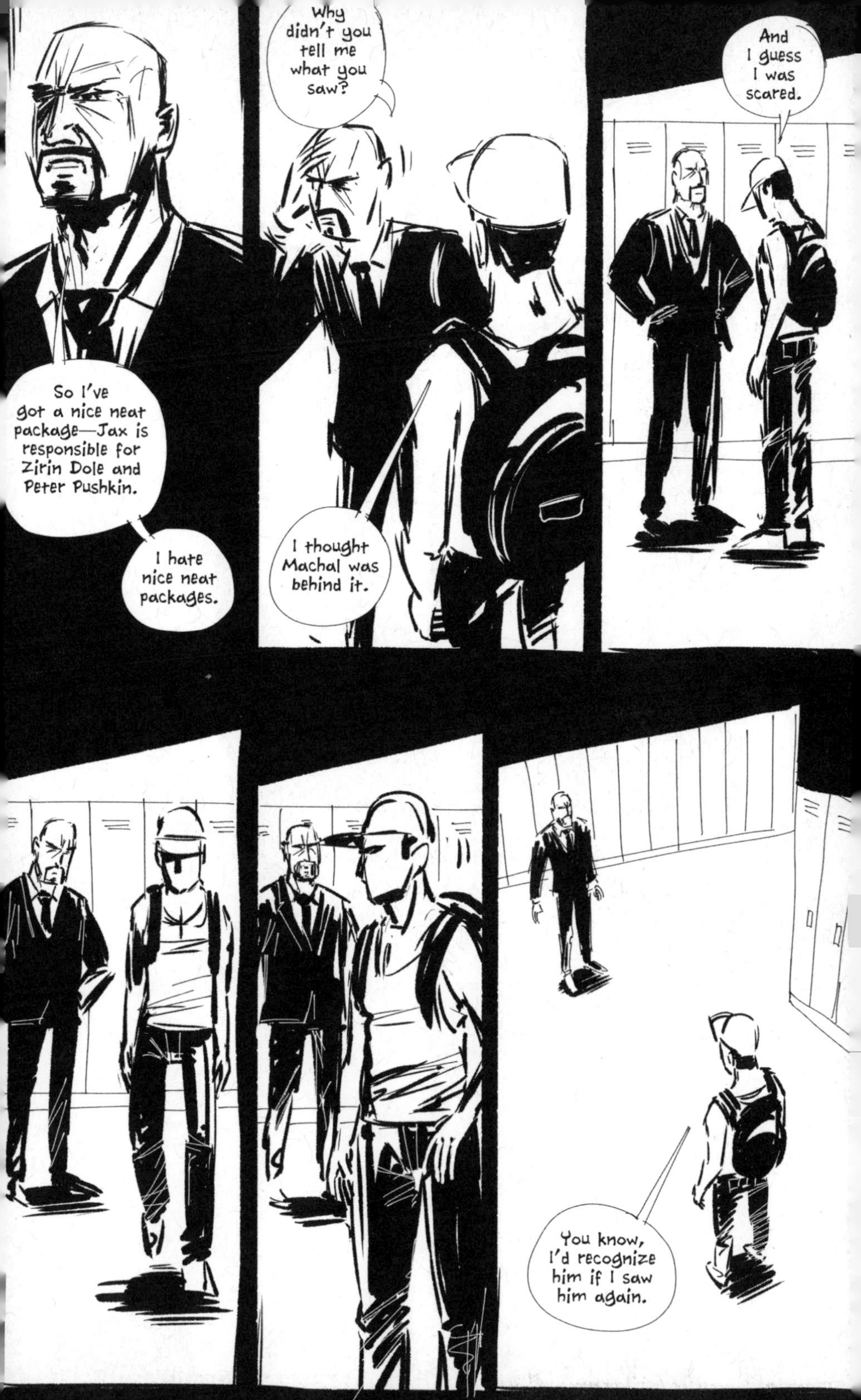
So I've got a nice neat package—Jax is responsible for Zirin Dole and Peter Pushkin.
I hate nice neat packages.
Why didn't you tell me what you saw?
I thought Machal was behind it.
And I guess I was scared.
You know, I'd recognize him if I saw him again.

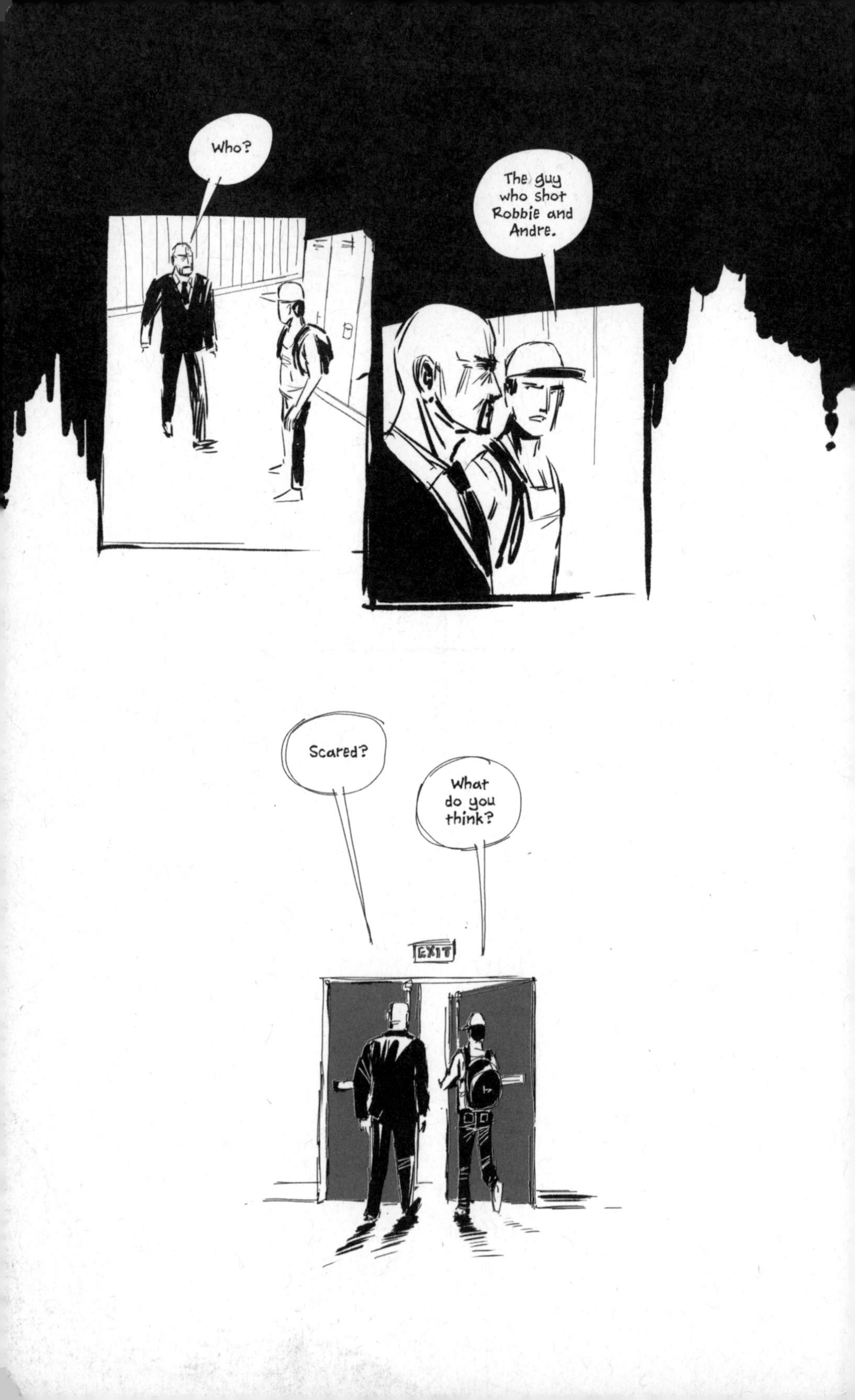
Who?
The guy who shot Robbie and Andre.
Scared?
What do you think?
EXIT